ONE BOSSY DISASTER

AN ENEMIES TO LOVERS ROMANCE

NICOLE SNOW

ABOUT THE BOOK

Trust me, I'm not falling for a human porcupine.

I don't do older men with baggage a mile long.

Billionaires? Nope, I'm Miss Independence, thank you very much.

And when a man with the emotional intelligence of a cucumber decides to boss me around?

Hoo boy.

Shepherd Foster and I are utterly incompatible.

He still can't get over the day we met when I questioned Mr. High and Mighty's judgment.

He's also holding the key—and the moolah—to my animal rescue dreams.

I'm only putting up with this torture for the cute otters, I swear.

And we're only camping together so I can prove him deliciously wrong.

My ideas *will* outshine Seattle's grumpiest egomaniac.

If only Shepherd's scowls and barbed words weren't attached to a body crafted for sin.

I still don't know how it happened.

Don't ask me why I let his cruel mouth kiss me into a smoldering wreck.

Don't remind me that messy nights in Eden with my boss carry a brutal price.

I'm worried I'm feeling... things for a man I desperately need to keep hating.

Because there's one way this ends if Shepherd damn Foster gets his hooks in my heart.

Disaster.

I: A LITTLE MISUNDERSTANDING (SHEPHERD)

*S*ome people just don't know how to keep things simple.

I lean back with a scowl that's melting my face, the executive leather chair creaking under me as I watch the latest sludge interview on my tablet.

My blood pressure is already surging to levels that will make my doctor yell at me.

Some people *do not* know how to keep things fucking simple.

We were business associates. *Professionals.*

Nothing more, nothing less.

Vanessa Dumas promised me from day one of this stupid arrangement that she was unfussy. Uncomplicated. Oh so easy to work with.

She was, to the best of my knowledge, a smart woman with an eye for strategy who understood our mutual potential to lend each other a hand.

Yeah.

Everything I thought I knew was dead wrong.

She doesn't know the meaning of the word *professional*.

On the screen, it's the typical gaudy crap. The interview room is plush with a red sofa and white walls and a hostess with a giddy smile like she's just walked onto the set after three shots of vodka.

The blonde hostess—Martha Rubina—is clearly doing her damnedest to prevent age from stampeding all over her face with plumped lips and an artificially tight forehead.

Opposite her, Vanessa has made a special effort for this spectacle. Curling her hair, wearing too much stoplight-red lipstick.

She licks her lips as her gaze flicks at the camera and then away nervously.

Fake nervously.

"So, can you tell us how it all started with Shepherd Foster?" Martha asks, leaning forward like Vanessa's answer is the most interesting thing since Al Gore invented the internet.

It'll be a lie, of course.

I've read the headlines.

Not that good old Martha will mind.

She wants a story, viral links, and water cooler talk for the next week, and Vanessa knows how to deliver.

"Oh," Vanessa says breathily. A voice she never bothered using with me when she knew that airy, giggly shit wasn't my thing.

Hell, she knew *she* wasn't my thing.

Our 'relationship' was a casual forgery from day one—I made that clear from the outset.

I needed a plus-one to shut up the press and fend off swarms of real single women.

She needed a lifeline with my connections, and the networking at the various events I'm obliged to attend were perfect. Preferably without a thousand nasty rumors swirling in my wake.

I thought I had a woman on my arm who would dissuade the real gold diggers and shit-rakers from the tabloids, and she had her chance to send her career into the stratosphere.

Win-win—or so I thought.

I even covered all the damn expenses. Couture designer

gowns, ego slaying shoes, glittery handbags big enough to swallow an elephant, the works.

The entire steaming enchilada.

No, she wasn't getting me, but I was never on the table. Dating is the last fucking thing on my list of experiences, right next to eating fried wombat and a nice bout of hantavirus.

When I laid my cards out, I made that perfectly clear.

Vanessa knew precisely what she was getting into. With me, it's always strictly business.

Absolutely no romance.

I have a reputation for not getting involved, and I gave her zero indication it would be different with her pretty smile.

I knew better. I'm too smart to fall into the fake-love-turned-real trap that claims so many other billionaires in this town.

When I needed a fake girlfriend, I intended to keep her fake and at a safe distance.

But I watch the way she smiles so innocently, my lip curling with disgust.

How did I miss it?

For all the arranging and agreeing we'd done, I never saw it coming.

I never once imagined she'd ambush me in the back of my limo.

She was the one who threw her leg over my lap and thrust her tits in my face like Thanksgiving dinner.

The memory makes my teeth grind.

We'd been at a movie premiere—some indie flick gone big— and the only reason I was there at all was because the producer, Dane Jacobs, also headed Homes for Seattle, one of the charities my company supports.

I went because I had to, and I brought Vanessa as a favor.

A fucking favor she repaid by telling me she had so much more to offer if I'd just get over my rules and let her ride my cock all the way to happily ever after.

And damn, did she offer.

My skin crawls at the thought.

It's not that she's not attractive. Most men would go to war over a woman like her with straight red hair that's almost auburn and naturally plump lips.

Still, *attractive* doesn't mean insta-love.

It certainly didn't mean I wanted to get it on in the back of a car with a relationship prop after an event I had little interest in.

On the screen, she flicks her hair over her shoulder as she tells the world her version of our relationship—how we met, which is almost true, and what happened after, which is where the lying starts.

"I didn't even think he was interested in me at first," she says slowly, teasing out her words. "I mean, look at him. He's gorgeous and brilliant and so wealthy, right? I didn't mind his past—and he hates when people talk about that, so I won't."

Fuck, I might just break my own jaw today.

"We kept running into each other at charity events," she continues, batting her eyes. "But one day... one day, he pulled me aside. Shepherd kissed me and told me that he thought we could really *be* something special."

"Wow. That sounds so romantic," Martha the host says, batting her lashes back at the liar.

I snort, unable to help myself.

Bull. Shit.

"Oh, it was! I thought I was the luckiest girl." Vanessa's smile drops. "We went everywhere together. I mean, you've seen it..."

The screen changes to a press photo of the first time we went out together, over eight months ago now.

I remember that night. The first time in ages the cameras were aimed at me, but I wasn't the focus. Also the first time in a good, long while they had something else to talk about besides my soaring star in business or dark whispers about my past.

"This is you, right?" Martha asks.

Vanessa's laugh is more like a trill and annoying as hell. "Yes! Although I don't know what's up with my eyebrows."

"So what happened between you two? You looked so happy!"

"Everything. Everything I ever dreamed of, being swept up by a man like him. It was almost like a movie, falling so fast and so hard. There wasn't time to slow down and think until—well, I can say now, I suppose. After six months, Shepherd asked me to marry him."

"No!" Martha gasps, feigning shock.

Like the producers didn't have a written statement from Vanessa and an approved bullet point list of subjects before they agreed to put her in front of a camera.

"Yes, yes, and I was just as surprised as you are now. But I loved him so much, I... I just wanted to be with him forever. You know how it is. Obviously, there was no other answer." She sighs, her face crumpling. "I thought he was just as serious about me. I thought we'd be happy together."

"What happened?" Martha's face lines with concern.

Vanessa glances down. "I still don't know, really. Maybe he met someone else? Or maybe he just got bored with the sex," she says, pulling at her finger like she's searching for a phantom ring I never gave her.

Damn, she's deviously good.

If my desk wasn't topped with solid marble, my fist would be going through the thing right about now.

"You mean it was that abrupt? He just dumped you with no explanation?"

"Without a word," Vanessa says dramatically, her voice rough.

God Almighty.

If this is her acting debut, she's killing it at my expense.

"I don't know what happened, Martha. I *don't know.* Sometimes, I think it was all an act, whenever he said he loved me. He's a cold man. It isn't all his fault, no, but he's so... so heartless to do what he did. I never knew anyone could be so cruel."

"Funny. I never knew anyone could be so damn annoying," I mutter, muting the interview.

Enough.

Like I'd ever consider being chained to a backstabbing creature like her for more than five minutes, never mind a lifetime.

How the hell is history repeating itself like this? Another fucked up black hole rumor mill for Shepherd Foster, CEO of Home Shepherd and apparently Bad Luck Inc.

This time, it isn't even true.

I never wanted anything to do with her.

I should've listened to my gut and never made this goofy-ass arrangement in the first place.

I should've known. My life isn't a rom-com movie where I'd actually fall in love, so it had to end in tragedy instead.

"Well, give it to me." I tap the screen with my index finger. "How far has this crap spread?"

Hannah Cho, my assistant, jumps to attention by my desk.

She's been waiting patiently while I fume for the past five minutes. If I didn't know better, I'd say her spine must be steel.

"Too far to stop it," she says. "You're watching her on the biggest morning gossip show in North America, which means it's too late to scrub the internet. Too many eyes have seen it, saved it, tweeted it, and sent it to TikTok."

Wonderful.

"You are now Shepherd Foster, brilliant CEO and cunning heartbreaker. Congratulations." She pauses for a breath. "In some eyes, I'm sorry to say, an *abuser* of women."

"I never touched her once, dammit," I growl.

"Emotional abuse, sir."

"I was *never* emotionally involved with her. The whole arrangement was fake as hell."

"Oh, no doubt. I knew it from the second she claimed you went all Prince Charming on her. That's... not you, Mr. Foster." She nods intently. "Regrettably, I'm afraid you'll have a hard time convincing the internet. The reality of the ruse won't win you many sympathy points, either."

I wince because she's right.

6

The age of social media means no secret stays sacred for long, and some lies never have an expiration date.

Worse, it's the age of the ambush.

I didn't know what Vanessa Dumas was doing after I brushed her off until it was already public knowledge.

"What are our options? Anything yet from PR?" I demand.

Vanessa's perfect, red-lipsticked mouth moves on the screen as she tells another lie I don't care to listen to. No doubt she's squawking about how wonderful she thought we were together, and how she was so sure we were madly in love.

Hannah hesitates. "I'm afraid—"

"There must be favors to call in." I push my chair back and pace across the rug in the center of the floor, all slate-grey to match the building's décor. "We have a few friends in the media. Maybe even at the network that signs Martha Rubina's paycheck."

"...it's already live and approved, sir. You'd need to bring out a big stick and make a lot of noise to put the cork back in this bottle."

Yeah, and Legal would love to whack me with a big stick if I even consider lawsuits over this, considering it was my own ham-fisted idea that started it.

"A press conference then," I say. "I'll go straight to the people. Tell my side of the story, set the record straight, and be just as loud as she is."

Hannah only tucks her hands behind her back, which I know from experience means *hell no* before she says a single word.

"No, sir," she clips. "If you push back, you give them more attention. The more you protest, the guiltier you'll look. And considering your past..." She clears her throat.

"Don't say it. Believe me, I know," I snap. "The louder I bleat, the more people will go digging, and then I'll be one big open wound."

I've been dealing with this fuckery for my whole adult life, ever since the day I flipped and helped take Uncle Aidan down. And that was *before* the goddamned mess with Serena.

My particular past required moving a goddamned mountain when there were guns and bodies and the whole world knew my uncle was an Irish mob boss. Never mind the whole tragic dead wife thing.

I resist the urge to throw something at the wall.

"So, what then? You want me to stay silent while she drags my name through the mud for the thousandth time?"

"I want you to be the bigger person, Mr. Foster. Billionaire CEOs don't acknowledge petty rumors," Hannah explains patiently. "Doing so will just give them fuel."

"Yeah, yeah. Above the fray and all that."

I drag my hands through my hair and bite back all the caustic words I want to hurl at Vanessa, who's still running her mouth.

The smug smile on her face behind the crocodile tears tells me how much she's enjoying this.

What the hell happened?

I just wanted it to be fucking simple.

"There is one more option, I think." Hannah clears her throat. "It's clear Vanessa Dumas wants something. I suspect she's using this for leverage to get her foot in the door with TV execs to launch her career."

That's the problem.

No one uses Shepherd Foster.

"I *was* helping her career. That was the whole deal," I grind out. "Bringing her to these events gave her attention she wouldn't have had. If it was too slow or she couldn't figure out the rest, that's hardly on me."

"I never said it was, sir."

"Well, I'm not buying her silence, Miss Cho. She's cost me enough."

"Obviously not."

I stare at her.

She's been with me long enough to know I'd rather fight a

pack of wolverines with my hands tied behind my back than roll over for anyone. Maybe some parts of a man's bullheaded upbringing never die.

Besides, if anyone finds out I paid off Vanessa with favors, won't that be worse?

"No deal. I'm not bribing her with more favors or anything else. I won't stoop to sleazy backroom tactics."

Hannah doesn't blink.

I'm not my damned uncle, is what she really hears.

"Of course not, Mr. Foster. I'd never imply it."

I glare at her, but her expression doesn't change.

She's a hard woman to read, and normally, that's what I like most about her.

Today, it's one more uncertainty.

Fuck, she's the best assistant I've ever had, and that's partly because she's impervious to any of the crap I throw at her.

If I didn't know better, I'd say she's a biological android, flawlessly programmed to be professional, polite, generous, and capable.

Not warm, necessarily, but I don't need buttery smiles.

When it comes to an executive assistant, I need efficiency, and Hannah's skills are almost terrifyingly so.

I know she's not here hashing out the bad news without some defense percolating in her brain.

Idle gabbing is not how Hannah Cho does things. She's solution-oriented like a crossbow hunter is arrow-oriented. She's already mapped out all the possibilities of how this might go down today, tomorrow, and for the next three years.

"Will you sit?" I say, gesturing to the chair. "Tell me what you're really thinking."

Hannah perches on the edge of the chair. Her bob is glossy, not a hair out of place, and the lace blouse emerging from her pant suit clings to her neck. She's severity itself, no-nonsense and simple, which I like. The only piece of jewelry she's ever worn is a silver chain necklace from her grandmother with a small dangling swan.

"I have an idea," Hannah says. I knew she would. "One that *doesn't* involve a poorly thought out press conference or any weakness on your part. Perish the thought."

I drum my fingers. "Go on."

"It involves the new Young Influencers program."

"The what?" I frown at her, drawing a blank.

She sighs like she expects my total cluelessness.

"The latest goodwill program Home Shepherd sponsors. It allows young social media influencers interested in philanthropic work to shadow the CEO for several months so they can gain the executive experience helpful in running a nonprofit."

What the hell?

I agreed to that shit?

"Right," I lie. It doesn't tickle the faintest memory, and I can't believe I signed off on something so time-consuming, but fine.

"It's intended to give our young influencers an inside view of leadership. They get to see how philanthropy programs at our level work, plus a chance to enjoy your insights," she explains.

"I understand the concept."

"Yes, sir."

On my tablet, Vanessa is still yammering about the broken vow that never happened.

I try not to snarl as I turn it off and push it aside.

"Look, you know how I feel about influencers," I say.

It's almost the same world I despise, all rumor mills and pretty faces with ulterior motives.

The worst kind of fame and infamy.

It's repulsive, the way they leech off people for views. Anything for a leg up.

"I do, Mr. Foster," Hannah says coolly.

"So tell me why I don't remember authorizing this program,"

I growl. "And while you're at it, remind me when I'd ever agree to spend time with a social media addict."

"You didn't, sir. Because I just came up with it."

I stare at her blankly.

She's too good.

That also explains a few things. Although not why she thinks this is a good idea.

"I'm going to give you two minutes," I say curtly. "I warn you, Miss Cho, I'm going to take a lot of convincing."

Hannah smooths an invisible wrinkle from her pants and looks up at me, her deep brown eyes opaque. In the years we've been working together, I've never managed to get a good reading on how much I annoy her.

I suspect that's how she likes it.

But this rips me out of my comfort zone like a car collision. I want to know why she thinks it's a good idea.

Disregarding my time limit, she takes a minute to collect her thoughts, steepling her fingers before she starts.

"Frankly, we need a fresh approach to our public relations, especially when they involve *you*. Due to the nature of these rumors—and the ugly fact that we didn't catch them before they were splashed out in the open—we need to think creatively."

"And you think some vapid influencers are the answer? That *is* creative," I say sharply.

"I understand you're not the biggest fan, however, they have a lot of leverage with their reach. You could use it to your advantage. We'll also thoroughly vet our candidates to ensure they've been involved in charitable causes before."

Yeah, right.

I snort again. "What makes you think any of them would say anything positive about me?"

"Because they'll all be clamoring for a spot in this new program. Even if there's a scandal hanging over you, sir, that doesn't diminish Home Shepherd's power and prestige," she says smoothly. "Especially if the reward for successfully completing the shadow apprenticeship is a sizable donation to the charity of their choice."

"I see."

I hate that I can't argue.

I hate that it doesn't sound half-bad.

And Hannah knows it as she gives me a serene smile. "Rather brilliant of you to think of something so gracious, huh?"

I fold my arms and eye her sourly.

Have I mentioned I hate this shit?

Some airhead who spends their days posting ten second puppy videos from animal shelters following me around, yammering and demanding selfies.

Godawful.

Any influencer with a working brain will want something I can't give. I don't buck up and *smile* for the same cameras that might as well shoot me in the face.

They'll drive me mad in a matter of days.

And what, them talking about a marvelous work opportunity is going to cut through Vanessa's bullshit?

Remind the world for the millionth time that I'm clean and kind and all that happy crap?

"You're still skeptical," Hannah says.

"How could you tell?"

"Consider it an engineered distraction," she throws back. "No, you can't address Vanessa's accusations directly and come out on top, but you *can* remind people of what you're doing here. Under your fearless leadership, Home Shepherd has done a lot of good for this world."

"They won't forget Vanessa that easily. They never do. Not since Aidan Murphy and the trial of the century," I grind out, the memory so foul I can chew it.

"They will when her story doesn't change—or especially if it does—and you don't give it the time of day." She leans forward. "Keeping your head down and doing what this company does best *is* your response, Mr. Foster. I don't think you appreciate just how much weight these influencers have."

Too much.

Still, it's the best of several bad options, and Miss Cho has a point.

My fault, really, for not realizing Vanessa isn't a stable woman who takes rejection nicely. I should have prepared for this when she didn't respond to my nice email and an offer for one more all-expense paid trip to the conference of her choice just to show her there were no hard feelings.

I just don't know how Vanessa thought I would ever be seduced.

Hell, Hannah handled most of our correspondence, and my assistant isn't exactly a grinning cupid.

But this whole influencer scheme will only be temporary.

It's an honest way to manufacture some good news with the name Shepherd attached for the press.

Me, I can sacrifice a little time if it solves the Vanessa Dumas problem and lets me focus on real work again.

I've been meaning to expand the corporate philanthropy program, anyway.

Right now, we're posting record numbers thanks to our watchful lights. Every high-end home in North America wants a custom porch light that doubles as a solar-powered door camera.

It doesn't feel right funneling all that money into my pockets. They're heavy enough as it is.

Maybe it's the guilt that comes with growing up a mob boss' nephew.

Maybe it's my atonement for sins I didn't commit.

Or maybe it's just me doing what I always do best—running from any whiff of drama. Anything and everything that gets in the way of honest money and fresh ideas.

Regardless, I don't have time for an ongoing stew of rumors.

"Fine," I say. "If you think it's a good idea, I'm not about to argue with you."

"Excellent choice, sir."

I glower at her.

Hannah doesn't even blink.

"If you're going to pick someone from social media to follow me around like a lost puppy, at least make sure they're squeaky clean," I warn. "I don't give two shits who just as long as they'll get the job done."

She allows herself a small smile.

"Of course. Have I ever let you down?"

I don't dignify that with an answer she doesn't need.

She already knows the reason I keep her on is because when she's in charge, I can take my hands off the helm.

That's hard when I hate relinquishing control.

"Wipe my calendar for the weekend. I'm going to clear my head," I say, pushing my chair back and shrugging my suit jacket on. The evening sun is big and orange, hanging heavier and lower as it slips below Seattle's glossy horizon.

If I'm going to get out of here before sunset, I need to get moving.

As always, she takes everything in with a polite nod. "Another one of your excursions, sir? I can't say I blame you."

"Yes. I'll be back Monday."

"I'll have some candidates ready for you then."

"Good." I switch off my computer and leave my tablet on the desk without a second glance.

God, what a fucking headache.

Why did I ever drag myself out of witness protection when it was all said and done with Uncle Aidan?

I have regrets.

If I'd kept the name Billy Jordan, I could've had a nice, boring life in Gilbert, Arizona. I could've been married and settled on a nice middle-class income with a couple orange trees.

No criminal baggage.

No Serena and her mess.

No fucking billions and cutthroat women thinking they'll have the cleavage that's able to restart my heart.

Instead, I've got Shepherd Foster's problems and money and no fucking orange tree whatsoever.

Like I said, I have regrets a mile long, and there's only one thing that ever gets my mind off them.

II: A LITTLE TOO FAMILIAR
(DESTINY)

*A*lki Beach feels like walking into heaven, if heaven's mornings are made of high winds and fresh salty air.

Soft sunlight spills across the ocean below a blue sky that yawns on forever, and there's no one else around to interrupt my quiet time.

Beside me, Molly, trots along with her long pink tongue lolled out. Only the best dog ever.

Early morning runs like this are all I need.

Early morning runs and Molly.

Oh, the seals are a nice perk, too.

They're half out of the water today, basking in the sunlight like overgrown potatoes with flippers. I'm too far away to see them for sure, but I'm almost certain their eyes are closed in contentment, despite the wind.

Beautiful.

I stop to catch my breath and Molly notices the seals. Her ears prick and her head cocks to the side.

"Not a chance, girl," I tell her, wrapping her leash around my hand. "Those seals don't need your kind of trouble."

She whines in protest.

Of course, Mol would never hurt anything. But at ten

months, she has a lot of energy for a rangy young husky and not a lot of common sense.

She doesn't know she'll definitely scare the seals.

This is a good photo op, though.

The lighting is pristine, soft and flattering despite my sweaty face. If I face the sun, I'll even catch the seals in the background.

"Ready?" I kneel so Molly's head rests next to mine. She huffs in excitement and licks my face. "Okay, on three. Smile for the camera. One, two..."

Molly looks to where I click my fingers, her pretty blue eyes sparkling in the sunshine as she huffs a breath.

I swear she's more photogenic than I am.

I take several quick shots and skim through them as I start walking again. The seals come out best in the third shot, so I start editing.

It isn't much, no more than a minute's worth of flipping through filters.

My brand is candid, not overdone.

Just a little contrast tweaking to bring out the seals, a soft filter to make the most of the morning sun, and I bring up a box to post it on Twitter and then Insta. My tongue pokes out from the corner of my mouth as I type.

Big hello from Mol and me on our morning run! Anybody else spot the seals? Remember, when you see wildlife in its natural habitat, always be respectful. #AlkiBeach #harborseals #wildlifeprotection

Not too preachy, but some people need the reminder.

Just yesterday, I saw someone post a video of their friend trying to catch a seagull. They probably thought it was a little harmless fun, but they don't know how fragile animals can be.

My phone vibrates a couple minutes later as Likes start pouring in, peppered with comments. Each one is a little dopamine kick, sharper than a double espresso.

For once, it's not just the scenery or Molly's cute face that has people lighting up.

It's a cute selfie. My hair is all over the place from the wind and my face is pink.

"What do you say, Mol?" I show her the screen. "Cute or nah?"

She boops her nose against it, leaving a messy smudge I need to wipe away.

I laugh loudly.

"Yeah, you're right. They love you more."

She wags her tail and I kiss her furry head.

Getting Molly was the best adult decision I've ever made, even if she's demanding and needs to pull me out of the house four or five times a day.

I'm convinced I have half my followers thanks to her.

Molly runs beside me as I spring into a healthy jog again, the fresh breeze kissing my face. The leash is still wrapped around my hand, but I don't give her any room.

Most of the time, she's reliable.

Her recall is good.

I've done so much training with her that I'm pretty sure *I* would respond to a cooing voice and smelly salmon treat, but the doggo knows what I expect by now.

Though I'm guessing she'll always have one weakness.

Birds.

Any kind, from the smallest hummer to the biggest screeching eagle, causes her to lose her senses.

If she was chasing a seagull off a cliff, she'd go right over with it.

If the bird dove into the water, Mol would swim too.

I love her, but when it comes to birds, she's a total doofus.

"Absolutely not!" I tell her as we pass a bunch of black oyster-catchers roaming the shore, their distinct red beaks ready for feasting.

Molly grumbles, one ear flopping adorably as she stares them down.

I know what she's thinking.

If I'm not supposed to chase birds, why are there birds?

"You have a point," I say, and she glances back at me. The sand is firm and I don't lose pace as we pass by them without incident. "But no. Birds are part of the ecology around here. You go chasing and eating them, and pretty soon we'll all be joining the dinosaurs."

She grumbles again at hearing "no."

Call me crazy, I talk to her a lot.

She doesn't understand most of my rambling, but that's one word we've worked on to death. Husky pups need to be told "no" a lot.

The beach opens up as I head to the point where the lighthouse juts into the sky. As lighthouses go, it's a small one, but I love getting to the point and staring out into the bay.

Just me, the sea, and nature.

Being here makes me feel like everything is all right with the world.

The sun has fully risen like a gold balloon by the time I reach the lighthouse. The wind picks up more, though, turning the gentle morning breeze into a proper gale.

It roars against my ears, tossing my hair up.

I slow to a stop, picking my way across the rocks and gazing out to sea.

From Alki Point, I can make out southern Bainbridge and Blake Island. On the other side of the bay past that, the wild growth of the Banner Forest National Park awaits.

It makes me smile.

How many times have I gone hiking there with Dad, Eliza, and the fam?

All that greenery is a big bowl of pea soup for the soul.

I've called this place home for most of my life, yet it still takes my breath away—even when the wind wants to shove me in the ocean.

I'm used to seeing people boating out here. Most mornings, the bay is littered with sailboats and little fishing ships.

Not today, though. The rising wind is enough reason to tell me why when I see the waves.

They're rolling bigger like restless beasts rising from a long nap, the wind spitting spray off the top.

Brine coats my cheeks, and for the first time, I shiver as I check my phone.

Dang.

There's even a wind advisory for small boats. As I scan the waves, I don't expect anyone down by the boat launch.

Definitely not a man holding a flimsy green kayak.

"Oh no," I mouth, noticing he's only a few feet from taking off on a one-way trip.

As one enormous wave swells halfway to Blake Island, I lunge into action, running toward the launch with my hands over my mouth.

"Hey! Hey, wait, mister. You can't go out in weather like this!"

Are you freaking crazy? I want to add. But there could be a thousand reasons. He might be a tourist or a risk-taker or just some guy who never checks his phone and underestimates how pissed off the sea is today.

He stops and stares, all dark hair and slashing blue eyes that ground me midstep.

I jerk back so hard I'm almost winded. Even Molly goes into an instant heel at my side, watching him warily.

"There's a major wind advisory. Looks like it's already over thirty miles per hour out there. You really don't want to go out there," I say quietly as he watches me like a statue.

Okay, yeah, definitely freaking crazy. It kind of comes with the territory in this town.

"I'm aware of the weather, miss," he says sharply. "I also have eyes. I've done the route to Blake Island over three hundred times in worse weather than this. Thanks for your concern, but no thanks."

Holy hell.

He's talking polite, but the wave that crashes behind him hard enough to spray us both obliterates his argument.

"You can't go out there, dude. That's the kind of mess that drowns people," I say. But the more I talk, the frostier his icy look gets. "If you've been out to Blake so much, you must know how many people wind up in a bad spot and need rescue? But this, this is easily avoidable."

"So is this conversation," he clips.

Oh, boy.

We've got a live one, I guess.

My brow pulls down. "Um, don't you think it's a little *selfish* to risk people and resources if the Coast Guard has to roll out after you? I'm trying to avoid that."

He rolls his eyes so hard I think *I'm* the one who's dizzy.

"Lady, get a life. You're lecturing a grown man who's perfectly comfortable with taking his own risks. If I'm swept away, I'll find my way back. You can have the police standing by to arrest me for self-endangerment if it makes you feel better."

"Come on. That's not even a crime." I sigh as he turns his back, shooting me another cutting gaze over his very broad shoulder. "I guess no good deed goes unpunished, huh?"

He shrugs, pushing his kayak down at the edge of the very unsettled water before he looks up at me again.

Even Molly has her ears back, studying him like she's trying to decide if his stupidity is a threat. I'm sure it's just my mood rubbing off when she's extremely sensitive, but ugh.

I can't believe this.

"If you want to do good, Miss Intrusive, kindly butt the hell out and let me enjoy my day," he says.

Yep.

He's officially the rudest, coldest, most reckless man I've ever met. Part of me wants to give him a friendly push right into the storm the rest of me is working so hard to keep him from.

Decisions, decisions.

"Whatever." I try to say it nonchalantly, hating how much

anger creeps into my voice. "Pardon me for giving two shits about saving your life."

The waves slap the shore too close to us again, and I can't hear all of his response clearly as Molly shakes off the water.

But it sounds like "...you'd do better to care more about your dog. Get her the hell away from the water and stop pecking at strangers who don't need saving."

I'm actually speechless as I watch him push away, climbing a ten-foot-tall wave less than a minute after he's on the water.

It's not remotely safe.

He's a ginormous idiot and a half.

Only, I guess I'm the bigger one for standing there and taking his abuse. If he doesn't give a damn about his safety, why should I?

This man is either wackadoodle or as wildly overconfident as he is short-fused.

Still, I squint at him as he fades into the choppy waves, certain he's on the verge of needing a rescue any second.

When I'm right, I'll do him a favor and call it in.

I peel off my windbreaker and throw it around Molly while we watch and wait.

I don't mind the chill. In fact, it helps cool my blood a little after this massive prick made it boil.

I'm honestly mad that he's fighting the waves as well as he is.

Slowly, calmly, like he lives for nothing but spitting in the face of danger.

The raw power in his controlled movements feels angry, like someone with something to prove to the universe.

Holy hell, no.

No, this can't be blind arrogance.

This is more like *rage*, a fury taken out on the ocean itself because nothing else is strong enough to withstand him.

I watch in irritated awe for a few more minutes with my heart climbing up my throat.

I'm expecting him to weaken any time as his muscles fail him, to show me a satisfying flicker of fear.

Any second now.

...it never happens.

Somehow, this maniac withstands the ocean, climbing over every swell, grinding his way toward Blake Island a few brutal crawling feet at a time.

I already had the Coast Guard's rescue contact pulled up on my phone, but now I hesitate.

Watching him is hypnotic.

I've never seen anyone take on the ocean like he has a personal grudge with Poseidon and he's determined to win.

And weirdly, he *is* winning.

To me, nature isn't something you conquer. It's part of life and it's our responsibility to watch over it.

But this man has declared open war on it with every cleave of his paddle.

His naked aggression twists my heart like a limp rag.

Even though the sea keeps trying to swallow him up and serve some humble pie, it's failing.

My God.

He must be enjoying himself.

I wonder if he knows I'm still standing here like a freezing idiot, watching and trying not to care about his fate.

Why else would someone throw themselves out there?

The adrenaline rush, sure. This area attracts junkies seeking their next high on wild risks.

Crazy, but what do I know?

Once I'm sure he isn't doomed and he's rolling up on the island's shore, I turn away from the man and his weirdly compelling battle—just in time to find Mol trying to eat a whole-ass hermit crab.

"Molly!" I pry her mouth open and dig the poor thing out. At least the shell saved it from her sharp little teeth.

I drop it back in the water, hoping it isn't too traumatized.

"You can't do that," I say, and she wags her tail, staring up at me with wide blue eyes. "Those aren't the right kind of crabs for dinner."

Mom, you don't know how wrong you are. Her goofy dog grin only widens. *Crabs are dinner. All the crabs,* I imagine her saying.

"You're the worst. But I love you."

I glance back at the man on his stupid mission, but he's finally out of sight.

For a second, I panic, wondering if I should've kept watching to make sure he's all right after all. But then I see his kayak bobbing on the shore, this pale green thing tied down and half-obscured by rolling waves.

Huh.

Okay then.

I guess I need to just accept the fact that he knows what he's doing and he's too big an asshole to leave the world so soon.

Totally not what I need on a quiet morning.

I distract myself from the weirdness with thoughts about the weekend.

Maybe I'll head over to Olympia for another stab at sea otter tracking. They're so rare and endangered I've never spotted them in the wild, but I'd love to.

The Department of Fish and Wildlife is practically begging for civilian reports.

If I get a lucky hit up north, maybe I can help them preserve the species.

My internet followers would *love* that, and obviously it would be an amazing opportunity.

But not even thoughts of adorable endangered otters are enough to stop me from thinking about that sea freak toying with drowning like it was nothing.

What kind of man has that big a grudge against living?

And why?

"This way. Let's get out of here, girl." I jog away from the point so I can no longer see him.

I pull out my phone and check my notifications.

There are a bunch of Insta Likes and comments adding up, plus a healthy trickle of new followers. I swipe past to a few new Discord messages.

I'm in this chat with a bunch of other local people where we hash out new ways to grow and gripe about what it's like to be an influencer.

Every so often, someone shares a cool new opportunity.

Usually, though, it doesn't blow up unless there's something serious going on.

Today, the messages are coming fast and furious.

Too curious, I open the chat and read through the messages.

ClaraDoesChickLit: **OMG OMG YOU WILL NEVER GUESS WHAT**

MegTea: I CAN GUESS

c h a o s b e a r: what? whats up?

jennineedscoffeeornope: new program? deets?

ClaraDoes ChickLit: RIGHT RIGHT RIGHT

ClaraDoesChickLit: How do you always get it first Jenni? Omg

MegTea: Who did you blow? Like did he taste good?

I WRINKLE MY NOSE. Meghan Tea's whole brand is loud, crude, and she's never shy about reminding us she's number one in the pecking order.

I hate that she's in our group when her brand is mostly self-centered and not based around a coherent niche like cooking or travel or random acts of kindness. Mostly, her videos are the Seattle dining scene, where she gossips about everything banal and scandalous in this city.

Still, I keep reading as the messages pop in.

. . .

25

CLARADOESCHICKLIT: Ew Meg. F off and find your next story somewhere else.

jennineedscoffeeornope: babe I always got an ear out

ClaraDoesChickLit: ANYWAY it's a new Young Influencers program with Home Shepherd. Y'know the one with the hot messed up CEO? You guys it looks a-MAZING

I STOP WALKING to type a message.

DESTINYSCHILD: Home Shepherd, huh? The global security company?

SEVERAL PEOPLE START TYPING AGAIN, but Clara responds first. She usually does. I swear that girl has bionic fingers that type at the speed of light.

CLARADOESCHICKLIT: YES!! I mean, I know I know. It's kinda weird, but it looks like a really cool program and a great opportunity. Every Seattle library will slay if I get that money

MegTea: Whatevs. You do your little books. When I win, I'll feed the homeless. #peopleoverpages

NOBODY LAUGHS at her bitter joke.

I purse my lips as I think, tapping my chin.

Mol settles next to me and licks her lips.

Well.

I should look into this.

Free money and real opportunities to help people typically don't grow on trees—but for Clara to get so worked up, it must be good. She's more than a book snob when her high expectations extend to charity.

But the thing is, I've dealt with companies like this before I was old enough to drive.

Consider it one of the many life lessons that come with growing up a billionaire's daughter.

Dad taught me early and often to suss out ulterior motives.

Oh, sure, most places say they want to help the world. They all read the right script.

But it's really all about finding a fresh cause to make themselves look good and offset the real damage they do. Especially when it comes to Mother Nature.

They usually have a shitload of environmental damage to offset.

Dad knew that better than anyone, too, and he's invested a ton in making sure Wired Cup runs as the most sustainable regional coffee company around.

It's all about public perception, in the end.

I'm guessing the CEO of Home Shepherd doesn't give a single solitary fuck, especially if he's a walking mess like they say. I don't really follow rumors but the way they talk about him is enough.

He'll probably pawn the (un)lucky applicant off on an intern or corporate program manager in charge of philanthropy.

That will turn a great opportunity into something mediocre. A nice little bullet point on a résumé and nothing more.

See? It's never too early in the morning to be cynical.

I turn my attention back to the conversation.

*CLARADOESCHICKLIT: **OH AND LOOK AT THE PRIZE MONEY!!!***
Hang on, lemme find a link
    *MegTea: **Hurry up. Some of us have places to be Clara.***

. . .

Prize money?

I read back and realize I must've skipped over that part.

That changes things if the big bad company is offering real skin in the game.

Stroking Mol's head, I click the link and wait for it to load. If Clara sent *three* exclamation marks, that means something.

The webpage looks professional enough with simple, readable text and actionable links. I skim through everything until I find the real meat it's offering and—

And holy crap.

Holy meatballs.

Home Shepherd, Inc. is offering *two million dollars* as prize money to a charity of the winner's choice.

Two million effing dollars.

Look, I come from money, but a couple mil being handed out to a good cause isn't pocket change. I've never managed to raise a fraction of that amount.

The only way I could get that much is if I raided my parents' bank accounts, which I totally refuse to do, especially when they already give so generously from their own pockets.

Two million dollars.

That's a lot of incentive.

There's also a note about getting a chance to work with Mr. Hot Messy CEO in the flesh. I'm surprised he's personally involved, and it might be good leadership experience, if you can get past the likely personality flaws.

I haven't had a chance to work with many business leaders who aren't part of Dad's circle and biased toward liking me. That could be useful if I'm ever in a position to start a nonprofit.

The bad news, of course, is that a prize that big guarantees fierce competition.

Mr. Hot Messy CEO would get a big pile of good applications for a quarter of that amount. Even if he'd offered a hundred grand, he'd have people vying for the spot like hungry piranhas.

But two million dollars?

I have to remember how to breathe.

My mind is already spinning with hope, imagining everything I could do if I win the position—which is ridiculous when I haven't even decided to apply yet.

But it does say you can pick any charity you want, doesn't it?

Imagine what a local environmental group could do with a cool two million as a booster, all in one go. Heck, if I let my followers know, maybe they'll donate too.

But what would I choose?

I'm pretty sure they need to know upfront.

I chew my lip as I run through my options.

Maybe the Marine Conservation Club?

They do so much to protect endangered local species like sea otters, whales, harbor porpoises, and sea lions.

Reflexively, I reach up and finger the little onyx turtle necklace I always wear. My stepmom, Eliza, got it for me years ago and it's turned my luck around ever since.

So, maybe I could put in an application and let the rest sort itself out.

What could it hurt?

If a man can wake up this early to scream at concerned strangers and tempt fate dueling with the Puget Sound, I can certainly tempt it by getting off my butt for a good cause.

* * *

IT TURNS OUT, it can hurt a lot.

Mostly my head.

Especially when you freaking *win.*

"Stand up straight," the lady says from behind the camera. We're set up in the bright, airy lobby of Home Shepherd's headquarters. We could have filmed it on his office floor, but his décor feels less than cheerful.

What I actually mean is less *pleasant.*

Chrome and weathered grey slate are classy, for sure, but stepping in there made me feel like I forgot what the sun looked like in this fancy dungeon.

If the CEO chose that style himself, I can easily imagine what sort of man he is.

Stone-cold, with a personality as bland as his slate-tiled artisan floor.

I plaster on a smile.

Hey, it's not like I'm new to standing in front of a camera under stress. But when I applied for this program, this wasn't what I bargained for.

Honestly, I never expected to win.

Home Shepherd is a big deal in these parts. I've heard Dad mention them offhand for securing his shops and I couldn't care less about security services.

Plenty of influencers certainly applied when they heard about the massive payout for charity.

It's a little sweet to edge out the local competition, I'll admit.

Especially total brat influencers, like Meghan "Tea" Maven, who make their views off rancid gossip. Home Shepherd's big charity payoff would just be one more thing for Meghan to boast about, anyway, no matter how many homeless shelters she supports.

For her, it's a means to an end.

More about boosting her own clout than helping the world.

I'm not into the whole gossip thing, of course, but a lot of people are. She's been all over everything lately.

Compared to my paltry almost-a-million TikTok followers, she has well over five mil, plus a zillion more spread across Instagram and Twitter.

On paper, it should be a no-brainer. Meghan has a bigger platform, hands down.

For some reason, they picked me. I must've passed their vibe check, I guess.

"Okay!" Camera Lady says cheerfully, and I try to focus again. "That's lovely, Destiny."

It's not lovely.

My smile feels rubbery at the edges and I think my eyes look puffy from the three hours of sleep last night. I've been doing this all day, all these little press releases and photo ops to let the world know about the program and the fact that I'm joining it.

I already want to just crawl into bed and sleep for a solid day.

But at this point I'd settle for getting down to *work*.

My skin prickles with the attention.

My smile wilts, and I have to hoist it back into place again.

"So, Destiny, can you tell us why you're excited to work with Home Shepherd?"

Again, my smile becomes more of a grimace as I answer the same question I've answered a dozen other times this week. At least I have my lines memorized.

"It's an amazing opportunity," I say.

Clara, bless her heart, has coached me through this so many times it feels almost natural.

Camera Lady nods enthusiastically.

"Home Shepherd is such a big name," I continue. "They already do so much for making people feel secure. I know it's going to boost my platform."

The woman smiles encouragingly. I keep my body language relaxed and open as I continue.

"Of course, the chance to shadow such a well-known CEO is pretty thrilling, too," I say, really hamming that part up.

Somehow, I don't believe I actually *will* get to shadow him, but I know how corporate egos operate. We'll let everyone think I will and that I'm oh-so-grateful for the opportunity.

Including Mr. High and Mighty Foster himself.

No harm in signaling that I know where my bread is buttered and why I'm here.

"I'm looking forward to making new connections and learning how to make a difference from a business perspective.

A new one, I mean. I grew up with a big shot CEO for a dad, but that's always been a little too personal to be useful. I can't wait to get advice from someone who didn't used to buy my pj's. I can't thank you guys enough. It's a fresh perspective, and I'm totally game."

Camera Lady grins. "Do you think you'll take what you'll learn here with you?"

"Absolutely." My smile brightens, this time for real. "Mr. Foster is top dog in the home security biz, right? It would be pretty hard not to learn something from the best."

There, I've done it. Name-dropped him.

The stupid, petty part of me hopes he'll see this and realize what my expectations really are.

He hasn't sent so much as a note by pigeon. He probably has no intention of even meeting me beyond a quick handshake and a how-do-you-do.

But I want him to feel a smidge guilty—if that's possible.

There's actually not much about him available online, despite his reputation. What little Clara knows was secondhand from another influencer who said he smashed some poor woman's heart to bits with a flash-in-the-pan engagement.

That's what the only articles I can find are buzzing about, aside from tech security issues that mostly go over my head.

That's a bit of a red flag. Does he really only have one recent scandal?

Every time Dad sneezed, the press used to jump all over him.

As soon as I knew I won, I went full detective on Foster, searching for his LinkedIn, any social media profiles, any articles I could find about him.

His face looked weirdly familiar, too, but I couldn't quite place it.

Before his escapades with Vanessa Dumas, the man was a ghost, and nobody gets to play phantom with this much money unless they've spent a ton on sweeping up their dirt.

But all he had was some corporate bio, which I read in detail, and some articles about how he established Home Shepherd years ago and how much money it's making on cutting-edge innovations.

Aside from that, the rest was all rumors.

No social media.

No pictures of him having fun and showing off like billionaires in their prime do.

No slick images grandstanding with his charities, which is really weird when every rich guy with power has at least a couple sets or several big supportive speeches posted.

The only thing I could find were a few recent photos with the actress he apparently dumped or something.

I'm not sure I blame him, really.

She looks high-maintenance as hell.

But even those articles were mostly about *her*. The fact that *she* was on his arm, and how she feels, crying about the alleged breakup.

I could care less.

I care a little more about the fact that he's enormously private.

Is he even aware I'm alive? Does he know this program exists?

Or did some minion come up with this idea and he just signed off on it without a second glance? From the pictures, which show a handsome, stern man with piercing blue eyes and cheekbones that could cut glass, he doesn't exactly look friendly.

Or hyper-committed to charitable works that don't make money.

And now, to no one's surprise, I'm stuck here doing a bunch of publicity shoots and videos rather than anything substantive.

"Destiny?" Camera Lady calls with a frown.

I snap my smile back on my face for the rest of the session.

I definitely don't meet Mr. Foster that day.

The next few weeks fly by in a social media haze with more

mini events and publicity shots—anything and everything except real philanthropic work.

It's uniquely exhausting.

The thought of what that money might accomplish is the only thing that keeps me going.

There are two million annoying reasons to stick with this, despite my irritation, and I spend my spare time figuring out where I'll actually put the money.

Turns out, they let me submit a shortlist I can finalize later.

I haven't decided on a solid charity yet, but I've made a list of my top five. And revised it. And swapped out top place about ten different times.

But it'll be one of them.

They're all fine conservation organizations with good track records of preserving habitats for endangered species.

Not an easy list to narrow down. Since announcing I've joined Young Influencers, I've had so many charities reaching out to ask me to consider them. Not just in Seattle, or even the US, but organizations from all over the world.

As a side perk, since my announcement with all the promotion floating around, I've gained five thousand new followers.

So maybe it's not all a waste of time.

I hope so, anyway.

That's why I'm here.

To get the word out and make a real difference.

Finally, after the exhausting press junket dies down, my first day of real work in the office arrives.

The Home Shepherd offices are at the top of a high-rise stabbing up into the grey canopy of clouds over the city. When we reach the top floor, I try not to wince.

Despite the floor-to-ceiling windows overlooking Seattle in its busy midmorning glory, something about this place makes me feel like sunlight itself has suddenly ceased to exist.

Not to be dramatic, but it looks like the antithesis of environmentally friendly.

They could have at least dropped a few plants around to break up the clinical vibe. Some accent color. Even just *green*. We don't need flowers rioting everywhere, just *something* to offset the drabness.

"Miss Lancaster?" A slim Asian woman steps out from behind the desk and murmurs something to the other receptionist, who offers me a curious glance. "Hi, I'm Hannah Cho, Mr. Foster's executive assistant."

I'm no stranger to high fashion and class, but everything about Miss Cho is pinned so perfectly in place she makes me feel small. She's dressed in royal navy-blue and cream, her blouse fastened around her neck and her sleek bob flawlessly styled.

When she looks at me, I know she's making a mental note of every hair that's out of place, how bright my skin looks, and how hard I'm forcing this smile.

For a billionaire's daughter with a very important day, I'm sure I look like a mess.

It's a little scary how accurately she takes it all in without even breathing a snide remark.

Jesus.

Believe it or not, I *did* make an effort today. But against her militantly professional, picture-perfect attire, I'm convinced I spit toothpaste down my blouse. Or maybe, in the quick walk from the taxi to the front doors, the wind tossed my hair into a bird's nest.

Dad always taught me to be on time when that's a basic courtesy everyone deserves, but maybe I should have been more than five minutes early.

Did she expect me to arrive earlier?

"Hi," I say quickly before I can overthink myself into paralysis. I give a quick wave and tuck my hands behind my back. "I'm Destiny Lancaster. Nice to meet you, Miss Cho."

"Thank you for being on time. That's always useful here at Home Shepherd."

"Of course."

Of course it is. What kind of tantrum does Foster throw when people show up late?

She gestures down the wide corridor. "This way. Mr. Foster is—he will see you now."

I stop in shock. "Wait. I'm... I'm meeting Mr. Foster today?"

"Those were the terms of the program, yes. I regret that it's taken this long with his travel schedule. However, he's had a few meetings out of town this past week."

"Yes, but..." I don't have an adequate answer.

I wasn't expecting him to ever stop ghosting me doesn't seem like the right tone.

So I settle for a pained smile.

"That's fine," I lie. "Lead the way."

She says nothing else as she leads me to the executive office.

No surprise, it's an enormous, intimidating space with a giant, forbidding man at the center like he's the focal point of the entire universe.

He stands against the window, radiating pure arrogance, looking out across the morning day like he owns it.

The sunlight seeping past the clouds casts him in shadow, true evil villain style.

First impression?

I have a sense of imposing height stuffed inside a black suit, impeccably tailored with subtle grey pinstripes and understated gold cuff links.

Understated.

Classy, yes—but not in the cold, soulless way of his office.

So, there might be a hint of taste in there somewhere, and a man who understands that great wealth doesn't need to be ostentatious.

Then he goes and ruins my first impression.

He turns, sees me, and scowls.

Second impression?

Holy shit.

This can't be real.

It can't be him.

The walking asshat from Alki Beach looks just as big facing me as he did facing away, with a gloriously chiseled face that would be a whole lot more appealing if he wasn't glowering like I just spat in his coffee.

His jet-black hair and blue eyes are so familiar it stops my heart. So does that glare.

God, I don't think it's just the photos I've been scanning from the internet rumor mills. I can't believe it didn't hit me sooner.

But to be fair, I only argued with the kayaking maniac for a few minutes and his posture is everything.

It's the *way* he stands with those big shoulders bowed and that arrogant little curl of his lips.

The faded scar lashing down one tanned cheek I barely noticed until now, the huge folded arms—it all signals a man who's wrapped in pure aggression.

"What's this? Is this a joke?" His glare flicks from me to Miss Cho, who's standing right behind me.

What?

My jaw drops. This man looked me dead in the face and had the audacity to call me a 'what'?

Oh, hell no.

"The young lady selected for the inaugural Young Influencers program, sir," Cho says coolly, not even remotely ruffled.

It's like she expected this.

Like she deals with his attitude all the time.

Well, what else? If she works for him, she knows he's a titanium jerkface.

"If you recall," she continues, "we made our selection recently and she's finished the press material. I forwarded you her résumé, social profiles, and application."

"I remember," he snaps.

"This is our winning candidate, Miss Destiny Lancaster." Miss Cho gives a small sweep of her hand like she's presenting a lowly peasant to a Roman emperor.

It's so tiresome.

At least Foster *looks* at me for longer than three stormy seconds this time before he decides he wants to rip my head off.

His gaze burns with a braising contempt as it travels down my body.

Oof, forget my head.

It's more like he's ripping off my clothes so he can judge me.

Mind, body, soul, and everything in between.

I have to fight the urge to cover myself with my hands, and I'm not the type of delicate flower who ever wilts under a man's eyes.

Only, I can't just flick this guy off for giving me an angry eye-fucking I never asked for and go about my day.

I'm frozen as he drinks me in, his strong throat working. I swear the sound of him swallowing echoes through the room.

Yeah, I can't take this anymore.

"Well?" I clear my throat loudly, coughing into my hand for emphasis.

His nostrils flare before that stern gaze snaps back to Miss Cho.

"Find someone else," he snarls.

Then he strides past me, brushing my elbow without an apology.

What, what, what?

The door slams behind him.

He's gone without a single word meant for me.

Miss Cho looks like she's holding in a sigh she's too proud to release. She holds up a hand with a thin smile, looking exasperated, but in a patient way.

The woman might be an undercover saint if this is normal when it comes to babysitting Shepherd Foster.

"Please give me a moment. Sometimes Mr. Foster needs to be managed."

My mouth threatens to drop and I hold it in place with sheer willpower and clenched teeth.

Foster's assistant has just told me he needs to be managed? After insulting me in the worst way possible?

"Don't worry," she says. "Wait here and I'll be right back."

Then she leaves, following Foster out and stranding me in his cave of an office.

My whole head is ringing, pinched between humiliation and outrage and total confusion, but mostly one question that keeps blasting on repeat.

Girl, what the hell did you sign up for?

III: A LITTLE LIKE DESTINY
(SHEPHERD)

I almost make it to the elevator when Miss Cho catches up with me, her tall heels beating the slate tiles like a drum.

For a hot second, I glare.

I'm tempted to order her back into my office to clean up the mess she's made and find a suitable candidate.

Definitely not the nosy blonde mouse from the beach who never learned how to mind her own damned business.

Unfortunately, despite the fact that I call the shots, Hannah Cho can be incurably stubborn when she wants to be. She knows she's too good at oiling this machine called Home Shepherd and that makes her essentially irreplaceable.

"Are you going down, sir?" she asks politely.

I grunt in response.

She takes that as a yes, stepping into the elevator after me just before the doors shut.

Fuck it, I could run.

The thought of punching the button, stopping on some random floor, and bolting is remarkably appealing.

I *could* throw all caution to the wind and leave the elevator mere seconds before the door shuts and find another way out of this building. There's no way she'd be able to catch up in those heels.

Still, I stab the button for the first floor with unwarranted viciousness and deflate, leaning against the chrome rail with my hands stuffed in my pockets.

Beside me, Hannah stands rigid, gripping her oversized white tablet.

We both know what this is about as we stare at the bright-red numbers ticking down on the elevator screen in acid silence.

I know what she's doing, dammit.

Waiting me out.

Hannah has this way of radiating silent disapproval that would wear down a heart of iron—and all she has to do is wait for me to crack.

Works like a charm every time.

Right now, she probably has a thousand arguments against my knee-jerk reaction.

All the reasons why we should keep an impulsive, self-righteous lick of good looks and appalling manners on.

I have one better reason why we shouldn't.

It's a small fucking world.

Not nearly large enough to share it with a woman who interrupted a private moment, a personal eruption.

Hell, a woman who tried to *care.*

Only eight more floors to go.

The doors ping open and a man looks in. One look at me and he backs up, deciding he'd rather wait for the next ride than join us.

Sensible.

It takes all my willpower not to join him.

Seventh floor.

Sixth.

I set my jaw and finally look at her, casting a suspicious side-eye.

Hannah keeps her gaze dull, fixed on the screen counting down floors. Her eyes don't even twitch under my scrutiny.

"I could fire you right now, you know." I tap my fingers against my bicep. "Don't go thinking your job has divine protection. I'll explain it to God himself if that's what it takes to—"

"Of course not, Mr. Foster," she says blandly. "You're well aware I earn my keep here every day."

Damn her, I am.

"I didn't ask you to follow me," I snap.

"No."

"And yet you know I have no intention of bringing it up. Decision made and done. Get her out of the building."

Finally, she looks at me with one eyebrow raised. "Really, sir? That's rather impulsive. I think it would be a mistake and you should reconsider."

If she was anyone else, I would have chucked her overboard years ago for insubordination.

"Miss Cho, I don't need you to come charging in and questioning my executive decisions," I growl. "I'm also not sure why I agreed to this Young Influencers gimmick after all. We have an entire team of PR specialists for image concerns. Instead, I trusted your plan and you delivered one hell of a punchline."

"And you were very rude to the poor girl. Will you at least tell me why?"

My jaw tightens.

Fuck, here we go.

Every time I consider how to explain my ugly encounter with the girl on Alki Beach, it sounds a little dumber in my head.

Yes, I was an undiluted asshole.

Her only sin was persistence.

The first time she came at me with her concerns that I might drown was forgivable. Still, the fact that she continued, and the way she kept watching me as I pushed into the waves...

Whatever.

That's not the fucking point.

"Did you not see her?" I clip.

Hannah's cool gaze snaps to mine, unflinching.

"I do have eyes," she says calmly. "She's quite attractive. Is that your concern?"

"Ridiculously attractive, yes, but that's not it, exactly." I inwardly groan, still unsure how to tell her my beef without sounding like a total lunatic. "Also, Destiny is a ridiculous name."

The tiniest hint of a smile curls her lips. "Well, I can't be blamed for choosing that."

No.

I glare at my reflection.

I wish the attraction factor was just convenient cover.

When Hannah first came up with this idea, I never imagined her selecting someone so goddamn gorgeous. Let alone so annoyingly familiar.

Ridiculous name or not, she's elegant. Polished. Cool and sleek and so simply, yet fashionably striking that she probably turns grown men to stone when they pass her on the street like a little Medusa.

All blonde hair, slender neck, and frosted blue eyes. Model-perfect with a young body shaped like raw temptation.

On Alki Point, I couldn't see much beyond a pretty face I wanted to evict from my personal space.

It's worse today when she's in my office without the wind tossing her hair and a windbreaker hiding her body.

The dress she wore had one of those tiny black belts around her waist, just in case I missed the way her hips curved. Like any hot-blooded man could *ever* miss those hips.

Her type of gorgeous has its own gravitational field.

A force of nature I have zero interest in fucking with.

"You saw her pictures," Hannah reminds me in a tone that suggests she knows I never did more than glance at her résumé and certainly didn't bother checking out her socials.

"I'm disappointed, Miss Cho. I trusted you to pick someone suitable."

"And I did. I know you found it—rather unexpected, sir. But appearance was never a qualifier for the position. In fact, I'd argue that her being attractive is an unintended perk."

"A perk." I give her an ice-drenched look. "I beg to differ. What about a man? Isn't there a male influencer somewhere?"

"Not with her followers or qualifications. She's picture-perfect and squeaky-clean with an innocent, fresh face."

Innocent? *Her?*

Bah.

A fresh face, for sure, forever glowing with minimal makeup. Worse, I'm sure Destiny knows *exactly* how pretty she is.

The last time I banked on any woman's innocence, just look how that turned out.

"Not to mention her family connections," Hannah continues. "The Lancasters—"

"The coffee people? Wired Cup? As in Cole Lancaster?"

She nods.

That makes a little more sense.

Destiny dresses like someone familiar with high fashion, which becomes second nature when you come from money. The Lancasters have a vast regional coffee shop empire stretching from Montana to Hawaii and they're well known in these parts.

Wasn't there even some drama with her old man and his wife years ago? Some sort of headline-grabbing rescue story?

I can't remember.

"Yes, the coffee people," Hannah says. "But that's not the point."

"Then what the hell is?" I rake my hand through my hair.

Goddamn.

She doesn't seem to notice my irritation intensifying like a grease fire. In the five years she's worked for me, I haven't been able to provoke a single negative response from her.

Believe me, I've tried.

Not deliberately, but I'm the kind of boss who would try anyone's patience.

"Don't worry, I did some digging into her motivations. She's sincerely renounced her family's money in favor of doing honest nonprofit work," she says. "That's another reason she stood out in a field of well-qualified candidates. For Miss Lancaster, this isn't just about raising her own profile."

"So?" I demand.

She sighs patiently as we walk through the lobby.

"So, if you're seen working with her like a perfect gentleman, while she publicly vouches that you have no ulterior motives as a funder and mentor, then perhaps she's it. Your golden ticket out of any alleged escapades with Vanessa Dumas."

Shit.

I hate that it makes too much sense.

I rub the back of my head as we sweep through the lobby, twitchy bystanders parting for us like Moses and the sea.

Unlike my office, this lobby is all white and gold and busy as hell.

Interns with coffee in their hands and harassed expressions on their faces hurry toward the elevators, lanyards around their necks swinging.

Normally, it's the kind of chaos I enjoy because it's productive.

Today, I can't even bask in the joy.

"Look, Mr. Foster, all you really have to do is be decent for a few weeks with her," Hannah says. "Is that so hard?"

Miss Cho, you have no frigging clue.

"I don't appreciate the insinuation that I can't," I say, though it's a valid one, considering the way I've already handled this Destiny situation.

Like a magnificent asshole.

Hannah side-eyes me.

"I'm sorry, sir," she says, though she doesn't mean it. I think she just gets her kicks from calling me 'sir' when she's right and waiting for me to admit it.

Infuriating.

If I had a real leg to stand on, I'd have already argued back, but I don't.

So I fold my arms and watch the comings and goings of busy people rather than look at her. Everyone looks like they're already five minutes late, but there's lots of idle chatter in the air.

Hannah waits calmly, just as she always does.

I drop my arms and she nods in acknowledgment.

"Your shareholders are already feeling jumpy," she reminds me.

"What else is new? They're human fleas."

She pauses, choosing her words carefully. "Well, after other events in Seattle and certain CEOs going off the rails with erratic behavior, they're rather keen to avoid any disasters with Home Shepherd."

I sigh.

"Even if I *did* engage in a relationship with Miss Dumas—which you know I didn't—it was fake. Hardly in the same realm as buying a billion-dollar company for three times its value and then crashing it with no survivors," I snap.

"Of course it's different, sir. I'm just saying, it would be a shame if your stocks were to fall any more thanks to this, and people start making noise about your ouster. What's Home Shepherd without Shepherd Foster? You just need to reassure them that you're still thinking. You're not going feral."

"People are too goddamned focused on billionaires' lives," I mutter, scrubbing a hand through my hair. "Except when their goofy antics end in a happily ever after, of course. Just look at Brock Winthrope or Miles Cromwell. Shit, if I'd tossed out my brain and married Vanessa damned Dumas, no one would care what I did after that. They'd have our photos posted to a few wedding blogs and call it a day."

"...the trouble is that you and marriage don't mix, so it's a nonstarter. Never mind how Miss Dumas would make an objectively terrible partner."

Right.

That still doesn't mean my private life is up for grabs—although no one in the media ever gets the memo.

They're always on the hunt for new juicy scandals, and Vanessa has thrown them a hunk of red meat.

But without the public fascination with billionaires and what we do with our dicks, this crap would've died on the vine already.

As it stands, they're *still* talking about it online.

Still poking at my darker past in an effort to exaggerate rumors of the present.

If Legal hadn't assured me the fake relationship would come to light in any litigation—making me look even worse—I'd have shut Dumas up with crushing damages in a heartbeat.

"I agree it's unfair," Hannah says. "But this is the reality of the situation, and it's very much worth doing damage control. Since we have a perfectly good cause lined up... why don't you learn to crack a smile and play along?"

Play along?

Play the fuck along?

Isn't that what caused this problem with Dumas in the first place?

Hannah smiles unevenly as I pin her with a look.

If it were anyone but Destiny Lancaster, this wouldn't be so impossible.

If we didn't already have a sour history, maybe I'd give this more than a second thought.

Never mind the fact that Miss Lancaster is *disturbingly* attractive. The kind of face that could be splashed on billboards all across the US, beautiful and classy and unfussy.

It's a real fucking problem.

Frankly, I don't trust attractive women.

After Vanessa—who doesn't have a dime on this girl—and every other woman who's fucked me over in the past, I've made it a policy not to trust their motives blind.

Plus, Destiny is an influencer on top of it.

She thrives on public perception and personal brand popularity, regardless of whatever noise she makes about not being in it for the fame and followers.

Again, I see shades of Dumas.

Acres of beauty wrapped in an ego, designed to sell a product and market herself.

Only, this could be *worse* because Destiny is five times prettier than Dumas and probably just as accustomed to using her looks to get ahead.

That's not something I ever want to be a part of again. Not after the latest meltdown.

"I understand the theory behind it," I say. "While I admit I didn't pay much attention, I'm certain she wasn't the only applicant. We had over four hundred, didn't we?"

Hannah hands me her tablet. "Just take a look, Mr. Foster. One more time. Read her profile. You can spare me five minutes."

"Three minutes." I snatch it away from her and scroll through Destiny's Instagram.

Damn.

This isn't the same little fireball who ambushed me with my kayak.

Not the girl I saw in the office, either, barely holding in her real thoughts, all polish and cool professionalism.

In these bright photos, she's outdoorsy and candid, grinning at the camera with a ponytail and baseball cap on a trip to the Cascades.

I fight the urge to admire the dirt streaked on one cheek.

It's too messy and natural-looking to be pre-planned. Same goes for the creases in her clothes that really look like they were left there by a hard day of hiking.

Besides, I'm pretty sure no phony influencer would be caught dead with a husky in their face, slobbering all over their sunglasses. The dog's dried drool still shows up on the lenses a few pics later.

The photos are well chosen and authentic, I'll give her that. All flattering natural light and stunning backdrops.

She also isn't using her assets, posing in a bikini or some skintight jean shorts like most influencers might if they're using sex appeal to sell their brand.

Still, I'm naturally skeptical.

There's got to be a few skin pics somewhere here, right? A bikini set or a link to a certain 'Fans' site where desperate men drunk on good looks will throw money at her for a chance at getting in her DMs.

But no, the more I scroll, the less skin I see.

There's a trip to Alaska a year ago. Whale tracking, by the looks of it, and she's stuffed in a bulky orange jacket on a rickety science ship.

The woman's out there in the wild, taking selfies at safe distances from wildlife while she's out jogging in the brush among the bears and foxes. No dog this time.

She plies the seas with researchers, willing to be wet and miserable to save creatures who don't know their entire species is under the gun.

When it flips to Hawaii, I flick through long posts about endangered monk seals. From the comments, it looks like she actually gets people to pay attention to the plight of the animals beyond the adorable images. Her write-ups are thorough, informative, and attached to cute animal pics intended to tug on the heartstrings.

The same lanky husky shows up in the later shots, a smaller puppy then, frequently licking her face.

I keep scrolling, gritting my teeth.

Yes, I'm still searching for that inkling that she's not a good person. One more walking ulterior motive like everyone else with good looks who plays up their generosity and good deeds.

I'm annoyed that I can't find it.

No smoking gun.

It's just as infuriating how much she glows in every photo.

Not because of her makeup or layered clothes hiding a body made for sin, but because the vast majority of her shots are so natural.

It's damnably compelling.

I stop on a familiar picture of Alki Beach from the day I went out kayaking and tap on a Reel next to it.

In the video, she's still red-faced from yelling at my stubborn ass, the wind tossing her hair back in a messy ribbon that slaps the side of her face.

Somehow, she's still got her shit together enough to talk at length about harbor seals.

This version of her, all wind-swept hair and bright smiles, is almost hotter than the tall, dressed-up bombshell I just chewed up in my office.

Yeah, fuck.

There's a disarming sweetness about her that's too appealing to simply gun down and send her packing like I want to.

It shouldn't quell my paranoia so easily.

Yet, it's oddly reassuring to see all this evidence that her energy *is*, actually, focused on the environment.

"Do you see it now?" Hannah taps the top of the tablet, clearing her throat.

"She's... not as bad as I initially thought," I admit grudgingly.

"See? I promised you I'd pick the best person. That's her. No sign of greed or glad-handing whatsoever. Miss Destiny Lancaster truly is our best candidate for shining you up, sir."

Fucking sigh.

I know she's telling me the truth.

She always does.

I'm just trapped in my own stubborn jackass of a brain and I know it.

Still, I can't just unceremoniously kick this girl away.

Especially when her sterling image is exactly what I need to sideswipe the Dumas scandal and redirect Home Shepherd's reputation from the personal mud flying around.

If this woman—startlingly pretty and all about philanthropy—can reassure the public that I'm not a bodice-ripping mafia brat intent on fucking and dumping everything I don't get killed, she'll shut down the rumors.

She'll make people forget and I'll look like Mr. Fucking Clean.

It's too perfect.

What I need, what Hannah wants, and what Destiny offers, all tied up in one neat package.

There's a touch of smugness in Hannah's smile as she reads the capitulation on my face. This is what I get for hiring a PA who's too capable.

Snarling, I shove the tablet back in her hands, and she tucks it against her chest.

"Fine. We'll keep Miss Lancaster *for now.* Go put her to work, keep her busy, whatever. Just don't let her go anywhere."

"Yes, sir," she says as I head back to the elevator. "Oh, and purely my personal recommendation, but a little apology might not hurt."

Sure.

About as much as a little kick in the nuts.

"Whatever. Just stop gloating, Miss Cho."

"Gloating? Perish the thought, Mr. Foster." Her smugness remains.

"I only agreed to this because it's the right thing to do. Also, I maintain we could have easily replaced her with someone equally suitable."

Someone less pretty and considerably less intrusive.

Even a *little less* pretty would do.

A girl with big ears or missing teeth, or a Wyoming farm boy with a nose fatter than a carrot.

"Of all the applications we received with the criteria we set, Miss Lancaster's brand was the best fit, Mr. Foster. That isn't just coming from me. I put together an eight-person committee who—"

A raised hand signals that I've already heard enough.

The best.

I'm starting to believe it.

I don't fucking want to.

Just like I don't dare give Hannah Cho any response that makes her head bigger than a hot air balloon as I turn and stalk back toward the elevator.

IV: A LITTLE WAR (DESTINY)

I stand there fuming for several minutes.

Miss Cho asked me to wait, but I don't know how long she expects me to stay in the office of a man who insulted me and rushed out like I caused an allergic reaction. I'm not even sure I still have a role at Home Shepherd.

What the hell is his deal?

Okay, so he probably didn't know who was picked for the program. But am I really so toxic, one past screaming match over the world's dumbest kayaking trip aside?

I made the effort today. I got dressed up.

I nailed the application process and the endless PR sessions.

I did everything a good employee should on her very first day, never mind a glorified intern for a nonprofit program.

This is a freaking *charity program*. No one pays me to be here beyond the pile of prize money. I'm far more okay with that than anyone who actually needs an income.

Whatever.

I'll wait twenty minutes, I decide, eyeballing the empty chair in front of his desk.

Do I dare sit? Or would that burn another bridge for touching his property?

He's probably a total wacko about that too.

Do I even *care* what impression I'm giving now?

Yes, unfortunately.

Although if he's behaving this erratically, maybe the tabloid stuff wasn't the pointless gossip I figured. Maybe I should have paid more attention.

But screw it.

I drop down in the seat in front of his desk—which is almost comically vast. His enormous leather swivel chair behind it makes me think of a throne as I pull up the story.

Mr. Foster and the actress, Vanessa Dumas.

I speed-read the article.

Long, messy story short, he was involved with her before changing his mind and dumping her abruptly.

No, not just involved. *Engaged.*

Exactly the kind of scumbag behavior I'd associate with guys like him who have way more money than common sense and more clout than character.

He probably thought he would have his fun, and when he got bored of her, she could skip off and pick up the pieces of her broken heart alone.

Which, from what I can see, she's doing very publicly.

Hmmm.

Victim or not, Vanessa isn't so much picking up the pieces as flaunting them like hunting trophies so everyone can take a good look.

Still, it doesn't erase his assholery.

It's easy to believe he's a heartbreaker. He's handsome enough, in a coldhearted lizard blood kind of way.

I figured out money and good looks were a deadly combination when I was fourteen. You'd need to be a saint *not* to let great wealth go to your head.

Oh, plus that faint scar on his cheek that makes him look mysterious and dangerous in an annoyingly sexy way.

If this Vanessa did fall hard enough to get bruised, I can kind of see the appeal.

Totally theoretically, of course.

He's so not my type.

Shepherd Foster is my anti-type.

I only find a guy attractive if his maturity has grown past the moody Neanderthal stage. But I get why she *might* find him attractive.

How, objectively, the jet-black hair and ocean-blue eyes and that slashing faded scar might entice some girls who let their butterflies do the thinking.

At least this program finally makes sense, though.

I'm here so Shepherd Foster can save face.

Sighing, I scroll through another article bursting with sensational claims.

Vanessa is outing all his dirt, even poking at some organized crime rumors I don't quite understand. When I try to search deeper, nothing turns up.

Huh.

The way it's played up, the crazier it seems, and the less confident I feel about believing anything.

Everything that came down with Dad after my mother died spoke volumes about where truth ends and entertainment begins in the media.

Bad rumors spread like wildfire when the right people repeat them like mockingbirds. It's all too easy for hearsay to become fact in the public eye.

That's the world of billionaires, though.

A world I swore I never wanted to be involved in, having seen enough of it growing up.

All scandal and image management and security concerns.

No flipping thanks.

Ugh. I should've known this opportunity was too good to pass up.

No one's motives are that pure, especially CEOs of powerful security companies.

But by sticking this out, I'm going to get the funding for my conservation work. That's the important thing, all that really matters in the big picture.

I stare at my phone thoughtfully. There's a stark black-and-white portrait of a perfectly scowly Foster staring up at me like the judgmental prick he is.

What kind of man is he for real?

The messy picture Vanessa Dumas painted or something more human?

Before I can dwell on it, the door behind me flies open. In stalks Satan with his usual bold, forceful strides. Miss Cho follows in his wake, wearing what seems like her normal serene expression.

Irritation flicks across Foster's face as he sees me in the chair, but he thrusts out a no-nonsense hand without waiting for me to stand.

A power play.

"Shepherd Foster, CEO," he says crisply. "You've already met my assistant, Hannah Cho."

Wow.

I guess she really did 'manage' the tantrum right out of him.

I sneak a quick glance at her, but she doesn't show a flicker of emotion.

Foster doesn't move, waiting demandingly.

"So, we're just going to pretend this is our first meeting?" I say, folding my arms.

His eyes glint like knives. "I'm going to swallow my damned pride and start over, Miss Lancaster. The rest is entirely up to you."

Lovely.

We're caught in a breathless staring contest for the next thirty seconds.

He's not offering an apology for going off on me, and I'm not expecting one.

I'm honestly tempted to leave him hanging for a few more seconds or to neglect his handshake altogether. He was *disgustingly* rude, after all, when all I wanted was to keep his dumbass from becoming the richest person to drown in the Sound.

But I'm stronger than temptation and smarter than my snark suggests.

"Destiny Lancaster." I stand and shake his hand lightly, dropping it as soon as I can. His fingers feel oddly warm, strong, too firm to call it diplomatic or comfortable. Another power play, I guess.

Another burst of irritation snaps at his eyes, but he just crosses behind his desk and drops into his chair. "You can go, Miss Cho. I've got it from here."

She pauses for a second, looking at me for half a beat before nodding.

"Of course, sir." As commanded, she turns and shuts the door gently behind her.

Yawning silence.

Three seconds feels like thirty years.

The large glassy modern clock on the wall ticks obnoxiously loud. I wonder if he wants that thing to intimidate everyone who comes into his citadel.

If he's hoping it's going to work on me, he's SOL.

"Sit so we can talk," Foster says, waving at the empty seat next to me. "You already made yourself at home once."

"What was I supposed to do? You stormed off and left me here alone." I don't mean to say it, but he's pissing me off.

Just because he's filthy rich doesn't mean he has to be a colossal dick.

His gaze lands on my face, direct and forceful like always. I have to fight not to flinch under his scrutiny.

"Do you need an apology? Is that what you're waiting for?"

"You *were* rude," I grind out. "And pretty psycho."

"I was," he admits, with absolutely no regret or remorse. "I suppose you only had my well-being in mind that day at Alki Point when you threatened to sic the Coast Guard on me."

My lips thin. "Oh, please, it isn't even about that—"

"My apologies, Miss Lancaster."

I've never heard a less sincere apology.

Somehow, I ignore my urge to spin around and exit the room.

"Now," he continues, "I need to bring you up to speed on our expectations. I'll give you the company tour now so you know what you're getting involved with."

A company tour with this guy? Not Miss Cho?

I can hardly imagine anything worse.

"Peachy," I whisper.

"For the next two weeks, you were supposed to be working with the Director of Corporate Giving, but regrettably she's just starting her maternity leave. Unfortunate."

He doesn't look like he thinks it's unfortunate.

Bastard.

"Right now, there's only a program intern, but he's well versed enough to explain how everything works with our grant process. I'm sure he'll be grateful for your cooperation and a chance to reduce his considerable workload."

Oh, now I see.

The big press junket is over, so he's pawning me off on a minion.

Just like I expected.

This awkward trainwreck of a meeting is probably the only time I'll see Shepherd Foster. That's a small silver lining.

Still, I smile tightly and decide to push my luck.

"I'm sorry to hear that, Mr. Foster. I thought I'd be working directly with you?"

He stares blankly.

"Did you?" Either he's not used to being challenged or he really didn't know that was the deal.

"Unless, of course," I continue, "you're the kind of CEO who doesn't know the ins and outs of his own program."

His eyes narrow.

Gotcha.

That awful clock ticks between us as he stares at me, his stern eyes hiding everything but his flaming irritation at being in this room with me.

Then he gives a small cynical smile.

"We work with *Homes for Seattle*," he says, naming one of the biggest charities in the city. "With *Doctors without Borders, CARE, the International Rescue Committee, Direct Relief.*"

Some of the biggest global charities.

Of course, he knows about those, though. They're famous and worldwide.

"You've heard of *New Leaves Tree Recovery* as well, I imagine," he continues. "Every year we donate a substantial sum to *Friends of Arctic,* the only conservation group to ever increase polar bear numbers near Hudson Bay. Last year, we partnered with Winthrope International to host a global conference for Hawaiian bird conservation. I gave a presentation on efforts I funded with a local, Dr. Cash—at my personal expense—to find a living Kaua'i 'ō'ō. The bird is probably extinct, but I'll agree with that call only after we've scoured every rock on Kauai." He raises a challenging eyebrow. "Are those too famous for you? Too personal?"

I think my jaw is hanging open.

I can't even argue.

"Additionally, we work with *Nairobi Waters* and a new earth-quake and disaster recovery charity set up in Turkey and Iran, a banana soil rehabilitation group in Brazil, and *True Blue Blooded* to stop the over-farming of horseshoe crabs by big pharma." He keeps going, rattling off charities ranging from international rock stars to the local and obscure.

And... and he knows the details.

About every single one.

Holy hell.

This man isn't bluffing.

He's not pretending just because he thinks it'll impress me. And he doesn't even glance at his computer screen to cheat and read off information.

The man knows his shit.

When he's done, he folds his arms over his broad chest, reminding me again of those shiny gold cuff links and his sheer size.

"I could bore you with more details, Miss Lancaster, but that's not why we're here." He watches me swallow too loudly. "Tell me, though, who exactly did you think you were dealing with?"

I bite my tongue.

Not because I think he's right or he deserves my consideration.

He might know what he's talking about, but he's behaving like an asshole. The arrogant, entitled superprick I met the second he stormed away with his kayak, thinking he could wrestle nature and win.

I'm still a little sad that he did.

But he *wants* me to rise to the challenge.

That's what this whole thing is—a test.

No way am I going to let this man *bait* me. I'm not intimidated by his big showy knowledge—and just because he knows the names and a few of the whys doesn't mean he cares.

He's probably one of those freaks with a photographic memory or something.

"Very impressive, sir." I give him an artificially sweet smile.

That gets through if nothing else does.

His biceps bunch, and he looks like he's gritting his teeth. A muscle pops in that impossibly sharp jaw.

Honestly, I would have preferred it if the exterior matched the interior. It would be easier to hate him if he looked more like his gnarled gargoyle of a personality.

But Foster turns away from me abruptly, shaking his mouse to wake his screen.

"Whether you're with me or the intern, you'll get your two million. Isn't that what it's all about? The zeroes on the check?"

In some ways, yes.

But admitting that would be like exposing my throat to a vampire, so I just watch him coolly. I can practically see his blood pressure climbing.

"Just so you know, I'm not impressed by big money, Mr. Foster," I say. Though he doesn't look at me, the corner of his mouth twitches. "I grew up rich."

"Cole Lancaster? Yes, he's done quite well for himself selling everyone their morning high," he clips.

Now he's making it personal?

My eyes snap to the half-empty mug on his desk and I glare.

"Emphasis on 'everyone,'" he growls. "I'm not immune to your father's brand. Half of Seattle grew up on Wired Cup, and this office runs on their Pioneer Campfire blend."

Nice save, damn him.

"Whatever. Money isn't worth much unless you make it useful," I say.

"And how do you define useful, Miss Lancaster?" he challenges.

I actually don't mind.

I want to meet him head-on.

I *want* to push his buttons and find his weaknesses, the things he truly hates. I want to flay him open and see what's really under all the jagged antisocial rock.

His dormant volcano temper is weirdly compelling. Like walking into a lion's den with a big, juicy burger and wondering how long it'll be until you wind up lunch.

"Useful?" I let the question linger, then I smile. "How about saving creatures who can't save themselves without it?"

"Animal conservation?" Foster's eyes narrow. For a second, I see the way my words press into him. The weight of them sit uncomfortably against his skin. "We might have one thing in common then, Miss Lancaster. Shocking, I know."

Oof.

I'm speechless.

And he closes off, shutting his flicker of emotion behind an icy wall I imagine he throws up a lot like a shield.

The air in the room thickens.

Adversarial, charged, yet somehow, questioning.

Can we set our own crap aside? For the greater good?

I don't know.

He's taken up arms, and so have I.

I'm not sure who even decided to declare war, but it doesn't matter now. There's no earthly way I'm backing down and giving him the satisfaction of thinking I'm a quitter.

Especially not when there's so much good on the line.

I hate how his eyes are so gorgeous, though. Blue and sharp and compelling.

I can't imagine them ever being soft, but now with our gazes fused, I notice flecks of brighter color. Grey and yellow and brown. All the fragments that make up that ice-blue.

It reminds me of the sea a little, reflecting the world around it while it looks on with its own unyielding strength.

This man has an ocean soul.

Vast and immovable and stubborn.

Kind of beautiful in a scary way.

The difference, of course, is that the ocean is more forgiving than Shepherd Foster. It brings life and only shows its terrible wrath every once in a while.

Generally, the ocean is *good*.

The same can't be said for him, no matter how many precious maybe-extinct birds he's gone searching for.

Mr. Foster is one of those hardass, brass tacks billionaires my father always tried to avoid.

I bet he probably fires people for breathing too loud and sends his executive team home in hives.

I can practically feel a few rising on my arms as I look at him. I'm allergic to prolonged exposure to jackasses.

But he's still watching me, searching my face like he wants to read every thought.

If he can, then he must know how much I despise him—but he probably knew that anyway.

Chin raised, I stare right back.

The charged air skitters across my skin, reminding me how long it's been since anything has made me feel this on edge.

"So, are we done making eyes at each other or is this part of Young Influencers too? I mean, I guess I can do this all day if you really want. First one to blink is a sucker."

When he turns away, I swear I see a hint of a smile he immediately squelches.

He looks back with pure scorn and raises his hand.

"I'll spare you the eye drops, Miss Lancaster. Now, if you'll retract your claws for twenty minutes, I'll give you the tour."

V: A LITTLE TRUCE (SHEPHERD)

*T*his woman is baffling as hell.

I've never met anyone quite like her, and it's pissing me off.

So much I'm hard-pressed not to show how much it irritates me.

Usually, I regulate my emotions well. It's a necessity when you're CEO overseeing billions and a Foster, considering how many idiots I've interacted with who will judge you based on rumors.

Honest business doesn't let you show your cards, let alone your innermost demons and desires.

My poker face is normally impeccable.

I smile when appropriate, rattle off the right script, and shake hands with the greediest corporate dunces America ever coughed up without batting an eyelid.

All fine and dandy.

I don't enjoy that aspect of the job, but it doesn't matter.

I do it anyway without breaking a sweat.

I know what's expected.

It's not like I can't handle being unable to read some people.

Hannah Cho taught me that no matter how often you see

some folks, no matter how well you can predict their behavior, you can't always read their minds.

Again, fine.

But Destiny Lancaster?

She's a different scenario altogether.

For starters, I'm used to people sucking up. When you're this rich and this connected, most people are interested in impressing you.

Not her.

That makes me sound like an arrogant asshole—and it might be a little true—but that's what I expected. I thought the influencer we hired would be giddy about the opportunity.

Not pissed because I didn't meet *her* expectations.

Hannah assured me she was the one, and her platform and attitude seem right, but she's not the gushing type. That's such a surprise I don't know what to do with it.

"The lobby looks nice," she says before we exit it.

The lobby. *The fucking lobby.*

"I'm glad you approve," I clip.

She glances at me but says nothing as I take her through Home Shepherd's relevant floors. When my people see me coming, they pretend to be hard at work, averting their eyes, and she glances at me again.

I pretend not to notice.

From the incisive way she takes everything in, it's clear she understands what she's seeing. A well-oiled kingdom with a religion of efficiency and excellence in everything we do.

Of course, she never compliments me on any of that.

Fair, when I never compliment her elegance, her poise, her figure, her carefully controlled expressions and tone as she greets names I struggle to remember.

Everything she says is thought out.

I think she's taking reams of mental notes with those light-blue eyes. Whenever she looks at me, her expression frosts over.

But sometimes, when she watches someone else, she reminds

me of the sporty girl in the Instagram shots. The one I shouldn't be so eager to see again.

Stop it, you fuck.

She's not here to smile and look pretty and certainly not for your amusement.

But when she does?

Goddammit, I'm shredded.

She's so bright and lovely I can't look away.

If Destiny Lancaster's superpower is blinding the world with her sweetness, she's already given my miserable eyes third-degree burns.

Even if I wonder how much is real and how much is just her being diplomatic.

Every face she wears is for profit. For effect. To sell herself to the company.

From what I've seen, she knows what she's doing. She's too controlled to let anything slip.

Everything I see is for show.

Everything.

I can't forget that.

Mark Cantor, the intern, works on the ninth floor. So after the whistle-stop tour, I lead her over to where he's sitting.

Normally, the Director of Corporate Giving has this office, but in her absence with Mark picking up the slack, he's temporarily in here like he owns the place.

He grins behind his bushy beard as we approach and practically knocks the chair down as he hurries over to shake my hand.

"Mr. Foster! Always a pleasant surprise," he says like the talking golden retriever he is.

Seriously, the kid is such an ass-kisser he's probably got a lip balm subscription.

I nod at Destiny next to me.

"Mark, this is Destiny Lancaster. She'll be leading our Young

Influencers program and you'll be working with her. Destiny, meet Mark Cantor."

Mark transfers his hyperactive handshake to her.

"So nice to meet you!" He smiles at her, charming in an irritating, clean-cut way.

It's hard to pin down what annoys me most about him when it isn't his impeccable work record.

Probably the fact that he's always so eager to please, fawning over anyone he thinks might be able to forward his career. He's known around here as the bagel boy for showering the office with breakfast and pastries a few times per week.

But he's a working beak with a bright future, and Destiny smiles back at him, clearly pleased.

"Hi, Mark," she says warmly, shaking his hand. He blinks a little, probably more dazzled by her than he has any business being. "Apparently, I'm going to be working with you?"

"Yeah! I'm filling in for Rachel," Mark explains. "Otherwise, you'd be working with her. But I have to say, I'm pumped for the help. I've seen your Instagram. Awesome work! Cool dog, too."

Destiny laughs and eats it right up.

I flatten my hand against my thigh to prevent it from becoming a fist.

Little ass-kisser, and this time it's an ass he has no business being around.

"Thank you. It's nice knowing I have any kind of reach. Sometimes, you wonder," she muses.

"You kidding? You're on fire." He waves a hand frantically. "Have you decided on a charity yet for the big prize?"

"Not yet." Her lips thin thoughtfully. "I definitely want to take my time and make the right choice." She shoots me a sharp glance, and her lips curl into a humorless smile. "After all, it's not about the money, but how it's used."

"Oh, for sure," Mark says, desperate to please as always.

"Thanks, Mark," I say sharply, ready to put this conversation out of its misery. "When you're working, you'll be in here with him, Miss Lancaster. The room is big enough to share, I trust."

"Sure," she says, glancing around. The office isn't massive by any means, but it's perfectly comfortable, and there are two chairs at a large wraparound desk.

Mark smiles at us both. "I'll make you a space, Dess."

Brown-nosing prick.

He's known her for all of sixty seconds and he's already resorted to nicknames?

I don't know what it is about him, but sometimes he really grates on me.

Or maybe it's just this woman injecting a baffling heat in my blood that feels too much like jealousy.

Absolute fucking nonsense.

"We should get going, there's more to cover," I say, giving Mark a quick nod.

Destiny trails after me, scanning the environment as I lead her to another person she'll need to know.

"This is Carol Garcia, our Senior Product Manager," I say. "Carol oversees our product lines from discovery to development, then beta testing and launch. Carol, meet Destiny Lancaster."

Carol smiles.

At first glance, she might not look like much, but she's a powerhouse in a lean, short package. She makes a point of being intimately acquainted with all of our products in a way no one else at this company is.

I wouldn't go as far as to say she's invaluable—because no one truly is—but she does an excellent job of being necessary.

"Hi, Miss Lancaster," she says. "It's great meeting someone who gets to represent the fun side of Home Shepherd."

I grit my teeth.

True or not, 'fun' is not the word I'm looking for.

We're a security company for fuck's sake.

"Call me Destiny. Please." She extends a hand and they shake.

"You'll be working under Mark in Corporate Giving, but if there's anything you need, just let me know. I'm always happy to help."

"Well," Destiny says, flashing me a quick glance, "that depends if I'll be involved in any of Home Shepherd's products. Or if any of them are involved in charity work, I guess."

"If you're interested, you could take a look at our process," Carol says.

"Miss Lancaster is here to learn more about our charity endeavors," I remind her, clearing my throat.

"Oh, of course, Mr. Foster. But that's a good thing to get young people involved in, too. Did you know we're expanding into security services for campus safety?" Carol beams at Destiny and prattles on at length about our Home Away school initiatives.

I'm not entirely sure why she doesn't bother me the way Mark does, even when she talks like a chipmunk on speed. Maybe it's her efficiency and honest passion. Carol does the work of three people. She's due for a raise and I make a mental note to revisit it.

"Thanks," I say, waving Destiny onward. "I'm sure you two can get more familiar another time."

Carol sends Destiny a wink I pretend not to notice, and we head back to the elevators to the top floor. Mine.

Only my office and Hannah's desk are up there, though sometimes I think we're wasting space.

"I was wondering," Destiny says, "how involved you are in defense technology?"

Finally, a question worth asking.

"We draw the line at doing business with anyone funding active wars of aggression," I tell her curtly. "Both in the U.S. or internationally. Believe me, we had offers left and right from both sides of the latest European crisis. I rejected them all."

"You did? Wow. It's so political. Everyone wants everything in black and white. Nobody can stand it when you don't choose their side." A tiny smile curves one corner of her mouth as she nods, apparently pleased.

"My money and my morals were better spent on helping the people who fled that war. They had no say in it, after all. I had zero interest in helping anyone precision-target their drones into better murder machines."

Are her cheeks red as she quickly glances away?

Damn.

An odd satisfaction pulses through me before I remember I don't give a shit about how she sees what we do here.

This is about my vision for the company. Her opinions aren't welcome beyond charity and positive influencer content.

"I know the security focus and our technology edge makes it seem like we're involved in defense schemes. The truth couldn't be more different," I tell her. "We're solely focused on domestic security for earning our keep. We want to make normal people feel safer, wherever they are."

"You do purchase military technology," she says carefully. "I did my homework."

"We do. *Old* technology," I emphasize. "We take the existing tech and repurpose it. It's a form of war-to-peace recycling, and because military-grade weapons and sensors are more advanced than you'll find on the market, our products are always better."

"But you're careful about who you sell to, aren't you?"

"Always. That goes from who we buy from, too. I have a long list of nations and NGOs I never accept as suppliers, and they're not always the ones you'd think."

Her eyes widen.

She nods politely and sends me a curious glance.

"So were you in the military then? You can guess I read a little about you... But there wasn't much in your Wiki bio, honestly, not after—" She stops cold.

I feel the way my shoulders stiffen.

My past is no one's business—especially not hers—even if my money and family make me a prisoner to human interest.

I just wonder which nightmare is hanging on the tip of her tongue.

After your dead wife?

After your meathead mobster fuck of an uncle almost got you killed?

She's wise to shut it.

The very last thing I need today is this little streak of sunshine prodding me over shit that happened long before I ever founded Home Shepherd.

She waves a hand like she needs to physically clear the air.

"Let me ask you this—have you ever thought about using your tech for wildlife conservation? Like Carol suggested?" she asks.

"How?"

"Well, for starters, so many endangered species need surveillance that won't disrupt their natural habitats," she says. "A lot of conservationists can't even *find* them. That's seriously like half the battle, sometimes. I've been on those ships. One time in Alaska, they spent eight of the twelve days just looking for the right pod of whales. I know it's a niche market and probably not big money. But with lots of grants floating around, there *is* a market, and it's crazy underserved."

For the first time, I stare at her without any irritation.

She makes a damned good point and it catches me so off guard I need a second just to process.

"You've done some research into this," I say.

She flushes. "I've lived it. It didn't exactly click that there was a solution until we were talking to Carol. It's worth looking at, is all I'm saying."

I nod, stopping just short of admitting this little firecracker might give me something more than grief.

"The technology in the field is good, but it could always be better," she says, turning and looking up at me.

Baby-blue eyes and flecks of green, different from mine.

They're suddenly lit up and sparkling the way they do in her photos and video shorts.

I want to fucking hate it.

The way she looks, the easy enthusiasm that doesn't feel like a soundbite, or some kind of clumsy olive branch meant to win me over.

"Just think about it, maybe?" she whispers. Then she gestures with her hands. That animated passion leaks into every word. "Being able to monitor these animals would make it so much easier to really help them."

I don't let myself leap at her idea, so I just nod again slowly, clutching my cards to my chest.

"I'll run it by Rachel when she returns from leave. Perhaps we'll set up a cross-department conference with Lyndon, my research head."

"Please do. It could have huge effects, and it would work freaking miracles with marine life. Underwater conditions are so harsh on the equipment, and the investment just hasn't been made into improving it."

She's right about one thing—with niche-level profits there's niche-level motivation to develop more durable research tools.

As I've discovered, most conservation groups aren't billion-dollar corporate conglomerates, either. They don't have the money to pile into new inventions when they're busy in the field or begging for the few scraps they do get from their wealthy benefactors.

It would have to be sustainable, too, but also affordable enough for individuals and organizations.

"Oh, and I was thinking," she goes on without giving me time to think through the implications. "You recently announced a prototype for the first silent civilian drone, right? The one coming in the next quarter or two?"

"You *have* been busy, Miss Lancaster," I say dryly.

My eyes flick down her body.

My blood heats viciously at the thought of her undressed and hunched in bed with her phone, reading my stupid bio and company history.

A young woman wasting precious minutes of her life on *me.*

"Obviously." She smiles sheepishly. "I like to know what I'm getting involved in."

And who, she doesn't add.

Fuck.

She has me by the balls.

I'm sincerely impressed, no matter how grudgingly.

"What about the drones? You have ideas, don't you?" I have to ask.

"Well, I was thinking... they could be *insanely* useful for tracking endangered species without scaring them."

"They're not designed for remote surveying, but perhaps." I look down into her face, trying to ignore her glowing excitement. She really is disturbingly attractive. "What are you suggesting? Be bold and say it, Miss Lancaster."

"A new line of business," she says immediately. "Maybe even a new product line? You'd be filling a gap in the market *and* contributing to conservation."

It might be a market gap, yes, but it won't be a highly profitable one.

Most conservation efforts operate off grants, donations, et cetera. I'd have to essentially give the damn equipment away for any of these groups to deploy it.

And judging by the way she's already framed this whole idea, she's bitterly aware of that.

It all comes back to what she said before in my office, about how money should be used.

We both know I have enough of it.

I've also never been brutally profit driven at the expense of all else—and it's not like Home Shepherd isn't profitable.

I can afford to take a loss on a single project, particularly if it's billed as experimental.

In other words, her suggestion has merit. It could be viable.

Still, I have no intention of telling her on the spot, even if I'm impressed by the fact that she's come up with this after less than two hours in the building.

"Just think about it," she says.

"I will."

"You'll consider thinking about it or actually consider it?" she presses.

I scowl at her, hating that I almost smile.

Coffee brat.

"I'll *consider* thinking about your proposal, Miss Lancaster. If you'll lay off ever thinking I respond well to smart-assed demands."

For a second, it looks like she's about to smile, too.

The corner of her mouth twitches, and her eyes warm, and God help me, she's more magnificent than ever.

Then I had to go and run my mouth.

She turns away, the fragile beginnings of the smile dying as she looks at the floor.

"So, what will I be working on while I'm here then, if I'm not working directly with you all the time?"

Damn.

I don't know how she keeps doing it, catching me off guard.

At this point, I should be prepared for her bullshit, and the sharp, uncompromising note in her voice when she asks.

"For the corporate end, you'll be working on grants and featuring a new product line," I say. "Mark will give you the technical details of how our corporate giving program should work in tandem with our product development team for this."

"What, because you don't know?"

I ignore her.

"Hannah will also give you access to the corporate system for the internal templates you'll use for your proposals."

She frowns. "Wait, what proposals?"

"The new product line *you* proposed, Miss Lancaster. You've got three days to sell me on this idea, drones for wildlife surveillance. I expect you to show your work in excruciating detail." I pause to enjoy the stunned look on her face. "If I like it enough, you can present your proposal to the entire board."

Fuck me senseless.

The way she looks right now with her eyes wide and mouth parted shouldn't be as enticing as it is.

I allow myself a few more seconds to suppress the intrusive thoughts of the sexy kind before I wheel around and stride away.

Time to escape while I still can.

* * *

FIVE MISSED calls from Vanessa Dumas that afternoon.

Every time I glance at my phone, another one appears, a buzzing middle finger flicking me between the eyes.

The only reason I haven't blocked her number is because I want to keep the call logs as legal evidence of harassment or blackmail, should she be so stupid to escalate this further.

She's been texting me, too, and her messages all range from apologetic to subtly threatening.

Telling me—and her audacity is something—that she knows I wanted it. That I was giving her 'signals' for months.

I should have sued her for sexual harassment the morning after she threw herself at me in the limo.

Then again, I never wanted to make this bullshit messier than it needed to be.

Hindsight is twenty-twenty.

I pick up the phone and bark into it.

"Miss Cho, get Miss Lancaster an access badge ASAP and make sure she has a computer set up in Mark's office."

"Yes, sir."

"I want a complete background check on her. Everything."

"A background check?" I can hear Hannah frowning.

"Did I fail to make myself clear?"

"No," she says after a moment. "But may I ask why?"

"Because I've entrusted her with a high-level proposal. She's not an employee. However, she should go through the same scrutiny as anyone else I've ever put in that position."

Because I want to know more about her is what I don't say.

Also, something doesn't quite add up.

The Lancasters have money. More than ever, judging by the hyped success of Wired Cup's big rebranding push years ago.

What I don't understand is why she, their daughter, is apparently left behind.

Why?

If you look at her Instagram, you might think you're getting a sporty, down-to-earth, fresh-faced girl who came from an average upper middle-class background in Ballard. Mostly makeup free, enthusiastic, passionate about her causes.

But here in the office?

This was a cool, sharp-witted professional.

Perfectly comfortable in large settings like this, facing down assholes like me who are used to being intimidating.

At no point was she overwhelmed by the scope of what we do. She even took time to research our future endeavors before she walked through my door.

I want to know why she left her family money behind for a life of clawing at charity prizes. Why is she doing all this on her own?

What's Destiny Lancaster's real story?

"Have you ever thought you might have trust issues?" Hannah asks blandly.

I sigh. "Don't you have things to do? Places to go? Important people to pester?"

"Not particularly," Hannah says dryly. "But fine. I'll make up something so you can dismiss me and dodge the question."

Goddammit.

"I could have you fired for that, you know," I say.

"I know. But you won't."

She's right.

Because for all the myriad ways her attitude gnaws at me, I can't afford to lose her.

"I'm cutting your pay," I snarl.

"What was that? A performance bonus, Mr. Foster? For all the good work I do? Thank you so much!"

"Find some work to do that doesn't involve my personal life, Hannah. I want that background check by tomorrow morning."

I can almost hear her smile as she ends the call, leaving me alone with a grinning Instagram pic of Destiny on my screen.

Fuck.

If she weren't posing with the dog and its big, goofy husky grin, I'd swear she posted this pic purely to torment me.

I drop my head into my hands and groan, wondering what I did in a past life to deserve this fate—fuck, this Destiny—certain to drive me mad.

VI: A LITTLE PRESSURE (DESTINY)

*S*haring an office with Mark Cantor isn't as easy as I thought it would be.

Don't get me wrong, he's a nice guy. A bearded marshmallow wrapped in human skin.

A little too eager to please, a little too perma-smiley, but I figured that was just because his boss was hovering over him when we met—and let's face it, most people would be scared into compliance by Foster's glower any day.

I'm not sure that man's face knows how to do anything else.

Does he ever smile in a *nice* way?

Does he laugh?

I can't imagine.

Except for those brief moments a couple days ago when he looked at me like he thought what I had to say was marginally interesting.

That's why he gave me this assignment, isn't it?

All I have to do is present my proposal to him, convince him it's a good idea, and *if* I pass, he'll let me present it to the board so they can rake me over the coals again.

Ha.

Still, there's no denying it's a fantabulous opportunity. I don't want to blow it.

So I stare at my work laptop and the PowerPoint slides, willing myself to find the right combination of words that sells them on this high-tech wildlife tracking experiment.

It's been two days since then.

Two brutal days of wondering how the hell I can convince Foster, assuming this isn't all some weird power game just so he can take my idea out back and shoot it between the eyes.

Part of me thinks there's no way this isn't an elaborate trap.

A trick so he can take me down a peg or two for daring to get in the way of his suicidal kayaking.

I bet he wants to.

I've persisted in pissing him off since the minute I got here, and there's nothing power-hungry guys hate more than being shown up. Or having someone around who doesn't fear them.

Especially if everyone else around here is like Mark the human puppy.

Or Carol, who seems to view him like the brilliant son she never had. Which is a weird vibe, honestly.

Before I even look up, I know Mark is over my shoulder again, hovering like an overgrown fly. I toy with the idea of asking him to buzz off and leave me alone.

If only a little honesty didn't make easy enemies.

Though he must not notice I'm visibly annoyed.

He's *relentlessly* positive. Almost to the point of denial, like he wants to paint over all of life's imperfections so he doesn't have to deal with them.

"How's it coming, Destiny?" he asks like he didn't just ask the same question half an hour ago before his coffee run.

Like I've written a single thing in that time.

I resist the urge to dig my hands through my hair.

I'm not a single sentence closer to winning over Mr. Cranky-face, and I know it.

In fact, I'm pretty sure I'm sucking so bad at this that he's actively avoiding me. Maybe he has a sixth sense for failure.

I've sent him emails, tried to schedule a meeting, and even waited outside his office, hoping he'll emerge like a hibernating bear so I can prod him with more questions.

If I could just find out what his top concerns are with an initiative like this, I could nail them.

But he always has a full calendar or he's just stepped out.

And no matter how pleasant Hannah Cho seems on the outside, she's quick to politely remind me that Mr. Foster keeps a godlike schedule.

I get it.

He's a busy man.

But he's also the guy who gave me this assignment.

He decided to take a chance on me after I triggered him into a tantrum.

Mark shifts his weight, waiting for my answer. I realize I totally tuned out of the conversation before it started.

"Sorry, what?"

"I was just asking about this slide..." He swipes a finger at the screen, which displays a quote from an interview I arranged with prominent marine conservationist, Debra Hollens.

"Oh. Yeah, I decided to pull the best parts from the interview and sprinkle them in," I say, bringing up the notes, which I transcribed late last night over blueberry tea.

He leans in, close enough to punch me in the face with his cologne, mumbling as he reads.

"Wow. Did she really lose a couple fingers to frostbite going after sea lions?"

I flick my mouse at the photo of Hollens waving, her two missing digits clear as day.

"It was an accident. They ventured too far in an arctic storm. She thought the sea lions were close enough to their camp, but they wandered too far and the wind picked up. It's like a maze out there and they lost their way. They're lucky they survived before search and rescue came and nope, no sea lions."

"Yikes! Talk about a sacrifice for science." He smiles awkwardly like it's the funniest thing ever before he notices I'm not laughing. "Uh, shouldn't that be closer to the front, Dess? It's a pretty compelling story."

I suppose he has a point.

"I'll move things around, yeah. Anything else?" I force a smile, so ready to be left alone.

"Nah, I'm good. Just chiming in to help you out." He gives me a look like a kicked puppy.

"Thanks, Mark. You've put me on the right track and I can take it from here."

As soon as he shuffles away, I look at the clock.

Barely one p.m.

Ugh.

I knead my knuckles into my eyes until I see stars.

I'm doing the best with what I have.

I had to go begging Carol for help so she'd give me the templates. I did all the research myself, put it together with references.

My interview with Debra Hollens was pure luck, and it was possibly the shortest interview *ever*. Fortunately, she has a way with words and sharing her life. She's the type of person where everything they say is interesting.

But her frostbitten tragedy is perfect proof of the many ways this would help conservation efforts—not just the animals, but human researchers.

I'm hoping—no, praying—that it'll help my case.

With Shepherd Foster, there's no room for error.

The one mistake he made with that actress has him more strung out than ever.

Also, after more digging around online and getting more details about the woman he supposedly dumped, I think I know why he's avoiding me.

Vanessa Dumas has a sizable online presence.

Her Instagram following—never mind her TikTok and Facebook page—has ballooned into six figures ever since she came out publicly about the big bad crimes he apparently committed.

It's not my place to judge, but... she doesn't look hurt.

She looks like she's *thriving* off the attention.

I mean, if I were in Foster's shoes, I might develop an unhealthy fear of attractive women too. Is that the real reason why he's avoiding me?

I'm almost sad if it is, if he thinks I'd pull a Dumas.

Besides, he's not *that* hot.

Not lose-my-mind-over-him hot.

Obviously, I have eyes and a pulse so I can see he's attractive. I get *why* gobs of women might have a crush on him.

They aren't me.

I've been around rich assholes my whole life, and I'd like to think it's made me immune to the toxic personalities buried behind their outer charms.

And I hate to admit it, but he's definitely hot enough for someone else to lose their wits.

It shouldn't be humanly possible for a man so cold to be scorching—but the fact that he's so forbidding and imposing makes him more attractive.

It's like a law of physics Newton forgot to cover, wealthy assholes and their animal magnetism.

Foster is a piece of forbidden fruit with arms and legs like tree trunks.

Raw temptation wrapped up in a pretty package, just out of reach.

But that's not what I'm here for.

I didn't apply for this gig so Mr. CEO could ghost me and I could waste my time away, stuck on his deliriously good looks.

God, am I as immune as I think?

I shouldn't have even *noticed* between all the sniping we've done.

He was too busy glaring for me to pay much attention to anything except for the fact that someone apparently set his eyes on fire.

Blue flame. Searingly hot.

Just like the rest of him.

I almost thunk my head down on my laptop. Only Mark watching me curiously from the other side of the desk keeps me from embarrassing myself to death.

"Not going well?" he asks sympathetically.

No.

No, it's not going well at all.

I'm hung up on the fact that my hot boss is ignoring me instead of just finalizing this dumb proposal and letting fate do the rest.

It can't be daddy issues.

If anything, the whole dead mother thing should've left me with an unhealthy mess of mommy issues instead.

Dad, like Foster, was an infamous grump before Eliza wore him down with her delicious pastries, coffee creations, and sunny smiles.

But Dad's special.

He raised me, and no matter what, he always showed more warmth at his coldest than Foster.

He also taught me how to focus. I definitely don't need to give a crap if Foster's all smiles or frozen stares.

The chance to shadow a CEO was another big reason I applied. It seems useful if I'm ever in a position to run my own nonprofit.

I've read through the company's history. Foster started this venture alone over a decade ago. He had jaw-dropping venture capital interest before he even hired his first employee.

By the time he turned Home Shepherd into a real working company, he was already known for philanthropy from his other ventures.

He created the vast architecture here from nothing but experience and some seed money.

Arrogant suit or not, he's the sort of man you'd want to learn from when it comes to building empires from ash and bone.

And honestly, bad attitude aside, I'm beginning to think I'd jump at the chance to trade Foster for Mark, who's finally typing away on his computer, humming obnoxiously to some pop song.

Mark wouldn't know the nitty-gritty about business if it smacked him in the face. All the pitfalls to avoid, how to make everything transparent and fully focused on doing *good* vs. just making money.

And Carol, she's perfectly lovely, but she's also not going to know the thousand-foot view.

As a product lead, she knows better than anyone what the company does on a smaller scale with its biggest assets, but...

The first time I met Foster, I didn't think he knew much either.

I thought all the research I'd done about how he'd set up his company meant nothing.

Until he dropped that mile-long list of charities Home Shepherd works with.

Until I dug deeper, talked to more employees, learned more history, and now it's possible—*possible*—that Shepherd Foster isn't just another greedy billionaire with an ego to feed.

Public disclosures show he takes home far less salary than he could, even if it's still a staggering amount. He has no golden parachute waiting on the other side in offshore accounts and vaporware companies.

By every measure, he pays his people well, triples their 401(k) contributions, and Foster Holdings' charitable contributions are legendary.

It's just kept weirdly quiet, without any big fanfare.

Just like charity work should be, honestly, and that's what bothers me.

Why isn't he like the others?

Why isn't the good he does an enormous dick-waving symbol of pride?

I hate to admit it, but I'm as impressed as I am suspicious.

Though the people here seem to want to do honest good without looking for praise and quick leaps up the career ladder.

Of course, the smears from Vanessa Dumas could be true.

I'm not stupid.

There's a distinct chance he's a sharp businessman and perfectly generous, but he's also a womanizing asshole. Maybe that's why he likes to be so secretive.

But if the rumors are only that, and this actress is blowing everything out of proportion for attention, what does that mean?

Is Shepherd Foster just a workaholic freak who wants to be left alone?

I'm still wrestling with the possibilities as I work until Carol taps her fingers against the door and pokes her head in.

"Hey!" she says. "How's it going with the big proposal?"

Mark looks up with a scowl, which is weird for him.

"Good," I lie. "Just fine-tuning the layout now."

"Nervous?" She gives me a sympathetic smile.

I hesitate. "A little. It's a quick turnaround. There's more I'd want to do if I had the time..."

"Don't overthink it! This isn't grad school and those suits grade on ideas, not fancy words."

Oof, yeah.

That's what worries me.

"The idea part is fine. Mostly. I just wish I had a little more practical experience to point to with something this new."

"You could always speak to Mr. Foster about it," she suggests. "I'm surprised he didn't give you more time. Two to three weeks is standard for a normal internal development proposal, and this is pretty close to that. It's not usually so tight."

No, of course.

Because Mr. Foster is a dark prince of all pricks who enjoys making me miserable.

"I bet he'll make time to see you if you hit him up," Mark says hopefully.

"Maybe," I say.

And by that, I mean he will, because I'm not going to allow him to dodge me until it's time to wow him like a surly professor waiting for my thesis paper.

I have to sell this idea, and that means talking to him at least one more time before I turn it in.

Carol smiles at us both. "Well, definitely give me a shout if you need anything!"

I half wave as she ducks out and the door clicks shut behind her.

"She's so nice," Mark says distantly. "Really helpful."

Yeah.

Shame she can't help me much here. I give him a quick smile and turn back to my laptop, tightening up my sentences and adding footnotes almost as long as the main presentation at the end.

The evening crawls by as I work and Mark hangs around like a baby monkey, clingy as ever and making flat jokes, throwing out suggestions I don't need every hour.

I try not to let my inner bitch out while I politely shoot down his help.

He's not jealous, is he?

Sometimes, it almost feels like he's poking, asking without really asking *why* Foster gave me this opportunity like it's a golden cow and not a Trojan horse meant to drive me bonkers.

When the day winds down and I can't keep my eyes on the screen for another minute, I wait while Mark packs up his stuff. He hasn't stayed late yet in the time I've been here.

Foster, on the other hand...

Foster must not stumble out of this tower until well past

eight o'clock at night. He's still online in the company chat at least that late, but not open to direct messages.

I check his calendar, which Hannah sent me when I asked when he'd be free. I see his last meetings for the day are all virtual, which means he'll be in his office.

Nowhere to escape annoying influencers with a burning need to pick his brain.

So I push back from my chair and power down my laptop.

Mark looks up with a bright smile I can't quite read.

Man, does he ever run out of energy?

He's twenty-six, like he told me the other day, but he could be nineteen.

"Are you heading out, Dess?" he asks, joining me at the door before I lose myself in the bustle of other tired people heading home. "Want to get a drink?"

Oh, God.

My heart flies up my throat.

...is he hitting on me now?

He doesn't look like he's flirting, exactly, but shy, soft boys like him never do. He's not the kind to wink or make some obscene comment.

"Not yet, I have a few more notes to read through," I say. "Thanks, though."

"You're not leaving?"

I grit my teeth.

It's none of his business, actually.

"Just heading to the ladies' room," I lie, for no particular reason.

He doesn't need to know how desperate I am to see Foster.

"Oh, well, I can wait for you—"

"Mark, no. I have a busy night. Family stuff." Another lie, and I ignore his slight pout.

"Ah, okay. I'll leave you to it. Don't lose any beauty sleep over this place... it's so not worth it," he mutters as he ducks away.

Now, it's making more sense.

He resembles a put-out little boy, sulking as he heads in the opposite direction from the bathrooms.

When I glance back, he's gone.

I don't dare wait any longer and rush up to Foster's office.

"Miss Lancaster?" Miss Cho says from behind the desk. "Are you here to see Mr. Foster? I'm afraid he's—"

She's not fast enough to finish that sentence, much less hop out of her chair before I'm speed walking past her.

She can't catch me before I rip Foster's huge black double door open like I'm entering a dark knight's lair.

Just like before, his office is dark, all chrome and slate and glossy power oozing from every pore.

Only today, the last hints of summer sun stream in through the window, bathing everything in soft red fire.

I have to admit, it's kinda beautiful as the light spills in against the polished shadow and moody greys. That pitch-black color he seems to love might have a hint of forest green in the light.

The light even gilds Foster himself as he glances up from the screen at the intrusion, his face twisted with surprise.

It's an improvement.

When he doesn't scowl, he's slightly more lickable.

A dangerous thought.

Then his brain catches up with his eyes and his face twists sourly, and all is right with his miserable, grumpy world.

"Do you not know how to knock, Miss Lancaster?"

I shut the door behind me while Miss Cho stands there helplessly.

She doesn't strike me as the type to listen in, but I don't want our conversation leaving this room. If I've come this far, I deserve a little privacy.

Mostly, because I'm about to do something highly embarrassing.

I'm going to ask this soulless gargoyle of a man for help.

I try to keep my emotions under wraps as I step forward and sink into the chair in front of his desk, steepling my fingers.

If we're going to do this, I might as well be comfortable.

"You ignored my calls and my emails," I say flatly.

"I was busy. Did Miss Cho not tell you I'm the boss?" He waves a hand at his screens, his jaw pinched.

"You're not busy now..."

His scowl only deepens.

"You have no clue what I'm looking over right now to keep this machine running—which I would be doing faster if you weren't here disturbing me." He looks past me. "I've got this, Miss Cho. Kindly go make sure nobody else barges into my office."

Hannah exits the room while I bite back my snark. Plus, the burning need to know if he's ever been polite just once in his life.

"What the hell do you want, Miss Lancaster? You're here for a reason," he snarls.

"I need more time."

The lines on his face loosen.

He doesn't shake off the anger entirely, and he doesn't smile, but it's something.

He clasps his hands together and leans forward.

"If you can't do the work, you're welcome to give up now. You'll still collect your donation to a conservation charity of your choice. I didn't say that up front, but why prolong this torture for both of us if you won't pretend to do the job? Take your money and run."

Bastard.

Just keeping my expression neutral hurts my face.

He won't win.

He won't bait me into losing my shit, even as he insults my intelligence, my work ethic, and my person in a single quip.

"Because. I have the chance to do way more good than a one-time donation here. That much is clear from working fifteen-hour days on this proposal," I explain. I squeeze my fingers together until my knuckles threaten to pop. "It's not that I don't have it ready. I'm basically done."

He raises an eyebrow but says nothing.

God, would it kill him to show some surprise?

"I could turn it in and present it to the board right now if you want. It's just that I need more time because *you* need more time."

"Excuse me?" He frowns. "More time for what?"

"To go to the Olympic Forest with me."

His chair spins slightly as he jolts back with a snort. "And why the hell would I go tromping through the woods with you, of all people?"

Ouch. Would that really be so atrocious?

"Sea otters," I throw back simply.

Foster stares at me like I've lost my mind.

I'm hard-pressed not to start laughing my head off.

Weirdly, it's almost cute to see this grouch look so gobsmacked.

Don't get me wrong, I expected him to be surprised.

No way did he see this coming, though.

Not a chance.

But I never expected his blank look, clearing the harsh scorn he's been beaming my way from the second I walked through his door.

And holy shit, I didn't need to notice how blue his eyes are with curiosity.

They're practically gems set against the sunset spilling in, glowing like sapphires, glinting and transforming his face from Ice King to Judgmental God.

I can't help it.

I'm staring helplessly as I press my lips together, fighting not to laugh—and failing.

"Sea otters," he repeats like he's testing to see whether he misheard me. "You want me to drop everything to see otters? Is that a serious proposal?"

...well, when he says it like that, he really does make it sound off the wall.

"I mean, I've been planning an otter stakeout past Olympia for ages," I say. "If I can't spot them in person, I'd love to check out their habitat, at least. I love those little guys and—it's research, okay?"

"Research," he repeats dryly.

I wonder if he has a button under his desk for security. Am I three seconds from a pack of stoic brutes dragging me out of the building?

"For community reporting to the Washington Department of Fish and Wildlife?" I venture. "They welcome public assistance with sightings and tracking. The otters are endangered and also really hard to find, so the state's always keen for any help."

Finally, it's getting through to him.

The sour disbelief leaves his face, but although he nods, a muscle in his jaw ticks.

Good.

I've gone and pissed him off again, just like I expected.

If I can sell him on this trip, then convincing him to use company resources for animal tracking ought to be a breeze.

"Technically, this *is* part of my presentation. The perfect chance to demonstrate future applications and observations for your technology out in the wild," I say, shifting forward so I can balance my elbows on the table and face the music in those glinting blue eyes.

Dad always used to nail me on posture when I was a little girl.

Elbows don't belong on tables, bad manners, especially in a business setting, and I know that.

I also know I should be prim and proper and remind Foster that I'm not the bad-mouthing kind of pretty girl Vanessa Dumas is.

Also, these are *otters* we're talking about.

Debra Hollens and her awesome interview are great material. Perfectly convincing but also a bit predictable.

But the otters—they're my ace in the hole.

They're for winning Foster over and bringing this home.

"Just think about it." I hold up my hands. "Just for a second, okay? I know you're a nature guy from—um, that morning we met. Say no more." I beam him a strained smile.

He's so not amused.

His nostrils flare.

"The otters are notoriously difficult to spot in the wild," I continue. "And since the government is asking for civilian help, Home Shepherd has a perfect green light. Your drones could *change* their tracking like nothing else. And if it works in a real field test like this, it could help for way more than just otters."

I expect him to laugh me off if he doesn't have me dragged away and unceremoniously dumped in the back alley next to the dumpster first.

Or at least give me a cruel, mocking smile and revoke any chance I ever had at involving Home Shepherd in this scheme.

Instead, he just looks at me like he's never seen me before.

Which is alarming, because the earlier scowl returns, gaining in harshness like a gathering storm.

I've never seen a man look so broody before—which is saying something when I grew up with the broodiest single dad in Seattle.

Then his hand starts moving.

Oh, here we go.

Security and the hounds are coming in three, two, one...

He presses a button on his intercom. "Miss Cho, can you come in here, please?"

This is it.

At least he's using Hannah to send me into exile nicely for having the audacity to suggest we travel into the wild after otters.

I meet his gaze, daring him to lay into me one last time, but instead he raises his gaze as his EA walks into the room.

"Miss Lancaster has just suggested we travel to Olympia this weekend to see the sea otters in their natural habitat," he says, utterly impassively.

It hits me that I'm holding my breath.

Because I have no flipping idea what he's really thinking.

"Well, *hopefully*. Like I said, they're pretty rare, and sightings are never guaranteed," I correct in a small voice. "But if we get lucky, we might spot something."

His gaze lands on me for a burning second before it shifts back to Miss Cho.

"Yes, you've made the concept quite clear. Hannah?"

Oh, no.

He's using her first name?

It must be serious.

"Definitely not." She answers a question he never spoke out loud. "I'm visiting family in Portland this weekend, Mr. Foster."

"All weekend?" His forbidding brows descend lower over his eyes.

"I'm afraid so." She doesn't sound like she's that upset by it. "You'll have to count me out on this one. However, I can make your travel arrangements. I'll make sure the lab releases a proto- type to you personally."

Wait. What.

Foster groans.

I stare at both of them in disbelief.

"Does that mean... you're coming?"

"Yes, dammit," he mutters. "Although frankly, I have no good reason why I'm actually considering it."

"Like otters aren't enough?"

The joke fails catastrophically.

But then something resembling a microscopic smile tugs at his lips.

"Otters," he agrees. His eyes linger on my face. We've been in the office so long the sun's light has finally dimmed and the automatic lights are brightening, painting his face in softer white-orange hues.

Meaning, I can see every gritty detail.

From my research, I know he's forty-two. That means he's seventeen years my senior, but he doesn't look like it.

To say he's aged well is like calling Taylor Swift a singer. He's still young and rough in all the right places. More like a mountain carved gracefully by time than a man who drinks his weight in green juice every morning, running from his own mortality at the crack of dawn and choking down a fifty-supplement cocktail.

His jaw is firm and sharp.

There's only the smallest hint of salt and pepper in his hair—and I don't think he dyes it—a distinguished badge of age.

And although there are faint lines around his eyes and mouth and across his forehead, they're barely noticeable in this light.

Maybe it's the lighting, though.

It's got to be the reason.

The *only* reason why I notice how lush his mouth is, too. His lips look like they could lay down the law or soothe any woman to sleep with tender kisses, and it's horribly easy to imagine him doing both.

Especially when he's not scowling.

Um... he's not scowling now.

My stomach doesn't quite flip over, but it lurches.

I don't even hear him at first as he dismisses Hannah and looks at me, his eyes slits as he leans back in his chair.

"One question for you, Miss Lancaster."

"Yes?"

He blinks and his face goes impassive. "How well can you handle a kayak?"

VII: A LITTLE RESTRAINT
(SHEPHERD)

I must be out of my fucking mind.

Absolutely certifiable.

Taking a novice kayaker on the long route from Olympia city limits into the wilds of the Olympic Peninsula?

Stupid.

And doing it alone?

Alone? With a beautiful woman?

They should have me institutionalized.

If Hannah Cho were here, she'd have done the smart, mature thing and booked us a boat ride to Olympia or a seaplane into the boonies.

Anything but this.

Which is why I'm still wishing she was available for this excursion.

Then I wouldn't be here, too distracted by the thought of a rigorous summer paddle with a young woman who has no business shaking me the hell up like she does.

But here I am, standing on this pebbly beach, waiting for Destiny and regretting every life decision I've ever made since Hannah first said the words 'Young Influencers.'

Christ Almighty.

If this leaks out to the wrong people—*the* Shepherd Foster tromping around the wild with a gorgeous young woman and a glorified intern—I'll be ruined.

Dumas couldn't have torpedoed me better in her wildest revenge dreams.

Hell, she'll probably up her attacks and slander out of pure seething jealousy now.

I can already hear the tabloid rats squeaking.

Foster's new fling! Younger, hotter, and sweeter than Miss Dumas? Did we mention younger?

New heartbreak, ahoy! Meet Shepherd Foster's stunning new victim.

A new mistress for Aidan Murphy's nephew! Will she come out of it alive?

Fuck.

I swallow a lump of tension that feels like solid lead.

What I should have done is vetoed this whole idea, no matter how adorable she looked trying to sell me on otters, batting her eyes.

Olympia, field testing our drones, the damned otters, everything.

The fact that she's scared to death over her presentation tells me she put the proper effort in.

The proposal is probably fine without this excursion.

The wind smacks my face, disrupting my melancholy.

It's a brisk morning as I pace around the beach, checking my equipment for the seventh time.

If we're going to do something monumentally stupid, we'd better do it right.

I've got everything that was on my list. Hopefully, Destiny comes prepped with everything I instructed her to bring.

I offered to provide it myself, but she insisted on lone wolfing it.

Here's hoping she hasn't gone for the budget options.

A rough and tumble venture like this requires the right gear, and I always opt for quality.

Five minutes before our agreed meeting time—eight a.m. to make sure we're in full light—Destiny arrives, already in her wet suit.

I'm lucky my jaw doesn't hit the ground.

Full body with curves for miles stuffed in a skintight suit.

Long legs, man-eating hips, the slim dip of her waist, all on full display like a brunch buffet.

Every blessed bit of her begging for my hands.

It's so tempting I have to ball my fingers into fists and stop just short of fucking biting them.

Jim Carrey in *The Mask* has nothing on what I'm feeling as I try to tear my eyes off her prancing around in that wet suit.

She raises a hand when she sees me, oblivious to the fact that I'm one brush away from blowing in my pants like a boy on prom night.

"Hi," she says shyly.

Hi? Fucking hi?

At least she came prepared, I suppose.

"You're here," I say curtly.

On time, I don't say.

"I figured you'd appreciate me being punctual, especially when we're doing something like this. Thanks again for taking a leap of faith, Mr. Foster." She nods at my kayak parked by the shore and the still water nearby. "Is that your ride? She's a beauty."

"She's sturdy and efficient," I clip, looking over her shoulder to see what else she's brought. "Where's yours?"

"Oh, that's the one." She jerks her thumb behind her. "Do you mind helping me carry it down? I had to fight hard enough to get it on my car."

"You tied it up there by yourself?"

"Well, yeah. I'm too old to call my dad for help lugging around heavy things, and too stubborn to go begging random guys. I'll show you." She rolls her eyes as she starts back up the beach.

She's wearing sneakers right now, but there's a waterproof backpack slung over her shoulders, and I can make out boots dangling from it.

By the looks of it, she's gone out of her way to buy the full kit.

Impressive, considering she only had a couple days to pull everything together.

"I can handle myself out here, in case you have any doubts. I'm not a china doll," she tells me as she leads the way to her small VW Bug.

It's blue—Wailea blue, I think, remembering that special shade of paint from Maui—and there's a slight dip in the side where it looks like a dent has been popped back into place. Whale-shaped air fresheners hang from the rearview mirror.

It looks like a car that's been well used and well loved.

Not at all what you'd expect from a billionaire coffee mogul's daughter who must have a trust fund large enough to leave her plenty comfortable for life.

Although it's old and dented, it's been lovingly polished, and I think she had the paint touched up recently.

"Um, this is Ladybug," she says, patting the roof affectionately.

My eyes snap up.

Somehow, defying commonsense safety and possibly the laws of gravity, there's a kayak strapped down with webbing.

A very *nice* kayak.

I reach up and run my hand along its side without thinking.

"This is a decent piece of equipment, Miss Lancaster. Congratulations."

Assuming you ever use it for more than a weekend hoofing it with your boss, I think grimly.

"Is that such a shock?" Destiny folds her arms. "You don't think I'd figure out how to shop?"

No, actually.

Most people who are new to this addiction tend to buy the flashiest boats. The brands that get promoted with young, hip models who spend more time on their haircuts than paddling on the water.

This is a Boundary Rider 520 with a sleek green hull.

Versatile, stable, and pricey but reliable.

"I could have lent you one of these if I'd known," I tell her. "I only use this brand."

"I appreciate that," she says blandly. "But I didn't want to borrow from you. Not any more than I already have, I mean."

I dart her a look, unsure whether or not I'm being insulted.

I look her car over again.

It's definitely at least ten years old and must have decent miles on it, considering her active lifestyle.

Another surprise.

"You're certain you can comfortably spend over two grand on a kayak?"

"I can easily afford it, if that's what you're worried about," she huffs out. "And um, can you not look at Ladybug like that? She's not falling apart..."

Goddamn.

I can't get over the fact that she named her car Ladybug.

Although, with the bulbous wheel arches and the arched roof, it's almost fitting.

"It's not that I can't afford a better car." Destiny spears me with a narrowed gaze. "I'm riding Ladybug into the ground because I love him."

Him?

Her car is a fucking him?

I catch myself the instant I notice hot jealousy spiking my veins.

Shit, I knew this entire trip was a big fat mistake.

Then I see the corner of her mouth twitching.

It's a tiny, quick movement. Blink and you'd miss it.

In half a second, she has her face back under control, but it makes me wonder if maybe she's doing this to mess with me.

This little blonde pixie with her hair tied back in a ponytail and her face makeup free. She looks more like the sporty girl I saw on Instagram today.

Not the prim, hyper-focused, no-nonsense girl who came to my office and lured me into the unthinkable behind her pristine mascara and flawless poses.

I don't want to fucking like it.

Yet, against my better judgment, I feel a smile brewing that makes me bite my tongue.

Damn, she got me good with the whole stupid car thing.

"It's a good kayak," I say, unstrapping it and lifting it from the roof, careful not to scratch anything. "One of the downsides is, it's not easy to handle by yourself. Particularly if you don't have much experience."

"Lucky I have you then, right?"

Lucky.

That's one word for it.

I take one end of the kayak and let her lift the other as we haul it back down to the beach.

There are a few other early risers milling around now, people dog-walking or recovering from the poor decision to stay out drinking until the wee hours of the morning.

While I follow her I decide I should have taken the lead. I wanted to let her set the pace, in case she needed to put it down and rest, but it doesn't seem like she needs to.

There's an honest fitness level behind her trim looks.

Instead, she marches on ahead, giving me a direct view of the peach masquerading as her ass.

That damnable wet suit cups it too perfectly, turning this into a proper death march.

How had I even missed an ass that magnificent?

Now, I see everything.

The perky way her hair swings behind her like sun-kissed gold threads.

The long line of her legs and the small of her back, begging for a claiming hand.

Her innocent face, every time she turns.

So innocent it makes me throb to defile her.

Fuck me.

I need to get my head back in the game. Safely out of whatever lust pit it's fallen into and gotten stuck in.

Yes, she's hot.

She knows she's hot.

Her entire image, her brand, her career, is made partly from her allure and the rest comes from her brain.

Like anything in life, it's a commodity and an asset. I should be too smart to fall for it.

Key word being *should.*

"Do you know," she says, barely winded when we rest her kayak beside mine, "I can't believe I never thought of this before."

I stand beside her.

It's easier like this, staring out across the inlet to the islands and the long route north up ahead.

"Kayaking, you mean?" I ask.

"Yeah. It's a cool way to see wildlife up close here, without disturbing it with loud noises or pollution. The back roads can be rough on vehicles, too. I've lived my whole life in the Pacific Northwest and I'm shocked it never occurred to me before."

"I've seen plenty of seals up close and personal. A few orca encounters, too, up in the San Juans," I tell her. "If you can handle it, there's no better way to get around these parts."

"Is that a challenge?" She narrows her eyes.

"If it is, Miss Lancaster, you're welcome to prove you're up to snuff."

We share a whimsical look—the usual charged defiance—but also something lighter.

Something I don't want to think too hard about.

"Let's get moving, then. There's only so much daylight to make time and make you look like a clown," she says.

I snort loudly. "You couldn't do it last time you caught me with a kayak, so now you're desperate."

She razzes me before she jerks her head away, checking her boat over one last time.

This girl.

Confidence looks good on her, and I think I like this version of Destiny a lot.

I grit my teeth and shut down the urge to let my eyes drift to her ass again.

I don't have to like her at all.

The only thing I need to do right now is show her how to kayak well enough so she doesn't die on the way to the Olympic Peninsula.

That's it. End of story.

"It's going to be a long day," I say. "And it's going to be hard. Have you eaten?"

"Overnight oats with all the blueberries I could handle. Breakfast of the gods." She nods, a short, sharp motion. Her eyes remain steady and serious. "But at least the weather's good today, right?"

I look up.

It's better than good, basically immaculate.

This is probably the warmest day of the year so far, peppered with intermittent clouds to lend us shade without baking in the sun.

"I wouldn't have taken you out if it wasn't," I mutter.

"So, killing your minions isn't high on your list of weekend activities? Good to know!" She flashes me the barest hint of a teasing grin. There in a flash and gone.

Then it's like she remembers who I am and her face shutters.

Whatever.

Fine. We're not here to bond or fuck around or anything like that.

This is business, plain and simple. An unorthodox chance for a bright young mind to sell me on this conservation tracking while I test out my own technology.

"Have you been on the water much before?" I ask.

"In recent years—for sure. I didn't go out much when I was a kid for reasons... but once I found my sea legs, I went a little crazy. Boating, jet skis, paragliding, canoeing, you name it." She hesitates, like she wants to elaborate before shrugging instead. "I've never tried kayaking, though. I'll try to catch on fast."

I already knew that from the evasive way she answered when I asked her in my office.

I'm regretting this entire venture. No CEO of a company goes to this extent just for a project proposal, and not even a moneymaking one at that.

Even if some part of me wants her to succeed.

I *want* her to convince me, dammit.

And maybe something about the way her eyes light up when she talks about those damn otters made a difference, too.

"No time like the present." I nod at the gently lapping waves. "Let's get started."

I already know, theoretically, that she can swim.

But as we stride into the water, the sting of the cold muted by my wet suit, it's easy to see she's more competent than I've given her credit for.

With just a few simple pointers, she knows what she's doing.

Her fingers trail across the water as it crests against her stomach. She throws me a grin before diving neatly through the surf. Her body cuts through the water like she was born for it, and she surfaces a minute later, flipping her hair back, now darkened to bronze.

Glassy droplets roll down her skin, accenting too much, and I hate that she's laughing. Real belly laughter.

"The look on your face," she says, splashing me. "Lighten up."

Summer or not, this is still the ocean, and she just dove right in without a single complaint about the cold.

I'm almost annoyed.

"Told you I could swim, so we can get that out of the way," she says. "Are you happy now? Sure I won't drown?"

"Show me more," I say, moving alongside her as she goes under again.

My body acclimates to the cold like I'm part penguin. Or maybe my blood just runs hotter than usual from watching her turn into a mermaid.

She might not know how to kayak, but she's a damned good swimmer.

"Okay," I say after five or ten minutes. "Enough."

"Satisfied?" Destiny cocks an eyebrow at me.

Not a good word to use when she's looking at me like that, her wet suit clinging to every curve.

Shit, at least most of her is still underwater.

I need to stop thinking about sex and focus on the lessons I'm supposed to be giving her.

"We'll practice technique first," I say, leading her back to shore. The pebbles shift under my feet, and I swipe my hands through my hair, wiping away the moisture.

Luckily, there's not much of a breeze, though I know it'll pick up once we're out there on the water.

For now, though, it should protect us against any chills.

"Ready when you are." Destiny rolls her shoulders as she grabs her paddle.

"Not even close. You forgot this." I tap her pack and show her how to stow it on the kayak so even if it does capsize, she won't lose everything she's brought. "Did you bring spare clothes and a sleeping bag like I asked?"

"Obviously. I'm not up for sharing one, dude."

That wins her an instant scowl.

"And the first aid kit?"

She sighs. "*Yes*, Mr. Foster. I went over the list you sent me three times like a good student. Oh, and I added some flapjack. Homemade."

"Flapjack?" I frown. "Pancakes?"

"No, no. This is a British thing, I think. My stepmom introduced me to it a couple years ago when we were camping. Syrup and oats, all packed neatly in a bar." She sees me make a face. "Don't be a dick until you try it. I must've hiked more than five miles on a couple of these bars before I even noticed."

"Sounds as exciting as low-sodium porridge."

Shaking her head, she rifles around in her overstuffed bag and pulls out this abomination.

"Quit grumbling and try it. It's high-calorie and slow-release, and it's actually pretty good for an on-the-go bite."

I stare at the ziplocked bag in horror. It *sags* with the sticky oat mixture, barely separated into pre-cut bars.

"This is flapjack? This baby food turned to stone?"

"It's great for ages five and up. I'm pretty sure it's even good for high and mighty businessmen with an emotional maturity not a day over two years old," she says, wagging a finger. "Trust me."

"I'll take your word for it, Miss Lancaster. Someone needs to keep a cement-free stomach if the other person gets sick."

Before I can blink, there's a hard brick of sweet-smelling oats in my face. She holds it under my nose.

"Less talking. More chewing. Don't tell me you're scared of a little fiber?"

Fucking hell.

If it'll shut her up, I suppose one measly bite of this sugar-gruel won't kill me.

I sink my teeth in like a wild dog and tear off a piece, chew mechanically, and swallow.

Huh.

Not terrible.

Thankfully, she has the good sense not to gloat, even when I grudgingly take the piece she snaps off and wrap it in foil for later.

"Now that we're all fueled up..." She tucks the rest back into her bag and fastens it so it's waterproof again before slotting it into her kayak just like I showed her.

I think it's an act of defiance more than anything—proving she doesn't need to be told twice.

She's not afraid of a challenge, and she's certainly not holding anything back.

Ignoring how much her weird attitude amuses me, I hold out her paddle.

She takes it, fingers brushing mine, and I ignore that too.

"This is your greatest tool when you're out there on the water. Treat it like an extension of your own arms."

"Yes, sir."

I glower.

"See these rubber rings?" I nudge her hands into place so she's gripping the right spots. Awareness jolts up my body when I sense her skin against mine.

Dummy, get a grip.

Don't let the oats go to your head.

Destiny freezes.

I clear my throat, knowing this entire endeavor depends on us trusting each other.

"Sorry," I whisper raggedly.

"No, it's fine." Her voice is taut with concentration and she doesn't look at me. "Is this right, bossman?"

"Yes, but don't grip it so hard. Loosen your fingers a little." I demonstrate on my paddle, showing her what I mean and leading her through the motions with the right grip.

She mirrors me almost flawlessly, though her movements are still a little stiff.

"The paddle is part of you," I say.

"Um, maybe not yet." Her eyes narrow as she assesses what she's doing, then glances up at me. "Why don't I look like you?"

"Practice. You'll find the right movements after a few hours on the water. For now, let's try something else." I leave my paddle where it is and stride around her until her back is almost touching my chest.

Then I lean around her, my hands beside hers.

Of fucking course, our thumbs brush.

Just the lightest touch, and it's still too much.

Ignore. *Ignore.*

Destiny inhales sharply, and I guess she's uncomfortable because she takes an involuntary step forward.

Well, why not?

She does have a massive fucking idiot here who keeps invading her personal space.

We don't have that kind of relationship.

Even if I thought we should, I'll never go there.

Especially because that one second slip was enough for me to notice the coconut smell of her hair, fresh and inviting and lethal. One more temptation calling me to my doom.

One more feature I shouldn't notice, let alone dwell on with the same damnable stickiness as her oat brick in my stomach.

"I'm lacking sleep," I rush out. "I didn't mean to—"

I stop.

To what? To touch her?

For fuck's sake, where is my mind?

"For making you uncomfortable," I finally finish.

"Huh? No, it's nothing like that." She stares at where my hands were just seconds ago. "I'm pretty sure I got over cooties with guys in gym back when I was in ninth grade. Just show me what you need to."

Bad, bad idea.

Still, I move onward, positioning myself behind her, forcing my brain to think of nothing but kayaking and sea otters.

There's no woman here.

No Destiny with her fruit-scented hair and sunny smiles and handfuls of curves that want to take my soul.

This universe is otter-centric.

Nothing else matters.

Otters, man.

"You need to move from your core," I strangle out, moving the paddle like my life depends on it.

At first, there's an easy resistance in her arms, but it soon melts away and she's gliding with me.

Her back knocks against my chest.

By some miracle, my dick doesn't go off like dynamite when her ass brushes me.

"Like this?" she whispers, so focused on the task.

"Better. Swing lower next time."

We try it again. This time, I stop leading and she picks up the slack.

"Good," I say.

To my surprise, she doesn't toss the praise away like a rotten apple.

She just nods, and when I glance at the side of her face, I see how severely focused she is.

Holy fuck, why does she have to be so unbearably cute when she's on a mission?

It's like all her energy flows into this one thing with laser intensity.

That's too familiar and too close to home, something that's served me well.

I can practically see the way she zeroes in on what she's doing, every iota of her being aligned with this.

I can feel the innate power of her body.

Her movements are fluid, yet strong.

If I ever thought she only posed for pretty, calculated photos without any real effort in the field behind them, I was wrong.

This girl works out.

Her core is strong enough to make the journey without breaking her, if we take it slow, even if she'll be working new muscle groups I will myself not to imagine.

"This is good. Keep it up," I tell her.

It's anything but *good.*

I should move the hell back now, knowing she's making progress.

We're still too close, practically touching.

The reason I can feel her strength is because her back is fully pressed against my chest.

When did she move closer?

Or was it me?

Regardless, I feel the way her chest swells with low, steady breaths. The pinch of her shoulder blades, their movements, the softness of her hair skimming across my hand.

Her fingers brush mine again, but she doesn't seem to notice anymore.

Me?

I can't *stop* noticing, and though I'm supposed to be the responsible one, I don't shift my position.

She's a tall woman, even if she still has nothing on my height, but here in my arms, she feels so delicate. Small and fragile and unbearably precious.

"I think I'm getting the hang of it," she says warmly.

The unexpected delight in her voice catches me off guard.

My body catches up with my sex-drunk brain, and I drop my hands, stepping back.

"If you think you're ready to head out, we can make some decent time." My voice is tight, but if she notices, she doesn't comment.

"Yeah, I think I'm ready for the kayak now."

I talk her through a few more basic safety tips as we prep, like not letting go of her paddle, and how to get in and out of the kayak safely without tipping over.

Basic stuff, everything she needs to know.

"Do you usually teach kids? Is this your spiel?" she asks when I'm done.

"What?"

"Do you think I'm just clueless?"

"*What?*"

She strides over to the kayak and eyes it for a second before climbing in, hands braced on the sides and feet sliding inside. She bends her knees, finds the right position, and glances up at me.

I didn't need to know that in the sunlight, her eyes almost look more turquoise than true blue, like the sea above the sand.

"Sorry, that was harsh, but... I think you've seen my pictures. Did you notice I spent three weeks in the Boundary Waters canoeing and again in Montana last year?" she asks dryly. "But thanks for the lecture about how to get in a boat."

"Safety first," I mutter. "This is technically a corporate outing. You'd better believe I cover all my bases."

"Fair enough. It's not safe if I wind up dying of boredom over super basic stuff, though." Her grin eases the sting, and she points at the water. "Okay, Captain. Onward."

Miserable little dork.

It's infuriatingly adorable.

"We'll practice in the shallows until I'm sure you've gotten the hang of it," I warn her.

"Ugh, fine. I guess if it doesn't take all day..."

"That's completely up to you, Miss Lancaster," I throw back.

Her jaw drops before she realizes I'm joking.

Then she smiles, bright and unrestrained.

Fuck, I didn't need to know how beautiful that is.

Especially not today.

We push on fully away from the shore and the shallows.

For a second, she looks unsteady before relaxing, just breathing and dipping the edge of her paddle into the water. It's calm today, so the waves don't offer much resistance.

"Don't hunch your back so much," I say.

She straightens, and immediately her technique improves.

"There. Now just follow me."

She glances over with a grin like she wants to bust my balls again but doesn't commit.

We practice close to shore first, getting her accustomed to paddling as efficiently as possible without overexerting herself too early. Pacing is critical.

She picks up everything quickly, and soon we're moving down my personal checklist.

"One last thing," I say.

"There's more?" Destiny groans.

"You need to know what to do if your kayak capsizes, Miss Lancaster. Anything might happen out here."

"Okay, Foster. Fill me in." Despite the attitude, it's clear she's enjoying herself. "Are *you* going to capsize?"

"That's only happened twice, and never seriously. Because I don't panic."

I explain how to extricate herself and her gear if, for any reason, she finds herself upside down. Panicking doesn't seem like her thing, but I talk her through a few basic techniques to prevent emotions from sinking her in the moment.

To my surprise, she doesn't offer a wisecrack in return.

For once, she just listens, and when I show her how to rock her boat and use her weight to flip it, she nods.

Then, without another word, she flips her boat and goes under.

Shit.

I should've known this dramatic little brat just had to test it out.

Fine, let her.

I watch while the bottom of her new kayak glistens in the sun, waiting impatiently.

After a solid minute, I start to worry.

She hasn't come up yet.

I allow ten more seconds for signs of movement, and then I stop thinking.

I'm up, plunging in after her, cutting through the water until I find her sleek black form, grasping her waist.

She's not stuck, thank God.

All that matters is that she's safe and I've got her now.

She struggles a little from the shock of my arms grabbing her, then she must remember what I told her if she ever needs an assisted rescue.

She goes limp as I drag her to the surface.

The air is cold and biting as we tread water that suddenly feels far less friendly.

Her body presses against mine, fully molded, and I'm holding her so tightly she couldn't escape if she tried.

The warmth of her body seeps through her wet suit—even through mine—and I can't make my arms unlock from around her waist.

Fuck, if this was her idea of a joke, I'll send her packing on the spot.

I'm close enough to see the diamond beads dripping from her eyelashes.

She looks at me, no sign of a smile on her face.

Her hands are splayed flat against my chest. I wait for her to apply pressure, to push me away, but she doesn't.

Fuck.

I didn't think it was possible for her to be any sexier, but drenched like this, with water against her parted mouth, she's pure nectar.

For a long second, there's silence.

Only our breaths, panting and frantic, this crackling charge like the air itself waits for us to breathe again, the space between us seared.

Then she breaks into a nervous laugh, swiping her wet hair back from her face and pushing back from me. Her face is pink now.

"Oh my God. I... I thought it would be easier than that. I'm sorry."

I look away before I can't.

"Are you all right? You scared me shitless." My voice is hard. Adrenaline thrums through my veins.

She laughs harder then, wiping her wet face clean.

"Yeah, sorry, I'm fine," she splutters. "I can swim. You *saw* me."

"I saw you go under, Miss Lancaster. Do not bullshit me."

"I was coming back up. I was *trying*. The kayak, it was just heavier than I thought."

"I told you it would be," I growl.

"Yes, I see that now. I'm sure I would've made it, eventually. I have a life vest... I mean, even if I *wasn't* coming back up with the boat, I'd have surfaced eventually."

"Now you see why you don't laugh off safety lessons," I snap, though it's fucking humiliating that I'm reacting like this.

I know she can swim.

I know she probably would've swam up eventually.

Still, she was under there for over a minute before I fished her out.

My instinct keeps screaming *react.*

To this, to *her*, I don't know.

Yet the blood won't stop roaring in my brain.

"Well, thanks for the help. You were so quick," she says, treading water. I glance at her, and the first thing I notice is how dark her eyelashes look when they're wet.

I look away again. "Try not to give me a heart attack again."

"Hey, I mean it." Her voice trembles, trying not to laugh. "It was very noble of you to worry..."

"Call me noble again and I'm taking you home," I bite off.

She coughs and when she recovers, she's all serious. "It's nice knowing my safety means something. Especially on the water."

The water, again.

Why does that mean so much to her? There's a story in her eyes she's not ready to share.

"You're a human being. Also, I don't want the lawsuit that

would come at me if you drowned. Would your father hire a hit man?" I mutter.

"Only for guys who date me," she laughs. "You're safe and still totally at my mercy."

"I'm starting to regret the rescue. I could still hold you under."

She stares at me and her mouth falls.

"...was that a joke, Foster? *Two* in one morning? Who are you?"

"Call me Shepherd."

Call me Shepherd? What the hell?

Apparently, I really want a lawsuit. Or maybe I'm vying for a bullet from her old man.

I'm definitely coming closer to welcoming harassment charges with every word out of my mouth. Just *begging* history to repeat itself.

Maybe my ruthless asshole of an uncle was right when he said I had a self-destructive side. Once, I was young and stupid and went driving after smoking my weight in weed.

It wasn't long after he had my father whacked for the insurance money, and Mom was buried in the bottle and long Sunday dinners with her sister. I only found out the truth years later, long after he was behind bars.

I was barely in the game yet, only dabbling with what he'd let me do, driving trucks with contraband TVs and laptops and kitchen crap they knocked off from corrupt dock workers.

Uncle Aidan seemed honestly concerned when the cops he bribed picked me up.

Right up until we got back to my parents' empty place. Then he smacked me across the back of the head so hard my vision stayed blurred until the next morning.

"Don't let me catch you trying to blow yourself up again, Shep. Ever. The older you get, the more you fuck up, you fuck me over, too. Now stand up like a man."

Miserable fuck.

Ironically, I'd wind up being a key part of fucking him over a few years later, just not the way he expected.

"I don't have much use for comedy," I tell her, brushing over the *Shepherd* moment. Hopefully she forgets. "We're here to field test my drones, Miss Lancaster. And to find your damned otters."

"Don't Miss Lancaster me, Shepherd. Not after you saved me."

Shit.

So much for forgetting.

Her expression also tells me she doesn't believe a word I say.

If only she had a clue what was running through my head.

When you've lived a pitch-black comedy of a life like mine, the only humor you have left is dark and depraved.

She nods and swims back to her kayak, at least, which has floated to a stop a few feet away. I collect her paddle and mine and haul myself over as she turns the boat upright.

Annoyingly, she's mastered climbing in on the water almost as gracefully as she does everything else.

I want to hate it.

I *want* to keep hating everything about her sunny, self-righteous little ass, and the fact that she's here excelling at everything I've taught her, making *me* seem like I'm overreacting.

It feels like the sky is falling.

Or maybe I'm the one going down flat on my face.

It might explain this familiar dizzy feeling of everything spinning out of control.

I'm used to that shit.

The trouble with falling is, there's always a hard landing.

"Thanks," she says when I hand her the paddle again. "I appreciate what you're doing. Even just for agreeing to this, really."

"Whatever. It's basic safety protocol." I won't meet her eyes and let them drag me down. "Now let's get going so we'll make some progress before dark."

VIII: A LITTLE DRAMA (DESTINY)

I'm too stunned to breathe when it sneaks up on me.

Somehow, I'm out here having the time of my life.

I won't lie, when Mr. Foster—*Shepherd*—suggested we actually go ahead with this trip, I was nervous.

Not least because it's extremely easy for anything and everything to go wrong out here with him, practically alone.

Not that I think he's a murderer or anything—when he's trying to clear his name, he's not going to dismember me and hide the parts unless I *really* grind his gears.

But it turns out, he knows his stuff.

Oh, plus being on the water paddling is actually fun.

When I was a kid, I was terrified of the ocean. Wouldn't go near it, not even when Dad made enormous efforts to make me feel safe on tranquil beaches without a cloud in sight.

There are so many unknowns.

Like, sure, I was scared of sharks and jellyfish.

But the thing that haunted me most was what happened to my mother when her body washed up on a peaceful stretch of shore next to our family coffee farm in Hawaii.

My parents didn't have a great marriage. It was stormy and toxic and ultimately, my mother smashed his heart.

Even so, Dad was devastated. He never had a chance to fix it, much less end it and move on.

He buried his feelings in chronic work and a defensive short fuse that didn't go away until Eliza crash-landed in his life.

Thank God she did.

Besides being the catalyst for making him function like a human being again, she also saved me from a lifetime of ocean deprivation.

It wasn't even the fact that she brought us closure with the past.

She encouraged me to explore my passion for animals at a time when I was a major brat, staring down the barrel of taking over a coffee empire I had zero interest in.

She reawakened Dad's kindness, too, and together, they got me on boats with dolphins and turtles and then into the ocean with nothing but a paddleboard.

They showed me a lost love I've been absolutely smitten with ever since. I can't imagine what my life would be if I'd let fear hold me back.

I also can't believe I've never tried kayaking before today.

Once the ocean bug bit me, I went ham on outdoor sports—surfing, canoeing, parasailing, you name it—but somehow kayaking never made it onto my list.

Maybe because there's still a hint of uncertainty with new things, and any water activities with live currents have the potential to go so wrong.

But it also has the potential to be incredibly satisfying.

Yes, even with an unrepentant grump for a teacher.

I steal a glance at him and try not to smile like a starry-eyed moron.

He's doing his broody thing again.

Mouth pulled tight, eyes dark, staring into the distance like he's contemplating the secrets of the mountains, his stern blue eyes narrowed and focused.

With him looking the other way, I can linger on that hard

jawline, the way he's made up of so many sharp lines and dips and walls of muscle.

That wet suit doesn't hide much, either.

And because I'm a hot-blooded woman, yes, I checked him out back on the beach.

I hate to admit there was a hint between his legs that he has a reason for that mammoth ego.

And his abs—

Sweet Jesus.

I had to switch my brain off before the daydreams started. It's already awkward enough with Foster without picturing him gloriously naked every time his lips move, okay?

The man works out.

He doesn't skip leg day like most guys or... any day, really.

He'd be less intimidating if he had skinny chicken legs or basic biceps or a narrower chest.

Honestly, that would make this entire thing easier if he was just a walking attitude without the Michelangelo looks.

The attitude isn't a total turnoff when he's not all supervillain.

The way he rushed in when my dumb face got stuck under the kayak—

God.

No, the man isn't half-bad when he tries.

And that confession feels like it might cost me everything to admit.

Before this morning, I came here expecting to see the boss-hole everyone in the company knows, up close and personal.

A cold, unfeeling, perfectionist lump who never developed enough patience to hold his shit together without screaming the minute I upset him.

Oh, he has high expectations and a low tolerance for failure, for sure—but although he's grouchy, he's never cruel with his criticism.

He's never off the mark.

I consider myself a fast learner, but even when I make mistakes as we ply the waters, he corrects them firmly yet politely.

No big sighs.

No passive-aggressive eye-rolling.

No pointed comments about how I should be picking up on this faster.

That helps me relax and improve at my own pace.

By midday, we're paddling along at a reasonable clip.

Sure, my arms and lower back are burning, and my palms might be a little chapped by sunset, but I barely notice.

It's too fantastic out here with a clear view of Washington's soul.

A hundred shades of green, imposing rock rising from the sea, picturesque yachts and sailboats and a few massive cargo ships gliding around us lazily in the distance.

The wind carries the songs of nature, birds and fish and hikers and fishermen laughing from the shore.

Shepherd certainly doesn't get any less gorgeous as the day wears on.

The sun sweeps high overhead as we go, traveling north past Harstine Island into North Bay.

The sunlight dances off the waters like it's pointing to sin, toying with the dark hair on Shepherd's head.

The rest of him is highlighted in the ruby red glow of evening reflected on the water. He's a silhouette shadow of the gods.

And those gods make me watch him kayak, gracefully moving through the water so effortlessly with every mile.

Now I know how your average Greek girl felt watching Hercules work out.

I lean back in my seat, tipping my head back and closing my eyes as I wipe my brow. When you've been under the summer sun long enough, it heats you up.

"Enjoying yourself?" His voice is wry yet gently amused, and suddenly next to me.

When I look over, I see he's stopped, waiting for me to pull alongside him.

It's a weirdly human moment.

Almost like he doesn't mind—or maybe he even likes—the fact that I'm having a good time.

Whoa, girl.

Let's not get carried away.

"It's nice to just hear the sea. I always forget how noisy Seattle can be until I come home," I say, lifting a hand so I catch the breeze in my fingertips.

"I know what you mean about the silence. Half the reason I spend so much time on the water is so I can hear myself think."

I wonder about the other half.

"Yeah. It's good to be alone, just the two of us here." I snap my eyes open, regretting my words, just in case he could take that the wrong way.

But he's just looking at me contemplatively.

Not like he's about to make my slip more awkward.

Because we *are* alone now.

And that's something I haven't stopped thinking about ever since we embarked and the little towns along the shore became smaller and sparser.

"Alone, yes. Fifty or more miles from every demanding asshole and bitter disappointment. Even money can't always buy that much solitude, Destiny." He glances away again.

It's fascinating how he relaxes when he paddles, like he's truly content, even though he's still vibrating raw power. Still, something about his giant, tight-wound body just loosens up here.

Though honestly, I'm a little more fascinated hearing my name.

It rolls off his lips like a tiger's purr, a new word he has to taste to understand.

No, this isn't the same man I met on Alki Point, all bluster and deep grudges against life.

That man didn't seem like he could ever find any peace without a heaping risk of drowning and hypothermia.

I think I like this version of Foster better.

Dangerous thoughts, I know.

But I don't have a prayer of stopping them as he looks at my face, then away, like his eyes might bleed if he stares at me too long.

"We've only got a few more hours of good light. We should rest and then bring it home."

The minute I stretch my arms over my head, my aching upper body agrees.

Apparently, his version of a rest is to paddle up to shore so we can stretch our legs while eating another piece of flapjack.

"I'm happy it won you over," I tell him between bites of my own. "I knew you had a sweet tooth in there somewhere."

His eyes flick to me, already narrowed. "Woman, I have a calorie deficit from five hours of steady kayaking and nothing more. Also, any interest in homemade sugar highs stays strictly between us. Don't make me put it in an NDA."

He's so ridiculous I laugh.

"A little late for a nondisclosure agreement over snacks, isn't it?"

He doesn't reply, ripping off another Shepherd-sized bite of his bar instead and chewing like he means business.

O-kay then.

"I'm so stiff," I say, rolling my shoulders for the tenth time and trying not to wince. "Ow. You weren't kidding about the workout."

"You'd have an easier time if you'd quit hunching your back," he says, tapping my shoulder blades. The contact jolts me. "Sit up straight in the boat. Let your arms take the strain."

"Um, my arms definitely *are* taking the strain," I say pointedly, waving them like overcooked noodles.

"They could be taking more. Some growing pains have to be expected, like any sport. It takes a while to break yourself in," he says with an almost straight face.

But one corner of his lip curls.

I can't tell if it's a fun smile or something more vicious.

I also get hung up on that whole 'break yourself in' part.

Holy hell.

For the briefest second, I saw that look.

He was looking at me like someone he wanted.

"Watch out. That's like the third joke you've told today," I say so I don't dwell on the other possibility. "You're really going to ruin your supervillain mystique if you keep that up."

"Like hell. Bad reputations are easy to get and nearly impossible to erase," he says grimly. That almost-smile, almost-desire look disappears. "I wasn't joking."

"Don't deny it! You absolutely did."

"That was a statement of fact."

I wave my flapjack bag at him. "I don't think so. I bet you're just a sadist who likes inflicting pain."

"I'll let you decide, Miss Destiny," he growls, his gaze flicking from the last piece of flapjack to my face.

With a sigh, I hold it out to him as a peace offering. "Have at it. I don't want to overstuff myself for the last leg of the trip."

"As long as you don't stuff it in my face again," he grumbles.

I can't help laughing.

This time, when he picks up his hunk of flapjack and stuffs it in his mouth, there's an honest smile in his eyes.

* * *

A LITTLE WHILE LATER, with our bellies full and our muscles stretched, he nods at his kayak and stands.

"Let's get going."

"Yep. Definitely a sadist," I mutter.

He rewards me with an amused snort.

We don't talk much as we set off again. I fidget with my small turtle necklace, pulling it out of my wet suit.

It's brought me so much luck over the years it feels like an extension of my own skin.

But he does continue to teach me, barking back key information as we go.

He talks about the differences between ocean currents and freshwater, how to get through tricky inlets, how to push against choppy waters, what to do when you can't, and how to survive when you're being swept toward sharp rocks or a big-ass boat.

He should know, I guess.

Part of me wants to poke him again about his death-wish kayaking trip the day we met, but I don't.

I'm smart enough to know when to zip it and just enjoy a nice evening.

Oh, and no lesson would be complete without a nice, long lecture about avoiding ferry and shipping lanes. That's huge.

Kayaking in Washington isn't all just paddling around in the pretty sunlight and looking for seals and orcas.

We stop a few more times in calmer waters for my benefit.

Amazingly, Shepherd doesn't even seem winded.

I have to remind myself where my arms actually attach.

It's hard. Really hard.

But it feels *good* pushing my body in new, unexpected ways.

It feels even better when he offers approving glances, and when I steer myself around a half-sunken buoy that comes out of nowhere, he mouths, "Good girl."

Oh, God.

I think I just died.

Overall, though, I'm hit with this weird sense of familiarity.

I'm listening intently, of course, but I'm far more glued to the way he moves, especially as our journey stretches on toward sunset.

When we hit a sharper current around some islands, he paddles harder, digging into the water like he owns it.

Tight, controlled motions.

Not tense, but powerful.

Like he's his own force of nature, demanding respect, powered by the same mysterious anger I saw the day we met.

This last strait is challenging, for sure, with currents pulling and threatening to knock me off course.

I should be more focused on navigating, but all I can think about is *him*.

The madman from Alki Beach.

How I watched him moving like this with the same feeling back then, only now, I get to see it up close and personal.

The same powerful strokes.

The same strange sense of warring frustration and joy that he takes out on the elements.

Even now, though we're pushing against the current, and he doesn't look like it's truly straining him. He only slows down to look back at me with concern.

"I'm good!" I call, flashing a thumbs-up.

But every time he dips his paddle into the water, I feel the sheer force behind it.

It's enough to steal my breath away.

Later, when we're through the worst of it, he glances over. When his eyes lock on mine, they're wild and hot and strange.

They make me tingle all over.

The butterflies swarming my stomach weren't there a second ago.

Why, Shepherd? Why do you row with such a grudge?

What made you so angry?

"Is there a reason you're staring?" he asks sharply.

My face snaps away with a blush.

Oops. I didn't realize I was.

"No reason. I just... I wish I could borrow a little of your stamina," I say, my voice worn.

"Miss Destiny, if you saw my true stamina, I'm sure you wouldn't be breathing," he says darkly.

What the what?

He can't mean—

I don't ask.

I don't dare.

My mind splits into innuendo-tainted chaos.

A terrible vision flashes of Shepherd's hard body over mine, his jaw set and his eyes blue flames, growling my name as he works me over with the same brute energy he uses on the water.

His eyes narrow and his throat bobs as he swallows slowly.

Oh, God, am I really still looking?

He's my boss, he's my *boss*—but instead of waiting for some snappy comeback, he just nods.

"It's rougher up ahead. Be ready," he warns.

No kidding.

The water gets choppier still, fizzing and rushing around us hard enough to spin my bow off center.

And just when I thought the worst was over.

We're passing through the narrows, without much room for mistakes around the rocks jutting out into the water.

The challenge makes me grin.

So does the chance to impress this man who's rapidly driving me insane.

"I was born ready, dude," I call back.

His eyes ignite as we set off together, paddling side by side at close range.

We're almost close enough to touch as we plow forward.

I know he's probably taking it slower for my sake, protecting me from taking on more than I can handle if he has to intervene. But the fact that I'm here with him, in the middle of nowhere, matching him stroke for stroke, feels oddly special.

Almost intimate.

I hear each splash as his paddle dips into the choppy waters.

My breathing synchronizes with his.

His paddle grazes mine, and the impact jolts up my arm like it's his bare skin.

This freaking man.

He makes every part of me overly sensitive, and every bit of spray sends a shiver through me.

Adrenaline and fear and wonder rush through me as a wave shoves my kayak against a rock.

"Destiny?" Shepherd glances over in concern.

I shake my head, righting myself before anything dramatic happens.

"Damn nice save," he says.

Yep.

We're doing this, and I'm going to get through it without him diving in to come to my rescue. My lungs work hard, but I keep breathing through the saltwater spray.

My legs tremble as they brace against the footholds.

Stroke by stroke, I become a human rope of fire.

No arms.

No spine.

No pain.

Just a numb, chugging movement.

Forward!

With every wave, I know there's a chance the next one could tip me over. And if it does, the rocks out here could scratch me up pretty bad.

This is the danger he mentioned miles back.

The jarring change from pretty sightseeing to *holy shit, no,* before you can blink.

But I'm not scared.

I'm here with Shepherd, immersed in it, and honestly, it's flipping incredible.

There's a silver lining to how rapidly things change on the water.

Just as I'm preparing for another intense stretch, I'm jerked back by my own exertion.

Without warning, we break past the sharp currents into calmer waters. And I can actually take a second to enjoy the adrenaline shot to my veins.

I set my paddle down, shake out my arms, and take a few badly needed breaths of briny air.

Then I do the only thing I can.

I laugh.

Arms spread wide to the sky, I throw my head back and just let myself be for one glorious second.

If he wasn't looking at me like a crazy girl before—

No. I don't care.

It's too much, this giddy feeling of accomplishment, all while I've just shared something so intimate with this bizarre, broody suit.

When I can finally straighten up again and breathe normally, he's still looking at me.

Probably trying to decide whether or not I've lost my mind.

Honestly, I wonder, too.

But he must see something I don't.

Because Shepherd Foster gives me a smile.

A rare, genuine smile, spurred on by what we've just shared.

The unexpected sight makes my heart skip in the wildest of ways.

And I have *absolutely* no clue what to do with that.

So I just smile back, shaking my head.

My heart soars halfway to the sun. I'm still a little scared because this is uncharted territory—just like all of today.

But my heart settles as he nods quietly, and we paddle on, together, into the evening light.

It's deep into dusk by the time we reach a small island just past Eagle Creek, and it hits me just how crazy this trip has been.

I. Am. Exhausted.

I'm fairly fit, but this was such a gauntlet I'm practically glued to my kayak and rendered boneless.

The plan is to camp overnight at the marine park before venturing out in the morning to scout for sea otters or signs they've been here.

A few recent sightings have me pumped.

But as I brace my weary arms against the side of the kayak, they give way.

Everything that came so easy this morning, even when we stopped for lunch, now feels impossible. I can't freaking move.

I didn't even notice my legs doing that much work, but now I'm aware they're also jelly.

Shepherd hops out of his kayak and parks it on the finer sand, without noticing how dead I am at first.

I shamelessly stare at his ass because I can't do anything else.

It's magnificent.

I'm also far too beat to feel any regret over checking out my boss.

I'm a hot-blooded girl, okay?

I have needs that get neglected a lot when I have a busy life with goals and not too many boyfriends worth keeping around.

I have eyes and Shepherd's body is too wicked for a man over forty.

The whole older 'daddy' thing never did much for me before, but with him—

No.

Nope, we'll blame it on adrenaline and exhaustion.

Finally, he turns around to look at me.

I gesture hopelessly with my paddle in the air.

"Um, a little help? I can't get out." I make another half-hearted attempt to stand and fail comically.

Shepherd stares at me for a second before he laughs.

He *laughs*—a real belly laugh—and it's a happy sound that vibrates through me.

Not cruel, either, but warm and understanding.

There goes my heart again as he strides over to where the waves meet the beach.

He grabs the front of my kayak effortlessly and hauls it out of the water.

No sweat.

No big deal.

No small favor with bigger muscle.

Damn, I'll admit it.

Right now, I am thirsty as hell.

I've been ogling him all day and he still hasn't stopped getting hotter.

"There," he says when I'm safely on the sand. "Can you get out now?"

I try.

I really do.

But my body simply won't cooperate.

I guess my legs forgot they're supposed to be a flesh and bone team, and my arms feel totally disconnected from my shoulders.

"This is so embarrassing," I say, but he just releases the end of the kayak and steps closer.

"Save it, Destiny. You worked your ass off today and there's no point in feeling shamed. Even if I'm going to carry you."

What?

He bends down, and before I can register what's happening, he does it.

Picks. Me. Up.

As in, I am in his arms right now, damsel in distress style, legs hooked over one arm while his other arm lends back support.

The world spins as I weakly wrap my arms around his neck.

And oh.

Oh.

He's almost superheated with exertion through his wet suit.

The shelter of his arms makes me aware just how massive he really is.

I'm so used to being the same height as most of the men around me—often taller—but this guy makes me feel small.

That's a miracle in itself.

And he's breathing harder now.

I'm pretty sure he wasn't when he dragged my kayak up onto the shore. His arms tighten around me, drawing me closer.

I'm not sure I'm breathing.

Scratch that, *definitely* not.

There's a wild look in his eyes.

My arms are locked around his neck and we're so close, I can feel his heart beating so, so fast.

He isn't alone. Mine strums like a guitar plucked by a rock star belting out a nasty breakup ballad.

What is even happening?

"It's normal for first-timers," he says softly, and I blink up at him in confusion.

Shepherd Foster is never soft.

...and first-timers?

How do I explain that although I'm way younger, I'm not inexperienced. I've had my fair share of male attention, though none of the boys I've dated have ever swept me up like a storm.

"Kayaking," he clarifies, eyeing my blank face.

Oh, crap.

And I thought I was embarrassed before.

Except, it's too hard to feel bad when I'm being hauled around by this bear of a man.

"It'll hurt like hell for a while. Eventually, you'll get used to it. You need to rub the feeling back into your legs. Can you manage that or are your fingers cramping?" he asks a little too gruffly.

I've got nothing.

I can't speak.

I'm a little worried that if I attempt speech, I'll say something garbled and terrible. Or worse, make some kind of comment about the dusky blue of his eyes in the fading sunlight.

It's not easy, especially when he's all Poseidon right now, smelling like salt and exertion and a testosterone brushfire.

His lips are more incredible than ever up close.

When you look at them, you can't look away.

From a distance, they seem thin and striking, but up close, they're so full, like they were made for kissing a girl completely senseless.

On a scale of awestruck to smitten, I'm a solid *I'm screwed.*

There's a strained moment of crackling tension.

I try to look away from his mouth, but I can't, and it's not because my neck feels like wood.

My eyes aren't working either—or maybe they're working too well—and all I can see is the way his bottom lip is slightly fuller than his top and—

I don't know if he kisses me first.

Or do I kiss him?

Can you really pinpoint the precise second a storm rips open and unleashes its lightning?

One second, I'm staring at his lips like a woman possessed.

The next, his full, delicious mouth presses down on mine with a growl that's all thunder, reaching up inside me.

Just a brush of parted lips and unexpected potential that feels like a cloud-to-ground strike.

I feel it in *every* searing bit of me.

His pressure.

His voice.

His claiming, harsh tension, snapping as he loses his own fight, as he *gives in.*

For the briefest second, I belong to Shepherd Foster in a way that makes me worry I'll be fit for anyone else.

Again, all lightning.

Blink once and it's over.

We jerk back, physically rocked, staring at each other in shock.

I see my horror reflected in his eyes, which are so dark and conflicted now. Thrashing blue fire on unsettled water.

Crap, crap, crap.

We just kissed.

I just kissed my boss.

Or he kissed me or—

Whatever.

It doesn't matter. This is an insta-termination waiting to happen. He's had so much trouble lately with that actress accusing him of the worst, he'll have zero tolerance for more trouble.

Eep.

Could he even press charges?

I don't know how he can prove anything.

But if I didn't instigate it, I certainly didn't *mind.*

I wanted it as bad as he did—and we both tasted desperation.

Even though he's still holding me up, I feel like I'm falling.

If I could hit the ground, I would.

It's too humiliating.

I have to borrow courage from next year to even look at him.

But he's not glaring at me. There's no anger smoldering in his eyes, no barbed words on his tongue.

His face glazes over as he moves, carrying me to a large drift-wood log.

Though he's not looking at me, exactly, he sets me down carefully and kneels in front of me.

I'm expecting him to walk away, if only to pull his thoughts together.

Honestly, I wouldn't blame him.

I definitely don't expect to feel his hands massaging my calves.

My brain short-circuits.

I stare at him in utter disbelief because this isn't happening.

Surely this can't be real.

After that messy, accidental kiss, he can't possibly be—

Oh, but he is.

And it feels divine.

His thumbs dig into my sore muscles with a manly, yet gentle precision.

A groan slips out of me so suddenly I press a hand over my mouth.

You'd think, being numb and kissed dumb, my legs and my brain wouldn't feel anything, but they definitely are.

And it's not total mortification.

His fingers are warm and my face is flushed, but he doesn't look up.

He doesn't meet my eyes.

He just works my torn muscles into butter like he's trying to smooth them back together.

I whimper again.

I can't help it—the human connection, the unexpected massage feels amazing and it isn't all the sensuality, either.

His skin rubs roughly against the rubber, and his hands are big.

My calves aren't small, with all the cycling and running I do, but he can practically wrap his hands around them.

He works his way up slowly, up to my knees, still rubbing and kneading at a steady clip.

I bite my lip until it hurts so I don't make more humiliatingly sexual sounds.

Though the higher he gets, the sexier this feels.

When he reaches my thighs, my legs open.

Just a bit.

Just to give him access to my thighs.

Nowhere else, obviously.

His breath is slower, but heavy now, his hands methodical, squeezing higher and higher, reaching toward my hips.

Holy shit, is he going to—

I squirm against a wet heat between my legs, my core pulsing.

Don't judge.

There's no straight woman on Earth who could experience this and *not* be ready to hurl herself at this man.

Especially after that kiss, all soul and instant addiction.

It may have lasted a few seconds—barely a moment—but it branded me from the inside out.

That's never happened.

One tiny brush of lips basically reached my clit.

And he still hasn't uttered one word.

I can't tell if he's just ignoring the fact that it ever happened —but then why is he still touching me?—or whether he just doesn't know how to touch the subject.

"O-okay," I stammer when his thumb drops across my inner thigh.

He's still working muscle groups I didn't know I had, but if he doesn't stop, he'll push me to an orgasm for the ages.

I stare at his face, willing him to look up.

He doesn't even meet my eyes.

Cryptic, magnificent bastard.

Irritation floods my blood, dampening some of my arousal. "Shepherd? Did you—"

"Don't say it," he snarls.

One hand moves off my thigh, moving to my lips.

He pushes a finger over them with a cutting glare.

"Don't talk, Destiny. Nothing you can say right now will do a damned bit of good."

Eek.

I clamp my jaw shut, confusion colliding with frustration.

So, what then?

He really doesn't want to discuss it? Or even acknowledge what happened?

What's *still* happening?

I'm so lost.

I squirm again, trying to find a position where I can't notice how wet I am.

For a second, his massaging stops.

I can't decide whether that's good or bad.

All I know is, whether he's actively touching me or not, I still feel him *everywhere*.

"We should talk about it."

"No," he says bluntly. "We shouldn't."

"But why? I just—"

"Nothing happened, Destiny. Nothing worth talking about and it's no one's fault. Just a mistake caused by too many hours on the water and too much shit stirred up in our blood. What the hell is there to say?"

My nostrils flare.

He's kidding, right?

I have *so much* to say, but right now, I can't find the words.

His reluctance definitely makes it harder, and extra difficult to not pick an outright fight with him.

"I don't know if I can just up and ignore it. After something like that, we should—"

"We shouldn't and we won't. I told you before, there's nothing worth talking about."

Jeez.

He's seriously going to keep denying it?

"Look, Shepherd, I know you didn't mean it to happen. Neither did I. But—"

"No buts," he says, still not looking at me. *Still* touching my legs in that firm, certain, incredibly sensual way he has that makes my muscles gel and my panties damp. "I said we're not talking, Destiny."

I could push.

I *want* to push him so bad.

But he hasn't just up and fired me, and the set of his jaw suggests he isn't going to let me get away with a sane conversation right now.

So I change tack.

"That was you. The real you," I whisper.

He sends me a quick, annoyed glance. "Must you keep talking?"

"No, I don't mean—" *The kiss.*

I clam up.

But I reach around and fumble with my zipper, yanking it down my back and exposing my bare skin to the air.

His gaze flashes to my red bikini before he drops his head and stares at his hands, which are still going.

If anything, they've moved higher than before.

Focusing takes everything I've got, but I find the watertight pouch with my phone inside and fish it out.

"What are you doing?" he asks sharply.

"Relax, I'm not about to take a picture."

Finally, sadly, he pulls his hands back and sits next to me.

"Then what are you doing?"

"Showing you something." My cell phone finally switches on, and I open Instagram, thankful I have a signal out here in the sticks. I scroll through the pictures until I find the one I took on Alki Beach that day with Molly beside me.

I thrust it at him and he takes it with cautious fingers. "What am I supposed to be looking at?"

"There." I jab a finger at the screen, the tiny dot in the distance. The kayaker. Him. "That's you. After you yelled at me, another thing you won't talk about."

He frowns at the photo, and then his frown deepens.

"What's your point?"

"I kept watching you all the way to Blake Island that day, after we almost came to blows. It was a lot like the way you paddled a few times today. Like you're angry at the whole world. If you won't talk about the kiss, about—whatever *that* was—will you at least tell me why you're so pissed?"

I know I've gone too far before the words are out.

Before he gives me a dark look and pulls back, dropping my phone onto my lap.

"It's not the world I'm angry at," he says abruptly, turning his back as he stands. "Stretch yourself out and let's set up camp."

IX: A LITTLE DANGEROUS
(SHEPHERD)

I'm a certified fucking rock brain.

I kissed her.

Or she kissed me.

Or something.

It doesn't matter either way, because it was a terrible mistake and it can *never* happen again.

For now, I'll do my damnedest to pretend it never did. Even though I can still feel every curve of her legs under my fingers.

Another mistake.

They just keep tallying the fuck up, don't they?

Yes, I know she was capable of massaging her own legs.

Everyone knows that massages are intimate and often lead to sex.

So, what business did I have touching her?

What the hell was I thinking?

I stride away like she's radioactive, taking deep breaths of cool ocean air until I'm calm again, pacing around to soothe my own burning muscles.

I haven't done a long haul kayak route like that in months, and I'm stiffer than I should be.

My hamstrings twitch as I bend over and catch a glimpse of

Destiny doing the same stretch, bowing her legs out like a dancer.

Zip up your damned wet suit, woman. That's too much sideboob for any man to handle.

Frankly, I'm astonished my heart hasn't exploded yet, let alone my head.

Because when she unzipped right in front of me, I thought I was about to have a cardiac event.

Wouldn't that be a nice surprise for Hannah to deal with? My dumb, dead ass coming home in a body bag and a scandal-ridden company in chaos.

When all the blood in my body rushed south, it's easy to mistake it for a heart attack.

My semi became a full raging hard-on, and I was boiling with so much sexual frustration I could hardly string two sentences together.

She bends over further, revealing a full view of her ass, still clad in her too tight wet suit.

Goddamn, it's finer than a Georgia peach.

Forbidden fruit incarnate, made to lure me to sin.

I force my eyes to the front. Away from Destiny and her perfect ass and any rabbiting thoughts about seeing her naked.

Nope. Nah. Never.

I just need to get my body on board with my brain.

I stalk away from her, taking a few more paces toward the shore so there's no chance she sees what she's done to me.

Specifically, the evidence that I liked what she's doing more than I could ever deny.

There's no damn room in this wet suit. My erection presses uncomfortably against the material.

Breathe.

Hold it.

Change positions.

Then she moans a little, the same way she did when I first started massaging her. I practically lose it there and then.

Mind over blue balls.

Head over hormones.

Discipline over arousal.

Exercise does that, regrettably, releasing torrents of raging endorphins.

Probably why I lost my wits and kissed her. Or she kissed me. Or what the fuck ever.

It's definitely why I was so keyed up when I touched her, why she opened her legs for me, and—

Fuck.

Stop thinking about touching her, numbskull.

Yeah, easier said than done.

Shifting, I push my hands against the ground to straighten the tired muscles of my lower back.

I rivet my eyes to the beach as long as I can until I hear Destiny moving.

A quick glance in her direction tells me she's still following the same stretching regimen. And the fact that she's shed her wet suit, exposing the red bikini underneath.

The little outfit does an excellent job of covering very little yet still leaving plenty to the imagination.

Shit, shit.

The woman is a walking fantasy.

A wet dream come to life.

And now she's inhabiting this beach with me overnight. I won't escape her until tomorrow evening at the earliest.

Fine.

I'm used to self-discipline, even if this is a bigger test than I'm used to.

I keep my eyes straight ahead for the rest of our post-kayak stretch out, and when I'm done, I nod in her direction without looking at her.

"You should get changed before nightfall. It gets chilly faster than you'd think."

Without a word, she nods and disappears into the woods.

I take the opportunity to change into military-style cargo pants and a t-shirt and then get started on setting up camp.

We'll need a fire pit first.

Summer air alone won't do enough to dampen the nighttime chill this close to the water.

Before I can finish digging, Destiny returns, wearing nothing but a formfitting long-sleeved shirt, jean shorts molded to her legs, and sneakers with no socks.

Of course, she still looks like a dream.

One look leaves me fucking delirious.

Her hair hangs down around her face in soft ribbons. I immediately notice she's either forgotten a bra or not bothered with one at all.

Why the hell not?

Just past sundown, there's already a bite to the air, and it perks her nipples under her shirt.

God help me, I'm a prisoner to my own gaze, and I can't look away.

She sends me a long glance, and maybe it's just my imagination, but I think her gaze lingers on my shoulders before she turns away.

"What? Is there a bug on my face or something?" she asks innocently.

No, woman. Your tits are just draining my entire life force faster than a blanket made of mosquitos.

"A dragonfly, I think. It's gone now," I lie. "You want to lend me a hand getting this fire going? The sooner it's up, the faster we won't freeze our asses off."

We work together in silence.

I continue digging while she roams our campsite, collecting small pieces of driftwood and flat stones to help feed the fire and keep it contained.

"Since you did lunch, dinner's on me." I fish around in my bag until I pull out a big blue can of rations. "You good with Chicken a la King or beef chili?"

Her mouth drops. "Freeze dried rations? You?"

I shrug. "It's not fancy, but it does the job. Don't tell me you're afraid of a little freeze dried chicken with a fifty-year shelf life."

I almost laugh as she swallows thickly.

"It's... it's fine, Shepherd. You were pretty adventurous with the flapjack."

"Yeah, now it's your turn. It'll reward your bravery, I promise. This stuff sticks to the ribs all night. And if it's too rough on your belly, I've got a box of Pepto." I pull out the pink box and chuck it at her.

She instantly throws it back like it's on fire.

"Dude, no. I can handle my reconstituted noodles just fine, thank you."

That wins her a bitter smile.

Nice knowing she isn't picky about her diet in the field.

You never know when she's young and fresh-faced and a billionaire's daughter—no Mediterranean avocado salads when you're on the go with no town in sight—though I'm guessing she wondered the same about me.

After I get some water boiling to reheat the food, she unwraps her sleeping bag. I notice she sets it about as far away from me as she can.

Good.

I'm glad I'm not the only one who sees the need for space after—well, fucking everything.

So why doesn't it make me happier?

I follow her lead, setting my sleeping bag at the opposite end of the fire, though still close enough to get heat. It's already clouding up and it'll be cold tonight for sure.

Fuck, I hate this tension.

Even the wind feels like it's whistling just to highlight the awkward silence between us.

We haven't even discussed our plans for tomorrow, I realize.

Surveillance, yeah.

I know how to operate the prototype drone stowed in my bag, but I'm clueless about the finer points of stalking sea otters.

The last light fades behind the trees by the time the food turns into something resembling an edible meal.

Destiny stops, hands on her hips, and stares at the last shred of vermillion and red coming through the trees. The thin cloud layer above highlights the colors.

It's one of the more spectacular sunset finishes I've seen in a long time.

She fumbles for her phone, taking a picture of the sunset, searching for the perfect selfie angle.

I watch her without meaning to as I stir the food and dish up some pears and blueberries I brought along for more texture and fiber.

Why can't I quit staring?

She takes maybe five pictures, flicks through them, changes the angle, her hair, the light on her face, and then takes another set.

She's clearly focused on what she's doing.

There's something weirdly compelling about it when I realize she's not just showing off for Instagram Likes. The image is all about building her brand.

I check the food to distract myself, though.

So what if she's standing there, the dying light gilding her in rose gold?

Who cares if it's the most picture-perfect pose I've ever seen?

Not my concern.

Once she's done a few minutes of quick editing, or maybe posted the pics already, she heads back to where I'm cooking.

"Right on time. Dig in."

I ladle out our dinner and pass her a bowl to go with the fruit.

She inhales it cautiously, but I can hear her stomach rumbling.

I think we're both starved enough to eat a half-cooked

porcupine right now. Chicken a la King might as well be food fit for an emperor.

I throw together my own bowl and then sit on the other side of the large log we're using for a makeshift bench.

The more room between us, the better.

Even if this feels like a chasm.

In the fire's light, her loose hair is art. Golden and slightly tangled from the salt water, looking so goddamn beautiful and tempting I want to rake my fingers through it.

"Brief me on tomorrow," I say, partly to distract myself and partly because this silence can't go on forever.

Plus, I need to know what we're doing. The otter tracking is all her, and I expect she'll have a few areas picked to comb from the air.

She snorts at me. "You're definitely ex-military, aren't you? Giving orders like a drill sergeant."

"I asked a simple question." I glance up. "Tell me how we plan to find these otters without a lesson in manners."

Her sneakers dig into the sand as she stands, still chewing her food. The dancing light from the flames licks up her body. Another reminder that her bra is missing.

Fuck.

"What?" I clip, staring up at her.

"Why are you such an asshole?" she demands.

"For asking a question?"

"For how you phrased it."

I fold my arms.

I'm only two bites in and my food is getting cold, but I don't care. If she wants a fight, I'm game.

"Why are you such a mouthy damned contradiction?" I ask.

"I asked you first," she throws back.

"Hardly an appropriate question for your boss and mentor."

Her face tightens. "Yeah? Is that what you are? I didn't know the prize money meant putting up with this attitude."

I don't think I've ever met someone so grating in my life.

"Actually," I tell her, my voice calmer than I feel, "you're being paid an awful lot for an opportunity to waltz in and change my whole company's charitable direction. You're welcome."

Yeah, it's a low blow, seeing as the money isn't designed for her at all and she won it fair and square. I'm also the one who agreed to this field test.

Still, I can't fucking help it.

Destiny glowers.

Her lips thin and her nostrils flare, adding a redness to her cheeks. But it's her eyes that hold my attention.

They're so lit they're almost green, like the cool, forbidding depths of the forest.

Beautiful.

I don't care that they're spitting fire at me.

It makes me want to rise to her challenge.

If this woman has to drive me insane, I won't go down without a fight.

"You offered the prize, Foster," she tells me, her chest heaving. Her hands land on her hips. "Why do you resent me for claiming it?"

I give her a tiny, twisted smile. "That's a whole other question."

"You never answered my first."

"No, and you can add it to the list of reasons why you hate my damned guts."

She huffs loudly. "Here's another question..."

"Sure. I guess you're seeing a pattern," I say.

There's no way I'm going to answer her now—out of pure stubbornness if nothing else.

Childish? Maybe.

No, I don't give a fuck.

"You say I'm a contradiction like it's personal," she says. "Why does that bother you?"

Only a thousand reasons.

Annoyed, I stride away from the fire and rake my fingers through my hair, pulling my thoughts together.

"When someone is made of contradictions," I say, enunciating clearly so she can understand, "at least one of those contradictions must be a lie."

"I—what?"

I turn to face her. She's still standing by the fire, painted in shadow.

"So which part of you is the lie, Destiny Lancaster? What's true?"

Her face looks pale. "Why does anything about me have to be a lie?"

"I know who your family are. The Lancasters? You think I don't know you come from money just like me?"

Her father is a billionaire. That's not insignificant.

It also has me wondering why the hell she needs this two-million-dollar prize at all.

"What's your game? I just want to know," I say. "Why play at being a typical do-gooder with big ideas and no cash to fund them? Why doesn't Cole Lancaster help you fund an entire sea otter preserve?"

Color floods back into her cheeks and her fists clench at her sides.

"What, you've been cyberstalking me now?"

"Fair game. Let's not pretend you haven't done some digging on me. And do you really think I'd pay out anything for a publicity role without conducting a thorough background check?"

"Jesus, this isn't panhandling, Shepherd. It's conservation work. *Charity*," she spits. "Also, I give away practically every penny I don't need. My trust is mostly a fundraising tool. I lived on my scholarship funds while I did my post-grad work, thank you very much. My father would help in a heartbeat if I asked, sure, but that's not how he raised me. I was brought up to make it or break it on my own."

I fold my arms, hating that I admire her fuck-you grit.

If she's expecting a round of applause, though, she's sorely mistaken.

"Not that it's any of your business what I do with my family," she adds.

She's right.

It isn't my business at all.

Yet, I still need to know.

There's got to be more to this story than high-strung morals and an allergic reaction to daddy's money.

With a final shrug, I settle back down by the fire.

"Come finish your dinner," I say gruffly. "The food's getting cold."

She lingers another second and then grudgingly sits, eating the fruit with her fingers.

"It's not half-bad," she says after clearing most of her plate.

I nod, accepting the compliment.

That creeping silence returns.

Tense, but less suffocating after we've said a lot of what we wanted. It doesn't matter if I don't have any easy answers.

Hell, I know I shouldn't want them.

Destiny's right. Her private business means nothing to me, and it certainly isn't relevant to this wacko otter excursion.

"Do you really not know about the family drama?" she asks later.

I look up, slowly chewing a few last blueberries.

"I wouldn't have asked you if I did. I'm the last man alive who keeps up with tabloid dreck."

Especially when it's about yours truly.

"God." She huffs a breath and stares into the fire, twirling a lock of hair nervously. "I thought everyone knew, but it's been a few years, I guess..."

"Tell me," I demand.

She draws in a slow breath.

"It's a long story..." She takes a slow sip of water, and I watch as she swallows. It's excruciating how I can't look away from this woman at her most mundane. "You know about my mother, right?"

I nod.

I had Hannah dig up her history and forward me a profile, yes. Although I scanned it, I didn't take much in beyond the major points about her influencer brand and environmental work. I barely skimmed her family.

"Vaguely. She passed away, didn't she?"

"Yeah. It happened when I was really little, during a trip to our family place in Hawaii. She was murdered." She cuts off, and I think maybe her jaw quivers.

Fuck.

That was the part I didn't know.

I remember a lot of social media about Cole Lancaster unearthing some big mystery and rescuing another woman years ago. I had no idea that story came with such a dark underbelly.

"So, long story short, there was a ton of drama before we found out. We didn't know the truth for years," she says with a dry smile. "Dad never felt right when he was told it was a freak accident, my mother washing up like she drowned. He was so busy raising me and managing his company, he let it lie for years. Then he met Eliza, my stepmom. I think she made his brain work again. She got herself into trouble, too, and when Dad came charging in to help, that's how he stumbled on the truth."

"Closure. Everybody needs it." I wonder if she can hear how I've been robbed of my own.

What else can I say?

I'm the asshole who wanted answers, so here they are.

I almost regret asking, prying at her, when I see the haunted look she beams into the fire.

My food is going cold, but all I can do is stare at her, wondering why I had to pull it out of her in the first place.

"You can find all the details if you really want to, so I won't bore you with the rest," she continues. "But after it was over and Dad decided to get remarried, I was heading off to college. I figured taking a step back was the right thing to do. For me and for him. He's with Eliza now and they've got a couple kids. A second chance at the nice, normal family he always wanted. They're happy. They don't need me around reminding them of... of..."

Her voice catches.

Fuck.

"Destiny," I cut in, "I don't think your old man would ever mind you—"

"No," she says quickly. "No, this was my decision. Not his. We're not on bad terms or anything. We get along great. I just... I wanted my space, too. I had to figure out my own shit. And I wanted to give him a chance at having his new family without any reminders of what happened before. Dad deserves it, especially when things weren't ever great with my mom..."

A life without her in it, she means.

Shit, that's heavy.

My jaw is glued shut.

She doesn't seem to mind the silence now, staring into the flames as the tension eases.

Until she looks up at me again.

"I'm guessing you didn't abuse Vanessa Dumas," she says slowly.

Damn.

A secret for a secret.

That's the unspoken trade here, isn't it?

My shoulders square and I look into the fire, gazing until the bright-orange glow burns its imprint into my eyes.

"I never did, but why bring it up now?" Or ever.

"Oh, I didn't mean to poke you with bad memories or stress or whatever. I just wanted you to know that I get it. What this whole thing is really all about..."

"What *thing?*"

"The internship. Young Influencers. You know"—she gestures broadly—"the whole reason I'm here, making you pull your hair out."

"Right."

"You need a little spit and shine on your reputation. That's cool," she says too freely. "It's shitty that she did that to you. Running around, making all kinds of ugly accusations. Don't get me wrong, I'm on the 'believe women' train. But you don't out it by bouncing around talk shows and interviews like it's a book tour. Her story just feels calculated."

I shift so the fire isn't beaming in my face.

"You don't believe her?" I ask slowly.

Destiny lifts a shoulder in a shrug.

"Eh, she doesn't strike me as the type who goes around belting out the truth for its own sake."

"She's not," I snarl. "I made a mistake with her—and not the type she implies."

"Yeah, I figured. And I sure wouldn't be here if I believed her at all, camping with you on a remote beach." Her lips twist in a humorless smile. "The stuff she's saying about you... Jeez, if I thought it was true, I wouldn't come near you without an armed chaperone."

"If the bullshit she's claiming was true, I'd deserve hell. I'd be the first to admit it and face whatever damages a court deems necessary."

"You'd deserve something, all right." Her face relaxes, slipping into the first genuine smile I've seen since the not-kiss. "You shouldn't have trusted her."

"Now you tell me." I roll my eyes.

"Well, just for next time. In case you decide to get mixed up with somebody like her again..."

"Is that a warning?"

"Warning?" She tosses her blonde hair over her shoulder and grins at me. "Oh, no. I said I'm game for helping restore your reputation. Hey, if all we do is find these otters tomorrow, I'll sing your praises for the next three months every day on socials. Everyone will think Shepherd Foster is the patron saint of cute marine animals."

Dammit.

A rough chuckle slips out of me.

"You'll have your work cut out for you, convincing anyone," I mutter.

Logically, I know I should be relieved she understands this PR scheme and isn't bothered by it.

Also, if she can read me this easily, it means she'll be able to keep this as professional and impersonal as I need.

Even so, irritation grips my chest, knowing she's figured this whole thing out so easily.

Vanessa always tried to look deeper, too, hoping to unearth some dark secret or weakness she could exploit to win me over.

Look what happened there.

I fold my arms. "You really don't believe Dumas?"

"Like I said, it doesn't add up." Destiny shrugs, taking her seat again on the sand, closer to the fire.

"How can you be so sure I'm not the heart-wrecking scoundrel she's made me out to be?"

Destiny shrugs again and gives me a long look, starting at my chest and winding up to my face.

The firelight flickers in her eyes, teasing the green flecks from the blue pools. They're practically luminous in the dark like this, vibrant fireflies that seem to see my soul.

She sees too deep inside me, and I don't know what to do with that.

"Call it a hunch. A sixth sense. Whatever," she says.

"You see dead people who aren't assholes?" I say, referencing that silly movie. "Sorry to disappoint you, Miss Destiny, but I'm very much alive."

"Oh, okay. You're not as intimidating as you want to be,

mister, for the record. You billionaires are all the same. Tons of loud bark and no bite. Totally harmless."

The way she rolls her eyes tells me she's joking, but something about hearing that strikes deep.

Anger, frustration, all the shit I shouldn't feel erupts in my blood.

One second, I'm on the log, keeping a nice safe distance, doing all I can to keep her safe from me.

The next, I'm thunking my coffee cup down on the sand and crossing the gap to her.

Before I have another coherent thought, I drop down on my knees and push her back, pinning her to the sand.

My body hovers over hers like a man possessed and every breath feels like napalm.

Fuck, I don't know what I'm doing.

Some kind of primal impulse takes over. This manic urge to remind her I'm not harmless, to tell her not to get too close or think she can slide into my life like it's a pair of slippers.

She can't fucking *know* me.

Nothing good has ever happened with the people I invited in.

She should consider me dangerous.

Tainted.

Unhinged.

All logic deserts me as my brain catches up to my body, which is far too close to hers.

I can feel her under me.

I'm not letting my lips brush hers.

I'm not gripping her shoulders hard.

I'm not losing my shit.

And Destiny, she's barely breathing now, her chest pushing against mine with shallow breaths that make me feel her tits behind that thin layer of fabric.

Is she afraid yet?

For both our sakes, she should be.

My anger softens the longer I stare at her, though, replaced by a sharpening awareness.

The darkening night deepens around us.

The crackling fire grows louder.

The distant roll of the evening tide echoes in my ears, almost as loud as my heartbeat as I stare down at her like prey, willing myself to rip away the next second.

The softness of her body against mine *kills* me.

She's slender, but lush.

All graceful curves and toned muscle and unbearably soft skin.

Her lips are parted in a devilish invitation, calling my hands to all the wrong places, begging my brain to switch off.

I feel my cock swelling as I try to get a grip.

As I try to find my familiar ice-cold kingdom again where I'm alone and safe with emotions I understand.

Anger.

Self-loathing.

Irritation.

Not desire.

Not empathy for this strange woman.

Not giving two shits about her struggles, her dreams, and how damnably good her hot breath feels on my lips.

Mind over dick matter.

Be angry, you fuck.

Better, be indifferent. Be nothing.

"What about now?" I growl. "Still think I look harmless?"

She looks up at me fearlessly, her eyes smoky and her breath coming faster, demanding a kiss.

Her lips part wider.

Damn her, I can't do this.

If she's *aroused* because of me, because of this insanity—

If she truly wants this as badly as I do, I'm boned.

No question.

My entire body goes rigid, my cock pushing at the zipper of my cargo pants.

I want her so madly I can't even see straight.

"Are you?" she challenges. "If you're trying to make a point, do it. Don't back down now. Show me how dangerous you are."

I almost do.

I almost devour her on the spot like the carnivorous, unhinged thing I am.

I come close—*so fucking close*—leaning down as she lifts her chin defiantly, bringing our lips closer, less than two inches apart.

I don't know if she's doing it consciously or if it's only a dare made on raw instinct.

I just know that if I kiss her now, I won't be showing her how dangerous I can be.

I'll be a slave to the desire scorching the air between us.

One more mistake in a lifelong litany, and this one infinitely harder to take back than Vanessa Dumas.

I can't keep fucking up.

I can't keep multiplying problems.

Then Destiny shifts under me.

Her breath catches as her hips move against my cock, grinding through the fabric.

I groan at the unexpected rush, the heat, the pulsing roar in my ears as she lets out a soft, almost pleading moan.

Fuck me.

Yeah, there's no stopping this now.

I kiss Destiny Lancaster again like my mouth is a ring of pure fire, and she's the only thing in the universe that can quench it.

I kiss like I take and I take brutally, like I want to chew her up and spit her the fuck out.

Hell, maybe I do.

Perhaps I want to crush this madness she's injected, this poison, this corruption of my discipline.

Or maybe I want to claim her right down to the bone so I'll never be her emotional hostage again.

Either way, she's there for it in a way that surprises me, kissing me back just as roughly.

A moan explodes up her throat, all wild need.

She grabs my face with her hands, nails digging in, and refuses to let go.

Her mouth is soft. Pliant. Giving.

She tastes so fucking sweet I'm drunk already, spilling a groan into her mouth.

Her lips part and her tongue teases mine, and soon, this isn't just a kiss.

Now, she digs her hands into my hair.

I grind my hips against hers as she shifts again, opening up to me.

My cock rakes her pussy swiftly through the fabric, a monster ready to descend.

I feel fucking drugged, knowing how potent she is, hating and loving how easily this woman leaves me intoxicated.

All the adrenaline that's stormed my blood during this trip surges, becoming raw need.

If we don't stop, this could become something molten, something heady, something fatal—

Until something else *cracks* in the woods beyond the beach.

I pop up, bracing my hands in the sand on either side of her head, staring into the forest.

There's nothing.

An animal snapping a twig or a falling branch, maybe.

Only, when I look at her again, her mouth is still ruby red from my kiss.

Red and swollen and perfect.

She's so visibly aroused, those goddamned nipples hard against her shirt, aching to be sucked into compliance.

Damn her, I'm never going to walk away from those unclaimed tits and live.

The girl is a human sugar lick, so tempting I almost give in and destroy us both again.

But her eyes are wide, and the air is so cool. I'm excruciatingly aware that I'm breaking every social boundary known to man with this song and dance.

I'm breaking so many rules, and all I want to do is keep shredding them to tatters.

A horrible idea stabs my brain.

Was this why she brought me here? Was this recklessness *planned?*

I bitterly wonder if that's why she got me into the sticks and why she seemed so relieved the instant she found out Miss Cho couldn't join us.

The perfect ambush. A chance to seduce me.

So she could reduce me to the self-destructive beast I am.

And just like she hoped, I obliged.

Fucking idiot ass-clown.

Or maybe Hannah's right.

Maybe I do have trust issues.

Snarling, I back up, pushing off of her, running a hand across my burning face.

Destiny jolts up, too, brushing sand out of her hair as she stares at me desperately with painful questions hanging on her lips.

Why not?

What did I do wrong?

She doesn't ask, but I hear them anyway.

"Sorry," I grind out. "That was damn inappropriate, Miss Lancaster."

I stand and stride away from her, adjusting the bulge in my pants as I go.

I don't want to look at her now.

Will she be gone in the morning, leaving a mess of tears and new hell posts online? Joining the chorus of people who already think I'm a predatory shithead?

And after what I just pulled, I wonder if I am.

I'm hardly innocent.

Still, she has to know.

She must know I brought her into the fold for a charity gig intended to brighten the company's reputation, and nothing more.

It certainly wasn't to fucking kiss her face off like a goat hopped up on blue pills.

Doesn't matter that she wanted it, too—or maybe the fact that she does just makes it worse.

"Wait!" she calls after me shrilly. "Foster!"

I move faster, away from that blinding firelight and into the darkness where I can try to find my wits again and tether them down.

"*Shepherd.*" She chases after me. "Wait, just so you know... I'm not upset. You didn't do anything wrong."

Didn't I?

I whip around and glare at her.

Why can't she understand?

I can't do this, even if she's made it crystal fucking clear it's consensual.

Especially not if she wants this just as bad as I do.

I won't repeat my past.

I'm not trusting another pretty face, leading her into temptation, waiting for her to *die* because I'm that goddamned toxic.

"Shepherd... at least say something," she pleads.

"Get some sleep," I growl over my shoulder. "We have a long day ahead—if we still have one at all."

She halts just past the circle of stones around the fire.

"I mean, of course. Shepherd?"

"Go to bed, Destiny. We need to get started before sunrise." Without waiting for an answer, I march back across to the sleeping bag I laid out before and stuff myself inside.

I zip the thick fabric up to my chin like the miserable human caterpillar I am, keeping my back to her.

Here we go again.

Silence.

Only, this time it's like the grave.

Then I hear her cleaning the bowl that toppled over when I threw myself at her, rinsing it out with some water she's collected.

I grit my teeth and close my eyes.

I, Shepherd Foster, am master idiot of the known universe.

A horny, impulsive, goat-brained dimwit—and apparently, I'm still led around by my cock after all these years.

What the fuck?

I'm too old for this shit.

Sighing, I wrestle my phone out and squint at the eye-killing screen.

Barely nine p.m., but the exhaustion is natural.

I'm sure Destiny feels it, too, that weight turning her bones to lead.

No more good will come from talking tonight.

My eyes drop from the time to my notifications.

That's where I see a new text from Vanessa, asking to meet and talk this out like 'civilized people.'

Like hell.

My lips curl into a snarl as I text back, *I don't negotiate with anyone who makes their disputes public. Never contact me again without your lawyer.*

The end.

I just wish I'd grown a bigger pair and faced her games head-on, without being talked into playing my own.

I never should have agreed to Hannah's reputation management scheme.

To Destiny, to her otter hunt, to fixing this shit with someone else intimately involved.

I've always been a man who handles his own problems, just like I did with Uncle Aidan and his crew when I decided I couldn't live a life of violence and pure villainy.

One wrong move half a lifetime ago, and I could've wound up with a nice, clean, anonymous bullet in the back of my head.

That should be far scarier than struggling for self-control around a new pretty face.

Then why is Destiny Lancaster so damned good at leaving me petrified?

X: A LITTLE WONDER (DESTINY)

*T*his is so not how I wanted to see the sunrise.

When Shepherd mentioned camping, I had big plans to get a few shots of the morning and evening light highlighting this beautiful place. I thought it would be great for my followers—and for me.

How often do you ever get to do something like this?

Just drop everything to go into the wilderness and live a few days synched to nature's rhythm?

Almost never.

Not when you're a busy adult strapped with a career, a brand, a life.

Nothing that should involve making out madly with my boss in the sand and then tossing and turning all night because of it, so wet and heart-stung I still hurt in the morning.

At least I wasn't suffering alone.

Every time I turned over, I heard him rustling in his sleeping bag like a trapped insect.

I knew Shepherd was awake every excruciating minute, just like me.

Stuck in reliving the last twenty-four hours, plus a hundred lost chances.

Is he kicking himself for missing them like I am?

Or is he just too busy brooding like the surly, walled-off creature he is, wishing to all the gods of common sense that he never went on this otterly catastrophic trip?

It's shaping up to be worth every bad pun.

Even now, I remember too much.

His firm, comforting weight pressing down on me.

How swiftly he moved, seizing my mouth, growling with need as his tongue pushed against mine.

And what a tongue.

The man knows when to give, when to chase, when to tease.

If he just knew how to sort his own shit, we might be in a happier place. Not here, rising with the sun and trying like mad to rub the exhaustion from my eyes.

My panties are still wrecked from dreaming about cold blue eyes that can only ever offer conflicted kisses.

And that wild, wanting look in his eyes...

God.

I still don't understand.

Why did he have to freak out and run away when it tasted so good?

It wasn't me, right?

It's not that people don't find me attractive. I know, logically, that I'm relatively pretty, and guys have given me plenty of attention ever since I hit my main growth spurt.

But this is different.

No one has ever wanted me the way Shepherd Foster looked at me last night.

Fierce and desperate and entirely demanding.

Also, so familiar.

He wanted me with the same strength he unleashed on the ocean, and that's weirdly compelling.

My heart drums wild whenever I think about it.

I didn't plan this.

I came for otters and wound up being drawn to my boss like

a moth to flame.

This isn't me.

I'm not Miss Free Fall.

If I'm dating, I need a guy to wow me before any real attraction sets in.

I'm a third date girl for any sexy business.

After we've talked and connected and kissed a few times, then maybe. Or maybe I realize I'm too busy or too disinterested and I politely end it right there. My usual routine.

But this isn't me.

I don't recklessly throw myself at men without a basic human connection first.

Whatever we have, it's definitely not that.

Shepherd and I don't even *like* each other.

There's just this sizzling animal magnetism I can't deny.

A switch he flicked the second he hauled me out of the sea.

Even then, I was a goner, before the ill-fated massage and the kiss that plucked my heart out.

Holy hell, the *kiss*.

My whole body burns just remembering it.

The single most erotic moment of my existence, and we were *still fully clothed.*

Briefly, I consider touching myself while it's still dark and quiet and I'm covered up in my sleeping bag, but then I hear him moving around and I'm sure he's awake.

Ugh.

He'll know.

Then I'll never live it down.

So I just lie there in the dim light just before sunset proper, wide awake and exhausted yet fizzing with a lust so intense it vibrates with awareness.

For a second, I think about calling out, but I open my mouth and stop cold.

I can't do it.

Not in this state.

Sighing, I wriggle out of my sleeping bag and cool off for a second in the dewy morning air.

I think Shepherd does the same, taking a moment to collect himself.

He looks so painfully handsome in that tight t-shirt clinging to him like a second skin that I don't dare stare too long.

And it's a one-way glance.

He doesn't so much as look at me as he packs his stuff away.

His movements seem almost as stilted as mine, sore from yesterday's rigors, or maybe just intent on holding himself together.

Despite everything, I feel a tiny surge of victory.

If he's been awake all night too, *good.*

The prick deserves it after kissing me like Satan on a mission and then cutting me off cold turkey.

Never mind the fact that he wouldn't utter one word about it.

Adults talk... don't they?

When they make mistakes, they own up to them—and he clearly thinks yesterday was an epic mistake—and they also figure out a way to set things right.

But when it comes to Shepherd Foster, CEO and shameless jackass extraordinaire, communication is an afterthought.

Fine.

Whatever.

While he kicks dirt and sand into the fire pit, I sit up and pack my overnight stuff into my kayak, strapping it down firmly.

Soon, without speaking, we carry our boats down from the rocks where we secured them and get everything ready to go.

My limbs feel like they're encased in cement when I start paddling.

Muscles I didn't know I had scream with protest.

Luckily, a few parts of this stretch of coastline are familiar. This isn't my first time coming to the Olympic Peninsula.

Last year, I came out here for five days sea otter hunting and came back empty-handed, not counting a few pics of cute foxes and a marmot. But I didn't have anything to prove then like I do today, and the stakes are higher than ever.

"This is it," Shepherd finally says about an hour later, breaking the morning quiet. "Where do you want to start?"

After some thought, I pick a small trail through the woods that curls back to another beach through some overgrowth. It's one of those hidden gem beaches that rarely sees people, safe from the summer tourists. That factor alone might boost our chances.

We climb out and secure our kayaks against some driftwood before heading down the brush-crowded path.

"You want to tell me about these otters? I'm guessing you've got some expertise," he says after a few more heavy minutes.

Loaded looks and deathly silence. At least we're good at something.

"What do you want to know?" I ask carefully.

"What *do* you know, Destiny?"

I can't help the annoyed grin that spreads across my face.

He really has to ask?

It might be easier to ask what I *don't* know.

"I've always had a soft spot for otters," I explain, stepping over a fallen log exploding with moss.

It's so idyllic here with the morning sun straining through the budding leaves. Mulch and gravel cover the ground without so much overgrowth the deeper we go.

I take a breath, hold it, and exhale.

This is fine.

This is good.

I don't need to worry about what he thinks of me out here.

My body aches. I'm so tired I'm seeing double, but I'm here and present in the moment.

"I fell in love with them when I was a kid and learned they hold hands while they sleep. Can you believe how cute that is?"

"I can believe it," he says dryly. "Are you drawn to anything besides the fact that they're living cartoons?"

I glare at him.

"Duh. Their numbers have recovered a little recently, but they're still endangered. They're interesting creatures and they need our help. They have the densest fur of any mammal."

"What, they don't have enough fat to keep warm in the ocean currents?"

"Exactly." I grin up at him. Maybe it's the light, but it looks like he half smiles back. "We'd find them more easily in Alaska, but there's a small population here that's still going. The Washington groups used to have a pretty extensive range and ten times its numbers, but you can guess what happened."

"People, unfortunately. I know the feeling," he growls.

He couldn't be more right.

The edge in his voice almost makes me laugh.

It's not hard to imagine him giving up every dollar he has if he could make everyone in a hundred-mile radius disappear.

"So, what then? You're campaigning to put them on people's radar? For raising awareness?"

"I guess. The animals that strike a note with the public always get a leg up with researchers and big money. It may not be right, but it's a fact. It's sad that the sea otters are still relatively unknown, though. We need folks to see how important they are to the ecosystem. They do a ton, no matter how sweet they look." Any second now, I'm waiting for him to cut me off with a curt nod, but he doesn't.

He just keeps listening as I rattle off otter facts like a talking Wiki article, my past trips here, the professor I worked with a couple years ago who fought tooth and nail for a grant he couldn't get for better research into restoring their numbers.

"Basically, they're in a pretty similar place to polar bears, just less well known," I say. "Between the shrinking habitat and human industry mucking things up, it isn't good. If they don't get some serious attention soon…"

I don't finish, but my meaning is clear.

The otters are dead meat.

The Washington remnant, for sure, and probably the rest of the Pacific Northwest population after that.

A tale as old as time.

So many innocent things will die if we keep destroying their world.

This is why I wish more culprits had to pay through the nose for their damage. For every charitable billionaire like Dad or Foster who try to leave a minimal environmental footprint, there are three more rich pricks willing to slash throats at any cost to fatten their accounts. Too often, those pricks have the government regulators in their pockets, too.

"Polar bears," Shepherd prompts when I drift into silence.

"Right. Yes. So, just like them sea otters are a keystone species. They go after sea urchins, which eat kelp. Like, so much kelp. With otters keeping urchins in check, the kelp forests thrive. It's all about balance."

"Balance. That's why I'm here stomping through this mud?" He looks down, grumbling as he rips his boot out of a tarry puddle where the tide must've swept in overnight.

I stifle a laugh.

"That's where you stop getting dirty and work your magic. The drones can cover way more rough ground without us stumbling around, right? Think what it took to even get to this spot..."

"You have a point," he agrees.

He stops and glances around the woodland, wiping his boot on a rock.

It's quiet, but not dead silent.

Compared to the bustling city, sure. But if you listen, there's so much going on—birds and bugs and even the occasional fish dipping out of the water.

It makes me feel so alive and I'll love the natural rhythm forever.

"Don't get too excited," I warn. "There's no guarantee we'll see any, no matter how good your metal bugs are."

"These 'bugs' were a thirty-million-dollar project," he says. "If they're good at finding intruders who squeeze through the slightest window—and they're impeccable—then they ought to be able to find your lanky friends crawling around rocks in the open."

I scan the rocks offshore in search of them with my own eyes first.

They usually spend the bulk of their day out at sea and come ashore to rest. That's our best chance at spotting them.

"Keep your eyes peeled anyway," I tell Shepherd. "Our best chance to see them is when they're resting, or sometimes when they're on rocks, breaking mollusks." I mime the action before stopping cold.

Now I'm just embarrassed.

What is it about this man that makes me act like a complete idiot around him?

He knows what mollusks are.

And um, probably how a hungry otter gets breakfast.

"Understood—and thanks for the demonstration, Destiny." His lips twitch into another almost-smile that makes my heart skip before I wrestle it back under control.

This is so bad.

"Is their endangered status recent? As in, the last forty years?" he asks. "I mean, out here or Alaska, it's not too densely populated. They don't have any natural predators that I know of."

"How about humans?" I sigh because it makes me sad. "They were hunted for their pelts as traders came west and moved up the coast. Their population recovered a bit, sure, but more recently, pollution has been a massive problem."

He nods grimly but doesn't say anything more as I squint across the sun-spangled sea.

I stare at the churning waves, looking for any sign of precious, furry little faces poking out of the water or frolicking around the rocks.

"Did you work with them in your grad program?" he asks from behind me.

"A little. Not as much as I wanted, and not just otters. I was with tons of different research groups with a broad marine life focus, usually. The professors want you to gain a lot of broad experience before you really home in on any specialty. I've worked on protecting turtles, dolphins from fisheries, and I even did a stint in Hudson Bay with an international polar bear tracking group." Though it's a losing battle like everyone knows. "I guess the otters are close to home. They've always held a special place for me. What I'd really like to get involved with is preserving what's left of our sei whales. They're crazy rare now in local waters, but a few scientists I worked with swore they're on the verge of a comeback—if they just had a little more help."

"And what help would that be?"

I slide him a glance, slightly irritated he sounds so skeptical.

Not that I can blame him when so much conservation work feels like an impossible battle.

"Well, we just don't know enough. 'Knowledge is power' isn't just a cheesy catchphrase with animal research. It's everything. If this drone tracking helps with the otters, underwater drones could be huge for the whales." I hold my breath, waiting for him to call me an idiot.

Honestly, I don't even know how technically feasible it is.

"That's a big ask. Unmanned submersibles are the most expensive experimental drone technology around," he says. But he doesn't instantly swat me down. "I'll admit, I don't know much about sei whales except for the fact that they've been hunted extensively."

"Yeah. They're protected now, but very little is known about them, and that's the problem. Especially their social dynamics. We need something capable of keeping up that can track their movements and study them without being as intrusive as research boats."

"Meaning, the drones would have to follow a pod over a long

distance," he muses. "It could be done—but I assure you, the cost would make this otter tracking adaptation look like a church fish fry."

"Right."

"With that in mind, I'm not sure a conventional drone would be your best option. Even the best submersibles adapted for civilian usage still run on batteries, and any hint of adding more lithium to the ocean if something goes wrong is a net loss for everything down there."

He frowns, thinking.

I'll be honest, it's weirdly adorable.

I mean, if you can call a man who's built like a mountain *cute*.

"Well, what would you suggest?" I prompt.

"I said *conventional*. What you need is something that can work around the energy problem. A submersible that draws its power from the ocean itself," he says slowly as if he's magically pulling the idea from the ether. "The current motions might provide a small device with enough kinetic energy to power itself indefinitely. We'd still need a data link, too, but that would be easy enough to establish with an environmentally friendly power source."

"Careful, Shepherd. It sounds like you're really getting into this," I tease, then freeze up.

He made it perfectly plain that we don't have this sort of relationship.

He doesn't do *jokes*, or even fun.

Although geeking out like this is pretty entertaining.

Not that I would ever admit it to his grumpy face.

He probably thinks this whole conversation is borderline insubordination, what with me low-key asking for spendy miracle technologies when I haven't even passed the first big test today.

Or maybe he's already planning on firing me because I kissed him back.

In his uptight world spinning with scandal, that's a high crime for sure.

A breeze comes blowing off the water, tossing my hair.

I rub my eyes and finger comb it back into place.

I really must be dead exhausted if I can't keep my thoughts straight, let alone focused on the animals we're out here to save.

Being horny and sleep-deprived does awful things to a woman's mind.

I'm three seconds away from insanity.

Then Shepherd abruptly ducks under a low branch, and he doesn't look like he's on the verge of firing me.

I haven't noticed him rifling through his large bag until now. He pulls out a smaller hardshell case with a handle, sets it down gently, and opens it.

Inside, I see the neatly packed drone prototype, so pearly white it glows.

"Whatever the future may bring, letting you drag me out here hasn't been a complete waste of time. This is an interesting application of our technology," he says without missing a beat.

Perfectly seriously.

My heart disintegrates into butterflies again.

Just how?

How can a man who's never met a human smile look so attractive when he's hunched over his creation like a mad scientist?

His eccentric, grumpy butt breaks all the laws of men.

One guy doesn't get to be smoldering and cute simultaneously, yet here he is doing it, slaying my heart to smithereens.

I nod sharply, pretending the drone test is all that's on my mind.

My smile does its best to come out, and I bite it away again.

"You're right, Shepherd. *Super* interesting application of technology. Imagine what we could do with the robo-subs and the whales."

"Are you laughing at me?" He looks at me.

"Nope. Never." I force my lips into a straight line. "Sir," I add as an afterthought.

"Smart-ass otter brat."

"Yes, sir," I agree.

"Are you trying to sound like Miss Cho?"

Is that how I protect myself from another kiss that rips my heart out?

"I'm showing you a smidge of respect for taking a leap of faith with me today. Don't let it go to your head. Oh, and I couldn't ever be one tenth as serious as Hannah."

He snorts. "Yes, she's unbearably polite when she insults me to my face weekly. You, Miss Destiny, pull no punches."

There it is again.

The barest hint of a smile—and is he looking at me *fondly?*

Oh, boy.

"Are you a bigger dick to her than you are to me?" I whisper.

"It's a tough contest. I threaten to fire her constantly, but by now she knows I won't." He eyes me coldly. "You, I'm still working out how to tame."

Apparently, he's on the right track with this innuendo that feels like an uppercut.

"Is that your first priority? Playing mind games with your people?" I ask playfully.

He shakes his head.

"I fucking wish. Hannah Cho is a force of corporate nature. If you want to know why Home Shepherd operates as tightly as it does, she's the one to thank."

My eyebrows lift.

Whatever crap I was expecting, it wasn't that.

He gives credit surprisingly easily, like it doesn't hurt his ego to admit that someone else has a hand in his success.

God help me, I like that.

I like it way too much.

"As long as you pay her well," I say, teasing him again.

"Agonizingly well, as she's reminded daily."

That does it, I smile.

This is the side of Shepherd he doesn't like to show.

When he's talking about endangered animals and charities and how he treats his employees, he's not half-bad.

Even his stance is different now.

His shoulders are looser, less militantly stiff, the sternness gone from his eyes.

And he keeps almost-smiling when I look at him.

For Shepherd, that's a freaking lot.

It's the nicest thing just talking like this.

Like we're halfway to being friends instead of the iron bossman and his confused shadow.

Somehow, that matters.

Maybe because I've fought my whole life for a chance to find my own footing without needing to stake my life on Dad's reputation and money.

The fact that Shepherd accepts me even though I'm miles beneath him on the corporate ladder makes my toes curl in my shoes and my belly explode with—

Yep.

Butterflies.

I can't remember the last time I ever felt them.

And all because he's exhibiting basic human decency after making so many mistakes yesterday. My standards must be hilariously low.

"It's nice knowing you have a good relationship with your assistant," I say.

"What? Did you suspect she was terrorized on a daily basis?"

I flash him a look that makes him snicker. "You tried to terrorize *me*."

"Tried? How disappointing."

"Was that another joke, Foster?"

His smile disappears. "No, damn you."

I burst out laughing, scaring away some seagulls waddling on the shore.

So much for trying to be quiet out here and using library voices.

"Funny, right?" I move closer, nudging his arm with my elbow. "People are more complex than you give them credit for."

Wrong move.

He totally shuts down.

One minute, he's teasing along with me, looking almost human and like he might be having fun.

Then his eyes shutter.

His mouth thins.

He goes right back to being the irritable, unapproachable frost king he shows the world—the same man I met in his office when he insulted me to my face.

I do not miss that man.

I also have zero desire to spend more time with him.

Clearing my throat, I try to ignore the fact that I nudged him as we start moving again, still close enough to touch in our silence.

Ignore him, ignore him.

Right.

That's about as easy as ignoring a rampaging bear barreling at me.

Although maybe a bear would make less noise.

"Careful where you step with the leaves," I tell him, pushing aside a few long strands of grass. "We don't want to scare anything away."

"That's what this is for, isn't it?" Without another word, he throws the small drone into the sky like he's pitching a baseball.

It whirs to life instantly, hovering above us like an overgrown bee.

It's the total lack of noise that catches me off guard.

The little machine is bizarrely quiet, you wouldn't know it was there if you didn't see it.

I'm legit impressed.

"Let the bug, as you call it, do the searching from here, Destiny," he tells me, brushing his hand against mine.

I hold my breath, wondering if he'll take it, but he moves forward again.

Ass.

Mysterious, uptight, annoyingly generous ass.

We continue along the back of the beach quietly while I hold in my sarcasm. With the drone deployed and moving just ahead of us at a comfortable pace, it's all about the otters now.

My eyes feel sharper than ever.

Every black piece of seaweed, every distant ship, makes me think of them.

But no, after trudging half a mile along the uneven shore, there's nothing. My eyes are tired and my shoulders slump.

I'm already feeling defeated as the drone slows and scans, turning in the air a full three-sixty.

It makes me wonder if we should waste more time here or cut our losses while we still have plenty of time to move to a better spot.

But then I see it.

At least, I see *something.*

It's small, but noticeable, splashing in a tide pool formed by half-sunken rocks.

I throw up an arm, stopping Shepherd in his tracks, thunking my hand against his wall of a chest.

He knows better than to ask, but I think his excitement almost matches mine as a long, quick moving otter crawls out of the rocks, bats its eyes, and then dives back under again.

A second later, it pops its head up and flops on its back, gliding on the water like a drunken frat boy in a pool. It's officially the sweetest, laziest, most unexpected surprise of my life.

Holy crap!

Holy shit.

When I grab his arm and pull, wordlessly sharing my thrill, he doesn't protest.

Shepherd just nods and smiles when I look up from the amazing scene to see his face.

Meanwhile, I'm fumbling around in my bag like a madwoman, trying to find my binoculars.

"Relax. The drone's footage goes straight to the cloud, even out here, thanks to Starlink. It can zoom in fifty times without losing image quality," he whispers hotly in my ear.

Wow.

Even with the reassurance, I'm scared I'll miss this if I even dare to breathe.

My heart pounds so hard I think I'm seeing double.

My hands are shaking.

This is too much. *Too incredible.*

Beside me, Shepherd lifts his own pair of binoculars. I didn't notice him throw them around his neck, but he must've thought to earlier.

He passes them over, and together, we take turns otter watching.

No, otters.

Plural.

Several more of these living plushies emerge, grouping themselves together to sun on the rocks when they're not splashing around like hyperactive ferrets.

I do my best to count them so I can send the state database an accurate report, though it's pretty hard when my hands are this unsteady.

Five... six... seven.

Seven otters.

Wait, no, eight. Eight.

Eight sea otters!

I forget how to breathe.

I think this might be the best day of my life since Eliza and Dad taught me how to swim.

I'm watching endangered freaking sea otters in their natural habitat.

Otters playing in the surf, a peaceful little family. A viable breeding population.

Sighing gratefully, I pull out my phone and zoom in, snapping pictures like crazy.

I post a few pictures to Insta ASAP, typing a clumsy caption, then I bring up the Fish & Wildlife information form.

"What are you doing?" Shepherd asks, breathing the question more than speaking it out loud.

Um, trying not to die from the rush?

I can't fathom how to tell him how grateful I truly am that he's being so supportive.

All my energy goes straight into capturing the otters with my camera.

"I'm reporting the numbers now," I whisper, doing a little happy dance. "Man, I can't believe we found them! Way more than just one, too. This looks like a solid breeding population."

"Jackpot," he agrees. "The drone should get better footage than anything your phone can capture."

"Right? I wonder if we're missing more. If we have the drone do a quick survey, we could get a better sweep of the area and know for sure just how many there are around here. Maybe, if there are more groups like this out there... they might not be endangered someday."

"Done," he says.

I whip around and look at him. "Oh, what? I wasn't seriously expecting you to—"

Before I can finish, he taps at his phone.

An app that controls the drone, I realize.

I watch the sleek little bug with those freakishly silent rotors lunge forward, holding my breath.

Without any noise, the otters seem totally oblivious, thankfully. They don't look up, even as it flies ahead of them, gaining altitude to take in a wider section of the area.

I lean in to the high-definition video feed coming back on Shepherd's screen. He taps an icon that switches to something like infrared. But I'm pretty sure we only wind up with the same eight heat signatures.

No big loss.

You don't spit in the face of a single miracle.

We enjoy the quiet, watching for several minutes.

I don't realize I'm getting drunk on his scent until he moves, leaving me so dizzy I bang into his shoulder.

"You hit a sinkhole?"

"No, no, I'm just—I'm a little overwhelmed. This is too freaking cool." I turn away as my cheeks heat.

"Falling face down in the dirt won't do us any good, or the otters. Don't make me catch you if you can't keep your balance, lady." The sharp glint in his eye says that's not an idle threat.

I swallow thickly.

There's something about the way he says *lady* that reaches so deep inside me, stroking me like a kitten.

"Just imagine what we could do if we had regular drone flights, monitoring this place. We'd have a crazy good understanding of their movements, their diet, their breeding patterns, their population—everything!"

I might take him up on that offer to jump into his arms.

I'm just that giddy.

But when he looks at me again, instead of eye-rolling irritation, he stares back with something almost like fondness.

His gaze is softer in a way I don't think I've ever seen it.

It makes his face gentler, erasing those hard lines worn by scowling so much.

Something about his face draws me in more than ever.

Something about *him.*

And that same indescribable something must radiate off me, too.

When it happens, it shouldn't be such a shock.

His big hand catches my waist, drags me in, and then we're kissing in the breathless excitement of this lovely moment.

Kissing like it's the very last time.

And if it is, the man makes it count like his life hinges on it.

He claims me gently at first. Slowly, but not hesitantly.

Shepherd Foster doesn't strike me as a man who's ever hesitant when he lets instinct take control.

But his lips are so warm against mine, an extension of the same braising excitement surging through my veins.

There's pure celebration in the movement of his tongue and the charge he ignites under my skin. His growl reverberates through me, and I give back a buttery moan.

His communication isn't verbal, no.

But you'd better believe he speaks with his body, with every movement, toasting our win today with his mouth and hands and the delicious sting of his teeth.

I soak it all up like a sun-starved plant.

Every new press of his lips whispers all the affirmation I've been craving, and all the filthy promises I dreamed last night.

Destiny, I fucking want you, they say.

God.

His rhythm quickens, matching the desire in my chest, the hot need that's been braising my stomach, and as my teeth graze his bottom lip, the kiss changes.

It becomes wild, frantic, almost too much.

Messy and clumsy and greedy and intense.

Just as big a contradiction as Shepherd himself.

The heat knifing through my body is sudden and urgent.

I wrap my arms around him, phone and otters forgotten.

Well, not quite forgotten.

Even the hottest kiss of my life can't make me forget that there are precious otters close by.

That's why, when he bites my bottom lip again, I swallow my gasp.

This time, I won't let him get away with getting me all hot and bothered before he hangs me out to dry, wet and cold.

I push myself closer, grabbing his shoulders, molding my body against his.

Holy hell, he's *huge.*

A giant in every sense of the word.

It's almost shocking we fit together so well when he has at least five inches and a hundred pounds on me.

I'm tall, but he's Mount Flipping Rainier.

I have honed, strong shoulders, but his could make the sky itself rage with jealousy.

I'm a decent kisser—so I think—but he could shame every Casanova born for the last five hundred years.

Our hips slot together, and I tug at his shirt, raking my hands over his bare skin.

This man.

Holy hell, this man has muscle groups I thought were only mythic.

His skin is warm and silky under my searching fingers, but I can sense the hardness underneath. I stroke down his chest, feeling him freely, his pecs, his abs.

All eight of them.

Eight!

He can't even settle for a regular six-pack like a normal hyper-athletic male.

"Destiny," he rasps my name. "If you want me to stop, speak the hell up. Right now."

He pulls back for the briefest second, his chest heaving, a question flaring in his smoldering eyes.

He's waiting for an answer I never give.

I just bite my lip, and my eyes flick down slowly.

I trace the arrow of pure muscle with one finger, pointing down to his beltline, and he groans.

Then his hands are on my hips and we're moving.

A second later, my back bangs against a massive tree, just hard enough to rattle me.

I don't know how we got here, I don't.

But do I want this to stop?

My brain has one answer, and my body has another.

I'm liquid fire already. So wet it's almost obscene.

I'm thrilled and sleep-deprived and confused from yesterday, and I shouldn't be this aroused this fast.

Even fully rested, I shouldn't be *this* ready to go.

He could just slip inside me right now and take over.

And it's like he reads my mind, grinding his hips against me, making me feel how massive he is where it counts.

At least he comes by his monster ego honestly.

I knew that yesterday, of course, when we were kissing in the sand and I felt him, but this is so different.

I wiggle, maneuvering myself so his cock presses where I need it most, pursing my lips and releasing a slow moan.

Holy shit, this is hot.

Like Hollywood romance blockbuster sexy.

One hand rolls up my hip, holding me in place, while his other finds the bottom of my top and flips it up. When he notices I'm not wearing a bra, a hoarse noise catches in his throat.

Then his palm cups my breast and goes to work.

It's insane that I'm still standing as I wrap my legs around him, grinding more firmly against his erection.

My head spins from how good it is.

When he pinches my nipple, I press my lips to his neck so I can only make one sound.

"Shepherd!" His name tears out of me, equally curse and prayer.

Yes, yes, holy hell, yes.

Don't stop.

Not even for the apocalypse.

I yank my top off, feeling the cool air against my bare breasts. He does the same with his shirt a second later.

Then we're warm, hungry skin on skin, and possibly the most erotic thing ever.

I rock against him again, wondering if I can come from this friction alone.

That alone is insane, but again, so is every part of this.

He kisses me again, hard and demanding.

Honestly, I'm thrilled to *be* demanded with such brute energy.

Happier still to dig at his shoulders, sinking my nails in, really feeling him.

And when he reaches down and opens my shorts, pushing them down my legs in one rough jerk, I'm beyond ecstatic.

This is it.

There's no coming back from this, and baby, I don't want to.

Next thing I know, we're tumbling down in a clearing between the thickest brush. I'm so riled I don't sweat missing a blanket.

Dead leaves crunch against my back as we roll, but I don't care.

Not when he's thunder incarnate, teasing one moan out after the next.

Not when my breasts are aching and my core is pure liquid and I need him inside me now.

Now.

"Shepherd," I whine.

I don't recognize my own voice.

He snarls a response, then drags his own pants down, freeing his cock.

It snaps out like a lethal weapon, pulsing and veiny and dangerously hard, a bead of liquid already at the tip.

With shaking fingers, I grab him and squeeze, loving how he groans.

I get maybe five strokes in, enough to see the scary-hot glint in his eyes, before he decides he won't melt into my touch.

When he slides a finger inside me, the world stops.

"Fuck," he rasps. "You're soaked, Destiny. How long has this pussy been ready for me?"

I can't answer while I'm shuddering to pieces on his fingers.

Not even when he growls, "Destiny, *how long?* Tell me."

But then he slides another finger in, and I forget my protests.

"L-last night. It's all I could think about. Shepherd, please," I whimper.

"Good girl. If you give me what I need, then so will I."

I don't know what that means until his thumb lands on my clit.

I try to keep pace, stroking my hand up and down his silky length. He hisses a breath between his teeth.

We're quiet—so quiet—and all I can think is that this is already the best sex of my last few lifetimes, and he's *not even inside me yet*.

Shit.

I'm so achingly close it's embarrassing.

Will I ever live down coming for him in under three minutes?

I wish I could still care.

But I don't as his mouth finds my nipple and sucks so hard I gasp, as his thumb presses down, as he takes me apart with pure sensation.

Not as the most powerful orgasm ever made rips me to pieces and scatters me to the wind.

I throw my head back and see white.

He drags his cock from my hands and there's a vague sound of a package tearing. I'm too far gone to notice the condom.

When he kisses me again—another wild, searing, own-your-soul kiss that makes my knees weak—and slides inside me, I have to bite back a moan.

He fills me to the brim and stops, rasping as he pushes his forehead to mine.

So tight it might hurt if he hadn't put me through the perfect warm-up.

When he moves again, the ache dissolves into this pleasurable stretching sensation.

"Destiny, goddamn. Tell me it isn't too much."

"Shepherd, please. Fuck me," I moan against his mouth.

His thrusts resume, this time like crashing waves, gaining tempo with every vicious stroke.

Eventually, I regain my senses, just enough to move my hips to match his movements.

The otters aren't the only wild animals here now.

Not when we're mating like desperate beasts in rut, grasping and thrusting and losing our minds in total delirium.

I nip his neck, leaving marks, clawing at his back, urging him on with every movement of my hips.

All the wildness I'd seen in him on the water pours into me now—and I want to share his pain, his fury, his need to disperse this wild energy.

All his beautiful brutality and arrogance.

All the fierce energy of a man with secret, deep passions I'm dying to know.

And I am feeling every bit of that passion as his cock marks me from the inside out.

Every. Single. Stroke.

The man against the world becomes the man who finally breaks.

But instead of fighting to subdue me, to master me, to shatter me with pleasure, he gives me something far more precious.

He gives up his iron control and comes apart in an avalanche of thrusts and guttural curses.

For a second, he gives me the sweetest glance as his face screws up and he can't hold back another second.

My legs lock around him so tight as my pussy molds to his flesh.

And I let him give.

I let Shepherd Foster empty his soul into depths no man has ever reached, figuratively and literally.

And when we finish, crashing down together in the grass and clinging with shaking muscles, it's like the world itself celebrates our beautiful chaos with a bright new burst of color and noise.

XI: A LITTLE INTOXICATED
(SHEPHERD)

There's a twig poking me in the spine, and I'm pretty sure I've got grass blades in my mouth.

Grass and mud and God only knows what else.

Right now, I think I know how Adam felt after one bite from a divine apple turned his whole world to shit.

If Hannah Cho finds out what I did, she's going to peel my eyeballs like grapes.

That is, if I don't off myself first for being so tragically stupid.

I'm naked on my back with itchy leaves under me. Destiny curls up against my side like she belongs there.

I've got no fucking clue where my clothes are. I ripped them off and flung them to the hinterlands in my animal state.

I should move. Find them.

End whatever the hell this spell is before it makes escape impossible.

But I'm still catching my breath one rough, conflicted lungful at a time, and there are glimpses of a forgiving blue sky just past the trees overhead.

The birds call out like they're endorsing a sin this big.

Hell, we even saw the otters.

That's what made this happen, I think.

My self-control was firmly screwed in place and I was ignoring everything she did to me until those damned teddy bear snakes showed up.

Until she lit up like a hot July night bursting with city lights.

Then she was bristling with so much infectious happiness and gratitude, a lightning bolt couldn't have kept me off her.

In the heat of the moment, it was mind-blowing.

Earthquake sex.

The kind men won't brag about in dingy bars because you'll never admit you were ever that damned lucky.

Regrettably, the best of my life, and so rampant it didn't matter if it was outdoors on the grass and leaves and dirt. It could've been on arctic snow and dagger rocks and it still would've been too exquisite for life.

It was also psychotically unethical.

I'm sure I just broke rules of engagement in ways I don't want to contemplate.

Fuck, even if she's a tall drink of trouble and an intern, she's practically half my age and technically no different from fucking an employee.

Possibly *worse.*

It's easy to forget she's so young sometimes when her passion for animals comes out and she cares enough to do her homework. Her ideas are sincerely good, better than the bland boilerplate shit I get out of my PR specialists and Corporate Giving people now.

When we get home, I'll have to revisit that.

Right now, I'm too paralyzed to think about anything but this colossal blunder.

When Monday hits, I'm going to have the mother of all scandals on my hands—if and when Destiny comes to her senses and decides to out my fuckery to the entire world.

Vanessa is one thing, but she wasn't my employee. It's easy to work against her, too, when I know every word out of her mouth is a lie.

We didn't have sex.

I wasn't the villain.

With Destiny, I *am* the devil who couldn't keep his dick tucked in his pants.

I have no idea what to do.

What to say.

The second she gets home and starts chattering on social media about fucking Shepherd Foster, you can stick a fork in me.

Right now, I have bigger problems, though.

Like how if this grass tickling my nose doesn't stop, I'm going to sneeze in her face.

I hate to imagine her giving me the hell I deserve when she's so real with me.

The way she reacted to those otters was genuine.

Her enthusiasm was sweet and innocent and entirely authentic. Definitely not faked for any clickbait shit she might post about it later.

She might dress up a few smiles for the online filters and fight for the best angle, but I know she didn't manufacture that joy.

Or that smile just for me, brighter than the sun.

Which means I need to find a way of broaching this mess without hurting her.

Somehow, while we're still naked.

Her breasts press my ribs, her cheek lies against my chest, and my arm is snug around her waist.

My posture is a fantasy, a lie that I could be the man to protect her, instead of the chosen asshole who's about to blow her heart to hell.

This grass across my face is killing me, though, but I can't will myself to move.

Destiny's hand comes up and she trails a finger across my

185

skin, skimming her nails through the hair and scraping down my muscles.

If I wasn't too spent to speak, my dick would take a lot more interest.

"Hey," she says through a yawn.

"Hey yourself."

"You're tense," she points out.

Fuck.

Guilty.

I inhale slowly, thinking about how I can possibly approach this.

How do I convince her that this mistake can't come out publicly without seeming like an even bigger ogre than I already am?

"Shepherd, you can relax," she whispers, those fingers tracing down my stomach. Unwillingly, I soften under her touch. "I'm not going to tell anyone, if that's what's got you so on edge."

"You're not?" I try not to let too much suspicion cut my tone.

"No. It's okay. What happened out here was between us, and more than consensual." She hits me with that smile again.

Goddamn.

I feel like the biggest jackass ever born.

My breath stutters unevenly from my lungs, making her head bob on my chest.

"The choice is yours, Miss Lancaster. I can't ask you to bottle up your feelings. Not when I'm the asshole who uncorked them in the first place, when I should have known better."

"You're Miss Lancastering me again. That's something I *will* tell every tabloid rag from LA to Boston if you keep it up." She looks up at me and laughs, asking for a smile I can't give. "Come on. You were good—inhuman, really—but it's not like you cast a spell that made me jump your bones. I wanted this. I won't go blabbing to the world how you seduced me against my will. I wouldn't dare, but even if I wanted to, it just isn't true." Her voice quivers at the end, uncertainty chewing at her words.

Despite everything, I tighten my hold on her.

"You really are torching my reputation. I'm not supposed to be this readable," I say dryly. It's annoying, but I can't summon any disgust behind my heartache.

Disgust isn't an emotion that happens under blue skies with wild songbirds and a woman so gorgeous she could shame every pinup from the last hundred years.

I just can't believe my life has become an X-rated Disney film.

"But you're hurting. The stress, it's eating you alive." She stares up with large eyes. Her hair is tossed across her face, her ponytail a loose mess.

Well, I wasn't exactly tender.

"It's very fucking complicated. There are good reasons to worry," I tell her darkly.

"Because you regret it? Is that one of them?"

Shit.

Usually, I would snap that *of fucking course* I regret what was clearly a bigger misstep than triggering a landmine.

Unfortunately, I care about hurting her.

Although she tries to hide it under her bravado, I get the distinct impression that her feelings are raw. Sensitive. Exposed and questioning.

That last one is a meat hook to my heart.

"Because I can't let it be a problem for either of us, Destiny," I venture.

"I don't want problems," she agrees quickly, breathing again. "Not for you or me or for your company."

"Then there's nothing to regret, is there?" I stare at her.

She shifts so her head rests better on my shoulder.

Damn, I should really let her go now, but there's something horribly reassuring about feeling a beautiful woman's flesh on mine.

It's been so long.

I can't remember the last time I allowed myself this

indulgence.

"Are you cold?" I ask, noticing the tremble in her shoulders.

"No. You?"

I shake my head.

"I guess I'm just processing." She laughs a little then, her breath warm against my skin. "That turned me inside out, I'm not gonna lie."

"You're not half-bad," I agree, biting back a smile.

"Look, I know you probably haven't been with a girl since Abe Lincoln was President, but FYI. 'Bad' can't be in your vocabulary after sex like that." She smacks my cheek playfully. "Now do you think we scared the otters?"

Little brat.

I can't resist touching her, palming the dip of her waist, feeling how fragile and perfect she is against me.

For such a slip of a woman, she took my cock like she was made for it.

Even now, seeing her naked almost does me in, obliterating what's left of my well-worn sanity.

Knowing she was so wet for me made it even better.

The desire in her eyes almost convinces me this is something we *should* be doing.

Like she wasn't sleeping with me for attention or because she was temporarily overwhelmed with the excitement strumming every nerve.

Fuck, why can't I let her go?

It's been a long damn time since I let anyone in like this.

Cuddling.

On the goddamned barren ground, no less, but cuddling all the same.

And she's not pulling away yet, finding her clothes, making awkward excuses for why she has to leave.

There's a distant splashing sound that may or may not be the otters.

"I don't think we scared them away," I say. "Did you get all the pictures you wanted?"

"I think so. I got a few videos too." Her sigh is pure content-ment. "Did you see them all? There were eight."

I saw the little animals, sure, but they had nothing on watching her.

The way her eyes lit up, the breathless joy across her face, the way her cheeks flushed as she held her breath.

No one fakes that shit.

There's no pretending you have a heart as big as a Sweeter Grind cinnamon roll unless it's really there in all of its massive, sugary goodness.

Everything about Destiny Lancaster is one long lethal sugar rush, and I just caught hyperglycemia.

Part of me knew how much shit I was in even before her clothes came off.

When she looked at me like I'm the one who put otters on planet Earth after talking about them like we were old friends, there was no stopping the inevitable.

Not with the way she stepped up and offered her mouth.

An invitation straight to my soul.

The memory alone reminds my cock that once wasn't nearly enough as a dark realization sets in.

Once with a girl like her would be a bigger sin than delving into this madness in the first place.

I clear my throat, eager to distract my growing erection.

"We should come to an understanding," I say.

"You mean unlike with the kiss? So now he wants to talk," she teases.

I pinch the skin of her waist.

"Yes, you little smart-ass."

"Okay! You first. I'm dying to hear this."

My jaw clenches as I ponder my words.

Everything and nothing stews in my head.

Honestly, I hate this shit.

Words are hard when I know how destructive they can be.

Talking about forbidden sex ruins the magic, too, but there's no way around it.

"First, we need to talk about the fact that I had sex with you."

"Um, yeah, it happened. What else is there to say? Are you still trying to make it sound like you forced it? That couldn't be further from the truth."

I shake my head violently.

"That's not my point. The fact that it happened at all means we need ground rules, Destiny. Don't get me wrong, it was damned good. Still, that doesn't mean it should have happened or change the fact that—"

"The fact that you're still a huge, uptight, grumpy asshole? Trust me, I know." She sighs playfully, and I feel the way the air floods out of her. It makes me hold her closer. "But I know what you mean. I get it, and you don't have to worry, Shepherd. This doesn't have to mean more. And... and I'm mature enough not to let it go to my head and turn it into something it wasn't."

I want to believe her.

But then why does she sound so disappointed?

"It was pure impulse, yeah. It overwhelmed us in the moment," I say carefully.

"Yeah."

"Since we also agree that the attraction was mutual, we can be clear about what it was and wasn't." I hope it makes some sense to her because it isn't computing for me.

My brain still can't believe I'm having this conversation.

"I guess it's kinda pointless, trying to deny it," she says, pressing her lips to my collarbone.

The kiss feels so casual, so affectionate, so natural.

It renders me fucking speechless.

"Right or wrong, this can't continue. As soon as we get back to Seattle, this can't happen again," I grind out.

"Understood," she whispers.

"Not ever," I say firmly, mostly because my dick is taking a horrible amount of convincing right now. "Also, I appreciate you saying you'll keep this discreet. I had no business complicating your life, yet the fact that you're willing not to mess up mine more than it already is means a hell of a lot. Thank you."

"It's cool, I... I know," she says, shifting in my arms.

I press my jaw against her hair.

Damn, her scent floods my nostrils again.

Coconut and sea salt and something quintessentially Destiny.

"But it's fine, Shepherd. Really and truly. I don't drag things out publicly, no matter how ugly it gets. I'm not Vanessa Dumas."

No kidding.

I'm starting to believe her in a way I never did with Dumas.

The hand I have on her waist itches, hounding me to explore more of her.

There are so many dips and curves, so many virgin places I haven't mapped yet with my mouth.

Last time was too fast, too explosive, all animalistic need and primal itches.

Since we're not back in Seattle yet, there's time.

I want her again and this time I'll devour her as fast as I damn well please.

She wiggles closer, twining her legs with mine. It's like she can read my mind.

Her knee brushes my hard-on, and then there's no hiding it.

"Destiny, fuck."

What else can I say?

She knows I'm as hard as diamond.

What man wouldn't be with a blonde angel wrapped around him?

An angel he has roughly one more day with to squeeze an entire lifetime of crazy sex into.

She grins, twisting so she looks up at me.

Her nipples are puckered already, brushing my chest.

It's a heroic effort just keeping my eyes on her face.

"You know..." She taps a finger against my chest. "We're not back in Seattle yet."

"Damn right," I agree, taking her mouth.

She gives back a moan, nudging my cock with her knee.

The wicked grin I feel against my lips is one of the most beautifully filthy things I've ever experienced.

"Something tells me you're awfully attracted to me, Mr. Foster."

"Start Mr. Fostering me and you'll find out just how awful I can be," I growl back, twisting her words. "Besides, lady, if I wasn't attracted to you, this never would have happened to begin with."

I hover over her, pressing my cock against her clit, dangerously aware I don't know where my pants are and I'm not even sure I have a second condom.

"What I mean is, you're *still* attracted to me..."

"You think I wouldn't be? You think one damn time got it out of my system? How can such a brilliant woman be so dumb?" I whisper, stroking her hair. "I've been awestruck since the minute you barked shit at me on Alki Point."

She shifts her hips, her eyelids fluttering as her pussy grinds against my length, pressing a kiss to the corner of my mouth.

"Shepherd... I don't think you're picking up what I'm putting down."

"No? Try me." I shift my hand to her peach perfect ass. It's even better naked than I thought it would be. I'll be dreaming about that ass for *years.*

"So," she says, kissing me hotly, her tongue in her mouth twisting against mine with filthy promises. "Why don't we take an extra day before we head back? Make the most of the time we're here since this has to end the second we're back."

Damn her, I'm a busy man.

But one more teasing flick of her tongue has me ready to clear my schedule for the next month just to keep playing caveman in paradise lost.

She's that lithe and small and incandescent.

Without breaking the kiss, she squirms out from under me and climbs on top, spreading her legs and straddling me.

"Well?" she whispers, grabbing my cock and rubbing it against her pussy lips. "What do you say to one more day? And knowing I have an IUD?"

"One more damn day, Destiny. I—fuck!"

Every dirty dream I've ever had comes true the second her hot little pussy engulfs me.

She throws her head back like a dream, filling herself up, taking an unexpected control I need back before my nut hits far too soon.

It's hard to hold back, knowing I'm going to flood her.

I'm barely human as I reach for her breasts, kneading and squeezing until her eyes flutter shut with pleasure.

"C-careful," she says, her voice heavy, hazy with lust. "We don't want to scare the otters."

"Bull. You're the one screaming, woman," I growl, dropping a hand to her hips and quickening my rhythm.

"Don't be difficult..." she whispers.

"Then don't live in denial," I tell her, driving deeper.

The way her hands go tense on my chest, nails raking my skin, tells me she's well on her way to being gone.

Definitely two minutes later, when my thrusts throw her around like a doll and my hands grip her little ass so tight my fingers burn.

I'm greedy, even as I take her pleasure, pulling her in when her breath catches in that way that tells me she's about to come.

"Let it go, sweetheart," I whisper, dragging her face against my shoulder. "Bite me if you're worried about being too loud."

Goddamn, does she ever.

And she comes her ever living soul out with her teeth in my skin, growling her release.

I'm in deep fucking trouble now, and I don't just mean the explosive heat rampaging up my spine from my balls.

I'm going to wear her bruises on my shoulder like a badge of honor for the next week, and possibly forever in my mind.

I'll always remember how sweetly Destiny Lancaster comes for me until I draw my last breath.

There's no stopping the frantic tempo, the grinding, even when she's through the fiercest part of her release.

Then it's my turn and I can't hold back.

With a vicious sound, I fling her up and down on my cock, striking hard and deep and burying myself inside her until I erupt.

Fuck!

So much come rushes out of me I wonder if I've sprouted a third testicle.

I've never, ever filled a woman the way I empty inside her—and she's only the second I've ever had without a condom.

I don't fuck random bedmates without serious protection, and I damned sure don't brand them from the inside out like it's all I live for, like I *want* to knock this woman up.

Perish the thought.

The orgasm must've melted my brain.

Still, I'm hard and twitching inside her when I come down from the high, my chest heaving as I listen to her panting.

"Holy shit. Shepherd, holy shit."

"Yeah."

I hold her, letting my lips work hers, slowly and tenderly devouring her.

I never knew more than my cock could be so needy with a woman, but here we are.

She's a little mind reader, and she knows how I want it now.

Languidly.

Savoring every inch of her, feasting on her tits and pussy like a three-hour dinner. And she's right there with me, teasing me, her eyes lit every time I suck a nipple into my mouth.

It's so fuck-hot it's irrational.

If it wasn't for another twig poking my spine, two inches from crawling up my ass, I'd be right there with her.

"Hang on," I say, taking hold and losing the damn stick.

She giggles, wrapping her arms around my neck, her face pressed against me.

I lie back down, and she joins me in so much skin on sweltering skin.

It feels too good in the morning heat, too addictive.

It makes me forget that I'm still rolling around the grass and leaves.

Destiny grins up at me. Must be the endorphins, because the last and only time I've seen her look this happy was when she was watching the otters.

"Is it too uncomfortable? There's a blanket in my bag..." She presses her lips against my collarbone, then my neck, working her way back up to my mouth.

"I'm good," I mutter, pinning her down for good measure.

"Just good?" she teases.

Her mouth is mere inches from mine and I capture every breath.

Shit, I can feel the way her thighs tighten around me, calling me home.

"You know *how* good, brat." I press my cock against her as she laughs again.

The uncertainty from before vanishes, and she's lighter than air.

This time, it's not the otters putting that giddy smile on her face.

It's me.

The man who stopped smiling when his marriage blew apart and everybody thought it was blowback for helping rat on my gangster uncle.

The idiot who's currently doing his damnedest to invite more disaster into his life.

But Destiny is still laughing against me, stamping long, slow kisses up my shoulder.

I reach for her nipple, roll it slowly between my fingers,

searching for just the right pressure she adores.

"Oh," she moans breathlessly a second later. "You can go harder."

"Harder," I repeat, something carnivorous grinning inside me.

So she likes it rough, huh?

The lust pulsing through my veins makes me a human hand grenade as I pull her in so I can bite her tits.

The moan that slips through her teeth is the sexiest goddamn thing I've ever heard. No question.

"Quiet," I tease, my voice guttural. "You'll scare the otters."

"Shepherd!"

Goddamn, I hate that I like it so much when she says my name.

"I want you inside me again," she moans.

"Tell me. Tell me what you like," I demand.

My cock jerks, already aching to fuck her again.

It's a need so primal it feels like possession but this isn't the time to overanalyze it.

I want her. I'm going to have her like the greedy prick I am.

That's all there is to it.

She takes hold of me, running her hand up and down my shaft. I suck in a breath at the spiking pleasure.

"Careful, Foster," she says with a smirk. "Don't scare the otters, you said."

"If you think they haven't seen us mating before—" Before I can finish that sentence, she slides down, pumping my dick, and my whole heart stalls.

The first two times were heaven.

This time, it's heroin.

Pure, undiluted pleasure pulsing through my veins like a drug.

I let her take her sweet time, feeling me, adjusting her little fingers to my size.

Some women find it harder to even fit me.

Not my Dess.

She begs with her hips, stroking my length, and only stops when I'm finally pushing inside her, loving how I can feel my last eruption in her wetness.

"Oh, God," she breathes.

She laughs a little, leaning down until her forehead rests against mine.

"Yeah. Stay for a second." I run my hands along her hips, her ass, lifting her up and squeezing.

"Why?"

"So I don't fucking come in you already. It's been twice in twelve hours and it shouldn't be a risk, but it is. That's what you do to me, Miss Destiny."

She blushes as I kiss her and softens, so pliant and easy and so fucking sexy I'm losing whatever's left of my mind.

The first thrust is good.

The second, divine.

The third makes me a starving beast, especially when her plush lips part and I hear her say it.

"*Shepherd.*"

I push into her again, moving her until she's at just the right angle, the best where I reach deep inside her, where I can feel her squeeze around my entire length.

I rub her clit, intent on blowing her apart in ways she never imagined.

Her nails dig at my shoulder like she knows it, but I don't let myself go too fast this time.

I want her to lose it.

I want to feel her come on my cock again before I blow.

I want to destroy her and put her back together again.

Her breath comes shorter, faster, and I feel her little pussy fluttering around me.

"That's right, Dess." I press with my thumb, rubbing harder, cutting swift circles around her clit, though it's about all I can do to remember to move my hips and my thumb independently.

My focus slips away with every stroke, even faster after I send her crashing over the ledge the first time.

Destiny comes hard, pulsing around my cock, pleading for me to join her.

Not yet.

Not fucking yet.

And I know—I know—that whatever ugly, messy disaster happens next, I'll never forget the way she moves to straddle me, her hair beautifully messy, falling in well-fucked tangles on both sides of her face and her blue-green eyes half-closed and dazed with pleasure.

"Here's your chance to wow me, woman. Ride me as hard as you want, all the way home," I whisper, crashing my hand against her ass.

It's all the encouragement she needs.

Her mouth parts with surprise.

The pressure at the base of my balls builds like a brewing storm.

"Shepherd," she whispers, bracing her hands against my chest and swaying, finding the perfect spot inside her, and fuck, *fuck* it feels so good.

I'm done for.

"Shepherd," she gasps. "Shepherd!"

"Come for me, Destiny. Need to feel you first."

She obeys magnificently.

And all I can see are stars.

She tosses her head back, biting down on her lip so she doesn't belt her screams into the wild, and her body shudders with the raw force of her orgasm hitting like a hammer.

I feel the way she squeezes my cock, so tight my vision goes, and there's no holding back.

Growling with delight, I release inside her, vaguely aware of birds launching from the trees as the whole universe becomes a mundane backdrop to our perfect wrong.

XII: A LITTLE HEARTACHE
(DESTINY)

I can't believe it's over.

Even though I guess that's a grim exaggeration.

I still have my life, my work, and a half-grown puppy who always chases away the sad by licking my face. Molly noses in, coming in fast and furious until I need to push her away.

Yeah, nothing truly *important* is over, I suppose.

Nothing meant to last.

Just enough to leave my heart hanging like a deflated balloon in my chest, heavy with bittersweet memories.

But that's the thing about memories...

What happened wasn't important in the grand scheme of things.

So what if I had the best time of my life with a man I'll barely see again?

So what if we had gravity-defying sex at least eight times over two long days and he left me deliciously worn out?

Thank God for the private charter boat picking us up for the return trip, or else I'm pretty sure I wouldn't have made the kayak trip home with jelly for muscles.

Eight times.

And every single second was indescribable.

Shepherd just has this way of making it feel different every time.

He doesn't just bust out the same three moves in a different order.

We were tender, fast, furious, slow, gentle—and everything he did made me feel cherished.

With most guys, after a while, it feels samey. Even when it's perfectly satisfying, a girl can get bored.

I can't fathom sex with Shepherd ever getting bland.

It's his intensity, I think.

When he looks at me, he doesn't notice the sun shining or even that it started to rain on us the last time that evening.

Hair damp, skin slick, a shiver, it didn't matter.

For two whole days, I became his entire world.

And foly huck, the orgasms.

Plural.

So many Os I lost track, and always during the same session.

That's no easy task for any normal man.

Of course, Shepherd Foster is anything but normal.

God, just *thinking* about being with him makes my toes curl.

I've found the best sex I'll ever have—and it just had to be with my off-limits, older, unapproachable boss.

But was he *that* frigid by the end of the trip?

We spent most of our last day exploring, marking observation sites, testing the drone a couple times for longer range flights before we worked our way toward the marina to meet our ship in the morning.

Overnight, we camped out one more time under the stars, sharing his sleeping bag.

I'm still trying to forget his scent as I unscrew my thermos lid and pour Molly some water into a portable bowl as we sit on the bench on Alki Beach.

I let myself remember our final night, and I don't just mean the X-rated paradise he swept me away to.

The way he held me in his arms.

The way he cradled me, tight and strong and so *big*.

The way he was so present, there with me like I became the focal point of his universe.

Sue me.

I'm not being overly sensitive or romantic or anything like that, but it's enough to make a girl melt.

So was his grumpy, adorably groggy butt the next morning when I woke up to the smell of him cooking instant eggs and sausage over a fire.

Just seeing Shepherd Foster so liberated feels like catching a secret I'm not sure was meant for me. All the little things no one else would notice.

The morning breakfast wasn't a surprise, no, but the way he snuggled back down with me after we ate for a lazy extended morning was.

I never imagined the bossman *could* snuggle.

What else don't I know?

My life has been cleanly divided into two phases. *Before* and *After* last weekend.

Except, somehow Before feels like one long hazy dream in black and white.

After, now that's transcendent.

Like seeing the world in color for the very first time. A learning experience I wasn't ready for, and if there's a lesson, I hope to God one day I'll figure it out.

I'm still trying.

But I remember the mole on the small of his back.

The scar across his side that matches the one on his face. I spent a long time kissing both, asking questions with my lips he wouldn't answer.

Who hurt you Shepherd?

Who or what made your life so hard you pretend not to care?

Seriously, my knees have never been so weak.

Ugh.

I'm grateful there were other moments, though.

As Molly flops down by my feet, taking a breather, we linger by the park bench. I'm reluctant to head home and read over a new stack of sea otter studies.

Another night is creeping in, and that's when the memories come out to shame the bedbugs with their bite.

I'm not sure I'll ever forget our last real conversation about Vanessa Dumas after we pillaged each other for the last time.

I never thought he'd ever talk about it in such detail.

Especially not while we were still naked in the cool morning air, huddled together in layered sleeping bags and blankets across the sand.

* * *

"YOU WERE RIGHT," *he says against my hair, holding me so close.*

We're chest to chest, and his warmth soaks into me like a bath. I sigh against his throat.

"That's a big deal, you fessing up. What was I right about?"

"I never hurt her. Vanessa, I mean."

I pause.

That's not a massive surprise, but hearing him say it is.

I knew I wasn't wrong, but for him to come out and even bring it up...

"...do you want to talk about what happened with her?"

"Fuck it, why not?" He twines a lock of my hair around his fingers. "I think I just want you to know my side of the story. The truth. Someone else should, besides the lawyers who only listen because I'm paying them a thousand bucks an hour. Because you knew what she said wasn't true, but I never told you what was."

His heart starts pounding against my cheek.

I shift around, wrapping myself more firmly around him.

We just finished our last round of sex maybe fifteen minutes ago. My body still feels warm and content.

"I'm listening," I whisper.

"We had an arrangement, Vanessa and me. A rotten fucking idea

*from day one. She agreed to be a prop, to raise her profile by associa-
tion, all so I could swat down any rumors along with advances from
women I had zero interest in. To me, they were always a distraction. It
should've been simple. She'd accompany me to a few events. Just
enough to get our names out there as a couple. I'd give her a chance to
make connections for her career. I knew how important that was to her.
But one night she let the deal go to her head, or hell, maybe she planned
it from the beginning. She tried to fuck me in our car, and I wasn't
having it. I told her the next day the arrangement was done."*

I'm silent, slowly taking it in.

"Wow. And the rest, as they say, is history?" I ask softly.

His warm breath fans across my hair.

*"Yeah. She decided to go scorched earth and play it up. Guess her
ego couldn't handle the rejection."*

*"I mean, I get why she made a pass at you," I say, pinching his ass. I
didn't think I'd ever see a male ass so fine. "But she had no right saying
all that crap. Let alone accusing you of such crazy, devious things..."*

I search his eyes.

Is this just him opening up or new worries talking again?

I feel the way his hold tightens.

*Just a fraction, enough to tell me he's scared of what I could do to
him if I ever told the world about this trip.*

I press a lingering kiss to his sternum.

*"Shepherd, I don't talk about my sex life, my relationships, any of
that on social media. I grew up seeing how much media hatches could
piss Dad off, and I've never wanted a taste of that. My life is conservation, cute animals, and Molly. End of story."*

When I mention relationships, he stiffens.

I look up, but he won't meet my gaze.

"Shepherd?"

"Yeah?"

"Are you okay?"

"Why wouldn't I be?"

Because he's stiffer than a board.

But I don't bother pointing that out when he's been so honest, so vulnerable. I'm sure he'll just get that look in his eyes that tells me how much he hates me for noticing too much about him.

For reading him too deeply.

"Okay," *I say eventually. I know my boundaries.*

Keep pressing, and he'll probably shut down, and I don't want that.

"Is Molly your dog?" *he asks, successfully turning the conversation.*

I see him holding his phone now, looking at my Instagram.

The guy is a natural.

Because let's face it, what dog owner doesn't want *to talk about their fur baby?*

I grin into his chest. "Yeah. She's the best husky in the world. I think I love her more than I could ever love any one human."

"Where is she now?"

"Oh, staying with a friend I met in my grad program for the week-end. Lena Joly. She's an awesome vet tech and a good friend. Molly makes her laugh and gives her mouth a rest from cursing like a sailor."

"Let's hope it's not at you." *He snorts with amusement.*

"Nah, no way. Only at everything else."

Shepherd murmurs against my hair again before saying, "Didn't know you were close to anyone from grad school."

"You didn't ask. I have friends. I'm not a hermit like you." *Just for fun, I decide to keep the name vague.* "Like Sam. We hang out all the time."

"Sam?" *he growls back, an edge in his voice.*

"Yeah." *I shrug.*

"Did you take a class in otter-nomics together, or what?"

"Close enough. We met in the library, actually, back when we were studying. We both kept showing up, sometimes looking for the same books, and having to take turns with a few."

If Sam was a guy, it would've been the beginning of a cute rom-com.

But I'm determined to leave Shepherd guessing.

We actually became instant friends. She loves dogs and whales almost as much as I do, even if she ultimately switched to a zoology program.

"I see," Shepherd clips, a line forming between his eyebrows.

God, he's too adorable when he's jealous.

"Do you want to know what else?"

"What?"

"We slept together all the time in college," I say quietly.

"I need to meet this friend. To talk." His arm tightens around me.

I let out a laughing squeal.

I just can't with angry Shepherd.

"Destiny, be serious. Tell me this boy's last name or—"

"Sam's a girl, you lunk," I force out through my laughing fit. "We used to have sleepovers all the time. As in, the kind where you sleep."

"Smart-ass. And here I was looking forward to a grudge match over who gets to sleep with you," he rumbles.

"Come on! It was funny. And, um, you're the one who said this needs to stop as soon as we're home. Remember?" I hold my breath.

"Yeah." His face drops.

He doesn't look up until I exhale.

"Come here, though, and I'll fix your laughing attack," he says, kissing me again, the back of his huge hand wrapped around the back of my neck.

He's as good as his word.

He absolutely cures me one bruising kiss at a time.

WE'RE WALKING off the small chartered yacht and he's carrying my kayak before he goes back for his stuff.

"You didn't have to haul it, Shepherd!" I call after him, running to keep up. "I'm not helpless."

"Maybe not, but after the time we've had, I know you feel like you were flattened by a Mack truck." He rolls his eyes at me, knowing it's too true. "You want me to strap it on Ladybug or what?"

"You remembered his name? How sweet!"

"God help me," I hear him mutter, but I think his mouth twitches up again.

That tiny half smile might just be my Achilles heel.

Before, I thought it was his abs and flashing blue glances, but it turns out a good smile can turn my stomach into a butterfly house. I try to swallow past the emotion.

It's not easy with that rock creeping up my throat, knowing this is it.

"Thanks," I say, helping with the straps. "I don't usually play damsel in distress."

"Shocking. You're rather good at it, Dess."

Dess.

When did we become nickname familiar and why do we have to go back?

I almost cringe at the thought of him Miss Lancastering me again, which he will if we only see each other in some stuffy, formal spotlight appearances for Young Influencers.

"Thanks. Did you like the way I fluttered my eyelashes?" *I bat them at him now, before stopping, because the weekend is over with its easy smiles and soul-shattering sexy times.*

We're almost home.

Back in Seattle, destined to be strangers again.

It's funny when you think about it, how a man you shared so much with has to be unfamiliar again. But that's the story of every bad breakup and heart-wrenching divorce, isn't it?

Becoming unfamiliar enough to smother love.

Somehow, this hurts worse because we never even had a proper romance.

Just a couple days of incredible, messy mistakes in the wilderness hinting at something too amazing to ever be.

Silently, I strap the kayak down on the roof of my car and Shepherd nods at me. "Are you sure you'll be okay when you get home? Are you going back to your family?"

"I'll be fine," *I lie. Somehow, I have to be.* "You don't need to worry about me. And I keep a small apartment here I sublease to a friend when I'm not around. I'm looking forward to some alone time to rest up, honestly."

His eyes narrow. "You're not just saying that?"

"Dude, I told you, I'm no damsel in distress. I just really like watching you carry heavy things." I would also really, really like seeing him in my apartment.

Which is so impossible he'd probably laugh in my face if I outed it.

But I hope I'm right.

I just need time to heal.

Why should the heart be any different from the muscles killing me in my arms and legs?

A day or two of downtime, and this ache in my chest should recover. I'll start to forget all about the grumpy billionaire and our otter excursions.

Time heals all wounds, they say.

...yeah, I don't believe it either.

"I'm not much for goodbyes," he says evenly.

"Yeah. Right. I guess this is it."

"Will you be in tomorrow morning?"

Oh, boy.

Is that hope in his voice?

"I'm no slacker." It's my turn to roll my eyes.

He smirks. "You were awfully stiff this morning and you don't have to be in the office. You can do the grant work remotely."

"Well, I need a focused workspace if I want to make this proposal shine. I've still got the board to wow, even if I've sold you."

I'm also trying like hell not to think about the sinful way he massaged my battered muscles that led to so much more.

"So, yeah, I'll probably be in," I repeat.

He nods, serious and unreadable again.

"Good. The hard part is over then. I'll email you my personal recommendation with the drone flight data. If your presentation doesn't convince them, that will." He sticks out his hand. "Goodbye and good luck, Destiny Lancaster."

Oh, God.

We're doing this.

Shaking hands.

Touching for the very last time.

Come tomorrow, we're back to being philanthropist rockhead CEO mentor and overly sensitive program apprentice again.

Nothing more.

I guess he's just preparing for the frozen distance with an impersonal handshake.

Except, as his fingers close around mine, it's the most sexually charged handshake in human history.

Help me.

I have a problem.

There's nothing sexy about basic handshakes.

But my heart rate spikes halfway to Jupiter, and I give him a professional nod before inhaling and stepping back, releasing his hand. Or maybe he releases mine.

All I know is, I'm so cold and my hand feels sweaty and I can still feel his calloused palms against mine as I rush away, trying not to tear up.

Thank God his back is already turned, and he's heading back to the boat to grab his own kayak.

I watch him for a single second with one hand on my car door before I tear my eyes away.

CEO and intern.

Strangers once more.

That's all we are.

All we ever should be.

There's no good reason I should feel like I'm losing a massive, hurting slice of my heart and heading home empty.

No reason at all.

A LONG WALK on the beach and taking the long way home through Pike Place, followed by an evening snuggling with Molly and a good book, still can't clear my head.

That's due to the most invasive, erotic dreams of my life that night.

Shepherd Foster has me tossing and turning and wishing I could forget so many things.

His delicious weight on my body.

His freckles, always so light and muted unless you really notice them in the light.

That nagging faded scar on his face hiding so many questions I want to ask.

The delirious way he kisses like a man laying claim, and now that I'm his, I've forgotten how to be anything else.

I wake up alone in bed, dizzy and disjointed as I look down. Mol must've overheated at some point overnight and crawled on the floor, flattening herself out like she sometimes does. I can hear her snoring softly.

Streetlamp-yellow creeps past the gap in my curtains, and I know I've officially lost it.

These aren't normal Destiny thoughts.

They're dirty, regressive, depraved.

I roll over and check the time, inwardly cursing the primitive instincts living inside my twenty-first-century body.

Half past five a.m.

Painfully early, but it's not worth going back to sleep now.

Molly leaps up beside me when she hears me moving with a big stretch, wags twice, and licks her lips.

"I can always count on you for an early breakfast, can't I?"

She licks my face in agreement.

At least I caught her awake before my alarm went off.

Normally, she bolts up like a crazy dog, bursting with excitement for bacon and cheese and her morning run.

I'm a morning person, too, even if I don't have puppy energy.

But for the first time ever, I'm dreading today.

As soon as I get moving, it's back to the status quo. The weekend, over and forgotten like one more fever dream.

Shepherd Foster, nothing but an illusion.

Jesus.

We never talked through what happens if we bump into each other around the office, either.

Am I really supposed to strut around with a polite nod, pretending I haven't seen him naked?

I wonder how I'll even look Carol in the eye without cracking up and revealing the insane secret that's burning me alive.

I slept with our boss.

And if she ever finds out, it's not my own reputation that worries me.

How will she see him, when she was so sure Dumas was lying and he'd never do anything like that?

She treats him like her own son, so patient in the face of his bluster.

And Mark... ugh.

He won't miss a beat asking about my weekend.

One little slip and the office blabbermouth will know that our trip resulted in the hottest sex west of the Rockies.

Otters.

Stick to otters.

We saw cute, endangered, wonderful otters and it was incredible.

That's what I need to focus on.

Just to drive it home, I grab my phone from the nightstand and unplug it, squinting at the harsh light from the screen.

My eyes are assaulted.

An avalanche of notifications fill my screen, and my phone becomes a vibrating brick. I was going to scroll through the pics I took this weekend, but instead, I see my name over and over again on—well, everything.

Google Alerts. I set them up for media mentions, just in case.

And tags.

So many tags.

Instagram, Twitter, Facebook, TikTok. Countless people tagging me, blowing up my DMs on every freaking platform.

What now?

Frowning, I open a few and let my tired brain try to process the words on the screen.

Maybe this is just a freaky coattails effect from the Young Influencers publicity. *I hope.*

Except, it's not that at all, and it's obvious as soon as I see the words.

I sit up in bed so stiffly it alarms Molly, who bounds over and presses her big rubbery nose into my face.

I might be crying.

Tears of fury and confusion and disbelief, wishing I'd never opened the link. But it's not just your run-of-the mill troll.

It goes to Meghan "Tea" Maven's latest video, posted overnight.

She's wearing her usual look, eye-melting lipstick and impeccable makeup that fits her snarky brand, plus jade-green cosmic nails that look downright lethal.

There's a malicious smile on her face as she introduces herself.

"Hiii, party people," she drawls. "It's your girl, Maggie, and I'm back with a whole freakin' tea party today. Remember billionaire scumbag Shepherd Foster? The same Shepherd Foster who just pulverized Vanessa Dumas' heart into little stabby pieces? Welllll..."

She stretches the word like her hideous smile.

I already know what's coming next.

She tagged me, after all.

The sound of my own ragged breath fills my ears, but her shrill, attention-grabbing voice still penetrates.

"Some of you might remember the Young Influencers program he started? Clearly, a desperate attempt to polish up his company and make everybody forget about his dirty misdeeds. Spoiler alert: we didn't. But the details are here if you wanna take a gander..." She points to the link her editor added to some tabloid garbage. "Dirty birdy benefactor aside, Young Influencers was an amazing opportunity with a very generous prize package. The money and terms are practically unheard of. A whole boatload of people applied. I know because I was one of them."

She pauses, staring into the camera with a shrug.

"What? Don't look at me like that!" she croons. "Before you get all judgy, don't act like you wouldn't take a pile of money from a dude who breathes small-dick energy too, if you could put it toward a good cause. Anyway..."

It feels like forever ago.

At the time, I was sure she'd be a top contender thanks to her reach alone, even if she's as charming as a drunken rattlesnake.

Instead, they chose me.

"As y'all know, I missed out," she says with a fake pout. Probably so everyone notices the subtle gradient from her wine-colored lip liner to the soft pink in the middle. "And who was the lucky winner? Destiny Lancaster! Yes, *that* Dessy, daughter of hardass hottie Cole and his coffee empire. You know I love my Wired Cup." She pauses to hold up a cup of coffee with a familiar logo with the most punchable look on her face. "And doesn't Dessy love to be Miss Invisibility?"

A picture of my face and channel appears beside her from my Insta link. I'm smiling with Mol, somewhere on Mount Rainier about a month ago.

Holy hell, no.

Molly whines and licks my face. It's like she knows how screwed we are.

I dig my fingers into her fur. "It's okay, girl. Don't get upset for my sake..."

It's almost worse that she can't understand why I'm upsetting her.

"You might notice," Meghan continues, "our Destiny doesn't have the same platform as some folks in this industry. That's whatever. That's fine. Everyone has to start somewhere, right?"

Her smug little smile looks painted on her face. "But well, let's be real—it was a pretty big surprise when she got selected."

"Jealous bitchface." I glower at the screen.

"I mean, let's think about it for a second. Home Shepherd wanted publicity, sure, and they wanted someone they could train, so they picked someone who doesn't have the experience or the exposure they wanted. Weird, right?"

The only weird thing I see is that smirk under your overdone makeup, I think grimly.

But the video keeps going.

"Unless," Meghan says in that lazy drawl that makes me want to scratch out her eyes. "Unless dearest Destiny did something awfully *juicy* to gain the CEO's favor."

A picture of Shepherd appears now from his corporate profile. He's his usual handsome, stern self in a charcoal suit with the light catching his glacial-blue eyes.

Again, she smiles too wide for her face. "I mean, it adds up. Simple math. When you look like a model and you come from a rich family—well, you can find the answer too, can't you?"

I don't know how I avoid throwing my phone.

This is nasty, salacious stuff.

People might have thought the same crap privately for all I know, but now that she's aired it in the open, everyone will think I went and fucked my way into my conservation money.

Worse, they'll think that a rich, powerful man like Shepherd Foster would totally screw a hot girl nearly half his age who threw herself at him for favors.

Especially after what happened with Vanessa Dumas, piggy-backing on the very scandal he's tried so hard to bury.

I barely notice she's still talking, wishing she'd shut up.

"...but maybe you think good-girl Destiny would never do something so spicy," Meghan says maliciously."Oh, I thought so, too. I wanted to give her the benefit of the doubt when she's all about cute animals and she rocks that whole do-gooder vibe.

But, well, there's that pesky evidence—and this evidence doesn't lie."

New pictures flick across the screen that stop my heart.

Pictures of us together.

Kayaking.

Cooking.

Smiling and laughing through various stages of our trip.

They're all aerial shots, so it must be drone footage, but how? *Who?*

Did someone hack the drone Shepherd brought along for our otter tracking?

I shake my head, trying to force answers into place that don't fit.

It really doesn't make sense.

Virtually no one knew we were *going* on the trip. I made a note not to tell anyone at the office, and I think Hannah Cho is the only one who knew there.

I can't imagine her backstabbing him like this when she's been a loyal soldier forever.

Even Lena, who looked after Molly this weekend, didn't know what I was away doing. It's common enough that she doesn't ask many questions.

I exhale a shaky breath as the pictures flick past.

I'm just waiting for a series of X-rated pics to turn up, but miraculously, they never do.

If it wasn't for the night and the tree cover, there'd probably be way more damning photos. This is just proof we were out there alone, close and intimate.

And that final shot that's half-obscured by some brush, but not enough to hide the fact that we're kissing...

Oh, God.

Dread crawls up my throat, coppery and bitter.

I wrap my arms around Molly and press my face into her furry chest as a darker thought hits me.

There's no obvious suspect with the right motive and access.

That means Shepherd will think I did this.

That's the bottom line.

The only explanation that makes sense, at least to him. No one else *knew.*

How could he not assume I lied to this face, and this was all a treacherous stunt to ruin his reputation for clout? Another character assassination.

Crap.

Crap crap crap crap crap.

Just twenty-four hours ago, I thought there was nothing worse than the fact that I might never see him again.

Now, it's staring me in the face.

How the hell do I make him believe me?

XIII: A LITTLE MALICIOUS (SHEPHERD)

*T*his job.

This *fucking job.*

Hectic mornings always feel like slamming back into reality from a fifty-foot drop, but this isn't just reality now. It's a concrete fucking floor.

I'm so livid I might burst a blood vessel.

If I could, I would fire every single person in this building.

As for Destiny—

No. Don't think about her.

I can't.

The second I dwell on what she's done to me, I'm going to come unraveled, and all of Hannah's protests that I need to keep quiet will be for nothing.

I bite my tongue and close my eyes.

Count to ten.

Resist the urge to hurl something through the massive windows, the only thing between my problems and a cold, indifferent city going about its business, blissfully detached from my shit show of a life.

Seattle looks damnably beautiful in the morning light, draped in silver and gold.

I hate it.

And Hannah Cho stands by silently.

Aside from suggesting in the strongest possible terms I should keep my yap shut, she hasn't said a word.

I glance at her and try not to yell at the video playing on her tablet.

It's déjà vu all over again.

The same thing we went through with Vanessa.

The same bullshit we were trying to stop.

But that was child's play compared to this.

I never fucked Vanessa Dumas, for one.

But Destiny? That little hellcat got under my skin and made me forget the rules.

Now, I'm paying the price for my little sin trip to Eden.

I'm the only one to blame.

Seduced by another pretty face until I believed she was authentic.

All because a forty-two-year-old man with cigarette burns on his past let his cock do the thinking.

Pathetic.

The video comes to an end as the girl in the overdone makeup and cat ears or whatever the hell it is on her head sweeps a hand at the camera and tells her viewers to follow.

Who knew the harbinger of my doom would look so ridiculous?

Whatever vile shit she's spewing for views is working.

The video already has six hundred thousand views and I know those view counts lag. Millions of followers, mostly kids who've probably never heard of me before logging on to watch my real-time detonation.

Pure bullshit.

I'm deathly quiet, but my anger is a wordless force that almost makes Miss Cho flinch from across the room. She closes the video and looks at me again.

Still steady. Still calm. Still worried and trying so hard not to show it.

"Sir?"

"Obviously, Destiny Lancaster is off the program. Scrap the whole goddamned thing," I bite off. "Once I calm down, I'll decide if this is worth a lawsuit."

She doesn't say anything.

Unusual.

"Also, I'm going to have words with her. It can't be avoided. Send her up the second she steps foot anywhere on my property —if she deigns to show her face."

Maybe she won't. That would almost be better.

Maybe she knows I'll have a shit fit worthy of a Greek tragedy, so she'll stay home and reap the consequences of her newfound celebrity status there.

Hannah purses her lips.

A clear sign that she disagrees with my strategy.

I shouldn't care, but dammit, I do.

Silence is Hannah Cho's greatest weapon. She wields it in meetings like an assassin's sword. Unshakable, implacable calm whenever she disagrees.

I grind my teeth together and pace the floor a few times, waiting for her to speak.

Of course, she doesn't.

"Well?" I clip. "You obviously have something to say, so spit it out, Miss Cho."

She flicks her gaze up to mine, her eyes dark and cool. "Mr. Foster, I don't believe Miss Lancaster is behind this hatchet job."

I squint at her.

"You don't...? How the hell can you possibly think that?" I snort. "I see it now. She suggested the otter trip so she could get us alone in a remote place. How she hacked my own goddamned drone, I can't begin to fathom, but I'm going to find out. You have to admit, it's deviously logical after Miss Dumas kicked off open season on my reputation."

Devious because it worked.

I fucking *let it,* as easily as dropping a rotisserie chicken in a piranha tank.

I let my little head dictate my destiny.

She showed enough skin and too many angelic smiles, and I came running like a scraggly coyote with a bone.

"You're certain it was ours? There wasn't another drone following you?" she asks.

My jaw snaps together. "Certainly not. Do you really think I'd have gone ahead with it if I thought we were being followed? Besides, we're the only private entity with a completely silent drone. Unless Destiny is with Naval Intelligence or an under-cover alphabet agency, she couldn't have dreamed of getting access to the lab."

"No, sir. That's my point." She brings up pictures of the shots in Meghan's video and holds up her tablet. They're probably all over the internet by now. "But did you notice how close these shots are? If there was a drone following you, I'm sure you'd have noticed."

I frown at the pictures.

Maybe we wouldn't have noticed while we were camping and busy as hell under the trees, but we definitely would have out on the water, where there was nothing but wide-open sea and sky and so much silence.

And Destiny, too, in that tight little wet suit.

I finally see Hannah's point.

Any regular civilian drone would've been noticed quickly from its noise alone at an altitude that low—*except* for our proprietary ultra-silent stealth model. The same drones that are still prototypes and haven't been released to the open market yet.

Destiny couldn't have gotten access to the research lab.

Then who the hell did? And how?

The handful of prototypes are all armed with chips that set off security alerts if they're removed from the lab without an override code from the executive level or a senior researcher.

If Destiny *had* somehow gotten access, she wouldn't have known about the tracking chips, I'm sure.

But anyone working in product development...

Fuck.

Maybe Destiny didn't do it.

Maybe it's an inside job, but not her.

Again, who?

I collapse in my chair, scrubbing my hands over my face, trying to hold my head together.

There would have to be a massive payoff for anyone on payroll to stick their neck out doing something so heinous.

Vanessa Dumas bribing an insider to keep smearing me is a real possibility—she certainly hates me enough—but she's already gotten her way by forcing our scandal into the limelight. There isn't enough worth her resorting to corporate espionage.

I could say the same for Destiny, too.

Like a pin stabbed into a balloon, the pressure blows out of my chest. I breathe past the crushing weight that's sat there for the past ten minutes, tighter than a boa constrictor.

It wasn't her.

Dess didn't fucking orchestrate this.

For now, that's enough.

The relief melts me alive. Hannah watches me slump in my chair, suddenly rendered boneless.

I don't understand why it matters so much, yet I can't deny that I feel a hundred pounds lighter knowing she didn't betray me.

She never used me.

Hell, she's as much of a victim as I am.

The anger still blazes inside me, but the sharp sting fades.

I run a hand through my hair.

"It wasn't Destiny," I say crisply, letting it sink in further.

"I don't think so, either, sir," Hannah agrees.

Goddamn.

I nod sharply. "We need to figure out who. Are we missing a unit?"

"I'm having Carol Garcia check inventory now. She was the last one in the lab during that time, but it was during your excursion."

I swallow a few more curses, wishing like hell something made sense.

Hannah narrows her eyes, taking in my expression. "Forgive me for saying, Mr. Foster, but you seem relieved."

"Do I?" I'd hoped to hide that.

"I wouldn't mention it if you didn't..."

There's no point in pretending. Not to my mind reader of an EA, who's mastered the art of deciphering my every expression.

"Perceptive as always," I say.

"May I be blunt, sir?"

"Are you ever anything less?"

"...did you sleep with Miss Lancaster?"

Fuck.

There's no easy answer to that.

Obviously, I want to tell her I didn't—that I would never, ever dream of doing something so monstrously stupid.

But I did more than dream.

And definitely not just once.

It was the best damn boneheaded move of my life, absolutely ravaging Destiny Lancaster for several days in paradise.

Before I can force anything coherent out of my mouth, there's a knock at the door.

Hannah doesn't have time to get up.

Not before Destiny sails in without waiting for an invitation, swinging the door shut behind her.

'A sight for sore eyes' doesn't do this justice.

Her face is flushed, the color high and bright on her cheek-bones, and she can't meet my gaze.

She looks miserable, though.

Probably worn to the bone from tromping through the office with everyone staring at her on the walk of shame.

Something I'm not used to feeling wells up in my chest behind the usual anger.

Protectiveness.

Her lashes are damp and her eyes are red-rimmed. It looks like she's been crying.

"Sh-Shepherd." Her voice cracks. "I... I know how it looks, but I *swear* I... I didn't—"

"I know," I growl.

"Huh?" She looks up. "You do?"

She immediately looks a tad less wretched.

It's clear she's been beating herself up over how I'll react.

And hell if she wasn't right five minutes ago—if Hannah hadn't intervened, I would have been the human volcano she's imagining.

I would have forced her to pack up her shit and leave, effective immediately.

Now, the very thought physically hurts.

"I do," I say, and I can't help myself.

Everyone standing here already knows, so fuck it.

I walk around the desk and pull her against me.

Comforting isn't something I have much practice with, but for her, it comes too naturally.

She turns her face into my chest and takes a deep, shaking breath.

Then another.

Slowly, she inhales me, and I let her take whatever she needs.

I hold her tighter, combing a hand gently through her hair, letting my fingers smooth the flyaway gold strands of her stress back into place.

"No one will hurt you. No one, Dess. I promise you."

The worst of my days under Uncle Aidan flood back, before the military shaped my violent urges into something useful.

All I can think about is how much I want to strangle whoever did this with my bare hands.

My reputation has taken another hit, but that isn't the first time.

That doesn't *matter*.

No, it's the fact that if this wasn't what she was planning, this might be enough to ruin her entirely. And without her parents' money as a backup, she has no safety net in place.

She can't lose her kindhearted dreams because some mysterious prick has an axe to grind with me.

I've seen her passion for nature and animals firsthand. I believe she genuinely cares about making an impact on this sleazy damned world.

Her breath rattles again as she struggles to hold it together.

The fury rushing through me feels so potent, my vision goes black.

The only thing I want to do right now is find the conniving asshole responsible for this and crush their windpipe.

I'm going to destroy them.

If not physically, then I'll take them for everything they have.

"Hey," I say, running a hand up her back. She slowly relaxes, wrapping her hands around my waist and locking them in place. "Can you breathe for me, sweetheart?" I whisper.

"I'm... yeah. I'm just so sorry."

"Have you had any hate messages?" Of all the questions I could ask, it's the most pressing.

"I'm sorry," she repeats with a hiccup. "I'll speak to my fans. Do whatever I can to quell the rumors."

"I know. I'm not asking about that. I never disputed it." Caressing the back of her neck, I tilt her head back so I can look her in the face. "I'm asking if you've gotten hate messages? Wretched trolls or people fishing for personal information?"

The way her expression tightens tells me all I need to know.

"I have a lawyer on speed dial," I tell her. "He'll be here within the hour. We can get the police involved."

"No!" she rushes out, then stops cold with her lips sealed tight. "I mean—we don't need to do that."

I don't understand.

She takes a shaky breath. "I mean it, Shepherd. The worst thing we can do is feed this drama. This comes with being an influencer, and I've been lucky not to stumble into it until now. Just delete, block, and move on."

"What the fuck, Destiny? You can't ignore a threat this big—"

"They don't have my home address," she interrupts. "It's not a big deal. There's more important stuff at stake here, okay?"

I grit my teeth. "The minute you feel like it's getting out of control, you tell me."

"Shepherd—"

"You're just as much a victim here."

She sniffs hard, blinking back tears, and it's such a sad, pitiful sound that my heart squeezes.

"I'm willing to hold off until we know more. Still, I don't think this will just go away if we ignore it, Dess. It's too fucking big for that," I say, hating that every last instinct screams 'attack, now.'

"Well, I have a platform. I can be public in a way you can't as CEO of a huge company. There are bound to be people who believe me. I think. If I tell them, maybe they'll help..." She trails off and glances at Hannah, who's pointedly staring out the window. "If anyone finds out..."

That's the million-dollar question.

"Did you ever tell anyone about our weekend plans?" I ask firmly.

"No one. Never," she says immediately. "I mean, Lena and Sam knew I was going on an otter trek, but that's nothing new. I've been doing it for years. So, nothing out of the ordinary."

"And no one else could've found out?"

"No. Unless they saw the pictures I posted along the way, but we were already out there. I never tagged a location once. I went back and looked." She falls back and stares up at me, her eyes red-rimmed and tired, but sincere. "I know because I basically live online. It's easy to assume people will know where I am all the time, but I'm very private with my personal life. That's how I grew up. I'm also not an idiot. I made sure all of my location sharing was off."

Yeah, and this definitely counts as her personal life.

Our personal lives.

I glance across at Hannah with a heavy look she beams back.

It had to be someone in the company. No question.

Hannah's knuckles go white against the corners of the tablet as she holds it against her chest. That almost hurts as much as Dess going to pieces in my arms.

Hannah is *furious.*

Which means she'll tear the company apart one department at a time until she finds the source of this treachery.

Whatever it takes, she'll ferret them out.

Good.

That's what I want from her, relentless bloodhound mode.

Even if I can't turn her loose to do the hunting alone.

The next look she gives me, laden with suspicion and under-standing, tells me she knows what we got up to this weekend no matter how much I dodge and deny it.

With Destiny in my arms, I can't argue it didn't happen. It's obvious to anyone who sees us like this.

And that's why I can't let anyone else see us when we're so rough and too real.

"That's all, Miss Cho," I say. "You can get back to work. Send me an action proposal once you've pulled it together, and I'll grant you whatever resources you need."

"Thank you, Mr. Foster." With a brisk nod for both of us, she marches to the door and heads out. I can almost see a trail of fire in her wake.

She's going to be a one-woman hellraiser until she has answers.

Destiny pulls back then, like she's just realized how close we are.

And maybe she's remembered what we agreed before we returned to Seattle.

This is definitely not the norm, but neither is the fucking sky tearing up and raining shards of hell-drama on our heads.

It feels impossible.

We've already crossed lines that can never be uncrossed. We obliterated them.

Still, I let her step back, allowing her the space to think.

It's a blustery summer day, the wind trying to clear a thin haze from wildfires further north. It makes the clear sunshine of what we shared on the Olympic Peninsula feel more distant than ever.

So does the silence settling between us.

The drone images that were posted online hit me fast and furious.

None were too incriminating, but I know how it looks to hungry bystanders with an appetite for scandal.

Me, Mr. Broken Engagement, spending intimate time alone with a new woman almost half my age.

Destiny laughing like I hung the sun in the sky.

She laughs a lot, but the way she did with me felt different. Or at least, that's what I fooled myself into believing.

"At least Hannah seems to know what to do..." Destiny says at last.

"That's her. Be glad she's on our side."

"She's definitely efficient."

"Terrifyingly so." I nod at the chair in front of my desk. The same one she sat in, casual as can be, the first day she arrived.

To think there was ever a time when I despised her.

It's unthinkable now.

I sit in my chair and we stare at each other, separated by my desk. I want to reach out and smooth the sadness from her face.

Hell, maybe kiss her again, if only so we can forget this hell for one bleeding minute.

Scratch that.

I definitely want to kiss her.

That greedy fire in my blood demands a lot more, too.

I grit my teeth, forcing the unsettled thoughts away. We agreed this was going to be the end, and it should be.

Mind over blue balls.

Remember how much trouble it's caused already.

"Shepherd," Destiny says, then pauses. "Mr. Foster..."

"If I can't Miss Lancaster you, you're not Mistering me, woman," I growl.

Her unexpected smile feels like witnessing a miracle.

"Fine, but... what do I do now? What do we do?" Her tongue moistens her lips. I look away too quickly. "When I came up here this morning, everyone was—"

"Staring?" I interject.

"And whispering. Muttering a lot behind my back."

"I'll have Miss Cho put a stop to that. She'll send an internal memo about the unfounded rumors today," I say. "But since you're here, you should go back to work."

Her eyes dart up to meet mine, horrified. "In the office?"

"Where else?"

"But—"

"The worst thing we can do is acknowledge it. The second worst is pretending it's going to stop us from moving ahead with revolutionizing wildlife tracking. Scandal or not, it doesn't change the fact that our little outing convinced me your idea works." My eyes search hers and I wait until she breathes. "Your presentation to the board is today, Dess. Finish prepping. Use everything we discussed and you witnessed over the weekend."

"You think they'll still *want* to hear it?"

"They'll listen. If anyone breathes a word about unrelated hearsay, I'll gladly stand in front of their firing squad." By some miracle, I don't snap at her.

There's a chance that if I do, her entire body will shatter like blown glass.

She needs courage right now.

Destiny isn't usually this fragile, and that worries me.

"We can't deny we went out together," I continue, making sure my voice is gentle. "However, if anyone wonders, the fact that you're presenting our findings reinforces the idea that we went there to gather intel on the otters and our proprietary technology. There are a lot of good points begging for you to make them. Focus on that, and mute your phone."

"Shepherd, I—" She takes a deep, slow breath and looks at her lap. "Okay."

"I know it won't be easy," I tell her. "But if anyone says anything that tries to sidetrack you from this work, refer them to me immediately."

She blinks at me. "Won't that look suspicious? If you come charging down to defend me?"

"I won't come personally unless it's a board member," I say. "I'll send Hannah. One look is the only warning they'll get before a termination notice shows up."

A tiny smile touches Destiny's lips. It feels like a victory.

"Okay, yeah, I can manage that," she agrees. "I'll pull everything together in time for the presentation."

"Good girl." I watch her for another long moment as she blushes, fighting the warring instincts in my blood.

Then, against my better judgment, I let the hammer fall.

"One more question. Will you come by my place tonight after the presentation? We need to talk strategy."

XIV: A LITTLE SIGN (DESTINY)

*T*he only thing that gets me through the day is the thought that I'll see Shepherd tonight.

The whispers suck, sure, but what's behind them feels infinitely worse.

When I walk through the office, all eyes are glued to my back.

At first, it's pretty openly. But after Hannah's short, sweet email threatens disciplinary action against anyone who talks about other Home Shepherd personnel, they shift to more subtle disgust.

I can't hear the rumors, of course, but I know they're flying.

I'm *her*.

The cutthroat slut who slept with Shepherd Foster to get ahead.

At least I must've been good to land a small fortune in charity money and a trek through nature with the bossman personally.

No email—no matter how stern or official—will wipe the slate.

And thanks to that message, everyone in the office who might not have heard the news certainly knows now.

The only question is how many people believe it.

Knowing my luck, everyone.

And whether they believe it or not, no one resists speculating.

When everyone on my team gets called into the nine-thirty meeting, I head into the kitchen to grab a coffee before it starts. Most of the chairs are empty, and I take advantage of the relative silence to eat lunch early.

Turns out, misery makes you crave carbs, and I think I'll eat the entire pound of this pasta salad I brought.

"Destiny, hi," a woman says from behind me.

I jump.

She's a short, neat woman with auburn hair. "I'm Rebecca from HR. Hannah Cho told me to introduce myself."

"Oh," I manage. I haven't cried since last night, but my eyes are hot and itchy. I shake her hand. "Thanks. Good to meet you."

"If you hear anything, don't be shy. Speak up, and I'll make sure it's dealt with."

Her smile oozes so much sympathy, but I'm not sure how it makes me feel.

A little like the kid who has the hall monitor protecting them at recess, I guess.

"Sure," I force out.

"Everyone knows you're working hard on your presentation and you don't need distractions. That's the same courtesy everyone deserves at Home Shepherd." She gives me a sharp nod. Her hair is tied up in a tight, professional bun.

She resembles everything I strive to be in an office instead of the hot mess I am today. I feel like a piece of wilted lettuce.

"Thank you," I say weakly, pinning on a smile. "I'm okay, but I appreciate it."

She smiles like she doesn't believe that at all.

And she's right. I'm so not okay.

"For the record, I've seen the photos," Rebecca adds carefully. "It's not all bad. Now the world knows about the sea otters. Oh, and I'm not sure anyone knew how much Mr. Foster loves his kayaking."

The woman is a total cinnamon bun, sincere and sticky sweet.

This time, my smile feels slightly less painted on. "He's great at it for sure, much better than me. The trip was my first real try at kayaking and he taught me a lot."

She nods again. "You look exhausted, sweetie. Good luck with your presentation. You've got a few of us in your corner, no matter what. Carol wanted me to let you know she promised to strangle someone if they shoot you down."

I snicker at the image. Relief flutters in my chest, too, knowing I still have her on my side.

"Thanks, Rebecca," I say again and scurry back to my desk. When I stop by the water coolers briefly, three guys whistle, practically right in my direction before they turn back to each other and burst out laughing.

Idiot ass-clowns.

For a second, I toy with the thought of reporting them to Rebecca, but I can handle a few petty comments without tattling.

I shouldn't care.

Shepherd wouldn't.

Even with the Dumas thing, he seemed more concerned about how it would impact the company and the employees under his brand than his own credibility.

The man is a rock, strong and indifferent. I'm sure he'll throw off the bad thoughts just like he does the ocean waves.

But the difference between us is that I've made a living out of what people think about me.

The fact that people trust me on social media makes a difference.

If that trust is shattered, I don't have a brand anymore.

It's hard to shake that mentality.

So I shut myself in my office and focus on finalizing my big presentation. Eventually, Mark sidles back in with a look of concern.

"Destiny, I saw the email," he says. "How you holding up?"

Deep breath.

I so don't need this today. But I also don't want to be rude to one of the few people here who's still trying to act human.

"Fine. About as well as you'd expect."

"If you need anything, just shout," he tells me.

God.

You know what I really need?

I need to stop feeling like I made Shepherd's life worse.

I need to stop knowing that the world is always judging him for what they think he is, when that couldn't be further from the truth.

I need people to know that yes, we broke every official rule when we did what we did. And then I need them to put a freaking sock in it and stop judging so much.

Through the glass windows, I can see how they glance around, their smiles cruelly curious.

Whatever.

People with dull lives thrive on whispers.

It's just, the scandal is me.

I'm a real person, with feelings, and every little whisper or sideways glance feels like another stab of the knife.

Online, you can ignore it by turning off your phone, blocking messages, swiping away the haters.

It still sticks, but it's not like this.

Here, I'm a fish in a bowl, and it takes guts to try to get some work done.

So that's what I do.

For the next few hours I bury my head in the project, looking over slides, data, testimonials. I whip my presentation into the best shape I can.

Then I gather up my things as Mark gives me a wide smile.

"Good luck! Bet you'll kill it. I couldn't help noticing how polished it looks."

"Thanks, Mark."

Amazingly, I'm not annoyed with him today.

Carol also stops by outside the glass, tapping until I look up and see her offering a smile and a thumbs-up.

She doesn't know the exact details about what I'm presenting, but when I outlined the concept, she was totally encouraging. She loves to see the tech she helped bring to life used for good causes.

With any luck, their well wishes will rub off, and the bigger picture will win out.

This cause is so much bigger than me or Shepherd Foster and one dumb scandal.

Because we've got a whole mess of otters to save and time keeps slipping through our fingers like sand.

* * *

I'm WAITING outside the conference room when my phone buzzes and turns me into a little lump of dread.

Daddykins flashes on the screen, something I knew was coming for days, as soon as he found out.

Do I even want to know?

No, not really.

But do I really want to put this off for later when I'm already a ball of nerves, waiting to find out how fast the board rolls its eyes at my proposal and spits it out?

Holding in a sigh, I swipe the green icon. "Dad, hi."

"I'll sue them all," he snarls in perfect Cole Lancaster fashion. "Every last one of those pricks who thinks my daughter is dog chow for their damn amusement."

"Hello to you, too. How're Eliza and the kids?"

The loud squeal behind him tells me Nicole and Elijah are

the same explosive little cherubs as always. I might be ancient to them, but I love my little siblings.

"Not relevant, honey. You know that. Destiny, you have to—"

"You have to stop charging to my rescue," I say firmly. "Look, I get it. I'm not exactly thrilled about what's going around online, either, but Dad... it's my problem. I can't have you bailing me out."

"I can and I *will* when protecting your reputation properly costs more than those distributions from the trust you barely touch," he grumbles. "Dess, you can't just let bullshit like this go. It takes on a life of its own. One day you think you're dealing with a particularly ugly frog, the next, it's a fire-breathing goddamned dragon."

I snort. "You're being too dramatic. It's really not fun, sure, but it won't kill me."

For a moment, he's silent.

"No. However, it might just permanently damage your ability to keep building up the brand you've worked yourself to the bone for. People are fickle, especially these professional charity types. Too many morals and not enough brains. Definitely no balls. One whiff of scandal, and they'll drop you faster than a rotten apple. They won't wait around to find out it isn't true."

I freeze, unable to speak around the boulder in my throat.

"It's obviously not true, Dess," he says slowly, waiting for an answer I can't give. "Is it?"

"Dad, I have a huge presentation in like ten minutes. Can we talk about this later?"

"Goddammit, Dess. Did he touch you? I swear to God, if he lured you in with promises in exchange for—"

"Dad!" I'm shaking, gripping the phone so tight. "No, he didn't force anything. We didn't trade favors. It wasn't like that at all and—and frankly, it's none of your business."

The silence between us is suffocating.

I almost want him to yell at me.

"You're too damn smart for me to get up in your life," he says quietly. "But Dess, you'd better put those brains to good use if you really want to get mixed up with Shepherd Foster. The man's not what he seems. He's—screw it. If you want to know, you know where to find me. Until then, I'll let you decide."

What the hell?

What is he even talking about?

I'm on the verge of tears, so ready to go full defiant brat on my father like I haven't since I was seventeen and bored out of my skull with everything Wired Cup.

But before I can tell him to kindly fuck right out of my life, I see the flashing screen.

He's disconnected the call, leaving the void between us.

And coming from Cole Lancaster, that's the most grown-up courtesy you can imagine.

* * *

THE PRESENTATION TAKES place in a conference room that feels almost tropical.

I drain sips of water every few slides with the board's haughty, overly professional eyes on me, slow-walking them through my idea.

And it's a damn good concept, I'll admit.

My research is solid and I know it. I've got stacks of evidence to back up my claims, and the personal experience we captured on the trail speaks volumes.

I even added the pictures from the weekend, boosting my arguments for the many ways this technology can revolutionize how wildlife organizations collect data on various species.

If this were one more college speech, I would've aced it.

But it's not.

These five men and one woman watch me with slitted eyes the entire time.

Somehow, I *know* they're not looking at graphs and otters, even if they're right there in front of their faces.

They're seeing the other photos from that trip that were posted online.

They're hearing TikTok and Twitter and tabloid garbage every time I open my mouth.

They're wondering if I seduced him or if I'm just the latest in a slew of young, dumb girls who didn't know any better.

They're thinking Shepherd Foster is another rich, older goat who creeps on younger women, then hands out professional favors like candy.

A chill sweeps down my spine every time their gaze zips over me. I'm extra glad I dressed modestly today.

Oh, sure, they nod along every time I stress how critical sea otters are to the coastal ecosystem. The woman frowns with real heartache when I point out how their population crashed in perfect correlation with invasive industries.

They give me all the polite applause I could ever want at the end, and a big, blocky man thanks me and calls it an impressive speech.

But deep down, I'm thinking I blew it.

The board won't sign off on a purely charitable venture like this when it's tainted by egos and nasty whispers.

They'll cave to the public spectacle around Shepherd and me. All made worse by the fact that it's compounding the mess with Vanessa Dumas.

I wonder if they're even plotting to remove him as CEO, assuming they can.

That makes my heart sting.

But I'm more surprised than anything to find Shepherd standing in the shadows in the back of the room when I pack up my laptop and leave.

How long has he been there?

Did he really take time out of his crazy schedule to come listen to me?

"God himself would've been convinced by that, Destiny. Hell of a job," he says crisply.

I'm drowning in butterflies, but I also feel weak.

"Well, maybe he can help sway the board then. I doubt they'll approve it, and it has nothing to do with anything I said..."

His eyes sharpen, searching mine.

I stand there in front of him, knowing that all eyes are on us now.

If their minds weren't made up during the speech, I'm sure they are now, seeing us together like this, standing far too close and whispering to each other.

"You made your points and you showered them with proof. That's what matters," he growls, his blue eyes dark and stern and so hypnotically lovely I lose myself in them without a fight.

"Thanks. I was so nervous." My tone is stilted, formal, so I offer him a quick smile to make up for it.

"Nervous? Bull. You were confident with your findings. I listened to the whole thing. Every slide was well thought out and documented."

"You know what they say... fake it till you make it." My smile trembles a bit.

"No illusions needed, Miss Destiny. Leave the rest to me."

My eyebrows go up as he starts moving past me. "What does that mean, Shep—" I catch myself "Mr. Foster?"

"I have to go." He glances at his watch, the one status symbol he seems to wear religiously. It's a ring of solid gold that must cost more than most people's annual salaries. "I have another meeting in five. However, I told you I'll handle this if they need more persuading."

It's so hard to stand. I'm almost giddy knowing he wants to fight for me, but also knowing he shouldn't.

It isn't fair.

If anything, it'll only fan the flames we desperately need to stamp out.

I can't let him.

"Shepherd, no. Let them make up their own minds. I'll either win or lose based on what I said. Nothing else."

"We completely agree. Nothing else. I just need to know it's the only factor they're considering. Call me their friendly reminder," he rumbles in the most unfriendly way, tapping his watch for the time. "I have to go now. See you tonight. In the meantime, Hannah has HR on your side if there's any more trouble."

"I know," I whisper weakly.

With one last pat on my shoulder—a hand that's removed almost as fast as it touches me—he turns and militantly strides on, leaving me alone to slowly make my way back to my shared office.

Mark greets me like a bright-eyed puppy.

He immediately slaps me with fifty questions about how it went.

Honestly, I barely care.

I'm still stuck on that long walk of shame back to my hole, the people passing, the whispers tossed around like frisbees.

I can imagine all the crap they're saying even if I can't make out a word.

I'm sure they're talking about the way Shepherd pulled me aside, if anyone saw it.

Sighing, I do my best to ignore this torture and make a few new social media posts to my Instagram. All otters, all the time.

I'm not posting a word about shit talk and kisses that never should've happened. If people don't like that, they can hit the Unfollow.

The trolls are bad enough to temporarily disable comments, though.

My DMs are overflowing, too, but I don't have the energy to go through and block them all. Later.

"It must be terrible." Mark doesn't sound like he's faking it this time. He nods at my phone. "That's not a good face. Are they still spamming you?"

"Eh, it's what happens when you get caught in something like this. I'm used to it." My smile stretches across my face like clay and sags almost as quickly.

This is definitely not the kind of attention I'm used to.

"You need anything? Coffee? Water? Something stronger to take the edge off? Our little secret, of course..." He jerks a thumb at people walking by beyond the glass.

"Well, I won't start drinking my problems away, but an iced tea would be amazing if you can run down to that machine in the break room," I say gratefully.

"On it! Then if you're not too busy you can help me with the grant applications. I'm just one guy, I can never keep up," he says. "A lot of outside charities are interested in working with Home Shepherd, but we can only sign on to collaborate with so many."

I nod automatically.

That makes sense.

And helping Mark feels better than stewing in my own misery all day, wondering when I'll get the disappointing 'thanks, but no' message from the board.

Still. As the clock ticks closer to five, knowing I'll see Shepherd tonight is the only thing that keeps me going.

I'm too excited.

Don't lose your head. He wants to talk, I remind myself.

Right.

Just because he comforted me in his office and made noise about charging to my rescue doesn't mean it was anything more than a few beautifully reckless days with a massive price we're both paying.

A temporary paradise where we played at being someone else before returning to the cold, hard minefield of reality.

Or was it who we really are, away from prying eyes?

Shepherd the stonehearted supergrump, a front for the warm, passionate man underneath.

The person he showed me was so kind. So gentle. So open.

He touched me so reverently.

Like there's this hidden warmth under the surface just longing to be kindled. And at night, that heat boiled over, branding me for life.

"Focus," I whisper, pinching my wrist. "Stop. Dwelling."

You know it's bad when you have to talk yourself down from obsession.

But yes.

That was then.

And now, for some unholy reason, he's invited me to his house, and yes, I want to go.

But this is a strategy meeting and nothing more.

Not another huge mistake waiting to happen.

Not another chance to bare my heart to Shepherd Foster, and let his burning, honest soul consume me.

* * *

GOOD LORD, Shepherd's house is *gorgeous*.

It's a pretty big contrast to the iron and glass cage he lives in downtown, all light teak wood and modern curves and arches with thoughtful finishes.

The floor looks like it's been sculpted out of one massive piece of dark granite. The dark contrast with the walls makes this soaring space with the high ceilings seem intimate and shadowed.

Masculine, but not overbearing.

I'm no stranger to fine hotels and ostentatious homes, growing up like I did, but this...

This place takes my breath away.

Sweet Jesus, save me.

It's so freaking masculine my mouth dries up and my heart flips over.

If it wasn't for Molly pulling insistently at her leash, I'd enjoy the view longer.

"Hello?" I call. "Anybody home?"

I'm pleasantly surprised and a little weirded out that a man who owns a major home security company doesn't lock his door, even if the house is surrounded by a gate with a digital intercom screen that must go to someone manning it twenty-four seven.

"In the kitchen!" Shepherd calls right back. "Come down the hall."

I fully mean to head straight down to join him. But as I walk the wide hallway flanked with golden sconces glowing like artificial torches, I get distracted.

The house is actually a proper ring around a glass-walled atrium full of wild growth and greenery. Is that a breakfast nook hidden in the flowers and trees?

Be still, my heart.

A stone path leads outward, splitting the house neatly in one spot as it leads directly down to the waterfront.

I should've guessed it would go to his own personal pier. Several kayaks are tied up there, dwarfed by a ridiculously large yacht.

It's not nice.

'Nice' is too tepid a word for this place when it's bursting with class and character with plenty of space to roam around in.

Best of all, it's not the fifteen-thousand-square-foot castle to one man so many rich people need to show off.

He can't host a small town with a freaking ballroom like other billionaires Dad knew. This seems like just enough, a comfortable place that feels like a real home for a larger-than-life man.

I'm beyond impressed.

It takes a lot to impress a billionaire's daughter, but somehow, he's done it.

I shouldn't be surprised.

At this point, I should *expect* Shepherd to subvert expectations.

After one last longing look around in the fading light while I rein Mol in, I follow the lights, padding my way to his kitchen.

Of course, it's enormous. Stylish, too.

The wall tiles are soft earth tones surrounding sleek green-black cabinets. A hulking island separates us from Shepherd, who stands in front of the range with his shirt sleeves rolled up.

So, he doesn't just cook when he's camping.

For a hot minute, all I can do is stare in awe.

I thought the otter trip showed me a generous slice of the real man.

Now, I know it barely scratched the surface.

There's something about seeing him like this in his home, suit coat and waistcoat gone, shirt sleeves rolled up, tie discarded.

The top two buttons of his shirt are undone when he turns to face me.

Oh, boy.

My heart does that flippy thing again.

Molly also perks up and chooses that moment to lunge, and the leash slips from my now-loose grasp.

"Shit! Mol, no!" I gasp as my thirty-five-pound dog leaps at Shepherd.

It happens so fast.

I can only watch in breathless horror as he—catches her?

Yep.

Just grabs her and hoists this big, squirming fluffball in his arms, cradling her like a baby as she wiggles with joy and licks his face frantically.

My heart? The one that was fluttering a second ago?

It pretty much melted into jelly at the sight of him smiling slightly in that way he has, weathering her frantic face slurps.

"Welcome to the manor, girl," he says.

It takes me a second to realize he's talking to the dog and not me.

My heart is too full.

I don't know whether to smile or shrivel up and die of embarrassment.

But how can I even have feelings like *this?*

Sure, we've had some hot sex and tons of unexpected drama, but I can't—

No. Not going there.

"I'm mortified. She hasn't been this crazy for months. I thought I'd trained it out of her, but... clearly, we still have work to do."

"No hard feelings." He sneaks her a piece of the strip steak he's been frying up and my gooey heart puddles in my shoes.

"Now you've done it," I say, finding my voice and rushing forward to pull my dog away. "You'll spoil her. She's already a little duchess."

"Royalty, huh? I guess pets really do take after their owners," he teases, planting a kiss on the top of my dog's head and finally setting her down.

Molly circles around the kitchen in glee, still licking her chops.

"A *demanding* princess," I argue. "Don't even comment."

"Certainly. She learned it from the best," he says, totally ignoring my warning.

I fold my arms, but he just throws back another one of those sly smiles and turns back to the steak. "Have fun snooping around my place or what?"

I gasp. "I wasn't snooping!"

"Weird. I'd have thought you'd have come right down instead of spending three minutes walking around."

"...you were counting?"

My face must be white.

Eventually, the longer he stares me down, I crack and start laughing.

"Fine! I had a little look. Couldn't resist. Nice boat, by the way." I motion to the ship perched near the small dock and boathouse down the hill, past the floor-to-ceiling window.

"I was hoping you'd notice. It does the trick for getting around when you're too worn out from kayaking or other activities."

Is he joking? Straight-up dicking with me?

I squint at his broad, muscular back, too shell-shocked to speak.

I thought he'd be the tense one thanks to this whole situation and the fact that I'm here in his house.

After everything else, I never thought he'd invite me over and treat me like this is no big deal.

I definitely didn't expect him throwing around innuendo like we're on a second date.

Oh, crap. Are we?

I shake my head like I can physically banish the thought.

"I like your house a lot," I say lightly.

Keep it calm and casual. Stay cool.

He's only grilling you steak and what smells like a delicious chimichurri sauce with his sleeves rolled up in a kitchen that should be on MasterChef.

This is fine.

Totally normal behavior, and not even a little bit date-like.

Yeah.

I really cannot go around thinking Shepherd is treating me like a *date.*

We're not dating.

We're not even screwing anymore.

This is purely a work meeting until it isn't.

"Thanks," he says smoothly. "I designed it myself."

"Wait, what? You're an architect too?"

"I'm demanding. I hired the right people to make my needs a reality."

No argument there.

He flips the steaks over. "None of the other houses I looked at had what I wanted, so I had to build it. It only took a hundred hours of my life with sketches and consultations and corrections."

I have to grip the counter with both hands.

Is there *nothing* he isn't good at?

"It paid off. This place is drop-dead gorgeous."

Molly lets out a loud yip of agreement that bounces off the high ceilings.

His next glance is assessing, but he just nods.

Deftly, like he's heard it a thousand times, and maybe he has.

This is a home that deserves to be shown, though he's so private I can't imagine he would.

I watch him slather the steaks in green sauce, line asparagus neatly on the side, and then spoon rosemary-scented potatoes onto the plate.

My mouth waters.

After animals and the ocean, my next dearest love might just be food. I'm not ashamed of it either.

"You don't have a chef?" I ask as we take our places on the island, opposite one another.

"No. No staff," he answers.

"None at all?" My eyebrows go up. Even Dad keeps over a dozen people on payroll just to manage everything when he owns several properties and travels a ton.

"A few cleaners come in twice a week, just to help stay on top of things. There's also my personal security specialist, Hank, now interning with Enguard Security out in California. I don't skimp on my safety."

I stare at him, waiting for more that seems to hang in the air.

It makes perfect sense that a man with his money who heads a world-class home security company would have strong personal protection. So why does it feel like more than that?

He reaches down to scratch Molly's head before I can ask.

I don't know if it's me, but his voice sounds a tad wistful. A tiny bit lonely.

Like maybe he's so used to it being this way he doesn't know how to imagine anything else. Just him and his small, distant house crew... but does that mean it's what he wants forever?

I don't know if Shepherd even *knows* what he wants.

"Your girl won't jump our plates, will she? Time to eat." He carries two thick, ceramic plates of steaming food over to this massive wooden table and lays them down.

Once I'm sure I've got Mol settled with an antler chew I fish out of my bag, I sit down across from him.

I'm not expecting to be totally bowled over.

The steak melts in my mouth, and I melt with it.

Even the wine he's paired it with is on point, elevating the meal from awesome surprise to exquisite shock and awe.

"I prefer a rosé," he explains as he takes a long sip, staring over the edge of his glass.

"Oh, so you're not a traditionalist." I smile into my own sip, and it's so good I could die.

I've always been a bit of a wine snob—probably comes with the territory when you grow up rich—and this ticks all my boxes.

"Not for everything, Dess. Sometimes a man must be inventive."

I look at the glass, running my finger over the slight condensation, letting the slight sharp bite of chill ground me.

"Well, this is nice and all, but should we get down to it? Talk damage control? You must have something in mind, but I'll go first." I take a deep breath. "I decided to feel out Meghan via DM personally since we were acquainted before all this. I've asked her if she's willing to hear my side to consider a retraction."

His face turns up sharply, but not with the anger I half expected.

"You think she'll go for it?" he asks.

"I don't know. Maybe. I don't think she's a *bad* person exactly, though she likes to play one for views. This sort of thing is her brand, sharing gossip and tea, but I know she calls it human interest." I pause and sigh. "I really don't know if she'll consider a truce. But there's no harm in correcting the facts since there's nothing much hidden anymore. No harm in trying, right?"

He chews slowly as he considers it, his muscular jaw working.

"If that doesn't work, we'll go direct. Put out a joint statement about adapting our product for conservation work and get the sea otter trip into the press release," Shepherd says with a stoic coolness I can't imagine feeling. "We'll be clear it's a work excursion without denying the claims head-on. In fact, we should do that even if Meghan *does* retract," he adds.

My blood pressure rises. I'm speechless.

"You mean there's still a chance at adapting—well, anything? Like moving forward with the tracking drones?"

He gives me another dry, heart-stopping smile. Reserved yet amused.

"I meant what I said, Destiny. It was a perfect presentation."

"But it isn't up to you. The board..." I trail off.

"Consider them convinced. I was open and honest, and I told them if they wanted to can me from being CEO, be my guest. I also made it clear there was real merit in your idea, and raising the company's global profile is a certainty if we give it a chance. What reason would they have for letting some he-said, she-said bullshit stand in the way of progress?"

Wow. Is that a hint of smugness in his voice?

I'm still too flabbergasted to speak.

"You can guess which way they came down," he continues. "Mrs. Medlin texted me two hours ago with their decision. With so many companies fixated on their public reputation for sustainability and mitigating environmental damage, it's too brilliant to ignore. You handed them a golden ticket, woman."

I flop back in my chair, raking a hand over my face.

Shepherd clears his throat. "Are you okay?"

"Holy shit. Yeah." I crack one eye open and stare. "You're being completely serious, right? Like this isn't some horrible story just to make me feel better?"

"I may be a hardass sometimes, but I'm not that cruel. I also noted there was still plenty of indirect profit to be made by investing in reputation management—a lesson I know all too well, personally. How many consumers try to make ethical shopping choices today? It's a tidal wave and it's growing. Perfectly logical, though I'd like to think my personal touch dragged them over to our position." He gives me that secret smile again I'm not sure I understand. "A bit cynical, perhaps, but it worked. That's the important part."

The messiest smile takes over my face.

My chest goes light as my heart stalls.

I have to check to make sure I'm still bound by gravity.

Without thinking, I reach over, drag his hand across the table, and sink my teeth into his finger.

He jerks his hand back like it's on fire.

"What the hell was that?"

"What does it look like? I had to make sure I'm not dreaming. This is too flipping good to be true."

"So you bite me when you're supposed to pinch yourself?" he growls.

I shrug, feeling my cheeks overheat until I break into another smile too bright for my face.

This is really happening.

Shepherd went to bat for my product line.

He believes in my work.

He believes in *me.*

And it's definitely not helping to quell the crazy butterfly swarm that's taken me over from head to toe.

I need to divert right now before I do way more than bite him.

So I wipe the smile off my face, rubbing Mol's head as she struts over and lays it in my lap, hoping for a few scraps, I'm sure.

"What happens if the rumor mill keeps spinning?" I ask. "If there are more of those pictures, X-rated ones..."

"They won't dare." His voice is so firm and unyielding. I half believe it from his tone alone. "I'm certain it's someone from inside the company. Miss Cho is on the case. She told me Mrs. Garcia found a few anomalies with one of our prototypes. Turns out, it wasn't ours at all, but a crudely modified consumer drone you can buy online."

"Wait, what? Someone stole your drone and replaced it?"

He nods sharply.

"Wait. Not Carol, right? She'd *never.*"

"It's unlikely, however, since she was the last person to access the lab before the crime, we have to look at her."

I'm almost dizzy at the implication. I can't bring myself to imagine the office mom could be so underhanded, so cruel.

There must be a better explanation.

I blink at him. "I guess that's logical, but why? Where's the motive? You think someone *inside* the company wants to—what, ruin you?"

And how did they know where we were going? They couldn't have followed us off my Insta pictures and stories when I only started posting them when we were well up the coast.

That's the part that makes no sense.

Was it in Shepherd's work diary or something?

Go look at otters with Destiny Lancaster.

"I think they breached our lab and had another one of my stealth drones trailing us. The units still struggle to penetrate dense tree cover, and the infrared mode isn't fine-tuned yet. So, the world can get fucked until we get to the bottom of this. Everything we did stays between us."

"Right." I release a long breath.

But did we have tree cover every time we had sex? The weekend blurs into one long haze of passions.

"They won't find out, Destiny." Shepherd's voice is so gentle. "Even if they did, it's not true what that rat influencer says, the way she's framing it. You know that, right? You were chosen for the program on your own merits, your own reputation and image. Hell, I almost made the mistake of locking you out."

"Lucky you for changing your mind." I grin.

"Yeah. My point is, the fucking came *after* that."

The way he says it is devastating.

It crawls right up in my feelings even more until every last part of me tingles.

Fucking.

It's the way his lips move around the word, maybe.

Or it's just the raw, frenzied image of us tangled together, making me half tempted to ask if he wants to do it again.

But my phone buzzes on the table beside me first.

Meghan's picture-perfect face appears on the icon beside the message, wearing her trademark smile.

A DM answering me.

Smug. Nasty. Triumphant.

One look at Shepherd tells me he knows it's nothing good.

I swallow nervously as I scan the message and meet his eyes again.

"It's her. She says she'll be in Seattle this week for a media convention," I say, reading the message again. "...and it looks like she's willing to talk in person."

XV: A LITTLE CONFESSION
(SHEPHERD)

$\mathcal{D}$estiny's face turns pale as she looks down at the phone in her hand.

I have the irrational urge to fling it aside and haul her into my arms.

I don't do that, of course.

Because although she's here in my house, eating the dinner I've been working on for four hours since I tossed the meat in the marinade, we set boundaries.

Fucking. Boundaries.

I have no right to cross them, no matter how much it kills me staying on the right side of wrong.

"I should go see her," she says.

I nod slowly, digesting the news. "Only if I come with."

Her eyes flick to mine and widen.

"You?" Her lanky dog nudges her nose into Destiny's palm, and she scratches the husky under the chin. "Do you think that's a good idea?"

"My mess started this, Destiny. I won't let you go alone."

Yeah, fuck, maybe I am taking this possessive bullshit too far.

But the thought of her meeting this flippant shit-stirrer alone makes my blood boil. Like any new wave media jackal, she could spin whatever story she pleases out of the slightest word.

Nice people don't stake their careers on gossip that eats through lives like acid.

"I don't know." She frowns. "Shepherd, if we turn up together—"

"It means we're a united front, committed to the truth."

"But what if she suspects we're just trying to bury it? And that a whole lot of something *did* happen?"

"Who doesn't suspect that now? Hell, they're right," I tell her. I swirl my wine before taking a sip, choosing my words carefully. "Besides, her olive branch could be an ambush. It's better you don't walk in there alone."

"I'm not helpless, you know."

"That's the point. You're far from it. Even the strongest know when they need backup."

"What happens if this is a trap and she's just waiting for us to walk in together so she can tell her followers we're a thing?"

"Then my lawyers will move so fast she'll wish she had birds eating her eyes instead."

"Eww." She wrinkles her nose. "It's not illegal."

"No, but I imagine what she's trying to achieve with unsupported smears isn't strictly immune to legal action, either."

Destiny sighs and ducks her head down against Molly as she embraces the dog.

I try not to be distracted by how charming she is.

She warned me that the pup is young and her training isn't perfect, but they both seem to have the bond any good dog owner should.

And seeing it's as sweet in person as it looks online only makes me angrier that there's some asshole firing potshots from the shadows, not caring if they tear down Destiny to feed their little lies.

It's more than that, too.

Like the fact that she's an addiction.

A sugar rush in slim, blonde flesh I can barely keep my hands away from when she's this close, here in the privacy of my home.

No office politics here.

Just us.

Alone and intoxicating.

Maybe the damned wine was a bad idea after all.

Still, I know the way I'm feeling has nothing to do with booze and everything to do with the beautiful creature across from me now.

"Okay," Destiny says finally. "So let's say we both go and have this sit-down. What's the best-case scenario?"

"Your frenemy publicly retracts her statement. Worst case, she doesn't and we're no worse off than when we started. Arriving together doesn't mean anything, Dess." Damn. The nickname slips off my tongue as easy as honey. "We're both in it now, whether we like it or not."

"Yeah, I'm... I'm sorry. I can't believe it's gotten so out of hand."

"Don't apologize," I clip. "You're not the one responsible."

"No, but I'm the one who suggested the Olympia trip. If we hadn't gone there in the first place—"

"There would be a lot of otters at the mercy of shitty tracking. Thanks to that trip, we know they don't need to be. Also, I'm the guy who brought you on board in the middle of a scandal that was already shitting up my life." I hold her gaze, knowing that's a dangerous thing to do. "No point in passing out blame. All we can do is act."

She sighs, her shoulders slumping. "I guess you're right. I'm still sorry this happened, though. I never meant for it to blow up like this."

"That's life. Existence is flammable."

And so are you, woman, I don't say. *Yet for some unholy reason I want you to turn me to ash.*

Molly jumps up as she smiles, bracing her big paws on

Destiny's thighs. She wraps her arms around the dog and sets that furry tail wagging.

"You're cute with her," I say. "Did you grow up with dogs?"

"No. My dad was so busy and I was sort of deprived," she says. "I think that's why I fell in love with animals so much. Typical story of the kid who wants what she can't have." She grimaces. "I was a huge brat back then, though."

"You? Never," I say with a snort.

"Hey!" She swipes at my arm, but her face breaks into a reluctant smile anyway. "You're not supposed to agree."

"Why wouldn't I? I thought I was the asshole here."

"Well, yeah, *that's* true." Her grin softens as she loses herself in bittersweet memories, her eyes going distant and glassy. "I used to be so demanding when I was little..."

"Demanding how?"

"Just like... whatever I wanted at the time." She shrugs. "I guess I was a little spoiled. I was Dad's little angel, you know? All he had left after losing my mom, and we didn't come from a big family. So I made a fuss whenever I wanted something. Good thing he didn't let me get away with it all the time, though." She smiles fondly. "That's one thing he always did for me—never let me get away with my shit."

"Is that why you're... the way you are now?"

Her eyes sparkle with challenge. "Are you trying to say I outgrew being a brat?"

"Don't put words in my mouth."

"You were, weren't you?"

I cock my head and give her a long, slow look that has her squirming in her chair.

My cock loves it too much.

"You're not so bad now. I guess."

"Coming from you, that's practically a mad declaration of love. Mr. Darcy, you flatter me." She leans forward, the apple crisp I had waiting for dessert completely forgotten. "Are you going to list my faults now?"

"Would that stop your head from growing bigger than the moon?"

"Too late."

"No point then," I snap.

And fuck.

I can't find enough faults for a proper list to throw back in her face.

Destiny's eyes heat before she trails a nail along the surface of the table.

I watch every movement avidly, imagining what she could do with that lonely finger trailing down my cock.

Her hands are a curse of the highest order, only rivaled by the rest of her.

Her nimble fingers.

Her smart mouth.

Her luminous blue eyes.

The whole time she gave her presentation, I couldn't stop thinking about the last time we fucked, slowly, wrapped up in the sleeping bag.

It was slow and sensual and too good to forget—and it left me fucking throbbing while those assholes on the board sneered at her, their minds already made up.

I'm more glad than ever I laid down the law and stuck my own neck out.

Not just because her proposal was smart, but because it was penance.

The cost of undressing this woman with my eyes, all while I'm trying to deny that I'm anything like the womanizing wolf the world believes I am.

Fuck, what's wrong with me?

What is my sickness?

It must be some black magic hidden in the curve of her neck, those long legs I always see straddling me, and an ass that could turn any man into a pillar of salt.

She makes me pure lust incarnate.

Ridiculous.

Ridiculous and fucking pathetic—especially when Destiny deserves vastly more than dick energy.

As her boss—however temporary—her work deserves my attention.

Her ideas are entitled to their fair shake in the world.

That's why I strong-armed the board into making their decision then and there.

It's amazing what a little shame can do. It made them override the rumors, plus they chose to keep me and take a leap of faith on her.

Wise decision.

"It's funny, you know, suddenly having this opportunity I thought was toast. But I guess after Mom died, I figured out you can't just stamp your feet and get what you want. Not even if you're a billionaire." She swallows thickly. I focus my attention back on her words. "So I gradually started figuring out what I wanted to do with my life..."

"And you decided conservation was your calling, bringing endangered animals to the masses," I say.

"Actually, that's my launchpad, but it's not the plan forever. It's one more step, just like school in Hawaii and then UC Davis for postgrad work. Someday I want to start my own marine conservation nonprofit. That's why I applied for this program. *You* were part of the deal."

I stare at her, surprised.

"I'll probably regret saying this, but having a chance to work with you almost meant as much as the money. It's not every day any charity program gives you a chance to rub shoulders with a hyper-successful businessman. And whether I like it or not, you need business thinking to keep a good nonprofit alive. Plus, I knew you'd be objective, something I'd never get with Dad."

Her soft smile fades quickly on the last word.

Curious.

It shouldn't be possible to find her any more attractive, but she manages. I watch her shift in the chair, leaning forward in a way that compresses her cleavage into pure sin.

"Anyway, I'm rambling. That's enough about me."

"You'll pull it off, lady. Anything you set your mind to." I mean it, too.

"God, I wish I had your confidence." She laughs.

"You have more than you give yourself credit for. Remember, I saw the whole presentation. You've got good ideas and a solid presence. You did your homework. You *can* carve your place in the big conservation world and save some creatures. If I can help speed that up, I will."

Destiny takes a long sip of her wine. "That's a big promise, Mr. Foster."

"Yeah, and I don't bet on losing horses."

"Flattering," she says, but her eyes ignite as she looks at me again.

With a parting nod, I stand to tidy up the table and clear away our plates.

Just in time, too.

One more second with her face-to-face and I'm pretty sure my balls would be smurf-blue forever.

All the while, I feel her watching me, which doesn't help them warm up to something resembling human coloring again.

"For the record, you're still demanding as hell, no matter how many nice words I've dropped on you tonight." I tell her.

"Ass," she whispers, but her lips are curved and her cheeks are flushed with soft heat when I glance back.

"You don't seem to mind."

"You have other attributes, too," she says, checking me out pretty obviously. "There are some benefits."

"Yeah? Why don't you enlighten me?" I'm enjoying making her blush to death, especially the way her eyes linger on my shoulders.

Working out has never been about attention.

I don't lift weights in my forties and pound through miles of coastal waters so girls will get butterflies in the gym.

For me, it's about erasing all the shit I'd rather not think about. The human brain is just another muscle, the only one you can pummel into exhaustion by running the rest of your body ragged.

But damn, when Miss Destiny looks at me with that teal sparkle, I can't help feeling good about myself.

I fucking *want* her to feast on every inch of me.

"You're quiet. Enjoying the view?" I ask.

"Maybe." She drains her glass. "The wine tells me to say yes."

I snort. "Time to open a new bottle, then."

I half expect her to tell me I'm getting us into trouble again, crossing all the flimsy boundaries we put in place. But she just tilts her head as she looks at me and holds out her glass.

"Top me off, please."

I grab another red blend and pop the cork, refilling her glass. She tosses it back almost in one go in a way that says she's thirsty for far more than fermented grape juice tonight.

Damn.

A shame, but as she licks her lips, she looks up at me again. I forget all those thoughts about the quality of the wine.

"A shame," she says, echoing my thoughts. "It's good stuff— really good—but I wanted to get a little tipsy."

"Why?"

A dangerous question.

"Um, so I have the nerve to finally tell you that I think you look really good in chef mode."

"Chef mode?"

"With your sleeves rolled up and relaxed, I mean. You're a lot like you were on our trip tonight. You're—" She stops.

"Say it," I urge.

"You're actually human," she finishes reluctantly.

That shouldn't gut me so much, only I know it's true.

I just wish I knew what the hell it means that Destiny Lancaster brings out that side of me so fucking effortlessly.

Her smile is pure midnight sensuality now behind the wine softening her face and damn if that doesn't turn me on.

"But you want to know a secret?" she ventures.

"What?" I lean in.

"The wine hasn't even kicked in yet. All that meat makes it a slow burn." The adorable way she hiccups and quickly covers her mouth says otherwise.

Little liar.

Fine, though. I'll play along.

"Guess you didn't need liquid courage to work up the nerve to tell me I'm not a robot. How generous, Miss Lancaster." I'm too close to her face, seething with the urge to kiss her desperately.

"Oh, no!" She holds up a finger. "No, you're not doing that again."

I prop my arm against the wall, leaning over as I look at her. "What? Miss Lancastering you again? I think I'll do it whenever I damn well please. Feels more intimate than your first name."

Destroyed.

The way she looks at me with her little mouth dropping up in delight slays what's left of my self-control.

My cock might murder me in my sleep if I let my conscience win out tonight.

I've been hard as a rock through most of the evening, having her across from me, and now I'm bursting at the seams with the signals she keeps giving.

"...there's one problem," she whispers, swallowing.

"What problem, Destiny?" I growl, drawing closer.

"We said it was over and done. One weekend and then... nothing. As much as I want it—and God, do I *want it*—are you sure you want to go back on that?" Even as she speaks, her fingertips graze up my shirt. "Also, I know what you look like shirtless..."

"Does a lion want to devour a thousand pound antelope on a silver platter?" I ask, taking her face with my palm and tilting her chin up firmly.

She goes so red it kills me.

"I was hoping you'd say that. Because I kinda want to see you shirtless again."

There goes the rest of the blood in my body, south of the border.

Fuck.

Fuck.

"Has anyone ever told you what a little fever you are? How fuckable?" I growl raggedly.

I'm touching her before I even know it, my greedy hands sliding up her arms.

She's still wearing the blouse-and-skirt ensemble she came to work in. The same outfit begging me to take her over my desk.

That can't happen tonight, but I can take her on damn near every surface of my house.

She's made me that insane, absolutely certifiable.

"We said just the weekend..." she whispers. The way her hand slides up my stomach and toys with the first button of my shirt says she couldn't care less what lines we tried to draw. "But I figured maybe we could make an exception for tonight, seeing as I'm here and we're already in trouble..."

"Woman, have I mentioned I love how you think?" I can't think straight. Not when my lips collide with hers, all braising heat and pulsing need. "Missing this chance would be an atrocity. Now, bed or wall?"

"Bed or *what?*" Her eyes go wide.

"You heard me. You have five seconds."

I don't give her that long before she's in my arms and we're rushing across the room. I plow our tangled bodies against the side of my fireplace, pinning her down and drinking deep, taking until she gasps.

"Oh! Shepherd."

Yeah, fuck.

Give it to me, sweetheart.

Give it *all.*

I do my damnedest to drive it out of her, teasing her little tongue until it darts out to moisten the pad of her bottom lip.

She's panting when I pull away, glancing at the ceiling like she can see through it to the bedroom and then straight to the stars. "Bed. It has to be."

My eyebrows go up in genuine surprise.

"Don't get me wrong," she explains. "I'd love to have you keep going right here, but... I don't think Molly would like that."

I whip around and find the husky staring, sitting behind me quietly with her furry head cocked.

Shit.

I'm not used to having a third wheel with any woman.

The primal part of me may be annoyed at having to stomp the brakes. The rest of me is amused.

How long has it been for her?

How bad am I for wanting to be the first man she's been with in nearly a year—or at least the first one she trusts around her dog?

Still, we shouldn't push it.

That's a good way to wind up with a barking fit of confusion ruining the mood when you're on the brink.

"Upstairs?"

She smiles, raking her nails down my chest. "Yes. Good idea."

The journey up gives me just enough time to process this insanity.

No, dammit, we shouldn't have sex again.

I know that deeply as I grab her hand and practically drag her up the long floating staircase with me.

She stares at the glass cabinets and backlit display walls with pieces of my life and meaningful art I've collected over the years, but she doesn't say anything as I lead her into my bedroom.

"Stay," she tells Molly firmly by the door, who now has a

small green alligator chew hanging from her mouth Destiny fetched from her bag. "Good girl."

"She can have the run of the house," I say, deciding not to put on music.

That's not what this is.

It's not a date, no matter what kind of unspeakable fuckery is about to go down.

And it goes down *hard* a second later, when her skirt hits me in the face.

When I turn, she's already naked.

"How?" I whisper, biting back a grin.

My cock lunges at my zipper, and for a second, I just stare at her.

My eyes have never been so ravenous before.

She's too perfect.

Long legs, gentle curves, toned yet soft at the same time, all anchored around that pink perfection between her legs underneath a small blonde strip of hair.

She tenses, her muscles defined as she breathes slowly, pushing her tits out like an offering.

I've mapped so much of her body and not nearly enough.

I hate that this already feels like so much more than a hookup, even if we're both throbbing.

Hookups, they scratch an itch.

This feels more like an antidote for my soul.

She's so much more than one more fuck I won't think about in a month, a year. I think we both know it, and honestly, it scares me.

Just not enough to stop.

Her spectacular eyes are almost wholly blue, deep and dark and inviting as her chest rises and falls.

"Not fair. You're still wearing too many clothes." Her voice is a husky whisper.

Goddamn, she's going to make me keel over before I can even get inside her.

"Greedy girl," I say, stalking forward. "Do I have to make you beg again?"

She licks her lips and nods.

I let her touch me, placing my hands over hers, guiding them down my body. As her nails drag down my chest, my abs, stopping at the insistent bulge just below my belt, I lose it.

My fingers are already working at my clothes.

This isn't a night for idle teasing, not when there's this much sex-crazed magic in the air.

Pants first. Shirt. Socks. Boxers.

When I'm as naked as she is, I pull her in, drawing her in with one rough push against the small of her back.

My dick hurts, growing hungrier by the second to be inside her.

Her gaze falls and stops on my pulsing cock.

Fuck, I'll never get tired of seeing her look at me like this.

I could see it every day for the next century, and it still wouldn't be enough.

"Mouth, woman. Let me feel it."

I watch her go to work, taking me to heaven one slow kiss down my body at a time.

When she's on her knees with my cock in her hand, it's a miracle I don't blow right there. But I regain control just as she starts making these slow, devilish strokes down my length, pushing her clasped fingers tightly against my balls.

And when the head of my cock disappears behind those heart-shaped lips, I think I'm in pieces.

No longer whole, and that's okay.

That's very, very fucking okay when she sucks like a goddess.

Her tongue works me like mad, pure sorcery as she changes rhythm.

Total delirium in every wide-eyed glance as I fist her hair.

"Destiny, fuck," I snarl, the only coherent words I can manage.

She isn't bothered as she sucks me harder, faster, her little hand working a cock that's far too big for her and her young blue eyes staring up insistently.

My breath becomes a groan, and that shame I should feel at losing my shit so early gets hurled aside by pure ecstasy.

"Destiny!" I pull her hair, winning a loud moan against my cock. "Fuck, that mouth, you're going to make me—"

With evil precision, her tongue goes there.

Right to the spot that must be my hardwired trigger.

Next thing I know, I'm seeing stars as my balls heave fire and I'm trying to hold myself back from shoving my cock all the way down her throat.

Just enough.

Just enough to push her limits.

Just enough to hear her moaning gag as I boil over, releasing in her mouth until I'm spilling out of her.

Fuck!

This is not coming.

This release rips me out of my own body and slams me back into it, and soon I'm fisting my cock, marking her tits with a few last ropes while her hand works between her legs.

She's still wearing me when she comes.

Damn good thing, too, or else I might be a little jealous at her fingers doing the work.

"That's it, Dess. Good fucking girl," I snarl, my eyes drilling into hers.

I cradle her head against my thigh until she stops shuddering, pressing my wrist against her mouth so she has something to bite.

Unlike roughing it with the otters, she can be as loud as she wants here, but I still enjoy watching her try to stifle the music of her orgasm.

Once she's on her feet, kissing me again, our rhythm slows but the hunger doesn't.

It's different now, yes.

Needier at a bone-deep level I can't describe.

I kiss her more deeply, and she claws at my back, raking her nails down my skin.

I'm sure she's leaving marks, putting her own unique signature all over me.

Good.

It's sexy as hell knowing she's into marking me just as much as I want to engrave myself on her.

Though her eyes are dark with lust, there's this strange distance in steaming desire.

She kisses me with a little bit too much desperation.

Finally, when I can't stand it and I haul her across the room to my huge king bed and throw her down, she averts her eyes and looks past me at the ceiling.

"My eyes are down here," I joke, waiting until she looks at me. "That's right. Look at me when I break you."

Good fucking girl.

Her eyes never leave me as I rub her pussy, pushing two fingers inside her sweetness, robbing one moan from her lips after the next.

She's so wet for me, instantly squeezing me until I see white.

I'm lucky I already came once, or I'd be a goner for sure, blowing my load inside her in under a minute.

Patience, patience.

The way my thumb rubs her clit drives it home that I'm taking my sweet time.

"Shepherd," she gasps.

"That's it," I growl.

That's it forever.

My name on her lips.

I want her eyes on me the entire time.

Not looking past me.

Not through me.

Not like she's somewhere else when I'm in full control of her tight little pussy.

"Destiny," I whisper.

Her eyes snap to mine.

I press my forehead to hers, holding our gaze, before I slowly work my way down to her tits and feast.

Her nipples are willing prisoners. I suck and massage and bite with just the right pressure that makes me think she could go off just from having them sucked.

Only, I'm not going to give her that chance.

She's already put her bratty mouth to good use, and it would be a sin not to return the favor.

So I do.

I kiss down her belly, that little landing strip, her right inner thigh.

I draw it out until she's clutching the sheets, holding on so she doesn't go airborne.

"Shepherd, Shepherd..."

My name floats off her lips again and again like a prayer.

When I know she's desperate, when I know she's red and seething and about to pass out if I hold back, that's when I answer.

My mouth finds her pussy and I eat her like my last meal.

This tongue delves deep, drags her to the edge, and then moves to her clit for the grand finale.

And what a fine fucking send-off it is.

Come for me, sweetheart.

Make that pussy scream.

It's the most beautiful orgasm I've ever witnessed.

Her clenching, shaking, whimpering, coming apart, hair lashing like gold ribbons as the pleasure pulls her under.

Destiny Lancaster comes like she'll never be the same after my tongue, and I'm proud as hell of that.

She's barely breathing again, falling into my next kiss, tasting herself on my lips, when I can't hold back.

I only wait until her eyes are on me before I push inside her, bottoming out in one long stroke.

Fuck, it's too perfect.

We've done this enough, so I know the rhythm of her body and the tempo of her pulse.

I know all the right angles.

I know I need to come inside her, coming on me, if it's the last goddamned thing I do.

She's so close, and so am I.

Pressing my fingers against her clit, we go hard while I stroke slow circles, thrusting like a surging river.

"Oh, Shepherd, Shepherd. Fuck!" she murmurs.

Her eyes flutter shut.

"No, baby. Look at me."

Be with me, I want to say.

But I don't, not even in the heat of this, because I don't know what she'll think that means and honestly, I don't know myself.

Her eyelids flutter. "So. Close."

"Then go." My breath falls against her cheek like a desert breeze.

I need—*need*—to see her come undone, before my balls lose it.

This is the last fucking time we'll do this.

Supposedly.

If that's true, this needs to count, this whole night where every hour feels like a breathless eternity that's never long enough.

I want her captured in the moment.

Not thinking about anyone else.

Not dwelling on the fact that we're doing everything we shouldn't.

Not tomorrow's trouble.

Just her and me, tangled up in this bed, alive with our own brute passions and driving each other out of our minds with filthy promises.

I slow my fingers as she squeezes around me, and she squirms, desperate for release.

"Look at me, Dess," I order again through clenched teeth.

267

"So demanding," she says, but her voice is tight.

There's no more play in her eyes as she finally meets mine.

That familiar pressure becomes a raging current against my spine.

I slow down a little more—barely.

I'm not coming before she does.

"Shepherd," she begs again. "Shepherd, please."

"Since you asked nicely..." I press my thumb against that sensitive nub, knowing she's ready.

Fuck, is she ever.

With one shrill moan, she comes apart under me.

It's almost violent.

Shaking the bed, crying my name, my entire body shaking with animalistic energy, driving to her very depths.

Just like that, I lose the battle with my own orgasm and I tear the fuck open.

I didn't want this to end, but there's something impossibly hot about watching her come for me, and I can't hold back.

With one more furious breath, I join her in the reverie, coming until my vision, my body, my everything are stars.

Destiny, indeed.

I'm deathly afraid she's going to be mine.

When I'm done, I know we should clean up. Yet I can't bring myself to roll out of bed and away from her when we're both rendered boneless.

She sighs, long and deep, and when I pull her into me, she doesn't fight.

Even though this is on the heels of one of the best orgasms of my life, there's something melancholy about the afterglow.

A tinge of sadness that started the second she looked away.

If this wasn't the last time, it's coming in the next few hours.

The very real curtain call.

A happy fluke, I guess, that she came to my house and this happened again. But we both know this can't continue.

After tonight, it's over and done.

If only that didn't make it far too real.

* * *

THE MELANCHOLY LINGERS like poison after a sting.

She's still in my arms, breathing gently across my chest.

Still, there's a blue aura I can feel, sadness creeping in.

I just don't know how to mention it.

Some shit, I can handle without breaking a sweat.

Business, character assassinations, former associates of Uncle Aidan's outfit who would've loved to slash my throat with piano wire if I wasn't so high profile...

I've built my new life around my career, and it's no exaggeration to say I know what I'm doing.

But this, this is uncharted territory.

I've never been one of those touchy-feely guys. The men who talk about their feelings without it getting weird.

In the life I've lived, feelings are something you hide, an annoying vulnerability that shouldn't exist at all.

Hell, even just *understanding* this feels harder than learning Coptic Greek.

I'd rather talk facts and figures.

Give me numbers, graphs, figures organized into a spreadsheet.

Data doesn't lie, assuming it's not manipulated.

People, as numbers and assets and liabilities, make sense to me.

They have a function and either they do it or they don't.

If they don't, they get one chance to fix it before they can fuck right off and stop troubling me.

Mostly, I'm barely in charge of that day-to-day minutiae anymore when I handle the big picture.

Shareholders, expansions, and reputations to keep.

This doesn't feel small, though.

It's about the size of Everest, all squeezed into this room.

Destiny, with her eyes shut and her breath steady and her hands balled slightly. This is like waiting for a time bomb to detonate.

Mainly, the fact that she's pulling away.

Walls have gone up around her, despite the fact that we're still naked.

I don't know how to reach her.

Not that we were ever close to have that connection.

This was just sex.

A lie I tell myself a thousand times and it still doesn't sink in.

No, fuck this distance.

The feeling is like an itch under a cast, right there on the surface but impossible to scratch.

I'm uncomfortable. Antsy.

Not at all what I'm used to, and all thanks to another human being.

Where the hell is my cynicism now?

How the mighty have fallen.

I can't actually be interested in keeping this madness going... can I?

And for me to be interested *first*? Before she breaks down in tears, begging me to stay?

Goddamn, that's infuriating.

I'm losing my touch.

No wonder she can turn herself off like a switch. It must be tough, being physically attracted to someone you're not emotionally interested in.

After all, we don't have much in common besides philanthropy and an appreciation for nature.

That's not enough to make a young girl like her fall for a mature bonehead like me. I'm twice her age, for fuck's sake.

I'm not down with the easy, casual sex young people in her generation enjoy, either.

Just look at my possessiveness when she said she'd never been with a guy when Molly was around.

The jealous way I wanted her to look at me.

I craved a connection, and she didn't.

Simple as.

I tried like hell to keep it casual, but clearly I missed the mark.

Because *clearly* this means more to me than it does to her.

She's from the same world of money that gets old fast, where life is materialistic and heavily performative in the public eye.

I can't stand it.

Privacy is everything, and she doesn't get that.

I've spent my entire adult life trying to shut the world out.

She's spent hers putting herself front and center for a cause.

Sure, she has her secrets, but that won't be true forever.

When she gets with a guy—the lucky future dickhead who's meant to stick around, and I hate him already—he'll just pop up in her pictures and videos with the same natural ease as her husky.

Also, I've got about ten thousand reasons for distrusting women.

I can't afford to get emotionally invested now, especially not in the girl who's already made my name mud through no fault of her own.

"Hey." Destiny glances up at me, her hand splayed across my chest, eyes wide and searching. "You're like a rock. So tense."

"Am I? Sorry."

"Don't apologize." Her breath is cool as she blows it out, long and slow. "I wasn't saying it to make you feel bad. I just want to know what you're thinking about."

Damn good question.

What *am* I thinking?

Right now, mostly how foreign it is that anyone wants to know what's inside my head outside of a professional setting. Having anyone scooping out my thoughts like the flesh from a coconut doesn't feel appealing.

But the gentle way Destiny keeps looking at me, the distance gone again, like she can just push it aside when she's worried about me, does strange things to a man's mind.

You know what?

Fuck. It.

"Did you know I was married once?"

"What?" Her eyes turn into dinner plates. "You were?"

I nod.

Too late to back out now, dumbass.

"Serena Jameson. I proposed to her before my second tour of duty in Iraq. She said yes. I was gone longer than intended, though, when my unit's time was extended. I'll spare you the details. What matters is, when I came home unannounced, I found her in bed with another man."

Destiny gasps. Her nails dig into my chest as her eyes darken with anger.

A warped part of me loves the way she looks at me.

"Oh my God. That's awful and unbelievable and... and you deserved better, Shepherd."

"That's what I thought, too. That's why we fought like wolverines when she leaped out of bed," I say bitterly.

It's like another life after so many years gone by.

At the time, it was like being eviscerated, but now it's just a cruel distant memory.

A glaring reason to keep myself separated from anyone who can inflict pain.

"She told me I never loved her. I was too cold, after I had so much poison earlier in my life," I say slowly. "Serena said I never made her feel loved, that I was just using her for sex. I wasn't using her, but in her own way, she was right."

"No way! Shepherd, she cheated on you."

"And people do terrible things for a reason, don't they? Every villain has a story and every crime has a reason." I look at her sharply. "Anyway, she said she couldn't spend the rest of her life waiting around for me to come home and shape up to be the man she wanted. She couldn't live with the way I made her feel—more like one more asset in my account than a proper wife."

"Jesus," Destiny breathes. "Holy shit."

My gut aches with phantom pain. I really wonder how deep I should go, but this is our last night, isn't it?

Why shouldn't she get to see all of me naked and exposed?

"It gets worse," I grind out.

"Tell me." She leans forward, slowly stroking my arm.

"The other man was still in the bedroom when I confronted them. After he heard us fighting for a little while, he snapped, I guess."

It's a rotten memory I've kept locked away in a vault.

Serena's betrayal was one thing, but this was so different.

So fucking unnecessary.

The Marines showed me plenty of gruesome shit, everything from half-starved kids to charred human flesh.

Active duty does that to every man who steps into a combat zone, I suppose, but this didn't happen on a barricaded Fallujah street where you'd expect it. This ambush happened right in my own home.

"I told Serena I loved her—as well as I ever could. I always had. But she didn't feel the same way anymore. We were too broken, too damaged. Too fucking betrayed. I was ready to walk away from the flaming wreck of our marriage and give her the divorce she wanted. Then her lover boy came barreling out with a gun."

Destiny stops breathing.

She's not the only one.

"Obviously, I tried to get her clear, push her out of his path, but the man was crazed—and clearly, he hadn't fired anything at a living person before. He pulled the trigger anyway. Shot Serena before I could get her on the ground. The bullet ricocheted and grazed me."

Deathly silence now.

Maybe she knows just getting this out is killing me.

Then her small hand comes up to my face, fluttering, and stops on that faded line on my cheek. I nod like my head weighs more than a boulder.

"She died instantly," I say coldly. "The man was still there, staring in disbelief. I knocked him out cold before he could do more damage, tried to resuscitate her, called the cops, EMTs, the works. But when he woke up, he claimed I provoked the fight. He insisted *I* shot her in a jealous fit and because I had PTSD. Lying fuckrat."

She's too stunned for words, but her hand tightens on my arm, so small yet so soothing.

"There was a massive scandal. With my past, people thought I did it—it's not unheard of. In crime of passion murders, it's often the partner. And she was unfaithful, after all. There was a big investigation and it went to trial."

"While you were still grieving," she murmurs, shaking her head sharply.

"It was rough. I had to face up to her betrayal and death and the fact that I was being accused of her murder. I also had the media up my ass for—"

I stop.

Goddamn, where do I even begin with my *other* dirt?

"My past. It always comes back to that."

She looks at me, her eyes glassy with confusion.

"I don't understand. What past?" she asks so gently.

I sigh out my soul.

"You're too young and you're not a crime geek. Don't suppose you've heard of Aidan Murphy?"

She shakes her head.

"He was my uncle and almost like a father to me, after my real dad died. He was also a heartless, bullying, drug-dealing fuck who spent his last years in prison after he was busted as head of the Irish outfit all the way up the Pacific Coast." I smile unevenly. "I was only seventeen when he went down, right after he drew me into his world. I also helped put his ass away by helping the Feds connect the dots."

"Holy crap. Um, is there any movie you haven't lived?" She looks at me fiercely. "I'm so sorry."

"Don't be. I was young and I spent a year in witness protection before I enlisted to sort my shit out. My family also lost damn near everything as the Feds combed through assets, trying to find out where Uncle Aidan's dirt ended and ours began. Point is, his trial was a big deal. So big that I had to hire a small army of reputation managers to clean up my history with it before Home Shepherd was ever a thought. Still, there's always a few breadcrumbs somewhere. A few people really into the mob stuff who remember. I was already fabulously rich, a rising star in the business world when the shooting with Serena and her killer happened. You can imagine the shit show when the reporters found out about the Irish mob connection."

I'm expecting tears, more sympathy I don't feel like I deserve.

Instead, she takes my hand, lifting it gently to her lips and kissing my knuckles one at a time.

"It's so horrible. I watched my father go through the same thing, so much pain and doubt about the past. I guess this is what he warned me about."

"Warned you?" My head snaps up.

"It's nothing, don't worry. He just... he heard about the scandal. He's too good at reading me, and I couldn't deny that one thing was true about the crap he was hearing. He told me not to get mixed up with you—and now I know why."

"Wise man," I bite off. I think my hollowed-out smile weighs a hundred pounds. "He's absolutely right."

"Shepherd, no. I'm sure he pulled strings to even find out all that. I couldn't when I looked it up. Whatever you did to bury the past, all the bad stuff, it worked. Mostly. And I guess now I know what you're so worried about our little rumors unearthing."

"It's more than that. Uncle Aidan, Serena, that was the past.

My old life. It might as well have happened to somebody else," I say darkly. "No one talks about it anymore, not after the lawyers and specialists I sent to clean it up. Forensics cleared my name in the end anyway. I couldn't have fired and hit her from the angle I was in."

"Of course. It isn't fair. You moved on, trying to live your life, and reinvent yourself..."

"What else was there to do?" I shrug. "I was innocent and—" I scrub a hand over my face. The silence hurts.

But Destiny holds me now, anchoring me to the here and now, both of her arms wrapped around my neck.

Much tighter than before.

It's weirdly comforting, even if she doesn't speak.

Somehow, that's better.

No mindless words of comfort or pointless assurances that everything is fine or that what happened was so horrid.

I lived it.

I know it was godawful.

She knows it, too, and she just holds me.

She understands I don't need words.

Just the sweet, companionable silence with her wrapped around me.

Right now, that closeness sinks under my ribs, like something inside me snapping back into place.

I close my eyes in the darkness and give in.

I let myself feel this, feel *her*.

My Destiny.

Fuck the bad puns.

She's still the realest and truest I might ever have.

Her arm is still hooked across my chest with her cheek resting on my shoulder, her little nose against my neck.

We breathe together.

I start to relax.

I hadn't realized just how tense I was until my muscles came unscrewed.

I sag back into bed, and Destiny is there with me.

A light scratch at the door sends me padding over.

The second I open it, the husky darts for the bed, her little nails scraping the floor.

Smiling as Molly licks her face, Dess looks at me curiously.

"It's fine. The bed's big enough for three," I mutter.

And damn, she feels divine in my arms all night, even with the canine lump stretched between our legs.

I don't dare let myself think she belongs here in my life.

That's a stupid thought, but having her here tonight definitely feels right.

I rub her back slowly, twining my hand in her hair.

When our lips meet again, it's like a reunion.

Slow and tender and so bittersweet it's hard to breathe.

Kissing Destiny tastes like coming home after a hard day and smelling a decadent pie.

She's a warm bath, a glass of wine.

A sip of forgetfulness I need.

If only it wasn't so addictive, greedily drinking her sweetness as the darkness fades into something brighter.

Goddamned stunning.

Just three days alone with her combined, and I've forgotten all the reasons I ever despised her. If only I could see myself with someone like her. After Serena, with *anyone*.

But I don't.

I can't.

My heart is scar tissue, and Dess deserves better than damaged goods.

Prolonging this shit by making her think I could ever give her something more feels catastrophic.

I should get up right now and walk the hell away.

She hooks a leg over my hip and looks down at me, her lips red and swollen. Her hair falls past her face and she brushes it back.

"I'm only going to say this once," she says, shifting so she's over me, the husky lump moving to the floor by my fireplace.

I'm hard again, and by the way she positions herself, she knows it.

"Just once," she whispers.

"Okay, once. What?"

"It's not your fault." She sinks down on me then.

The mingled wetness from last time makes me slide inside her almost immediately.

My hands clasp her ass like she's the only thing keeping me from drowning in regrets.

Now, I don't ever want her to leave this bed.

It's a crazy, possessive need that has me flinging her down on my cock until her toes curl and her lungs stop working.

"Don't need to hear you say it," I tell her.

"I know. Which is why I told you once, and I'll never mention it again."

I suck in a sharp breath as she takes my hands and places them on her breasts. She rolls her hips and I rise instinctively to meet her.

"Say it," I demand.

"I didn't know her, but you loved her. I get it." Her hands are still on mine, holding me to her as she moves, taking my strokes. "I just want you to know, Shepherd, she was wrong. So wrong."

I can't look away.

Her beauty blazes down at me like a tropical sun.

I'm not usually breathless, but right now, I can't breathe.

I don't know what she's doing to me. The whole world has inverted.

When she kisses me again, she tastes like closure.

Like painful endings.

Like new beginnings.

Slow, slow, she takes me deeper, her hips working faster, and I lie back and let her.

Let her go to town.

There's nothing sexier than Destiny Lancaster riding my cock in this moment.

I let her guide my hands, one at her breast, the other at the place our bodies meet.

This time, when she's close, she holds back.

I can feel her waiting for me.

Goddamn.

This isn't fucking anymore.

The distance we had before is gone, yet she's right here with me, eyes blazing and mouth open and breath so worn.

"Together. Please," she begs.

The sound of her voice pulls me over the edge as I thrust like mad, burying myself in her.

Yeah, I'm fucking falling.

Falling so hard I might never peel myself off the ground.

And we fall together, long and hard until this wild, gorgeous woman collapses on top of me, still panting for dear life.

I barely have time to pull out and wrap my arms around her before a huge, fluffy weight pounces on us.

"Molly!" Destiny squeals.

I'm fucking winded.

Groaning under the weight of a dog who looks too damn smug, almost like she knows exactly what we were doing. As Molly rolls right over, wiggling around the bed to find her place, the storm of emotion dissipates.

I can finally laugh again.

"Sorry," Destiny says, maneuvering the dog so she's not crowding us. "She does this thing where she crawls out of bed and then jumps back in later. My little cannonball."

"You're lucky I like dogs."

"Even on your bed?" She smiles.

"If she's a nice dog—and housebroken." I shrug.

It's probably a good thing we have this distraction, so we're not lost in what this means or doesn't.

Hell, or maybe I'm the one who needs the distraction.

Hell, maybe I'm the only one putting meaning into this where it shouldn't exist.

Destiny wraps one arm around Molly and the other around me. The pup slowly settles, content in her throne of tangled sheets.

"Just a few minutes, girl. Then it's back to the floor," she says with a yawn.

Molly licks my face, and against my better judgment, I close my eyes and pass out.

XVI: A LITTLE SIT-DOWN (DESTINY)

*T*o say I'm the worst person ever is an exaggeration.
Probably.

Like, it's probably a bit much to go ahead and walk the streets with someone ringing a bell behind me and calling "Shame, shame!"

Still. I feel like roadkill drenched in turpentine and set on fire.

Molly tugs at her leash, excited to be headed back to Alki Beach again, the place that always draws me back when the time comes to process my emotions.

I've been avoiding it the past few days because—

Well, because *Shepherd.*

Go ahead. Tell me it's hilariously stupid and pathetic.

Although, to my credit, I've also not wanted to linger around there in the public eye and risk feeding our little image problem. I especially don't want some idiot snapping pics of me looking pensive while jogging, heartache in my eyes.

There's nothing worse than the entire world seeing you all moody while you're sweatier than a melting popsicle.

But today, I decided I'm done hiding.

Life goes on, even when you're a billionaire's daughter stuck in a crazy, confusing thing you can't define with Seattle's most eligible bachelor.

The ocean air slaps my face, but it has that extra hint of summer warmth that makes it pleasant.

I've swapped out my running pants for shorts, perfect for keeping pace with an overactive pup who still likes to trip over her lanky legs.

I'm actually thankful one of us is oblivious to how messed up things are.

Molly tosses her head back in joy the minute we step onto the beach, trying to run headlong into the surf. I grab her leash tighter with both hands, holding her back as a group of harbor seals sun themselves.

I fall into my stride, my breath coming sharp and fast.

She's used to this routine, thankfully, and she falls into a well-behaved pace beside me, her friends from the sea temporarily forgotten.

What the hell is wrong with me?

I really shouldn't have stayed over at his place the other night.

I shouldn't have gone there at all, knowing how helpless I get around him.

The man deserves better after sharing so much of himself.

I couldn't be more wrong for him.

He's fought and bled for his right to privacy.

What am I? Just an influencer who basks in the public eye, thriving on the spotlight. It's the only way I know how to help the world.

For better or worse, our association makes me more popular —especially in the perverse way it is now.

But even if I wasn't an influencer, he thinks I'm too young.

He may be right.

If the man could ever bring himself to take a second crack at marriage, he'll want a wife. Someone who can do the whole wife *thing* instead of just floating around his life, warming his bed and going about her business.

Not great ground for something more.

Not that we could *be* anything.

For now, it'll be a miracle if I can help nail the coffin shut on the same scandal he hired me to avoid, rather than catalyzing it.

Molly barks and looks up at me with concern.

"It's okay, girl," I say, stroking her head.

I swear, the dog was a therapist in her last life. Or a guardian angel, seeing how well she reads emotions.

My breath comes faster now as I stop dragging and push back into a run, wishing the wind could wash away the feel of his hands on my body, his scent that shouldn't still be lingering, the feel of him inside me.

If only I'd left before the *wine*.

I didn't need more baggage, more bitter memories to try and forget.

I already come by that honestly as a Lancaster.

Even if he's hands down the best lover I've ever had.

Hot as hell, considerate, and devilishly good at working a woman's body. Even better at leaving kisses that linger like a sting.

I only get a few paces before I stop, feeling like I'm buried under a ton of bricks.

Yep, this is *bad.*

It's going to hurt like voodoo pins straight to my heart, isn't it?

Walking into that office soon and acting like he never touched me.

Like I didn't just lose myself in his eyes and come on him half a dozen times.

Like I didn't bawl my eyes out after he told me about Serena and his family secrets.

Like I didn't just slip dangerously closer to a mad, mad love for Shepherd Foster.

I have to concentrate on running, until the intensity passes.

I can't even lie to myself.

And his dead wife, it made me jealous in a messed-up way.

Annoyed and hurt that he ever gave his love to someone so unfaithful.

Sad at the way he sounded when he mentioned her name.

So vulnerable. So soft. So undeserved.

She's dead now, of course.

There's no point in holding a grudge against a dead woman over a man I'm not actually with.

But between her and that douchebag she cheated on Shepherd with, he almost got convicted of a murder he didn't commit. He certainly had the scabs ripped off a rotten start to life he just wanted buried.

They destroyed him once, and he's built himself back up, but hearing him talk about it when it's clear he doesn't talk about it with just anyone...

It's a lot.

Too much for my heart to handle.

Today, of all days, I'm aching and dizzy with bruises.

Stupid, again.

Absolute buffoonery for even getting this emotionally invested in him.

But how can I help myself?

I squint against the breeze and push harder.

Usually, I take my time, stopping often to admire the view.

Today, it's only because my body makes me.

My legs burn. My lungs are disintegrating in my chest. My head—hoo boy, where do I even start?

Even Mol looks like she could use a break, her big pink tongue hanging out like a ribbon.

Reluctantly, I slow down and come to a stop at the lighthouse, walking up to the observation point so I can look across the water.

I instantly smile.

My mind sees him out there, fighting Mother Nature with all his raw, quintessentially grumpy Shepherd energy—and this time I wouldn't even yell at him for risking his neck.

...no, that's a lie.

I'd totally yell because no inner ragies justifies risking his life.

But I blink and he disappears.

There's no one out there today except a few lonely fishing boats.

Molly rolls down beside me, catching her breath. I crouch down and dig my fingers into her fur, fighting this weird feeling of disappointment and the weirder urge to cry.

I'm not crying over this, I lie.

"Wow, someone's beat today. What's wrong, girl?" I say past my rock in my throat. I think I already know. "No harm in an early nap, huh? Let's head home."

Molly looks up at me and stretches.

Those trusting, bright-blue eyes I adore so much glow brighter than the silvery water.

You know what the worst part is?

Shepherd got along with her so easy.

It was nothing like the date-destroying disaster I've been fearing ever since I got her. Men and hyperactive dogs usually don't mix, and it's one more reason I haven't put myself on the market.

But Shepherd, he just took every playful lick and rude paw like they were already old friends.

I wonder if Molly's feeling sad because she knows we won't be seeing him again, and whatever beautiful, messy thing might've happened isn't meant for this life.

Scratching her ruff, I pick myself up with a heavy sigh.

I pretend to ignore the stupid, hollow feeling in my chest as I turn Molly around and jog back home to get ready for my next round of misery in the office.

The good times never last.

It's time to grow up and face the freaking music.

* * *

So, being an adult is hard—and also *weird.*

Everything feels shockingly ordinary at work today.

In the days since we last saw each other, absolutely nothing unusual has happened.

He's holed up in his office and I've stayed in mine, mostly with Mark, who hasn't been the biggest pest in the known universe, even if he's a bit of a chronic suck-up by nature.

He's actually given me plenty to do and we've worked well enough together through his massive slush pile of charity queries.

Also, a certain someone—probably Hannah, or maybe her minion Rebecca—squashed the rumors so effectively that people only stare at me now when they think I'm not looking.

Progress.

Carol gives me a few sympathetic smiles whenever we pass by. She ducked in to congratulate me on a fantastic presentation —and apparently on the fact that the product team is already working to adapt one of their prototypes to conservation tracking.

I'm modest as always, taking the kind words in stride.

Except there's that little bit of pride inside me that feels good because it *was* a great proposal.

I worked hard on it, and it feels good to have that work acknowledged.

"So, in case you wondered... a lot of people feel bad that they were wrong about you and Mr. Foster," Mark says encouragingly at lunch. There's a splat of mayo beside his mouth as he bites into his wrap.

The sun beats down on our heads, warmer now at midday.

"Yeah?" I force a smile, knowing he's just trying to make me feel better.

"For sure! I mean, it's pretty obvious there's nothing going on now."

Oof. Now I know he's just buttering me up.

Or maybe my heart just forgot that every juicy piece of gossip eventually turns boring.

"I'm glad people are figuring it out," I say again.

"You think it just won't fizzle, huh?" His eyes shine with concern. "Listen, I don't think you have anything to worry about. People *will* forget about it soon, if they haven't already."

He gives me a sympathetic smile, but I think he's forgotten the fact that if he's still talking about it, it's unlikely anyone else has forgotten just yet.

Ugh.

This day is dragging.

"You're killing it with the queries, by the way," he tells me.

I try not to glare at him.

Silence is to Mark like bug spray is to mosquitoes.

"Thanks. They're not so bad once we found a groove."

"Oh, yeah. I wish I always had an assistant this good."

I bite back the urge to tell him *he's* the assistant, technically.

Then again, he's actually on payroll.

The work is a necessity, and definitely not as exciting as being out in the field searching for endangered animals. But if my time at Wired Cup taught me anything, it's that even corporate grunt work contributes to a good cause.

Money doesn't just allocate itself to the world's million good intentions.

Someone still has to read emails and reduce charities, people, and dreams into figures that fit neatly in a spreadsheet.

That's what nonprofit work is. I get that.

But there's something disheartening about it just the same, being the person pushing the buttons and preparing the big decisions made by the higher-ups.

I rub the back of my neck and tilt my head to the sky. "Thanks anyway."

"No, thank you, Dess. What you're doing is awesome," he says, leaning closer.

His floppy hair falls into his eyes.

Bleh.

I guess he's cute, in a younger dad bod way, but looking at him after Shepherd Foster is like comparing a pug to a Doberman.

The worst part is, I keep scanning my phone, hoping for a text.

But after a single quick message to say he'll meet me tonight to see Meghan, there's been nothing.

Fine, whatever.

He's been so caught up with meetings and work and life.

Definitely too busy for a life with me and the trouble that brings.

I genuinely don't blame him.

So here I am with Mark, finishing my sandwich and hoping this doesn't get too awkward.

"Any chance you'd consider staying on after you're done with Young Influencers? You could do a lot of good for Home Shepherd," he says. "Like full-time, I mean. I'm sure you'd snag a position, easy. Though if you're like me, you won't get paid all that much." He laughs, though he doesn't sound like he finds it funny.

Weird.

Is he still hitting on me now that I'm basically the office slut?

When we're alone, sometimes it feels like it, but he's always careful to maintain this personal distance. I've also seen him being this awkward with other people, too, so I guess it's just his nature.

Just his way of gladhanding and sucking up.

Mr. Nice Guy until he's not.

I've known the type, and I wonder what kind of teeth might come up if you rubbed Marky Mark the wrong way.

But staying diplomatic with people like him is just part of the corporate world, and that means it's part of the nonprofit world, too.

It's not what you know but *who*, after all, that determines success when there's big money at stake.

"You never know," I say noncommittally. It's more polite than *hell no*. "Well, lunch is almost done. Should we head back in and tackle that big cat sanctuary inquiry? You know, the one from Dallas, North Dakota?"

I legit wonder why there's apparently a very good large cat sanctuary in small-town North Dakota.

I also wonder who names their small town next to Canada 'Dallas.'

We settle back in, making small talk about their proposal as we go through it.

I spend the next few hours watching the clock until finally it's time to leave.

Before Mark can ask what I'm doing tonight and I need a new excuse to blow him off for drinks, I grab my coat and haul butt out of the building.

Shepherd texts me just as I'm leaving. ***Meet me out front in the car.***

It's not another date.

No more steamy, emotionally-charged sex that shouldn't be happening.

Just a date with destiny, and the tougher challenge of talking Meghan Tea down.

My stomach knots as I step outside, raincoat slung over my arm in the afternoon sunlight.

Ready or not, I'm going to see him again. For the first time since we literally slept together and I slipped out the next morning.

No, that's not quite accurate.

Since *Molly and I* slept in his arms. In his bed. After the best naughty nibble ever.

Huge distinction.

Somehow, having Mol there for the afterglow makes it more heart-wrenching.

A company car, black and sleek, stops at the curb.

Shepherd opens the back door for me.

I push inside and fasten my seatbelt as the driver pulls away and Shepherd punches the privacy visor up.

"Here. Before we get into the Meghan crap," he says, handing me his tablet before I have time to figure out how I should be behaving around him now.

At first, I'm not sure what I'm seeing.

There's a flashing red dot in the middle of the screen. He zooms out to reveal the San Juan Islands just north of Seattle and Anacortes.

"Whales?" I let out an undignified squeak.

"Not just your humpbacks or orcas. There's a pod of sei whales up there. A small EPA research ship confirmed a few fishermen's sightings today," he explains. "If you'd like, we could take my yacht out to observe them."

Oh, God.

Does he know he's blowing up my heart?

I'm gaping at him, mouth open, utterly gobsmacked.

He must have remembered that time I told him how much I wanted to see sei whales.

I have to find some words.

But that's kind of normal when he wants to see me, I guess, especially outside of work again.

Shepherd wants to spend *time* with me.

And what he's proposing definitely isn't another secretive little hookup disguised as something else.

Damn this man.

Hope blooms in my chest like cascading wildflowers.

Deep breath.

"Of course, if you have more pressing concerns, forget I asked." Shepherd clears his throat, staring at me intently. "I thought you'd like a chance to see them well within the boundaries of our state. I'd like to assess how practical it might be if we refine our product designs to include submersibles for under-water observations."

I grin. "Sure, sure. That makes sense."

"What are you implying, Miss Destiny?" He quirks a brow. "I have no ulterior motive."

"You're such a bad liar. But I love it." I reach across and touch his leg, marveling that I'm allowed to do that.

This level of physical contact, at least in the privacy of the car, still makes me feel like I'm getting away with something impossible.

And there goes my heart again.

But I really need to be less happy about this.

Sei whales or not, it's only going to hurt more when it comes to a bone-crushing end, won't it?

Yet, I can't stop my dumb mouth from saying, "It sounds amazing. When do we leave?"

There it is.

That small signature smile of his that shames the summer sun.

The lines of his face soften just enough before he snaps back to being all business.

"We'll discuss the logistics later. Are you ready for this meeting?" he asks sharply.

I'm a little thankful reality smacks me in the face.

"I don't know. As ready as I'll ever be?" I fiddle with the buttons on my blouse.

Maybe I should've changed into something prettier. The restaurant Meghan chose—on Shepherd's generous dime, of course—is one of the hippest and most expensive newer places in Ballard.

I don't usually worry about whether my business casual is business-y enough to be intimidating. But this whole situation has me on edge as we dart through Seattle traffic in silence.

If this goes badly, there might be such a blazing fire to put out that there won't be any sei whale excursions at all.

"You look fine," Shepherd says as we pull up to the place, almost like he can read my mind.

"Thanks." Another deep breath.

I should probably do something about my lung capacity, given how often I'm needing to breathe lately.

"You ready?" He grabs my hand and squeezes so tight.

I want to cry.

But for him, I need to be brave.

"Yeah. Let's do this."

The restaurant is a high-end Italian place with intimate lights hanging over tables and tasteful ambient music playing in the background.

I spot her immediately.

Meghan Tea shines at a table in the corner, sitting with a garishly dressed woman beside her.

I wonder if it's her lawyer.

I didn't know she'd be bringing company, but since it's me and Shepherd, I guess it's only fair.

As we approach, the older woman stands and jabs her hand at Shepherd first, then me.

"Hi, hi! I'm so glad you two could make it." She kisses the air beside my cheek. "I'm Adriana Cerva, Meghan's mom and manager."

Meghan, surprisingly, barely looks up when we sit. Her usually perky, whip-sharp demeanor seems subdued.

Even her newer fire-red hair hangs limply around her face, and her lips are pursed in a way that's hard to interpret.

But it doesn't look like a happy face.

"Hey, Meghan," I venture, trying to feel her out for hostility. But she just glances up briefly, gives me the slightest smile, and then looks down at the menu again.

She's not reading it, though.

Her eyes are too still, almost like she's staring right through it to the center of the Earth.

Okayyy.

Not what I expected.

To be fair, we've only met once or twice in person, very briefly at social media marketing conventions. Pretty normal, considering we're on opposite sides of the influencer fence.

But I've seen her videos plenty with how much algo love she gets, even if they make me roll my eyes.

She's not like this in her content.

She's always perky, brash, and ready to swing her sarcasm around like a brandished sword.

Then again, with something this serious and her mom-manager along for the ride, maybe she's just playing it cool. I've heard of outrageous people having a professional side.

Maybe her mom even told her to rein it in or something.

"Food first, right?" Adriana says with a fake laugh that slides down my back like a cheese grater. The frosted blonde tips of her hair look bleached almost white.

The woman is a talking mannequin trying to cling to her youth.

That's my first impression.

Shepherd and I just order espressos as Adriana picks the most expensive pasta salads and cocktails for herself and Meghan.

She makes idle small talk as we wait, doing everything she can to drive home the fact that her daughter is *famous,* and she's the whole reason for making Meghan Tea a national sensation.

Jeez Louise.

If she flashes her Chanel bag at me one more time...

Beside me, Shepherd's face is pure ice.

That cool, hard edge he wears that makes it plain he's not impressed by her act in the slightest, even if he stays perfectly polite.

It's a level of badass indifference I can only aspire to.

Of course, Adriana doesn't like it.

The less he acknowledges her bragging, the louder and more obnoxious she becomes.

Meghan dips her head further with every outlandish claim, still freakishly quiet, barely picking at her food.

"I remember when I was friends with Hank Hodges. You know, the actor?" she says, waving a hand. "Very attractive man. Very attractive. This was before he was married, of course." The implication hangs heavy in the air. "We still call each other every now and then on our birthdays."

I take another sip of my coffee, desperately waiting for someone to get to the point.

What I can't stop looking at is Meghan, wondering how she can be so silent when she's the whole reason we're here.

Her videos were cruel, mocking and nasty, loaded with horrible implications.

But right now, I actually feel a tad sorry for her.

Adriana doesn't seem to notice her daughter's silence.

When she's not talking, she's gorging herself on the spread in front of her like a starving squirrel, bruschetta and stuffed olives and fresh mozzarella.

"How about we get down to business and free up our appetites," Shepherd offers when they're finally about to move on to the dessert menu.

Thank God.

"Ha, I was waiting for this." Adriana wags a finger. "I've heard about you, Mr. Foster. A ruthless corporate shark. And I guess you know a thing or two about negotiating like the Italians do with your past and all." She waves a hand.

Oh my God.

I try hard not to choke on my coffee.

"I'm Irish," Shepherd clips. "No doubt you've had your own experience with negotiations, though, considering your role in your daughter's business," he says smoothly. "However, we're not here to discuss my past, business or otherwise."

Adriana cocks her head sharply. Her bleached hair flops.

"No? Oh, okay. So we're here to talk about the present, then. Your relationship with *her*, right?" She points at me.

"I have a name," I throw back.

"Destiny, Destiny. Of course. Such a pretty name for a gorgeous girl." Adriana practically sneers. Meghan slumps lower in her chair, that neon-red hair falling across her face like she wants to disappear behind it. "My bad. How could *anyone* forget?"

Holy hell.

I've never wanted to rip at anyone's hair and find out if it's a wig so badly.

"Meghan said she might consider retracting the very personal claims made on her channel recently," I continue, refusing to let her get to me.

Adriana's sneer disappears as she cranes her head at Meghan like a snake.

"Is that what you said, sweetie?"

Meghan jerks up in her chair.

"You'd know, Mom," she whispers. "You wrote the message..."

"Oh, yes, that's right." Adriana's pink nails tap the tablecloth. "Well, as it happens, I would like to discuss this a bit more. There's been an interesting development." She reaches into her oversized bag and pulls out a set of glossy photos, then slides them across the table to us.

At first, I wonder why I'm looking at X-rated photos in a fine restaurant.

Then I recognize Shepherd's ass mid-thrust, and a spill of blonde hair beneath him.

Oh, no.

Oh, shit.

These photos weren't anywhere online. I didn't know they'd been taken.

The canopy of leaves is too thick and dense to capture everything, but there's just enough skin to know what's going on.

No plausible deniability.

And that's not even the worst part.

Anger vibrates through me.

It's like I've been defiled, having something so personal stolen and laid out here like we're discussing a flipping movie script.

Except *no one* should ever be subjected to this.

I try to find the words to even process this, but I never get the chance.

Shepherd's knee knocks against mine as he flicks through the photos, his expression deathly blank and unimpressed.

When he moves, I jump.

He throws them back at Adriana so hard they go spinning.

"Why the fuck are you doing this?"

"Like you don't know," Adriana snarls. "You're not a stupid man, Foster—even if you're inclined to make bad decisions with your dick."

"Obviously, I don't know, or I wouldn't have asked." He leans back in his chair, arms folded, still observing them both with arctic disdain. "I find it odd that you'd show a complete stranger pornographic material in public."

Adriana's face flushes, blotchy through her makeup. "So, that's how you want to play it? Fine. Whatever, Mr. Man. If you aren't willing to discuss a little settlement that could keep this nice and quiet and private, well, maybe I'll just have these pictures blasted out to everyone who wants a copy. I'll *ruin* you for screwing a subordinate."

I tense and go numb.

Beside me, Shepherd's icy gaze locks on Adriana like a sniper.

She doesn't seem to notice the danger she's in as she turns her attention to me.

"Look, I know what it's like, sweetheart. When you're young and gorgeous, men make you think you need to give your body away to get ahead. But I can still save your reputation, little lady. If I tell the world he *forced* you into this to get ahead, your name is cleared, and maybe you can even get him to cough up some damages."

I stare at her, my mind stalled.

Screw this.

"You're sick," I grind out. "He never forced anything. I'd rather hang up my whole career than make a penny your way."

"So self-righteous. Sad." Adriana tsks, shaking her head. "One little word. That's all it takes to make this go away and turn you back into Little Miss Perfect again. I'm sure your father would appreciate it, wouldn't he? What does he think of this sordid business?" Her lip curls as she says the words.

She's doing it.

She's actually using my freaking family against me.

It takes a special kind of fire-breathing bitch to harness my worst fears so effortlessly and without shame.

I'm already halfway out of my seat, about to tell this woman where she can shove her blackmail and her head, when Shepherd moves again, grabbing my wrist.

"I have a very low tolerance for bullshit, Miss Cerva," he says, his words falling like icicles. "Not with me, and especially not with a smart young woman with a bright future ahead of her."

I fully straighten, but I hold my fire just long enough to fix them both with a steely stare rather than the torrent of abuse that's trying to claw out of me.

Don't do it.

Don't give her ammunition.

"As for your 'proof'?" Sarcasm drenches Shepherd's words. "I fail to see how these photos correspond to me *or* Miss Lancaster. Your habit of spying on strangers isn't my business, aside from the corporate espionage that must've been necessary to facilitate this. Now, I'm used to ugly rumors. I've only dealt with them my entire life. Miss Lancaster, though, there's no good reason she should have to suffer the same frustrations—and she *won't*. I will only say this once. Leave us the fuck alone before you wind up in court, selling your damned purse collection for legal fees."

That "fuck" gives him away.

He's still got his professional voice on, but he's spitting nails.

Who can blame him?

"Don't even try to deny it. It's you and Destiny, clear as day," Adriana insists, her voice jumping an octave.

People in the restaurant are looking at us now.

Shepherd cocks a brow, staring at the crazy woman until that smarmy look on her face melts. I've never wanted to kiss him more than right now.

"Prove it," he growls. "That burden is on you."

Adriana levels a slow look and sighs.

"I was worried you'd react this way. So blustery and unreasonable. So stupid. Since you want to be a tightwad, there's one more way we can both walk away with our dignity intact. You restart Young Influencers, and this time you choose Meghan. Do it, and I'll come down with a bad case of amnesia. I'll forget all about your love life and Meghan here will happily take some videos down."

Speechless.

I'm flipping speechless.

My eyes flick to Meghan. She's hunched in her chair, looking like she wants to be anywhere but here, and that small germ of pity sprouts into real concern.

Something isn't right.

It's like she's a puppet, helplessly chained to her psycho mom.

"Even if you could prove it," Shepherd says, "and I'm not saying you can, but if you *could*, that would be interesting, wouldn't it? I'm awfully certain I could prove criminal blackmail if this winds up in court."

Adriana has a smug smile on her face. "How interesting. So you wanna see who has the fastest lawyers in the old west? Game on!"

"No game, Miss Cerva. Just very serious questions about how you obtained those photographs, and what your business was spying on private citizens in protected wilderness with proprietary technology." He pauses to let his words sink in.

I see the moment they sink in, and she actually has a flicker of fear.

"*Criminal* questions," Shepherd says slowly.

Her smile vanishes.

Her garishly manicured nails press the table, almost hard enough to break, scratching the tablecloth.

Shepherd turns to Meghan this time.

"Think real hard before you follow her lead," he bites off. "If you two have any sense of self-preservation, you'll pretend we never spoke today. You'll be smart. Shut up, get out, and never breathe another word to me or Destiny again."

I think Adriana might have been struck mute.

Her breathing turns loud, rattling as she stares up into Shepherd's face.

Even Meghan looks up, her eyes wide and uncertain, almost bugging out of her head as she looks between us painfully.

"Miss Lancaster, let's go." Shepherd stands and pivots.

With his arm in mine, he steers us out of the restaurant, leaving them gawking behind us.

Even with my back turned, I can feel Adriana's glower, and when I glance back—a big mistake—she fixes me with a look I recognize.

I've seen that look before once, on a family friend I loved like an adopted uncle who wound up doing the unspeakable to my father and Eliza.

It chills me to the bone.

This so isn't over.

This is a crazy narcissist who's just had her pride shredded, and I know she'd rather die than let it go.

XVII: A LITTLE BETRAYAL
(SHEPHERD)

*R*ain splatters the windows of the car as Destiny stares blindly at the glass divider.

I tell the driver, Carl, to just drive us around while we think.

Doesn't matter where. We just need to get the hell away from that shit show in the restaurant.

"Hey." I touch her hand. It's ice-cold and she jerks back, almost like she's forgotten I'm here, her eyes shiny and blank. "We will fix this, Dess. I promise."

"What does fixing it even look like?" she whispers.

"We're going to take Adriana Cerva for everything she has." I pull her into my arms, and she rests her forehead against the crook of my shoulder.

Her heavy breath goes right through me as she exhales.

Fuck.

It's an effort to stay calm, but for her, I manage.

Tilting her head up, I kiss her softly.

It's for me as much as it is for her.

Her eyes are all misty blue today. I miss the green in them. I never noticed just how much vibrant green she has until it's missing.

More than anything, I want to wrap her in my arms until she forgets this pile of bullshit.

"Dess." I cup the back of her head and pull her in for another kiss.

Gentle, gentle.

We're not fucking in the back of this car, no matter how much my cock likes the idea.

After a second, she softens and her mouth moves against mine. But soon, she moves back again and looks at me.

"What if someone sees us?"

"The windows are tinted, sweetheart."

Her smile doesn't reach her eyes. "So you can have hot sex in the back seats?"

"Don't tempt me." I brush a knuckle along her chin. "Tell me you'll be okay. Where's my bright girl?"

"Yeah. I will be. But they won't give up, Shepherd. I just know it."

"No," I agree, hating it like hell.

"And I froze up back there. I didn't know what to say. She wants to ruin me, and for what? All because Meghan lost out on the Young Influencers slot? Because she smells blood in the water and thinks you're dumb enough to be blackmailed? It's insanity."

Before I can answer, my phone vibrates.

So does Destiny's at the same time.

I immediately regret looking at the screen.

My alerts are going off like screeching bats with another damn video of Meghan Tea's, already raking in the views. It's only been up for less than an hour.

This shit had to be pre-recorded.

The girl who couldn't say a word in the restaurant suddenly has more energy than a hyperactive lab. Destiny's eyes gleam with unshed tears as she watches Meghan talk about 'wild new developments.'

She slings a crapload of new accusations about the forced

nature of our relationship. Glimpses of the explicit photographs her mother threw at us flash across the screen.

Plus, plenty of edited clips with Vanessa Dumas talking about how I used her. What else?

My rage is fucking nuclear.

Not for myself, no, but for Destiny.

Sure, I can sue them into the ground for defamation—and I absolutely will.

I can wring them dry until they're begging for mercy.

They're doing this the messiest way imaginable, so I'm sure the case would be a slam dunk.

But the damage is being done to Destiny's reputation every second this open sewer keeps flowing. Their only edge, and the one thing I can never take back.

I'm sure that's the point.

Everything legal moves at a crawl, no matter how talented your lawyers are.

Even if we take them to court and win, they'll keep piping this out for days, weeks, however long they have before they're hit with a gag order, and even then, they could keep using minions.

The public at large will lap it up as long as it keeps coming.

This society loves its filth whenever it involves the rich and famous, and the only thing they love more is when it's thrown to them like Komodo dragons with a slab of beef.

To hell with my reputation.

That was half shot to shit with Vanessa's accusations. I can weather the storm.

But this bright young girl, who wants nothing more than to help endangered marine life... why the fuck does she have to suffer?

Because she fell into my orbit.

Because I signed on to Miss Cho's scheme against my better judgment, but she's also not to blame.

Destiny is being savaged because I let myself think I needed someone else to save *me*.

Another woman hurt, and I can't stop it fast enough.

Just like Serena.

She might not die or provoke a scorned lover into shooting me, but she'll have to live with closed doors, harassment, hideous insinuations, plus every goddamned dickhead in a position of power treating her like an earthworm because of these lies.

Goddamn.

I really am poison ivy.

It's hard to look at her as she sits curled across my lap, nestled in my arms.

At least I can still give her comfort, for now, despite the way it makes me feel like a tool.

Her breath shudders as she lets the phone fall into her lap, leaning against me again. I pull her closer.

"I'm so sorry." Her voice is so faint I almost don't hear it.

"This isn't your fault. Don't apologize."

Hell, until she signed on to our program, she was just as squeaky clean as Hannah promised.

This is entirely on me.

Both for being a walking scandal magnet, and because I couldn't keep my dick in my pants when I needed to.

If I hadn't touched her and kissed her and erupted like a volcano on that trip, there wouldn't be any salacious photos floating around at all.

She deserves so much better.

"I'm telling you, I'll find a way," I promise darkly, though the words are empty and we both know it.

"You don't have to do this alone," she says. "We're both in this."

Maybe so, but dammit, we shouldn't be.

I hold her tighter, ignoring the widening distance she puts between us.

I can't reach past the blankness in her eyes.

Something about the meeting has clearly shaken her to the core, and no matter how close she is, her mind feels like it's a universe away.

I can't reach her now.

I shouldn't want to, but I do.

"You can talk to me," I tell her. "We're going to power through this. I don't give a fuck what lawyers that liar has—mine are better, I assure you."

After everything that happened with my uncle, witness protection, and Serena, I know the value of a solid legal team.

"I don't doubt it," she says, resting her head on my shoulder. "I just wonder if it's the only way to set things right..."

I already know it's not simply because it's too fucking slow.

But what else is there?

Closing my eyes, we breathe together, until the silence feels more natural.

Still, that doesn't mean it's right.

There's just nothing else left for us here right now.

I give the driver directions to Destiny's apartment, and after dropping her off, head back to the office to think.

It's late enough in the day, there's no one else working except Hannah.

"Trying hard for that pay raise, I see. Go home," I tell her later as I walk past her into my office.

"Soon, Mr. Foster."

I grunt and shut the door behind me, walking behind my desk and dropping down in my leather power chair.

This thing between Destiny and me, whatever it is, has to end.

This time for real.

We agreed it would after the weekend, and yes, I'm well aware I'm the asshole who can't stay away.

Dark thoughts swirl around me like a cloud of flies.

I should just release Dess from her obligations at Home

Shepherd. Hell, I should scrap the entire program, double the money she gets, and help her set up her nonprofit.

No one else can screw her over based on rumors if she's the chief.

Mostly, I need her away from me.

Before I can taint her more than I already have.

Snarling, I open the bottom drawer I normally keep locked and pull out a bottle of bourbon and a glass I only keep around for emergencies.

Tonight is a goddamned crisis.

One shot rolls down my stomach and explodes, fanning fire into my blood.

There's no turning back.

After I've unleashed the legal hounds on Adriana, I'll let her go.

I'll do whatever I can to send her off to a better life than the one she has if she keeps working under me, a walking target for more punishment.

This weekend, that's when I'll tell her. When we take the yacht out to talk and try to spot the sei whales one last time.

No sex.

No kissing.

Not even touching a hair on her head.

Just one last bittersweet joyride to enjoy her presence and the way she lights up my inner darkness like the sunrise made flesh.

One last parting hit of the addiction she's become from a safe distance.

Then it's cold turkey, and she'll be free to follow her dreams without being mired in my nightmares.

Fuck, after her, maybe I need rehab.

Is it possible to be physiologically dependent on another human being?

The thought draws a bitter laugh out of me and I pour a few more fingers of booze.

I swallow wrong on my next shot. It hurts like hell on the way down.

Whatever.

Today, I need the pain.

But before I can fall too deep into the torture pit of self-hatred, there's yelling from outside my door.

I shove the glass aside as I stride over and rip the door open.

I'm not ready for what I see.

Hannah, damned near frog-marching Mark out of the elevator toward my office, yelling at him to keep moving.

And Hannah Cho *never* yells.

Mark, he's a human tomato with a beard, sullen-faced and sulky and staring at the floor.

"What the hell's going on?" I ask.

"That's what I'd like to find out, Mr. Foster." She swings around to face me. It's like flicking a switch, and she's back to her impeccably controlled self. "Why don't you explain my findings, Mr. Cantor? Or I will."

Mark's jaw sets. He won't look up from the floor as she waits impatiently.

"Okay! My turn," Hannah says with a hint of a brutal smile. "Jacob from IT found the missing drone this morning—the real one—and turned it in. Its transponder was barely working. The unit was broken apart, sitting in a dumpster behind a Sweeter Grind café in Ballard. It seems Mark removed the tracking chip from the prototype before he stole it, but not the embedded backup GPS chip you decided to have installed for additional security. Presumably so he could use it to track you on your sea otter excursion."

My eyes snap to Mark like angry hornets.

I'm ready to tear his head off, but there's one nagging question first.

"How?" I clip. "The research lab is locked down tighter than a vault."

This time, Hannah smiles.

"Well, it seems he forgot his access badge automatically logs entry, even if he's not authorized for access. The only time he entered the product development lab was with Carol Garcia at the same time—or rather, with her badge. That's how he disarmed the tracking chip and stole the unit from the lab. Carol confirmed she lost her badge and went looking for half an hour, right around the time Mr. Cantor generously supplied her with a cinnamon roll and coffee at her desk. He had no business being there without her," Hannah rattles off. "Honestly, I might not have noticed the discrepancy enough to ask, except for the fact that Mr. Cantor brought three teams cinnamon rolls from the very same Sweeter Grind shop on five different occasions. Circumstantial, yes, but when I found him working late and decided to ask about his lab visit with Carol, he wasn't exactly cooperative."

Yeah.

I don't deserve this brilliant of an assistant.

With my arms folded, I turn my attention to Mark, whose jaw works tightly. His fists are clenched. I know the look of a man who's trying like mad to come up with believable lies to save his skin.

"Is it true?" I ask blankly.

He stays deathly quiet.

"Answer Mr. Foster, please," Hannah says, her voice as frigid as mine. "There's no point in lying, Mr. Cantor. I practically caught you red-handed."

Finally, he looks up, his eyes narrowed, staring straight at me.

"Fine, fine," he snaps. "Yeah, I did it. I took the drone. I also got access to Hannah's schedule book, so I knew exactly where you were. I traced the route from Destiny's pictures. I followed you with the drone. I took the pictures. There, happy?"

Not while this little punk is still breathing.

"And then?" Hannah presses.

Mark hesitates, his mouth twisting until he sighs.

"Then... then I sold them to Adriana Cerva." For the first time, he grins like he's proud of himself. "If you want me to say I'm sorry, I won't. Honestly, people like you deserve to be dragged through the mud. Greedy billionaire pricks, hoarding your money and handing out the easy rewards to girls you want to bang. You leave the scraps to guys like me, barely enough to make a damn living in this city. And dude, I know she's pretty, but she's almost young enough to be your *daughter.*"

My fist feels like it weighs a thousand pounds as I strain to hold it back from caving his face in.

"You done, little man?" I grind out.

He nods.

"Just so I understand, you decided to slink around like a coward and help soulless assholes spin rumors because you feel entitled to my money? My *life?* Is that it?"

His face wrinkles with jealousy again.

"What did you even do to deserve it, Foster? I'm glad I took those photos." He steps back and throws his hands up. "Fuck it, I should've done more. Ruined you forever, and that stupid girl, too. She's another Insta-slut, using her looks for favors. Sleeping with you to get ahead."

He's visibly shaking now. It's a whimper against the hurricane in my blood.

"You done?" I growl again.

"No. She pretends to be all sweet, but I know better. For a rich guy, you're pretty oblivious. She's a Lancaster. She's never worked an honest day in her life."

The bullshit he's spewing sends rage charging through me, but I don't need to do anything to him. He's incriminating himself perfectly well without my help.

Hannah gives me a knowing look. I already know she has everything documented and she's probably crawling out of her skin to play witness.

"Anything else you want to add, Cantor?" I demand.

"Yeah—fuck you! I hope you die alone of stomach cancer in a sewer. Always acting like you're better than us, than *me*."

Entitled little shit.

He can't even come up with decent insults.

"I think that should do it," Hannah says flatly. "Washington is a two-party consent state, meaning we can't directly record this conversation without his permission. However, every employee agrees to corporate security terms when they accept any position here. That includes consenting to anything captured by the security cameras in this hallway."

It's almost too good.

The way he's damned himself dawns on his face with a delightful slowness as it slowly sinks in. He's just shot his own legs off.

"A little friendly advice." I fold my arms, staring him down. "If you're going to lose your temper like a ten-year-old, don't do it in front of people who can bury you alive."

He's flushed red and speechless, his mouth moving like a fish out of water.

All that fuckwit righteous anger fades right out of him as he staggers back. "You... you can't do this. Recording people against their will—"

"Oh, you're a lawyer now? Did you even read the terms of employment the day you signed on?" I raise my eyebrows and his shoulders slouch. "Go ahead. Remind me of all the ways I've infringed your rights, Mark Cantor."

He says nothing as his face drops.

"Also, for the record, your salary is thirty percent above living wage and includes quarterly bonuses," I say. "That's ninety percent above the going rate for interns in the Seatac area. It was, considering your position, incredibly generous. Now, it's revoked. Consider yourself terminated immediately."

Goddamn, that feels good.

Hannah nods. "I'll have the paperwork sorted tonight with HR."

Mark starts to slink off, but not before I call after him.

"I suggest you plan on a late night finding a lawyer." I let myself smirk as he turns back to glower at me. "I should probably also thank you for the ironclad evidence you provided against Miss Cerva. This simplifies everything."

It does, and I should be reveling in it.

But it can't silence every disgusting whisper online instantly.

It can't undo the insinuations that make Destiny Lancaster look like a rich girl who traded her body for a leg up.

"Go on," I snarl, mostly for my benefit before I do something I can't take back.

The blood drains from his cheeks and his neck goes splotchy.

"You won't win this," he flings back. "Y-you can't. Just wait and see."

I give him a subzero smile.

Right now, I'm perfectly capable of wringing his scrawny little neck, but that's not going to help anything.

"I can and I will. I'll be pressing the highest level criminal charges against you for theft and stalking."

"What? Criminal? No, I—" His throat bobs as his voice breaks off. He has nothing left to say as fear chokes him. "I'll... I'll get a lawyer."

"Let's hope it's a good one," I growl.

With one last frazzled stare, he turns and starts moving.

I hold up a hand and look at Hannah. "Wait until he's in the lobby. It's always the timing that counts."

With a neat shrug, she leans against the wall, counting in her head.

Approximately thirty seconds later, she taps her phone a few times and holds it up to her ear.

"Hello, security. Hi, this is Hannah Cho from the executive office and I'd like to report a theft on company premises. Yes, he's still in the building. The police are standing by? Wonderful."

XVIII: A LITTLE LIKE GOODBYE
(DESTINY)

*I*t has been a weird, hectic few days.

The whole office is in a flurry, but I can't get a word out of anyone explaining why.

Carol tells me it's over her head and above her pay grade. She's not privy to any details.

Rebecca tells me it's all very hush-hush, and whatever wheels are moving are known only to executive and legal.

Yes, it involves a major legal case. That's the only thing anyone seems to know.

And naturally, both Hannah and Shepherd are busy as ever, buried in calls and meetings related to quarterly earnings when they aren't huddling up with lawyers.

My emails go unanswered.

Fine.

I get it.

If the company *is* embroiled in some major legal case, then it makes sense they're both tied down putting out fires. I just wish I could get more than a vague ***you'll know everything soon*** from Shepherd by text.

I have so many questions.

Like why I'm suddenly not sharing the office with Mark and his stuff is gone.

Sure, it's a mildly pleasant surprise not having him hanging over my shoulder, making inane comments.

But it's *weird*.

What happened? Why did he get canned so abruptly? Was he stealing pens by the truckload or hacking the vending machines?

No one seems to know.

A few people give my lonely little office odd looks when they see he's gone, but I'm thinking they just miss the parade of pastries and bagels he'd always bring.

I try to pick up the slack once or twice, bringing in Regis rolls and boxes of coffee from Sweeter Grind. It can't hurt to invest in a little goodwill around here.

I also press on alone, tackling the query pile for Corporate Giving, moving through polite rejections and sorting promising candidates for the higher-ups.

Onward and upward.

If I stay busy, maybe I won't think about the quiet tremors happening under the surface at Home Shepherd, but of course, I still do.

How could I ignore them when I'm sure it relates to our trouble?

But I've scoured the news a million times over and there's nothing new. No one has reported anything about Home Shepherd or Meghan or even Vanessa.

Even Meghan has been weirdly quiet since her last video.

The smaller influencers hoping to ride her coattails by covering the scandal are also spinning their wheels, and new videos have slowed to a crawl the last couple days.

Awesome news, in theory.

In practice, it's suspiciously quiet.

Best of all, the trip is today. This afternoon, we'll be embarking on Shepherd's yacht for a whale trip.

So I head out a little early, clean up, and then drive to his massive estate and wait for him to meet me at the door, bringing Molly along for the ride.

"Destiny." My name sounds so reverent in his mouth it makes my breath catch.

So does the way he pulls me into his arms.

It's barely been a week but he hugs me like it's been a decade apart.

God, he'll never not feel good.

It doesn't matter that his face is dark and shadowed, handsome but haggard with a five o'clock shadow.

His gaze passes over my face, and I wonder if he sees my worry.

The fact that I don't know what's going on.

Automatically, I wrap my arms around his waist and press my nose against his neck. He smells like salt and cologne and iron discipline.

How can any man smell so familiar?

Except, I know him intimately.

We've explored too much of each other to ever forget.

I even know what's behind his icy stares and permanent scowls and the rare smiles I cherish.

I know about his mobster uncle ruining his start to life, his traitor ex and her crazy lover.

I know the secrets that keep his heart bound in barbed wire twine.

And I think, maybe, I've gotten a glimpse of the real tenderness underneath the bleeding, hurt mess.

His grouchy mask is just that—a front for a hidden warmth and sweetness that makes me feel—

No.

Don't even think it.

But I do.

After my own little tragedy growing up, after I've tried like hell to deny what's been happening for weeks, it shouldn't be such a painful surprise.

Shepherd's arms feel so flipping good around me, proof that it's deeper than just sparking desire or comfort.

It's pure love, plain and simple.

And I don't know what the hell to do with that at all.

The tension locked in my muscles slowly drains away.

"Hey," I say, breathing the word against his skin.

I need to bite my tongue. Words I don't dare say aloud want to escape.

We're not there yet.

Not yet.

Not ever.

If I've truly, madly fallen for him, it's not a love that can grow and thrive. It's the kind I need to smother, no matter how many tears and emotional bruises it brings.

And I'm already breathing around a scratchy lump in my throat as I inhale him.

"Hey yourself. Sorry I've been so busy, but I think you'll be very happy," he says.

I'm not so sure.

Nothing compares to having him with me, grumping his way into my life and searing me with rough kisses.

I know it's ridiculous and it trails me like a shadow in the summery afternoon sunlight splashing over us.

"It's fine. I'm glad you made time for this," I manage.

"Of course. Wouldn't miss your sei whales for an extra inch on my dick."

That makes me laugh, and for a second I look up into a playfulness in his eyes, breaking through the darkness.

But it only lasts a second, and then it's gone again.

"Are you sure, though? I keep hearing there's some big legal happenings going on..."

He sighs.

For a second, I think he'll tell me what the hell's been going on. But his blue eyes search my face, the ice in them melted in the midday heat.

He doesn't speak.

Instead, he tips my chin up and his lips find mine.

He kisses me fiercely, greedily, like he can feel the same thread of our strange fate unraveling, just like I do.

His fingers brush my cheek.

Somehow, it feels like goodbye.

One final kiss made for engraving me in his memory.

I dig my fingers into his shirt, swallowing a whimper, trying to hold him closer, to *keep him.* But he breaks away, giving me a stiff smile that doesn't quite reach his eyes.

Molly whines next to me, pawing at my leg.

"Someone's impatient. Shall we?" he says lightly, kneeling to scratch below her ears.

No.

Let's stay here and talk about why you look so worried.

Let's talk about why you've been ignoring me and keeping this legal thing under lock and key.

Let's talk about how we ever walk away after everything we've shared.

But I force a nod, stifling so many questions.

"Now?" I whisper.

"We don't want to lose the light. It takes a good two hours to get up there and last I heard, the whales are active today."

"Okay. That makes sense." I force a smile as Mol leans against my leg, staring up at me with questioning eyes.

Ugh.

I don't sound good at all.

More like there's a lizard trapped in my throat.

He doesn't take my hand as he leads me through the house, and while he gets ready, I slide my phone out of my back pocket, scrolling through the latest notifications.

There's plenty rolling in from social media, mostly reposts and a few straggler replies to the latest drama when it first blew up.

Nothing new—except for a DM on Instagram from Meghan Tea.

"What the hell?" I whisper.

Shepherd strides around the house like he's on a mission, filling his water bottle now, so he doesn't notice.

Destiny, don't go. Don't go anywhere with him.

My heart stalls.

I read it three times.

That's all it says.

Two stark sentences that come out of nowhere and say so much without telling me anything at all.

I'm not sure what to think.

For one, she shouldn't *know* we're spending time together, though she didn't mention any specifics. It could just be an assumption.

Still, this feeling of wrongness catches at the base of my throat, making it hard to breathe.

What do you mean? I message back.

For all I know, it's another cruel mind game. And seeing the dynamic at our meeting, probably some scheme her mother put her up to.

I wonder how much she agrees with Adriana, though.

No, I don't know her. It's not like we were ever more than distant frenemies before this craziness blew up.

But when we *have* messaged before, she'd usually reply pretty fast, thanks to being the terminally online type. She's always on her phone, checking her socials and analytics, never missing the slightest chance to promote herself or jump on a fresh subject with viral potential.

The minutes tick by and my message stays unseen.

Huh.

She's probably just messing with my head, trying to shake me up with this creepy-ass vague warning.

But I'm not letting this wreck what might be my last time with Shepherd Foster.

"Dess?" he calls loudly from the kitchen, almost like he can read my mind. "Everything okay?"

I stare at my phone for a few more seconds while Molly flattens herself on the ground. Nothing but more notifications rolling in.

"I'm good," I call back, wrapping Molly's leash more firmly around my hand.

When he emerges and heads for the back door, I join him.

We walk down the sun-soaked path to the pier together with Molly weaving between us, her head up and her eyes bright.

"This is her first time on a big boat that's not a ferry," I explain.

"We'll see if she's impressed," he says. "I suspect fancy yachts don't do much for Lancaster girls."

I roll my eyes but laugh anyway.

His yacht is actually perfectly nice as far as rich guys and their toys go.

I expected nothing less, but as we get closer, I can appreciate just how sleek and modern it is, pretty but functional instead of grossly flashy like some others I've been on.

It's a tall beast with white sides and massive black windows. A few cozy lounge chairs are perched in the front for soaking up the sun, and each cabin below is equipped with its own floor-to-ceiling windows.

We spend a few minutes on the deck before he leads me inside the main cabin.

It's gorgeous and modern, no question.

Despite the weird tension that still has me checking my phone every few minutes, excitement bubbles up in my chest.

Sei whales.

We're going to be riding off into the sunset, sipping champagne, and seeing freaking *sei whales.*

Another dream come true, and all because of him.

The excitement must be contagious. Molly barks and spins in a circle, getting her leash wrapped around her lanky legs.

"See? She's almost as pumped as I am," I joke.

Shepherd smiles softly as he glances at me and then the dog, but he doesn't make any move to hold me again.

I'm worried that kiss was an anomaly.

Something he only did because he couldn't help himself.

Did he need it like medicine? To soothe the same melancholy that keeps eating me alive?

Sigh.

I hate goodbyes with a vengeance.

Especially when all I want is for him to hold me and kiss me just like he did after we left Adriana and Meghan stewing at the restaurant.

No one ever held me quite like that.

It made me realize it's been so long since I truly felt safe, sure about what I'm doing with my life.

All the drama in the world doesn't matter when I'm in his arms, anchored to his massive chest.

We can take on the entire world together.

Alone, there are cracks.

Big ones, splinters, a thousand different reasons we shouldn't be together.

I'm desperately trying not to hurt.

I don't even know how to enjoy the moments we still have left.

So I dig my fingers into Molly's fur for support, counting my breaths.

This is fine.

We're going to have fun this evening.

We're going to see the whales.

And whatever happens next isn't up to me.

"Is Molly holding up all right?" Shepherd asks as he joins me at the window, the husky happily watching with her tongue out. "Do you need—"

"She's fine." I wish I could say the same.

I stand up and scratch my eyes, just in case any tears sneaked out when I wasn't paying attention.

"Can you take her leash for a minute? I just want to take in the view and get a few quick shots."

He takes it and stands with her so gently while I circle around the observation room, taking in a near 360 degree panorama of the mountains and silver waters reflecting the sunset. I hold up my phone, snapping photos and a few short clips.

"This is seriously amazing. I've never seen a ship built like this," I say.

"Same as the house. I brought in designers who gave it my personal touch."

I smile like a total fool.

Of course he did.

This man is a force of nature, always leaving his mark on the world.

I just wish he didn't do it so effortlessly with me.

I walk the room slowly, and then we step outside to the main deck. The cool breeze is the sharp slap in the face I need to smother the weepy burn digging at my eyes.

A tan muscular man with greying black hair and a big smile approaches.

"This is Captain Juan," Shepherd says. "He'll bring us to the whales today, safe and sound."

Juan smiles, displaying white teeth. He's in his forties, I think, and he has the kind of wiry strength you see in guys who get their exercise from their day jobs rather than the gym.

"Pleasure to meet you, Miss Lancaster. You brew a mean cup of coffee."

"Destiny, please, and that's actually my dad. He's in charge of Wired Cup." I smile warmly enough, but my heart twists.

I haven't said a word to my father since he was basically ready to come at Shepherd for robbing the cradle. I shouldn't keep delaying the inevitable—especially when we'll be broken up soon enough—but lately it's just been too much to deal with.

"Ah. Please pass along my compliments." His smile is wide and easy, like the glinting sun on water. It should help defuse the tension, but it doesn't.

Shepherd and Captain Juan talk logistics for a few minutes and I try to say a few words. But my heart isn't in it when I know this is it.

The beginning of the end for my heart.

"Leave the navigation side to me," Captain Juan says warmly before he steps away. "You two just sit back, relax, and enjoy the ride."

Easy, right?

God, it should be.

"Okay to leave her here for a minute?" Shepherd asks.

I nod and he ties Molly's leash to the railing as we head to the front of the ship, standing together as the engine rumbles to life and hums beneath us.

"Away we go," he says, reaching for my hand. "You need anything else? I thought you'd be more excited."

Don't cry, don't cry.

"Oh, no. All good. I'm just enjoying the breeze and—this view. Wow," I lie.

Whatever eliminates the chance of breaking down in a messy heap of tears at his feet.

He half smiles, clasping my hand tighter before he looks back at the horizon.

As we chug into the bay and head north at a good speed, I glance behind us at the rapidly shrinking Seattle skyline.

We live in such a beautiful place with the ocean on our doorstep and the mountains cradling this city.

If this is it for us, it's a picture-perfect finish.

I really should shut my mind up and appreciate every second.

The wind streams across my face as we plow through the

open waves, the edge of coolness softened by the summer evening.

I hold up my fingers, feeling the way the breeze slips through them like invisible silk.

Seagulls cackle overhead, and for a second, I can believe we're alone in the world.

Nothing but us.

Shepherd and Molly and me. After we head back to her, Molly leans her head against my hip, enjoying the rush of air through her fur.

"Thanks again for doing this. I hope it isn't interrupting your work too much," I say, wondering if he'll tell me anything.

"Dess, I would've dragged you here. When I heard about the whales, I couldn't let you miss it." He glances at me kindly and then looks back, leaning on the railing.

When did our conversations become so stilted?

It's like the air clogs with everything we're not saying, and nothing else can get through.

"I've been dreaming about this since I was a kid," I tell him. "They're so rare. I mean, it's such an *unlikely* experience, you know? This group is the first one that's been spotted in Washington waters all year, I think."

"Yeah," he agrees. "You've got to seize your chances. Grab them and hold the hell on."

My heart twists again.

"...do you think we'll really see them today? I know it's never guaranteed, especially with how fast the weather changes up in the islands."

"Guess there's some thunder and wind later, but we should have a good window of opportunity." Shepherd walks over to the lounge chair where he set his bag down and pulls out his tablet. He shows me the pulsing green dot that looks like our last whale report, not far from Friday Harbor on San Juan Island.

"They were here around noon," he says. "No promises we'll find them, of course, but at least we know the area. You feeling lucky today, Miss Destiny? Like you're going to live up to your name?"

Damn him.

The way he smiles crushes what's left of my heart.

I have to turn away, blotting my eyes as I pretend to fix my windswept hair before I can face him again.

"Everybody used to make dumb jokes about my name in middle school. I don't need you joining in," I tease back, loving and hating how he laughs.

It's an amazing sound, almost as rare as those breathtaking animals.

This is such a perfect moment—and this pit in my chest is ruining it.

I feel every tear of my heart like thin paper ripping apart.

Slowly but surely, piece by piece, one lost second at a time.

Go ahead and call it cheesy and sentimental.

It won't change the fact that I'm losing him and I hate it and there's nothing I can do.

The thing they never tell you about falling for someone is that sometimes you don't land in their arms for a happily ever after.

Sometimes you miss, you hit the pavement, and you shatter apart.

His fingers curl around the railing with white-knuckled intensity that makes me wonder what he's thinking.

The yacht rumbles on, cutting a path through the waves with surgical precision, sending spray through the air that wets my face.

Is holding hands as good as it gets now?

If I threw myself in his arms, would he take me?

I grip the railing tighter, forcing my attention back to the rippling water until a thicker burst of spray splats my face.

"Ick, that's cold," I sputter.

Shepherd chuckles beside me.

How do I live without that laugh?

"Anyone would think you've never been on the water before."

"It got in my *eye,* dude."

"Let me see." He reaches for me, turning my face so gently.

I look up through damp eyes to see him looking down at me. His thumbs smooth over my cheeks, delicately massaging them clean.

I want him to kiss me so bad it's blinding.

The longer we lock eyes, the more my vision blurs.

Dark like mist on the water, willing him to reach down and close this frozen distance between us.

If I could, I'd kiss him right here with the captain and crew watching.

I don't care.

If I'm losing this after today, better for us to go out with a bang that sends our hearts soaring.

The sheer force of my desperation takes me by surprise, and I bite my lip.

"You're doing it again," he whispers raggedly, his hand caressing my face now.

"Doing what?" I mouth.

"Turning me inside fucking out. Dess, when you look at me like that—" He breaks off, inhaling sharply, and his eyes drop to my mouth.

Kiss me now, you emotionally-challenged idiot, I think.

This doesn't have to be the end.

I beam the thought to him so strongly I swear he *must* feel it.

Shepherd, please.

But I watch the conflicted thoughts on his face, how his breath fights with the wind.

And it's the intensifying wind that wins out as he drops his hands and turns away, gripping the railing with both hands.

No, no, no.

"Has anyone bothered you lately in the office? The rumors?" he asks, back to being all business. "Hannah said she had it sorted and shut them down, but I'd rather hear it from you."

323

"No, it's... it's fine. People look but they don't talk behind my back. At least, not where I can hear. I think they liked the cinnamon rolls I brought as a peace offering. She did a great job."

Nodding, he digs a finger into his collar, tugging it loose.

His hair billows back in the wind, so dark and kissed by the sea gods I feel jealous.

I still want to run my fingers through it so badly they hurt.

Yes, this is silly.

It's like I'm possessed by the spirit of every fifteen-year-old girl with her first crush.

Only, I *know* exactly where this longing came from.

Just like I know I'm hilariously powerless to stop it.

So I lean forward into the wind, taking its crisp slap across the face. Like that can somehow blunt the hold Shepherd has on my heart.

"Are you cold?" he asks. "We can always move inside, or I can grab you a blanket from the cabin."

"No, no. This is great. It's actually refreshing."

He looks at me without a shred of belief, this emotional elephant we're not acknowledging growing bigger with every word.

What I should do right now is find a good angle to grab a few shots and short clips to share with my followers.

They'd love this whole excursion, regardless of whether or not there's an awesome whale sighting at the end.

But I can't while I have this moment.

This experience with Shepherd is still ours.

It's too precious to let anything pull me out of it.

Plus, I don't want anyone else looking into this private little world we've carved for ourselves with the sun peeking in and out of the swirling pink clouds and the mountains staring down as our only witnesses.

All I can do is watch him as he stands there, too striking to breathe, staring straight ahead with his jaw clenched and a sparkle in his frosted blue eyes.

"Less than an hour now. We're closing in," Shepherd says without looking at me.

Time is going fast. *Don't remind me.*

My stomach knots and tries to climb up my throat until it happens.

His hand brushes mine, and when I look over, he's closer.

A second later, my fingers are tangled in his.

I flipping lose it then.

The tears come furiously, spilling out as I turn away.

He just keeps holding on silently, like he knows how much I need him.

"Give your tears to the wind, woman. Not me," he whispers. "Truth be told, I hate that we have to go our separate ways."

I'm choking so hard I can barely speak. "Th-then why?"

Molly sinks down near my feet with a sympathetic whine.

"You already know. We both do," he says gently, turning and pulling me into his arms.

And he lets me break, just holding me silently, shielding me from my own pulverized heart.

Safe for a little while.

"I never meant to hurt you. Hell, I didn't mean to wind up in any position where I could. You must know it," he says, tucking my head under his chin.

He just holds me while I'm speechless for what feels like hours.

I don't even know.

"You're smart as a whip, eager to fix this world's mistakes, and so young you haven't lost your shine. That's what I'll always love about you, Destiny. I'm grateful you let me see it. One day, you'll look back. You'll see all this as a bump in the road, nothing but a nuisance against how incredible you're bound to be."

I'm beyond speechless.

His words are so dangerously close to an *I love you* my whole being freezes.

The worst part is, there's no room to bargain.

No counterargument.

No convincing.

He's so painfully right it's like being skinned alive, so I do the only thing I can.

I let him hold me until I'm too numb from the wind and his scent to think about wishing for more.

LATER, we make our way inside to warm up.

The wind is picking up as we approach the islands, verging on uncomfortable.

We're still so quiet, but it's like we've found an understanding in the companionable silence with Molly snoozing on a rug at our feet.

I'm startled when she jumps up and looks out the window with her ears back.

When I spin around for a better look at what she's seeing, I can't believe my eyes.

"Destiny," Shepherd says at the same time.

My throat goes tight when the first whale surfaces.

I'm all instinct as I lunge toward the glass, soaking up the sight of the sleek grey body cutting through the waves.

Water sprays through its blowhole, and as a second beast surfaces, I find my voice again.

"Holy shit. Did... did you see that?" I think I might be close to crying all over again.

"I'm right behind you," he whispers.

And he means it literally as he wraps his hands around my waist, holding me up.

Just in time.

Looks like the emotional quicksand I've been drowning in hasn't ruined my luck today.

We might never see another one of these gentle giants, but they're here.

Here with us.

I'm floating, exiting my body and entering this alternate reality where this handsome, confusing man is breaking my heart at the same time he gives me a miracle.

Another whale bursts through the surf, splattering us with water, and I squeal incoherently. I don't mind the rain that's beginning to fall, slightly clouding our view.

Crying.

I'm definitely crying.

"They're so majestic," I say, wiping my cheeks, willing myself to stop going to pieces for one freaking minute.

But Shepherd is barely watching the whales. His eyes are on me, even as he grabs his phone with one hand and taps off a message.

"Just told Juan to hold position and keep a safe distance. They're yours as long as they'll stay," he whispers reverently.

Together, we watch them in awestruck silence.

Even Molly doesn't bark, observing as they ply the seas like bears pushing through brush.

I'm hit with a thousand memories of the last time this happened with the otters.

I didn't know what was coming then.

Now, the future is too clear, but I try to stay in the moment, just relishing the scene.

If only I could stop time.

Capture this instant, set it in amber, press it between the pages of my memory, chop it out of reality, and paste it into the scrapbook of my life.

My eyes are wide, trying not to miss a single thing.

Every second, I'm here.

I'm present.

I'm living a godsend with Shepherd and I don't want to forget.

As we watch the pod slowly make its way away from the yacht, back into the open sea, we remain speechless.

There's only his hands, locked around my waist, anchoring us to this unspoken final moment that's our parting gift.

But at least I know he's with me, even if my heart refuses to understand why it has to be our last.

My chest is heavy, weighed down with regrets, but the spark of joy from seeing the whales helps me forget the future.

Almost.

I'll never forget who brought me here.

I'll never lose the heartache.

When I finally get the courage to glance up, he's watching me with this fond, bittersweet, barely there smile.

It's definitely for me and not the whales.

He looks at me like he's seeing something precious for the last time, before it becomes a lost treasure.

Here we go again.

I'm splinters.

This time, the sudden pain strikes so hard I gasp. I have to look away before he sees it in my face.

The last time.

The last effing time.

Shepherd squeezes my hand as the whales sink back below the surface and the storm that's been brewing overhead picks up, pelting the windows with diamond droplets.

"Was it as awesome as you hoped?"

Yes, yes.

And no, not nearly.

I turn, leaning into him, needing to feel him one more time.

"Can you check my pulse?" I manage. "I can't believe we actually saw them. And crap, I didn't even get a picture..."

"I had Juan capturing everything with the ship's cameras. I'll be sure to forward you the footage. Should be easy enough to edit however you'd like."

Oh my God.

He really thought of everything.

"You know, even if part of this sucks... I'm glad we came," I force out behind a sob. "If this is it for us, I can't imagine a better finish."

Besides not severing our hearts at all.

He nods slowly, his hands burning my sides.

I wonder if he feels it too.

He gives a long sigh, but before I can ask what's on his mind, he says, "We'll keep working on adapting our surveillance technology to conservation. The drones are just the beginning."

"You really think so?"

"I'd be a damned fool to walk away from a brilliant idea."

So why are you walking away from me?

I wish I could stop smiling at him calling me brilliant long enough to ask.

Never mind the fact that I get his logic.

I'm too young and sunny and he's too dark and damaged and obsessed with his work, and we've been nothing but trouble since the day we met. And Dad might still put a price on his head, but—

But we shouldn't be breaking up something so good.

My smile mirrors his, full of sad frustration. My cheeks feel raw against the drying salt on my skin.

"Thanks again, Shepherd. I'll never forget it." My voice is so thick. "And I'm sorry if I ever misjudged you when you just keep telling me how smart and pretty I am."

"You saw me too well, Dess. That's always been the problem."

He glances down at me, a frown touching his eyes as his fingers brush my jaw. The caress is so light it feels almost imaginary.

He isn't wrong.

This man who's capable of such gentleness, such tenderness, such fierceness and courage, and yet he hides it all so well.

My eyes sting. I have to suck in a deep breath before smiling up at him.

He says nothing now, looking down at me, his eyes storming and dark.

Time loses all meaning until I feel Molly pawing at my leg, checking to see if I'm still alive.

Eventually, he clears his throat and looks back out the window.

The whales are long gone and the rain is hitting harder now.

It's like a middle finger from Mother Nature telling us that this special moment is definitely over.

"I want you to know it's under control. Soon, you won't have to worry about Meghan or her warped mother anymore," he tells me.

"Why? What happened?"

"You've heard about the legal drama, I'm sure. Mark was the one who stole the drone, and we have evidence. He was working with Meghan and Adriana. He grabbed a prototype from the lab and sold them the photos of us he took. His stupidity is our smoking gun."

My brain short-circuits.

Mark?

Overgrown annoying puppy Mark Cantor did this?

Anger ignites my insides, and I brace my hands against Shepherd's chest.

He's so broad, so big, I feel safe enough to absorb the shock when I'm in his arms.

"He... he hated me that much?" I ask. "Jesus. I never thought..."

I shake my head.

Mark never showed me more than awkward overfriendliness.

If anything, I thought maybe he had a work crush on me.

Or maybe he wanted to impress me because he had a compulsive desire to suck up to people and make them like him.

Just look at how he treated everyone else.

Look how he treated *Shepherd*, Mr. Brownnoser extraordinaire.

Or so I thought.

"I'm glad you caught him, but honestly, I'm furious. The fact that he was using me the whole flipping time—"

"It's not about you, Destiny," Shepherd interrupts, taking my chin. He tilts my head so I look him in the eyes again. "This was about me. About sticking it to the man in his entitled mind. He expected a promotion for breathing. The little reprobate thought he saw a chance to make some money and fuck me over, and he took it."

"Still. He used me. He turned me into a weapon against you..."

"No. He tried," Shepherd says sharply. "The kid would've used anyone who'd give him a leg up. I've seen his type a thousand times. Cutthroat little cowards who'll lie and cheat their way to the top, not caring who they step on along the way."

I nod limply.

My stomach bottoms out. But although thinking about how two-faced Mark is creeps me out, it's also a relief.

We finally have answers.

No, evidence.

A smoking gun, just like he said.

"Wait, so you have total proof they paid him off?"

"Enough to connect the dots." He grins. "My legal team never had a case handed to them so neat."

"Wow."

My brain is spinning as it snaps into place.

I can't believe I didn't see it before.

His nonstop whining about being 'just an intern,' his daily salary complaints, even though he drives a newer car than me.

The way he targeted me, always sucking up, trying to make me think he just wanted a friend or he was that hard up for a date.

"So, you're suing him to death, right?"

"Criminal charges. Only way they ease up is if he spills everything on the Cervas. They're not worming their way out of this. It's just a matter of time. I have the proof—unauthorized

331

access and material theft. All that's left to do is pour the heat on Meghan. Seeing how she acts, I suspect she'll come to her senses sooner or later. She'll crack and she'll tell us just how fucked up her mother really is to save her own skin."

Ouch.

Poor Meghan.

Yes, she's a massive tool and a phony—even if she's been under crazy pressure—but with a mother like that?

It's hard to despise her.

I really want to know how much she's been threatened and ground into compliance.

With any luck, she won't get the bad ending. This whole thing blowing open could be a fresh start for her.

Adriana, on the other hand...

I hope that witch gets whacked in the face by her own broomstick.

The message from Meghan flashes again in my brain. I purse my lips, wondering what that was all about.

Another pathetic scheme by her mom, probably.

Something meant to drive a wedge between me and Shepherd, if she wasn't fishing for information about our plans so she could cause more mischief.

Adriana Cerva really should've hired better minions than Mark.

I grit my teeth at the thought.

"Once she's discredited," Shepherd continues, "the ripple effect should finish off Dumas' claims. They've been dropping off the radar anyway, now that she's milked time in the spotlight. People lose interest fast without a steady stream of fresh crap. Then we can get on with our lives."

"Two birds, one stone," I agree. "Pretty awesome sleuthing."

And it is, if only it wasn't one more sign of the end.

We go silent, still sharing a smile as I pull away. I settle next to him and stroke Molly's neck.

It's colder now, the realization stark and silent and hurting, even if I'm thrilled we get to walk away from this in one piece.

Shepherd doesn't move, either.

We're both trapped in each other's presence, and I think maybe if I freeze in place, we'll never address the elephant in the room again.

But maybe we don't need each other.

What's that saying again?

All's well that ends well?

This is, technically, the best ending possible to something that was never meant to be.

We just don't have the courage to admit it.

But Shepherd blinks as he clears his throat.

"I was thinking," he says, "about releasing you from the Young Influencers program early. You'll still get your money, so don't fret about that."

"What?" I take a step back.

"I've decided to match the prize with an investment of my own. You're getting double—four million dollars," he assures me, like it's the only thing that's ever mattered.

Holy crap.

Of course, I care about the money.

I'm thrilled to have a sizable donation to a charity of my choice, but hearing the rest knifes me in the heart.

He's letting me go.

Officially.

"In the long run, it's better this way," he says. "You won't be around to suffer any more whispers or evil eyes in the office. I won't risk tainting your reputation further as the legal actions against Mark and the Cervas hit the news cycle."

"*My* reputation? Don't you mean yours?" The anger, the hurt, just erupts right out of me.

His gaze holds steady as it locks on mine.

"If that's what I meant, I would have said it. *Your* reputation is the only thing that's mattered since those photos dropped, Dess. You've suffered enough and I won't keep tarnishing you."

The air punches out of me.

My gut fills with lead, jagged and sharp.

The shards cut even as they drag me down.

Fresh tears sting my eyes and I have to turn away.

"Don't you think it's a little late for that now? Pretending we were never together?"

"Destiny—" He sighs.

"Is this why you really brought me here today? So you could soften the blow and then tell me to my face to leave?"

His face tightens.

The ending we saw rampaging toward us slams me in the face so hard I'm almost blinded. The elephant in the room, trampling over my heart and leaving it for dead.

I wonder if I already have ugly tears rolling down my cheeks when I notice I've bitten the inside of my cheek hard enough to draw blood.

This is so ridiculous.

I knew this big goodbye was bound to hurt, so why does it matter how he does it?

Why do I care so much?

I knew I was bad for him from our anti-meet-cute.

Just like I knew this was never destined to be anything more.

But my chest splits open, a black hole swallowing his words. If only it could absorb the icy stare etched on his face.

"We came here because I know how much this means to you. If I hadn't gotten the tip about the whales, this conversation would've happened in my office," he throws back.

"Okay. So now we go home and I fuck right out of your life? Easy-peasy, right?"

"Easy?" he snarls, hurt welling in his eyes.

I immediately regret my snark.

Even Molly pulls away, clearing the void between us to flop down on the rug in the center of the room again like she can't stand the pain vibrating the air.

"Goddammit it, Destiny. What did you think was going to happen? I'm trying to protect you. Can't you see it?"

Unfortunately, I can.

It just rips me apart to say it.

"...I just thought we'd face this together and I'd finish out my time," I whisper. "You know I hate special treatments. I agreed to the terms you set when I signed on as your influencer. You seriously want to send me packing so I can't do the work I was hired to do? Won't that look worse when reporters circle back from the legal drama again?"

"They'll agree it's understandable, considering—fuck, *everything*," he growls.

The rough confidence in his voice kills me.

I shake my head, turning away.

"For the record, I didn't want it to go down like this. I wish you'd understand that. The best way to save your future is to get you the hell away. Staying on and leaving yourself open to more bullshit, you can't tell me that's a good idea." There's an urgency in his voice that draws me in, forces me to look at him and assess whether I believe him.

Do I?

Yes.

Do I want to?

God, no.

But before he can say anything else—before I let him stomp on what's left of my heart—there's a sharp static crackle from the ship's intercom speaker in the corner.

The noise catches us so off guard we both whip our heads toward it. That's when I notice how much the wind has picked up, battering the giant windows so hard they're almost rattling in their frames.

Then Captain Juan's voice comes through the racket.

"All hands, all hands, this is your captain speaking. The ship has declared a weather emergency. Please listen closely to the following instructions..."

XIX: A LITTLE CRISIS (SHEPHERD)

*T*here's no time to think about broken hearts and sharp words.

The whole conversation collapses as Destiny and I exchange a look and head for the stairs.

By the time we get to the bridge, Juan is standing by the console, grim-faced, his shoulders squared.

A familiar look I've seen in the Marines plenty of times.

Body language is one of the biggest tells, and his stance says more than a thousand words.

Whatever's going on, it's fucking bad.

There's another frantic burst of radio static on his comm system before it cuts out just as fast. Juan tries to reconnect, flicking switches and checking digital readouts, but there's nothing.

No signal. We're cut off.

Fuck.

"What's going on?" I snap.

"There's a nasty storm blowing in, Mr. Foster," he says, every word tight. He's been on the sea since he was a kid; this is his entire life. If he's worried, that's a bad sign. "Coast Guard is advising all craft to get off the open water."

"What else?"

"Damn comm system has been sputtering out for the past half hour. I can't get radio and there's something interfering with our navigation. I sent George down to the engine room and told him to comb through everything. Haven't heard from him for the better part of ten minutes, though."

"Wireless?"

"Also down," he reports. "Haven't gotten a signal on my personal cell either for a couple hours."

Shit.

I glance around, stopping on the digital radar screen that maps the ocean and landscape around us.

We're further out than I realized, having followed the whales away from the nearest islands.

Right now, we're drifting toward the open sea.

"What's the closest port?" I ask.

"Victoria for a ship this size. Almost forty miles away." His dark eyes shift to me and then away.

"It's mostly rain so far. A *lot* of rain, coming down in buckets. Maybe we'll miss the worst of it?" Destiny says cautiously.

She's clearly worried, and though she understands what's going on, she doesn't realize we're in serious trouble. I can't decide if ignorance is a blessing or a curse.

I should have known it was too humid, perfect for kicking up these evening storms that like to plow through maritime traffic like a moose charging down a highway.

Normally, they're no trouble in the modern age. With instant communications sending storm advisories well ahead of time, we should have been docked and out of harm's way.

But without our comms and the engines fucking up, it's a different scenario entirely.

"We can't rely on waiting it out," I say sharply. "You can never tell what might happen when that wind picks up. If they're saying all ships to port, that's all the warning we'll get."

I end it there.

No sense in scaring Destiny even more.

Fuck, I can't believe this.

I checked the weather right before we stepped on the ship. Captain Juan also reads the atmosphere better than most meteorologists, and I'm confident he didn't see it coming.

It shouldn't even be possible for a state-of-the-art ship to wind up trapped in a raging storm like we're back in the days of pirates and schooners.

Yet here we are.

"Just get us near land. San Juan, Vancouver Island, wherever," I tell the captain. "If we can still chart a straight line back to the shore, we should be fine, yes?"

Juan nods curtly. "That's the rub, sir."

"What? Are the engines not working at all?"

His stone-cold silence says everything.

Oh, fuck me.

The worry curled around my heart tightens like a snake.

"George can't figure out the issue. It's not a safety shutoff or anything clogging the system. We're just drifting, maybe a problem with the fuel line," Juan says after a long moment.

For the first time, I notice I can't feel the engines rumbling underneath us.

When did they stop?

Destiny sucks in a sharp breath and moves to the corner, kneeling next to Molly.

I have to grit my teeth, curling my hands into fists so I'm not tempted to hit something.

"Define drifting," I demand, my voice low.

"System won't fire up at all, Mr. Foster. It's like they're all offline. Since George is roughing it out down there alone, I was about to check out the problem myself before the wind picked up."

Lovely.

Juan and Destiny both stare at me like they're waiting for me to pull a magic solution out of the ether.

If we don't have power or fuel to the engines, we're beyond boned. The repair won't be quick and might need to involve getting the right supplies out here.

"Hold on," I say, keeping my voice level. Losing it now won't help anyone. "Okay. We'll head down together and see what's going on. This is a good time to test that fancy autopilot system you talked me into installing last winter."

Captain Juan smiles. "Hell of a time for it, sir, but I think we can trust it for ten minutes. I've played around with it plenty under normal conditions, but this—"

"This is where it shines. If it can't keep us grounded in an emergency, then it's useless." I turn to Destiny. "Dess, I need you to stay on deck."

"What? Here?" The moment I turn and see her face, I know it's not going to be that easy.

Since when did Destiny Lancaster take my word at face value?

If I ever want her to do what I tell her, I need to earn that right.

And I guess I just lost it with the whole breakup speech.

The thought stings like seawater on a cut.

Her jaw works as she meets my gaze, her eyes blazing. She's all fire now, animated by adrenaline and fear.

"You don't just get to tell me what to do while you run off to the rescue," she says, giving me the side-eye.

"This isn't a game, sweetheart."

"Don't 'sweetheart' me. If there's a problem, I'm helping."

"Which you will, right from the bridge. Plus, someone needs to stay with Molly. Just make sure the ship holds its position on the screen. Notify me the second anything changes while we go below deck. The automated system should do the rest." I gesture to the portable radio sitting on the console for the crew, then take her wrist and haul her closer, refusing to let her look away from me. "Listen to me, Destiny. We can argue all you want later, when we're safe. Right now, I need you to *help me*."

Her nostrils flare. The angry glint in her eyes fades as she nods firmly.

Yes, I know this is the world's shittiest timing, being blind-sided by a storm and a major malfunction after she felt like I carved out her heart.

"I don't know what's going on, but this is my yacht. While you're here, you're my responsibility, and I'm damned sure keeping you safe" I tell her, trying to soften my tone, but I'm too aware that every second slipping by could be critical.

Judging by the giant green-red blob on the weather radar screen northwest of us, we haven't seen anything from this storm yet. The worst is yet to come.

If there's one thing we don't have, it's time.

The venom in her gaze cuts me.

"Promise me you'll stay safe, Dess."

"I will. For Molly's sake."

The implication is so obvious it guts me.

She thinks I don't care about her.

"Goddammit," I spit.

No matter what happens next, I can't have her stewing and stressing up here, thinking I'm such a heartless cock it doesn't matter if she lives or dies when the truth is so different.

I care too fucking much.

That's always been the trouble.

"Make me regret this later," I growl.

Before she can ask, I sweep her into my arms and crush my mouth down on hers until I'm stealing the breath from her lungs.

I only linger a second after I break away to make sure she's still standing.

"Stay with Molly. We'll be back ASAP."

She doesn't argue, and I have an odd feeling that's the last good news I'm going to get.

With her eyes still burning my back, confused and hurt and

stunned, I hurry the fuck up after Captain Juan, hoping I'll buy us enough time to kick myself in the ass for that kiss later.

XX: A LITTLE ACCIDENT (DESTINY)

*H*oly hell.

Everything moves at the lightning pace of that kiss, quick and powerful.

I'm still dazed, feeling like the whole world was just pulled out under me like a cheap carpet, all the colors of reality smearing with my emotions as it whips by.

It's the ugliest mess you could imagine.

Too flipping much to process.

I stand motionless on the bridge, trying not to look out the window as I distract Molly with treats. She came along happily after I retrieved her from the other room. She's definitely going to get her body weight in more salmon nuggets the second we're back on land for behaving as well as she is.

I expected a barking, nervous mess. The way she leans against me, stress yawning and too scared to move, almost feels worse.

Also, I'm noticing things I never picked up on before as the rain keeps pounding the ship.

The rumble of the engine is quieter—maybe even nonexistent—and our speed is basically zero if I'm reading those navigation screens right. We're drifting as far as the anchor lets us, rolling on waves that pitch higher every few minutes.

Sweet Jesus.

Dad almost got himself killed in a merciless storm a lot like this years ago, and so did my stepmom, Eliza. He saved her at the last minute.

They were insanely lucky. I'm just worried that the Lancaster gene for good luck in rotten weather skipped right over me.

I'm also really hating my name right now and those crummy jokes about fate.

It's so surreal I feel numb.

My brain still can't handle what that kiss means—if it wasn't just another emotionally-charged mistake intended to shut me up.

And all this after the frigid way he shut me down, the way he tried justifying sending me off into the sunset with more money and a cold goodbye.

That hurt like hell.

What even is my life?

One of the other crewmen comes rushing past, heading for the controls.

My breath is too fast, so I work on slowing it down.

Breathe. Just breathe.

Stay in the moment, they say. But it doesn't help when this is an especially crappy moment following a direct shot to the heart.

What did it all mean? Will I ever get the chance to figure it out?

All the sex, the secrets, the warmth we shared, this crisis gesture with his lips...

I don't know.

I hoped I could feel like this was all bigger than an us that can't possibly last. I wanted to finish out the terms of what I signed up for with Young Influencers, with or without Shepherd Foster.

Now I know I'm fooling myself.

All the charity money in the world raining down on my head can't erase these memories. But they're definitely on hold as Molly whines louder and I hug her, pulling her face into my arms.

"Don't fuss, girl. Get some rest. We'll be just fine. We'll be home before you know it."

I hope.

But Mother Nature doesn't care. The biggest wave yet lurches past, punching the yacht up and down like a toddler tossing around a rubber ducky.

I'm not one for motion sickness, but my stomach twists.

My free hand scrambles around, searching for something to grip, but there's nothing on the floor. Molly and I go sliding against the wall, helpless to prevent it.

Thankfully the impact isn't hard. But what about next time?

God.

My stomach churns like mad.

Sure, let's add some traditional seasickness to the heartsick fever I'm already suffering.

I can hear the younger crewman yelling into the radio and—is that a voice in the static coming back?

Progress, hopefully.

Needing a distraction while I'm stuck here and Shepherd deals with God knows what, I fumble around in my bag until I find my phone.

I'm shocked to see my wireless connection is back—and so is cell service.

There's one missed call from Eliza.

The sight of it almost jolts me with its normalcy, and I stare at the screen with a creeping awareness that I haven't spoken to her or Dad in over a week since he tried to play papa bear.

That's way too long.

...and what if the worst happens in this storm?

Sighing, I hit Eliza's contact, still stroking Molly's fur.

She picks up almost immediately.

"Dess!" she says, always so brightly. Her happiness squeezes my heart.

This is what she's done for my family.

She brought the sun and the stars back into the very dark void Dad lived in. An abyss he only broke out of for brief moments while I was growing up.

She's not my bio mom, no, but I love her just the same.

"Hey, Eliza," I say, trying to make my voice sound as bubbly as hers. Totally not like this might be my last call ever from a sinking ship. "How're you guys doing?"

"So good. I realized it's been a little while since we caught up, and your dad—well, he's been bugging me to call you." It's so everyday, the way she says it. My heart wrenches. "I'm making honey pancakes for dinner. Your little sister needs to learn about the breakfast for dinner tradition when she's young."

"Adorable! I miss your pancakes so much," I say honestly. "And your coffee... what's on the menu at Liza's Love now?"

It's like I can hear her beaming over the phone the second I mention the little café she started.

"Citrusy sunrise brew. We take a single origin Sumatran dark roast and infuse it with dark chocolate and citrus rind. Cole was skeptical as always until he tasted it. Now, he's basically demanding an IV drip."

Somehow, I'm laughing despite the fact that I might never touch land again, but I'm glad. She makes it come too easy.

"Just don't let him steal it for Wired Cup. Some things need to stay with the little indie places," I tell her.

"Oh, yeah. I can't wait to see what you think next time you come around. You've been busy, huh? Don't be a stranger, hon." There's a pause as she speaks to someone else. Dad, maybe. Or Nicole, Elijah?

"Soon," I promise, certain she's probing me about the argument with Dad.

"Tell me about life." Her tone shifts, double confirmation that she's fishing. "I heard about... well, everything. But I'm sure there's another version of the story than Cole's."

I snort into the phone.

"Yeah, I mean, it's been a wild ride. But the worst is over." I say it too quickly, but she doesn't seem to notice.

"I'm sure it was, honey. For the record, I was right behind your father when he offered to go to war with anyone behind that rumor crapfest. It's *messed up*, putting your name out there the way that girl did. Oh, and your mentor..."

My breath stops as I wait for her to say more.

"Are you really okay? That's the one part where I tried to talk Cole down. It's one thing to go after a school of sharks that want to hurt you. But whatever happened, let's just say I know enough about love to realize it's always complicated. And I know you're smart enough to figure it out on your own."

She's. Killing. Me.

She gives me too much credit.

If I were actually smart, I wouldn't be here nursing a torn heart while the man I love tries to save us all from an icy grave, would I?

"I'm fine, Eliza. Really."

I hate lying.

If she hears the quiver in my voice, she doesn't let on.

"That's what I told him. I said you didn't need us fussing over your personal life when you could handle it yourself. But if those stupid Twitter journalists keep coming—"

"We're good that way, I promise. Mr. Foster has lawyers, and he's working overtime to shut it down," I tell her, making sure not to call him Shepherd. "Give it time. They won't know what hit them next week."

There's a loud burst of static from my phone. I check the screen to make sure she's still there until her voice comes floating back.

"Wonderful! I'd expect nothing less from any man you've

been close with. Plus, I'm sure he doesn't want anyone thinking he's messing around with a girl half his age just for favors."

A girl half his age.

Ouch.

Yes, I know there's an age difference. I also know Eliza was similarly burned by an older man once, before she ever met Dad, so maybe that's what she's channeling.

And maybe I should have asked her for advice sooner before I let my heart get the piñata treatment.

"Destiny? Are you there?"

I rub circles on Molly's neck with my fingers. "I'm here, yeah. Sorry, a little static. How are the kidlets?"

"So much trouble. But my heart is overflowing," Eliza says fondly.

She launches into a story of their latest adventure at a theme park in California, but the waves pick up again. Soon I'm fighting too much nausea to listen.

I already know the ending.

Eliza is a great hands-on mother, and I love my little siblings, but right now, Mother Nature won't let me count my blessings.

At least I know my family is good and they're happy.

That's what matters right now, with my heart too cut up over Shepherd and the storm to leave me enough emotional breathing room for anything else.

"Must be windy where you're at! I think I can hear it," she says.

My eyes fill with heat and I steady my breathing, though Eliza probably can't hear it over the rushing wind. The tears are molten as they spill down my cheeks.

Damn it all.

I miss them.

I miss Dad.

I even miss my mom, wishing she'd lived long enough for me to really know her, to see if she'd ever turn into a better person than the bitter mess she was at the sudden, unexpected end of her life.

"Destiny? Am I losing you?" Eliza calls through some static, thankfully oblivious to my tears. "Your dad wants a word before I go, so I'll hand you over."

Oh crap. Crap.

I wipe my cheeks and suck in a shuddering breath.

It's the wind.

That's all, I swear.

I clear my throat like there's a frog trapped in it as he comes on the line.

"Hey, Dess."

"Hi, Dad." My throat closes and I wipe my nose on my sleeve. God, I'm such a mess. "It's good to hear your voice..."

"Are you okay?" he asks immediately. "What's happening?"

"Nothing, nothing. I'm fine. I'm just outside... enjoying the sea."

"Don't bullshit me, girl." That's my father, never one to mince his words. "I know when something's wrong. I can hear it in your voice. You haven't sounded like that since..."

He pauses.

I know what he was going to say.

Since everything went down with him and Eliza and that drama around Mom's death years ago.

"Destiny," he says firmly. "What the hell is going on? Is it the rumors?"

I hold the phone against my ear and take another long, shaking breath, releasing it past my gritted teeth until I can find my voice again.

If I could, I'd tell him everything.

If he could do anything, I'd beg for help, and honestly, he'd probably try. But one death defying rescue in a raging storm is enough for one lifetime.

I'm not putting him through that again.

Plus, Dad has little ones now. If there was even time for him to help us—and there isn't—I'd never forgive myself if anything happened to him.

"It's not the gossip," I say. I'm relieved when my voice doesn't shake and give me away. "That's almost under control. Like I told Eliza, Mr. Foster is taking legal action."

"Damn right he is. If he wasn't, you'd best believe he and I would be having words."

I wince at the thought.

Dad and Shepherd in a room, fighting over me.

They're both grown men cut from the same cloth, and grouchy as sleep-deprived badgers until you know them well enough to see the very different sweetness underneath.

"You don't have to worry," I tell him. "Stand down, okay?"

He hesitates.

"I will, but you know I don't like standing around when it's my daughter's life on fire," he growls. "But what is it then? What else if it's not this?"

"Dad, I—" I stop, trying to find the right words. "It's life stuff, okay? I've been doing a lot of thinking about my future, my career. You know, the hard stuff I need to figure out alone. Same way you did."

"If it's Foster, he'll need a goddamned fleet of drones to stop me from busting his fucking teeth out."

"Dad!" Unable to help myself, I giggle. My eyes burn but the tears dry on my face. "It's really nothing I can't handle."

More static blows up in my ear, and then his voice.

"You're sure?"

"Do I not sound like it? Dude, look who raised me, and you did a pretty awesome job. From teenage brat to national scandal and soon-to-be savior of otterkind." Okay, okay, maybe I am sniffling again. "And... and no matter what happens, you know I respect you to death. You were hard on me because you had to be. I'm glad you were, too. It made me who I am—and you can rest easy knowing your work wasn't for nothing. I'll tell you more later. But Dad, I can handle *this*. Please trust me."

He's quiet for a long second, and I'm scared we lost the connection.

"Sappy shit," he grumbles, but I can tell he's secretly pleased. "Just let me know if there's anything you need, sweetheart. I won't keep you."

"Oh, I will! Thanks and I love ya."

"Don't ever forget how loved you are by all of us here. You haven't stopped by much all summer. We miss you, Dess."

So much for thinking the waterworks were over.

Wiping a few more tears, I press the phone close to my burning face. "I'll come, I'll come. Very soon."

"You'd better," he clips.

I kiss the air as I hang up, and a tiny shred of agony in my chest eases a little.

Taking myself out of the family equation was necessary for too many reasons, but they'll definitely see more of me if I make it out of this alive.

I slip the phone back in my pocket just as the ship pitches and Shepherd bursts in.

He slowly staggers past, grabbing at whatever he can find for support as he makes his way forward.

Ice beads on the back of my neck when I get a good look at him.

Crud.

I've never seen him like this.

He's pale. His eyes are wide and dark and trying like mad to hold it together.

The unexpected sight chills me to the core.

The peace I found calling my family vanishes, replaced by the crackling radio from the comm system again.

It sounds like another storm warning, what I assume are Coast Guard warnings about the dire weather barreling our way.

"Well? What's the verdict?" I ask, dreading the answer.

But I have to know.

His expression is not that of someone who's fixed our problem.

Everything that's happened between us takes a back seat now.

We're in real danger. Shepherd knows it and he isn't trying to hide it anymore.

Maybe he can't, and that scares me more than ever.

I'm on my feet before I know what I'm doing, gripping Molly's leash tightly, crossing over to where he's standing.

"What is it, Shepherd? Tell me," I demand.

But the moaning wind and the punishing wave crashing over us steal my words.

Everything tilts and I start to slide—until he reaches out, using his better traction to keep me from slamming into a bulkhead.

I grip a whining Molly with all my might, holding the leash like a rope while her little nails scrape the deck for support.

It's a solid thirty seconds before we stop tilting.

"We found George down below, knocked out from sliding around and breathing in fumes. The fuel line was cut." He says the words with slow, deadly precision, leaving no room for any misunderstanding.

My heart hammers instantly.

Oh, no.

I *want* to misunderstand.

The fuel line? Cut? As in... someone sabotaged the engines and there's no way to fix them to get us out of this?

But before I can ask anything else, Shepherd pushes the young man at the control aside. "Get the hell below deck now. It's up to the automated system now, since we know it works. We need to take cover."

Then he's got me by the hand, and we're running to the back of the ship as fast as Molly can keep up.

The waves look like slow-moving mountains leering in from the windows.

Insidious and black, glistening in the dense grey hellscape that's going storm-green like someone broke the sun.

You might almost be tempted to think it's beautiful in a terrible, chaotic way. But this is slow, unrelenting death itself and it's heading for us.

I shake my head as we stare at it, not comprehending.

"Holy hell," I mouth. "What now?"

Shepherd tears his gaze away from the sea to look at me. The darkness, the grimness of his face shakes my gut as my heart leaps into my throat.

Dread turns me to stone.

"Shepherd?" I whisper urgently.

"Hold your dog, Dess. It's about to get very fucking choppy. This was no accident," he adds, his voice boiling with rage.

No accident.

We're stranded in a nightmare some lunatic planned.

Suddenly, I think I understand why Meghan sent me that message.

I think she also made our mistake and underestimated Adriana Cerva. The woman wants us dead, and there's a horrible chance she's going to get her way.

XXI: A LITTLE INDECISIVE
(SHEPHERD)

J didn't know it was possible to feel like shit stacked this high.

It's one blow after the next.

First telling Destiny that I wanted her to leave the company, leave my life—

No, wanted is too strong a word.

I didn't fucking *want* it.

It's simply the right thing to do, and I wish she'd understand. Even if the hurt in her eyes is turning me inside out.

What the hell ever.

Emotional torture is the least of our worries and she seems to realize that.

I watch how Destiny pushes her feelings aside, giving small tells that show me just how difficult this is. The way her throat tightens, the nervous sweep of her hand through the husky's fur, the slow, measured breaths that swell her chest.

The three rapid blinks.

Her luscious mouth turning into a thin pale line, robbed of its color.

The way she exhales tells me she's trying to air out her emotions.

Her eyes are still clear, though, and they're the most beautiful thing I've ever seen.

Hell, all of her.

If this storm reaches up and drags us to the bottom of the sea, I'll go down with her on my mind.

And I'm sure it's a one-way trip to hell, knowing my last living act was to cut out her heart and stomp on it like a drunken bull.

"Adriana," she whispers as she looks at me.

"What?"

"That's who's behind this. It has to be her."

I rake a hand through my hair as I process what she's saying. "Adriana Cerva? Meghan's mother? You think she's responsible for the cut line?"

It doesn't add up that a greedy, underhanded clown like her could do something so serious, let alone get aboard unnoticed.

Destiny nods and paces away from me.

The tears are gone, replaced by cold determination and the razor-sharp focus that sets her apart. "I think she was using Meghan as a puppet the whole time. We underestimated her."

"Dess, she hired Mark, who couldn't even find a way into the lab without giving himself away. You really think she'd find someone who could breach my ship's security?"

She frowns. "You saw her, you know how toxic she is. I don't know how, but I'm sure there's a motive, and where there's a will, there's a way. She could've bribed someone again. Crazy, nasty-ass pageant mom. I can't believe it either, that she might get us killed." Her steps quicken as she paces, taking advantage of what seems like a break in the yacht lurching up and down hills of water. "All this over money. That's the sick part."

It dawns on me then.

"Not money, no. The fact that we're about to nail her to the wall with Mark caught red-handed. This is self-preservation." Fuck, I hate that it makes too much sense, even if I don't know *how.* "If it's her, she's prepared to do anything to save her own skin. Just like she was with her daughter's brand."

"Yep. Success has everything to do with money. Her condition for keeping quiet was having Meghan take my place, or a massive payoff from you. And when you found out about Mark and what he did..." She inhales sharply. "Imagine how mad she must've been. Psycho enough to do anything."

I think again about the deflated young influencer sitting at the restaurant table with us.

At the time, I barely registered Meghan. Adriana was always the threat.

But now that I think about it, there was something very wrong with that picture beyond a greedy, overbearing mother. Meghan was hollowed out. Not at all the loud, confident force she is online.

Her mother controlled the situation from the very beginning.

She was the personality, and Meghan was always just a blank slate. A tool Adriana used for success.

The thought makes me sick with fury.

It's my turn to start pacing, all I can do to refrain from hurling my fists at the walls.

"Oh, God. Adriana wants us dead. I should have *listened*," Destiny groans, and there's such certainty in her voice, I find myself believing her now without question.

"Listened? What do you mean?"

Dess looks up miserably.

"As we were getting on the yacht, Meghan messaged me. She begged me not to go, but she wouldn't say what or why." She pulls out her phone and shows me the message.

Meghan never responded.

Maybe her demon mother saw what she'd done and punished her for it.

"She knew," Destiny says. "She knew, and she tried to stop us..."

Fuck.

"If she had someone trash the fuel lines, they must've known the weather, too," I say, angry that I didn't see it sooner.

"Of course. She wanted to make sure they'd get us out of the way. No Shepherd, no Destiny, no lawsuit coming down on her head. The only one left would be Hannah, but with the chaos of you being gone..."

Damn.

"She knew my past," I say, putting it together. "Even if someone figured it out, they'd think it was one of my uncle's henchmen. Some prick from a long time ago who finally got his revenge."

It's too perfect.

"Yeah," Destiny agrees.

There's a growling sound against the sides of the ship as the wind reaches highway speeds again.

Over my radio set to the bridge, I can hear Juan and Peter, the younger man, battening everything down and preparing for the worst.

Her nervous eyes meet mine in the darkness.

There's only Destiny now.

We're balanced on knife's edge, precariously close to losing everything.

All thanks to one rotten asshole's bitterness and meddling.

"She won't get away with this shit," I vow.

Dess shakes her head. "You can't tell me that, Shepherd. Not now."

Not after everything else, she means.

She doesn't say it, but she doesn't need to.

I've fucked this all up for her royally.

For both of us.

After trying to muscle her away against my better judgment, I don't have the stones to take her in my arms and hold her and admit I was wrong.

But now, as her chin comes up and defiance enters her eyes

356

like burning stars, that's all I want. Even if it's the last thing I ever do.

Goddammit, she's too beautiful, and I can't believe I talked myself into throwing her away.

"This isn't the end. I swear on my life," I grind out.

Fresh static bursts from the radio. The comms are struggling again, but Juan keeps working steadily to raise the Coast Guard.

That might be our only chance, a fortified rescue vessel with a helicopter—*if* this storm doesn't capsize us first.

Destiny digs for her phone and I find mine as well, but it's just like I feared.

No signal.

We're totally at the mercy of fate now.

A weird feeling comes over me.

I've seen my fair share of danger before.

No one expects death to sneak up on them without warning.

When I found Serena in bed with Blake and he came charging out with a gun, that was like watching my life flash before my eyes.

The rug being ripped out from under my feet when I least expected it.

The impossible, thinking the woman I adored didn't respect me enough to be faithful while I was overseas, risking life and limb.

This is different.

There are no roadside bombs, no hit men, no reckless lovers with guns. We may never learn who did Adriana's vile bidding to put us in this position.

Still, it feels like the ocean is coming with a vengeance, hungry to swallow me up for all the times I've fought and thwarted it.

I've taken stupid risks in my kayak for the last decade, and I never once forgot what I could lose if my focus cracked or I made a mistake.

The difference is, the only victim would be *me*.

Not her.

Not four other grown men.

Not poor Molly with her snout mushed miserably against Destiny's ribs.

When you go to war, you know there's a risk.

But this was supposed to be a safe evening cruise, dammit. A rare chance to spot some precious whales and do the send-off I thought I could manage.

It turns out, the universe had other plans.

Apparently, so does my fucked up heart.

The room wavers again, and when I can tell we're past the latest swell, I decide to try the radio.

"Juan?" I call. "How's it looking?"

He doesn't answer. The silence glazes my brow with sweat, and I'm expecting the worst until there's a soft banging on the door a minute later.

He emerges, weary and disheveled. I've employed him for years, and he's a neat man. I've never seen him look like he just crawled out of a trench.

"We're almost through the worst of it according to the radar. But the electrical system is strained, sir, and we're going to lose power soon," he tells us.

Destiny holds out her phone. "Do you have a signal?"

He shakes his head. "This is a dead zone sometimes in the best weather. Normally, not a problem with the onboard Wi-Fi forwarding calls, but without power..."

Yeah.

He doesn't need to finish to tell us how screwed we are.

"The system shouldn't be fragile," I snap. "What happened to the backup generators?"

"Not sure yet, sir."

"Fuck," I curse and spin away, looking out at the slashing expanse of waves through the window.

The storm is far from done, and if we've sustained serious

damage already, it could easily put us down before any rescue ships ever locate us.

"I need to go. I'll give you another update in ten. Hold tight, Mr. Foster," Juan says, barking a few more orders to his men as he walks away.

I slam the door shut, then pinch the bridge of my nose and inhale sharply.

Destiny comes to stand beside me, her fingers toying restlessly with something at her collar. When I look across, I see it's the tiny black turtle necklace she always wears.

I'm annoyed that I never bothered to find out why it's so special.

"I hope that thing brings us luck," I say, nodding at it.

Her eyes darken and she gives me a lopsided smile.

"It's more of a memento—and honestly, seeing how the original necklace got stolen years ago and this is a replacement from my stepmom... the turtle might be bad luck."

Well, shit, how comforting.

The look she gives me next is so broken.

I want to sweep her into my arms more than anything. Hell, I'll trade my life for the guarantee she'll make it out of this okay.

But I can't cause more turmoil, more confusion, more pain.

Not now.

I can't even find the words to tell her I love her.

Especially when I've hurt her a whole lot more than losing that necklace did, and that's not something I can just come back from.

In the distance, the sky churns, sending more rain and wind and waves at the ship, though ever so slightly less angry than before.

Why does this feel like a break before it worsens, though?

"So this is it?" Destiny rubs her arms, wearing a determined look. "I guess we just need to grin and hope for the best."

Yeah, fuck.

I guess.

I also want to erase that vulnerable hurting look that's still clouding her eyes. I want to kiss her one more time.

She can try to hide it, but I know why it's there.

I read her body better than my own.

Her hands are balled up, her knuckles white.

Her eyes are empty and scared.

Her breath comes too fast, no matter how much she tries to control it.

Her gaze doesn't settle anywhere for long, bouncing between the oncoming storm out the windows, the heightened wind, and me.

But there's so much determination in the tilt of her chin and the tightness of her brows.

I swear, if it was down to bravery alone, this girl could tame the storm with a single glance. She's that strong.

So is my need to do something incredibly stupid.

Instinct is stronger than staying paralyzed by fear as I grab her, pull her in, and let my heart whisper.

XXII: A LITTLE DIP (DESTINY)

I've felt emotionally confused before, but nothing like this.

The terror in the air is palpable, the atmosphere so thick it's hard to breathe. It's like an invisible wall between us.

But the minute I hear those words, the peril we're in might as well be a bad dream.

"Destiny, I love you."

Four simple words I never expect.

Yet it feels like they're the most meaningful words ever spoken.

The ship groans, rolling with the waves as they intensify.

Everything is gaining intensity, honestly.

Especially the way Shepherd looks at me as he kisses me and pulls away.

He's waiting for me to fall apart.

Honestly, I might.

Fear and love do that, two sides of the same coin.

They sever all the threads holding you together, grounding you, until all you can feel is the impossible, the flighty, the unreal.

His kiss rinses out my mouth.

Fear tastes like blood, gross and metallic, and there's no telling how long it would've sat sour on my tongue without his lips.

But as long as I'm here with Shepherd, still tasting him, I refuse to give in.

Not when he hasn't.

There was a flash of it in his eyes when his gaze locked on mine, but he pushed it aside and took charge the way he always does.

Before I can give him any reply worthy of the shock he's given me, he's moving, gesturing behind him.

"Come on. We can't leave anything heavy sliding around if this storm isn't done with us."

We work together in near silence, taking everything we can from the room and forming a chain of bungees he pulls from a big white storage box, passing them from one hand to the next. Where Shepherd pulls his weight, I'm right there with him.

We fasten down the furniture with oversized straps and ropes.

Juan pops in a few times, helping batten things down with brisk efficiency.

Everything is happening so fast, but it feels like this weird time bubble where the outside world doesn't move at all.

This yacht wasn't designed to be caught in a storm like this. That's what nobody tells you about multimillion-dollar luxury boats.

They're nice toys, elegant and fun to ride, but they're meant to stay out of harm's way when the going gets tough.

This is a pleasure boat. We're supposed to be lounging around boneless, sipping champagne and sampling caviar.

Not running around like hens on fire, securing what we can so we don't get crushed by a flying chair.

And even if we do it perfectly, those floor-to-ceiling windows scare me a little, imagining a hundred ways they could break and send violent water surging in.

But at least the dread speeds me along.

We do what we can while Captain Juan and Peter work the radios and navigation systems, whenever they're not tending to George in the sick bay below deck.

I can feel my heart beating in slow motion as I crouch down next to Molly in the corner. She's curled up in a canine heap, drained from the stress, but very much awake.

It's pounding nails outside again like an ominous rhythm counting down the fading minutes of my life.

I wish I'd been bored enough earlier in my life to look up storm survival at sea.

The wind picks up even more, just when it doesn't seem possible. The yacht pitches and rolls and screeches from the stress, metal and fiberglass and God only knows taking a beating.

Soon, I can hear Captain Juan yelling overhead.

"Almost there, girl. You're being so good. Just a few more hours." It's all I can think to say as I kneel next to Molly, pressing my face into her fur as she stress-yawns.

Her familiar smell comforts me, even if she's a few days overdue for a bath.

My stomach drops into my toes before it leaps up my throat again.

Molly whines, and the sound eats into me.

Stupid, stupid me. If only I'd left her with Lena for this trip...

"Shhh. You'll be okay," I tell her again.

I guess it's a blessing in disguise that she can't smell my lies.

She doesn't need to know there's a chance we won't make it through this.

She'll also never know the heartache of a man who keeps shocking me to my core with *he loves me, he loves me not* words and gestures.

All while we don't know if we'll still be breathing in an hour.

I count my breaths to stay calm, inhaling and exhaling slowly.

There's a sharp curse from somewhere behind me, and I stand up, untying Molly's leash from the wooden column around the wet bar.

Shepherd told me to stay in the observation room, but there's no way I'm going to sit down here on my own while he's out there risking his life.

I can't lose my nerve.

We're not going to die like this if I have anything to say about it.

All we have to do is get through the next few hours.

How much worse can it get?

I amble up the stairs as the yacht pitches and creaks, guiding Molly to the bridge.

It's blacker than ever outside. Not even a hint of sunshine breaking through the chaotic clouds that match the fuming waters.

And the waves... they've gone from stabbing white caps to lashing silver towers.

They toss us up ten feet at a time, the ocean forming mountains that want to swallow us whole.

If we completely capsize, there's no chance of escape.

I know that.

Another blast of wind rattling the windows makes me squeak as I stumble in to where Shepherd stands with Juan.

"What are you doing up here?" His voice is cutting when he speaks.

"Seeing how I can help. You need as many hands as you can get, don't you?"

He moves beside me carefully, widening his stance as we roll again. The nose of the yacht rises up a terrifying amount before we drop down the other side of the wave.

"Destiny." My name sounds so small through the shrieking wind.

"I can't do it. I can't stay down there," I flare. "Not unless you come with me."

"That's not going to happen. I've been doing this longer than you've been alive, and Juan needs all the help he can get."

"Then tell me what I can do. There must be something," I say.

Thunder growls loudly again.

Shepherd curses. Juan is pale-faced and tight-lipped, totally focused on the screen in front of him, system readings that are very—red?

So much red everywhere.

Even I can tell this ship is in serious trouble, more than I thought.

I secure Molly to the nearest crew chair, which is bolted to the floor up here, and give the leash a firm tug. Her eyes are wide and fearful.

"Stay. Let me do some work and we'll be home soon."

The worst part is how faithfully she listens. Even now, when so much is happening and she's clearly terrified, she trusts me to see her through.

If only I had the same confidence.

I comb my fingers through her fur and kiss her nose one more time, telling her she's a good girl. My words are nonsensical, reassuring and empty, filled with real affection and false promises.

But I will myself to believe them.

Molly's tail wags as I loop my arms around her neck.

"At least tell me the plan?" I demand, staring at Shepherd.

"We're pulling anchor since the comms are shot. With any luck, the current should push us toward land. Last Coast Guard vessel that responded was almost an hour out, and it'll never make it in this mess. We need to break out of the storm zone, so we'll steer the yacht as well as we can. We'll meet the waves head-on," Shepherd says.

His steely eyes are narrowed on the view in front of us and the mounting waves like skyscrapers.

How do they keep getting *bigger?*

365

My whole mouth tastes like copper now, and I think I bit my tongue.

Captain Juan slams his hand against the screen in frustration.

"This doesn't make sense, sir. It says we're taking on water in the storage bay, but Peter ran down there and said it was bone-dry. This crap must've fried our sensors. Hard to tell what's going on," he snaps.

Sweat beads down his neck in rivulets.

I dig my fingers into Molly's harness, holding on as I watch them go back and forth about the best course of action like two combat vets planning a raid. The tension between them almost hits breaking point.

And I guess that goes for everyone in this room, too.

It's not just worry lining their faces.

It isn't just concern wrapping hands around their throats with strained words.

The two men in front of me aren't sure what to do, and their uncertainty feeds my fear, potent and commanding.

Shepherd curses again, pounding the wall before he sends me a quick glance and turns his attention back to the instruments.

Screens are flickering now, strobing right along with the overhead lights.

And I realize there's something worse than getting pulled under by the storm.

The very real possibility that this ship might be pitch-black when it gets swallowed up.

Lucky me.

And my luck gets even better three seconds later when the lights blow out.

For the first time, I'm truly paralyzed in the roaring blackness.

I can't even get back to Molly, but somehow, I stumble into Shepherd and grip his arm for support. "Tell me what to do. Please."

"Just hold on to me, sweetheart. That's all you can do now. Hold the fuck on and don't let go."

I can't see the rain out the windows, but the sound, it's everywhere.

A thousand angry hammers pounding on the windows, the cabin, the mess of things strewn around the deck outside.

Endless streaming noise like a waterfall, and that racket means water, so thick and cold and imminent, even if we can't see it.

Oh, God.

There are no working lights on this thing anymore. Somehow, the power loss took out the emergency lights, too.

We're blind, spinning through the waves in almost total darkness.

If it wasn't for his arms wrapped around me, I think I'd pass out from the fear.

But he holds me so gently, stroking my hair, pressing me against his chest until I think I might just escape if I could only melt into him.

"Shit, shit. Destiny—hold on!" He senses the motion a second before I do.

The yacht groans like we're inside a whale as it heaves up higher than ever before.

There's a final blinding flash of light through the glass and we're—

Holy shit!

We're practically vertical.

The wall of water we're climbing blots out what should be lightning and clouds and endless killing rain.

My heart stalls.

I don't even worry about making Shepherd bleed as my nails sink into his skin.

A startled bark erupts just as we start falling, and for a weird second, it's almost like we're floating in zero gravity.

Dear God.

Please be all right, Molly.

Please don't let us die.

Please, please don't let this be the end.

A desperate plea, a prayer for an end that's coming way too fast as I'm tumbling in Shepherd's arms, too dizzy to know if we're still standing on the ground or completely airborne.

I just feel the bone-jarring crash a few seconds later and my vision shorts out.

Everything turns white and then instant black.

* * *

"DESTINY? DESS, WAKE UP!" Shepherd's voice floats down from a mile away, but it only takes a second to become so much closer.

I blink my eyes open as he shakes me.

"Oh, fuck. Thank God." He's holding me while I shake off a numbness that feels like I've been sleeping on my arms and legs for ages.

I blink my eyes awake and sit up in his arms.

"Can you stand? Go slow, lady."

"What happened? Are... are you okay?" There's a dull ache behind my eyes, but I'm grateful I'm still breathing.

"Took a nasty fall. We can't tell if the hull's been breached and we're taking on water."

Yep, here we go.

It wasn't just a terrible nightmare.

"Shepherd, is Molly—"

"She took less of a beating than you. Shit, if I hadn't pulled you aside in time, I don't want to think about it."

I look past to where he's staring and see a dent in the wall. Next to it, there's a heavy chest on its side with equipment spilling out, the bungees that should've secured it broken.

It isn't hard to see I would've been crushed.

"Stay with Molly," he tells me, gesturing to the dog.

She's standing up and looking at me, her tail curled and her ears perked, but mostly she seems relieved I'm on my feet again.

She's not the only one.

I settle in next to her, rubbing a bruise on my leg, while Shepherd goes to work with Captain Juan, who has a nasty new gash across his head.

The instruments are still out, but we've got a few faint emergency lights back.

The men work furiously at the main controls, manual levers and a steering wheel which take their combined strength to turn.

The only thing we have left is pure muscle, forcing the rudder this way and that, steering this thing manually. At least that must mean they were able to pull up the anchor and save us from being stranded out here.

We're still riding hills of waves, smaller now but no less deadly.

I fight to keep my eyes open through the lightning flashing through the windows.

If these are my last moments alive, I want to be present, even if it's just with my dog and the man who saved me.

Waves wash over the side of the yacht. I hope no one ever stepped out, because there's no way they'd survive being washed overboard.

It's raw. Violent. Impossible to believe, considering how the sea was so calm barely an hour ago.

Now, it's a chore to remember what daylight looks like, or how it feels to not be afraid.

I don't want to drown.

I almost regret downplaying everything during the last call to Dad and Eliza, but there was no good reason to have them sharing my misery.

It's all on the line now.

If we go down here, we'll disappear in the ocean. One more mystery lost at sea, a footnote of human interest.

Another wave crashes across the deck, slamming the windows. The silence in the cabin disappears in the growling rush.

Yep. We're climbing another relentless wave taller than most buildings.

Have I mentioned I don't want to drown?

As we crest with Shepherd and Juan fighting, Molly whining, the door to the stairs outside blows open.

Water streams in, so frigid it's like knives sliding across my skin.

Shepherd spares me another glance.

"Hold on tight. We're moving now," he tells me, voice strained and knuckles white from his grip.

"Starboard!" Juan yells, turning the wheel.

The yacht sways like a dazed dragon, groaning in protest, and I'm sure this is going to be it as another wave picks us up like we're a paper plane.

This one feels endless, almost as bad as the last one that knocked me out.

When we reach the top, we're nearly vertical again.

I hug Molly as tight as I can.

I know from the stress building in my stomach what's coming next and I try to brace myself.

Our descent is too swift, too furious, and the ship plunges back into the murky waters like a bad carnival ride.

The impact throws me forward until I lose my grip on poor Molly.

So much water billows in through the open cabin door.

A quick, angry wave grabs me, pulls me, freezes my fingers, dragging me toward the door.

"No, no!"

Before I can finish screaming, we're moving over hills of water again. The ship tilts and the flood that came in starts spilling back out—only this time, it has me by the ankles, and it's taking me with it.

I can't breathe.

I make a strangled, gurgling sound, muffled by water.

Shepherd turns, sees what's happening, and visceral panic crosses his face. He leaps across the room and grabs me, his fingers splayed, grasping, desperate.

He misses.

There's no stopping gravity. Not when I'm careening helplessly toward the open door, the mouth of ocean doom outside.

Then Molly lunges and her teeth snag my jacket sleeve.

She bites down hard enough to bruise.

Yes, enough.

It keeps me from losing my fight against the water.

Everything hurts and I'm winded, but I'm still alive.

Still on board the ship.

Still in this.

I throw up a hand, praying for something to grab on to. My fingernails slide across the smooth surface.

Then another wave roars in through the open door and this time, even Molly's tormented grip isn't enough to save me. I'm all out of chances.

Down.

Down.

Down.

I brace for the worst, pinching my eyes shut while a dark voice laughs in the back of my mind.

Irony of ironies.

Your fear of the ocean was always right, and you didn't listen.

I'm just hoping the final plunge that turns my lungs to ice and rams its way up my nose, my mouth, is quick.

I'm not expecting a hand.

Not a defiant grip, strong fingers digging into my flesh.

Shepherd swings me around so I'm almost out of the water.

We lunge backward, tangled together, hands searching and fingers wrapped around the freezing metal of the bolted chair against the wall.

It's way too late for any dignity.

As the ship bounces and sounds like it's splitting clean in half, I bury my face in his chest, too numb to feel his warmth.

But he's there.

I know he is.

Frozen, miserable, and angrier than the storm itself, but he's there for me.

The thud of his heart matches mine.

Alive, even in the jaws of death.

Still blinking water out of my eyes, I look over his shoulder.

First I see Juan, dead-eyed and staring in disbelief.

Awesome.

There's *another* killer wave charging dead at us.

I'm almost bored of dying at this point.

If we get out of this alive by some miracle, I will never not respect the sea.

Shepherd's swift movement is the only thing that keeps us watching and waiting for the end.

"Hang on to the chair!" he yells hoarsely.

"Wait, where are you—" I never get to finish.

Not before he's bolting for the door that keeps flapping with the wind, the latch broken or jammed. He looks like he's holding up an avalanche as he flattens himself against it, still staring at me.

Holy hell, no.

There's still too much water pooled around my feet, the floor so slick. There's no way he'll have traction if—no, when—the water blows it open again.

"Shepherd!" My scream tears my throat, but he doesn't move.

Then the wave hits and everything goes upside down.

I'm panting and sobbing and fighting but—I don't feel that familiar suffocating flood, do I?

He's actually doing it.

Like some kind of freaky, grumpy superhero, he holds back the deluge.

He saves us yet again.

I don't breathe until the ship stops turning.

The final impact isn't as terrible this time, or maybe I'm just used to being heaved around like I'm in a blender.

Everything goes deathly still.

I have to check to make sure Molly's still there. I swear, if I didn't know any better, she's holding her breath just like we are, waiting for the next wave we can't hold back.

But although we're tossed around for a few more minutes, the next hills of water are kittens after dealing with a lion.

Minutes pass.

Quiet grows.

The ship moves like it isn't about to break apart, and amazingly, there's no sign we're sinking.

I can't stand it anymore.

Flying across the room, I throw my arms around his neck before I know what I'm doing, and he's holding me just as tightly.

I'm sick with adrenaline, my limbs quivering, and he strokes the ropes of wet hair away from my face like he knows.

Of course he does.

"Are you hurt?" he whispers, leaning back and cupping my face, looking at me all over again. "Dess?"

"I'm alive. All thanks to you."

"Don't go soft on me now," he whispers. "We still need to barricade this door before my damn arms fall off." He switches his attention from me, searching for something not tied down or bolted he can use.

Eventually, he finds a long chain that spilled out of the storage chest and sets to work with Juan, wrapping it up tight.

The thunder grows more distant now, and the waves are more like the aftershocks of some tsunami, a shadow of the lethal danger they were.

I watch him the whole time, crossing the room to comfort Molly, trying to allow ample space while she shakes herself dry.

Capable, glorious, caring Shepherd Foster.

Molly whines and I let her lick the salt from my face.

I have no clue if it's from tears or just water. I don't care.

My chest heaves with emotion, more of it tangling up inside me with every passing minute.

We're still breathing, though.

We're alive and well as the darkness churns, an eternity passes, and soon, we're plunged into a calm black night.

XXIII: A LITTLE MIRACLE
(SHEPHERD)

*T*he night is long and frigid and miserable as hell.

Yeah, the worst is over with the storm passing, but it's no cakewalk as we struggle with the comms, checking our phones every few minutes for signals, holding our breath to see if another ship ever shows up to help.

I leave Dess to comfort Molly while Juan and I take turns manhandling the manual controls.

That was too fucking close.

Every time I close my eyes, I still see her being dragged out of that open door.

Almost gone forever.

And I know for certain what would've happened if I'd lost her.

I thought I knew before, but the fear that filled me then, the absolute terror of thinking I was watching her die, confirmed everything.

When the morning light breaks, everyone is exhausted from nothing but brief naps, yawning and rubbing bleary eyes.

We float into the sparkling sunrise, barely alive to tell the tale.

But we *are* alive.

Despite the odds, we made it.

Destiny unhooks her arms from the sleeping husky in her lap. Her eyes are wide and tired and she looks stiff, her wet clothes mostly dried into a clammy dampness if they're anything like mine.

Yeah, fuck.

One glance from her is all it takes.

I can't go on pretending this is something I can just quit the second we're on land.

Her gaze drifts from me to the window and she smiles.

There's a magnificent sunrise inching over the horizon.

Beautiful, sure, but after today, the sea will never hold the same magic for me that it used to.

"Any idea where we are?" she asks roughly.

We haven't spoken for hours, too drained and distracted, running on pure instinct.

As the storm faded and we drifted through the night, we had to keep working.

Juan glances between us and excuses himself, eager to check in with his crew.

We haven't seen Peter for over an hour, and with George laid up in sick bay, I hope they're both okay, along with the other guys.

But Dess is still here, staring, waiting for my answer.

"I don't know," I tell her, wishing I had a better one to give. "No land in sight. We really need GPS to have any clue."

She nods glumly and slumps back in her seat.

Bruises bloom across her arms and there's a big one on her cheek, no doubt from the sea flinging her around like a doll.

I'm aching, too. Battered. Hurt all over.

But I can't feel my own pain whenever I look at her.

There's just this soaring relief that she's alive, and fury at the soon-to-be destroyed motherfuckers who tried to kill her with their games.

"Sorry, Mol," she says, unfastening the dog's leash.

Molly sits up and yawns, wagging her tail like it's just another morning. Or maybe the husky knows how close we came to never seeing another sunrise again.

Fuck, I almost watched them die.

I thought if I survived this, I'd have to go about life knowing she wasn't in it, and the thought slayed me.

Now, I know.

I'm certain I'd rather die a thousand times than risk anything like that again, and she needs to know it.

"Destiny."

Her head jerks up and her eyes find mine. Her lips are swollen from the salt.

"Shepherd."

I take her hand and pull her up.

Instead of pulling away like I expect, she clings to me, her palms skimming over my arms, my chest, my back.

She's checking to see if I'm all right, or maybe if I'm real flesh instead of a hallucination.

"Hey, hey." I cup her face in my hands, marveling at how beautiful her eyes are in the dawn.

That green I haven't seen in ages is back, shining through the blue.

Barely two months.

That's how long we've known each other.

Does it matter?

Fuck no.

In that short time, she's hooked her way under my skin and in my heart and there's nothing I can do about it except man the fuck up and accept it.

You don't keep playing games after staring the reaper dead in the face.

And I try, even as she's swiping at her eyes.

"Sweetheart, don't cry."

She shakes her head. "Don't. Don't call me sweetheart unless..."

"Destiny—"

"I remember what you said, Shepherd. When the storm hit, I get it, that was the least of our worries. But now that it's over... I can't. I can't be nothing to you."

"I know. Fuck, you'll never know how much I understand."

"Then what am I?" She looks up at me, tears dousing the sparkle in her eyes. "Before all this happened, you told me you wanted me to leave Home Shepherd. You thought we should never see each other again. What changed?"

I hesitate, but I can't hold back the growl boiling up my throat.

"Almost losing you." I drop my forehead against hers. "Destiny, goddammit. I almost watched you slide out that door. It fucking murdered me."

Now, I'm the asshole who's trembling in her arms.

She steps back, searching my eyes, still in my embrace. Just far enough away so she can see my face.

So she can read the emotion there, the sincerity.

Can't she see I'm offering her all of me?

Everything.

Because that's all she'll be to me.

It's too late to go back now and carry on with denials. This lie that we could ever walk away, that what we have needs a time limit because we're too wrong for each other.

I'm officially done trying to bullshit myself into believing it.

"I love you," I say. Full stop. "Dess, I fell so damn hard, so fast. When I think about how quick it's been, I still don't understand it. I never will, and I'm okay with that. No one's done what you did to me, woman. I'd rather drown forever than ever let you go."

"Don't say it unless you mean it."

"I mean it, sweetheart. Just didn't want to accept it before."

"Shepherd." She takes a shaking breath and a tear tracks down her face.

I brush it away, hating myself for being the reason behind it.

I never want her to cry again. Especially not because of me.

"This is real," I tell her. "I can't go another minute without telling you."

Her eyes glisten and her lips quiver.

"I never should have thought about letting you go in the first place. Never should have thought it'd protect you." It's pouring out like venom from a wound. The most honest words I've ever spoken, wrenched from my chest. "The best way for me to protect you was always to stay with you. I know that now."

If I let her go, there's always another door, another flood that might take her away even if it's not literal.

How could I let that happen after this?

If she'll have me, I'll make sure nothing ever harms her again.

And I'm going to bring the full weight of justice down on Adriana Cerva until she's flatter than a crêpe.

If she'd only fucked with me, that would be one thing. She isn't the first and she won't be the last.

But she dragged Destiny into this, and if it wasn't for me, she'd be dead.

If it wasn't for me, she wouldn't have stepped on this damn boat to begin with, and none of this would have happened.

Now, I know there's no safer place for her than right by my side, where I can protect her.

"I don't need an answer now. You've been through a hell of a lot," I say, touching her face. "Still. I had to tell you right the fuck now."

"O-okay." The beginnings of a smile touch her face.

"Okay?"

"Okay," she repeats, leaning up to kiss me.

It's all I need.

Her lips taste like salt, tangy and wild. At first, her mouth is gentle, asking a question I can only answer with assurances.

Yes.

Yes.

Fucking hell, yes.

The kiss changes, charged with energy that crackles across our skin. I put everything I can't say into the kiss, telling her how glad I am that she's alive.

How much I want her.

How much I need her.

This is only the kind of kiss you get after a near-death experience.

It's electric, heart-torn, messy and biting and hands down, the best ever.

Her lips take my entire soul.

When I break away to breathe again, I'm actually dizzy.

Too spent and exhausted for words.

There's just Destiny Lancaster and her arms, her small hands on my face, her mouth on mine.

We both gasp for air at the same time, and I still want to kiss her again.

Again.

I'm a shameless addict.

A convert to her love.

I'll worship her for the rest of her life, if I can be a part of it.

And I know—I know what this means. This feeling, so vast and intense, tears me apart.

Her hands are in my hair. My hands are on her waist, her back.

Yeah, I'll never recover from this.

I might spend the rest of my life craving her, and I don't even care.

I'd keep kissing her until one of us passes out, too, if it isn't for the interruption.

Radio static.

The Coast Guard.

Canadian Coast Guard.

I lunge for it. "This is Shepherd Foster, owner of this vessel. Can you see us on radar? What's our location? Over."

There's a rustle, maybe the sound of surprise and the man speaks again, giving us the exact location. We've drifted so far we're just off the coast of British Columbia, not in US waters anymore.

I take a second to look out the salt-splattered windows.

There's nothing to see but water and a small fishing vessel to our right, just a dot on the horizon.

Destiny has her hand over her mouth, just as shocked as I am.

"We're stranded. Our ship was damaged from the storm," I say, keeping my eyes on her. I never want to stop looking at her now. "How soon can you assist? Over."

"Affirmative," a voice comes back. "Stay put and we'll send someone out for you as soon as possible. Over."

Help is on its way.

Fucking finally.

I hold out my hand to Destiny as she presses against me, her body so warm.

I rest my chin against her.

Molly, just as exhausted, snuggles against our legs.

Dess laughs, light and free as I kiss her head.

When Molly stands up and mushes her leathery nose against my cheek, I kiss her, too.

The relief is too real, humming in my veins like blood after a hard run.

We're alive.

We're together.

We have time.

Mostly, we have a chance to sort out what the hell we're truly meant to be.

* * *

IT TAKES the better part of the day to get us back to Seattle, and it's evening by the time the plane from Vancouver lands.

I take Destiny and Molly back to my place without asking.

No discussion, no argument, no emotional firestorm over what this means. We're all just too soul-drained to care.

We fall down in my bed together the instant we're through the door.

My gut rolls with phantom motion, still feeling like we're trapped in that storm.

Dess has the same far-off look in her eyes.

I run my fingers through her hair, and she digs hers under the hem of my t-shirt so we're skin to skin. We allow ourselves this bliss, this peace, for what feels like hours and it's still not nearly long enough.

Molly sleeps in a grumbling heap of long legs and fur at the end of the bed.

Goddamn.

I never thought I'd have them here again—especially not like this—but I couldn't bear it if she left me now.

"What do we do next?" she whispers in the darkness.

"We belt Adriana with everything we've got. One good sleep and I'll be ready," I tell her.

We sleep with that thought hanging over us, my legal machinery already moving in the background.

The lawyers will go to war without me lifting a finger, but it doesn't feel like enough.

Leaving a woman who tried to murder us to a mundane arrest warrant and years behind bars doesn't begin to touch the hell she put us through.

Of course, I don't want an open confrontation. Not until I'm positive Dess has fully recovered from her ordeal.

It's two more slow days staying in, making phone calls, and listening to the softly pattering rain like whispers from another world before we talk through our decision.

* * *

We set off in the morning and arrive at Adriana Cerva's townhome just outside Medina.

It's the typical plush, upper middle crust sort of dwelling you'd expect. A fitting space for someone who's done well, but never well enough when there's an endless appetite for Chanel and Prada and regular trips to warm beaches.

No doubt it's all from her daughter's mudslinging, and it's predictably tacky as hell. Her entire moral compass is based on its price tag, and I imagine it extends to her daughter, too.

Meghan is only valuable as long as she makes money for mama—and lots of it.

Fuck, if only I'd noticed how off things felt at the restaurant.

There's so much I should have done differently.

Still, the stakes are too high today to dwell on the past.

Destiny slips her arm through mine.

We've had a few difficult conversations, but they've all revolved around the immediate future. What's going to happen with Adriana, how we'll prevent my attorneys from having cardiac arrest when they find out what we're doing, what we'll tell the cops.

Honestly, I'm giving fewer fucks about Adriana's fate by the minute. I can't wait until this is over so we can talk about the future.

"Ready?" she asks in the back of the limo.

"It's all I've thought about since we came home," I say, helping her out of the vehicle.

Except the knowing look we share says that isn't true.

Destiny has taken up infinitely more real estate in my mind than revenge, no matter how well deserved.

We thought about calling ahead, but the last thing we wanted was to give her a chance to prepare, let alone run.

Destiny also talked me into letting her come along for the

ride. If I'd had my way, she'd never go near the woman again, but she insisted this was the only way to do it our way, and not just mine.

A few more steps, and here we are.

Dess reaches into her coat pocket and pulls out her phone to reassure herself it's there while I rap on the door.

When Adriana opens it, her mouth pops open with a wet smacking sound.

She's wearing purple blush lipstick and a black blouse that's unbuttoned just enough to show a little overtanned cleavage.

Got to keep up appearances, I suppose, even in the privacy of her own home.

The color drains from her face and she moves to block the doorway.

"Oh, no. Foster, I—"

She never finishes before I storm into a picture-perfect living room that looks like a model showroom, spotless and modern.

"I didn't say you could come in! What do you think you're doing?" She spits, finally recovering enough to yell at us as we head for the open kitchen.

She follows, her heels clopping against the polished wood. Her hand strays to her phone.

"Leave now or I'm calling the police. I didn't invite you in."

"Call them anytime. The conversation should be riveting." I throw her my coldest stare.

Her face clouds with uncertainty, and she's too paralyzed to move.

I give her a tight smile, mindful of the woman on my arm.

For Destiny's sake, I promised I wouldn't lose my temper. It takes searching every molecule I am to stay indifferent.

"Why are you here?" Adriana huffs out.

"I thought about coming in a sheet. I figured we could show up as ghosts," I say slowly. "However, since you never got the news you were hoping for about a sunken yacht tragedy, it wouldn't have the same effect."

"Sunken yach—oh. Oh, no. You're being ridiculous," she says weakly, her face rippling with shock.

Destiny tilts her head as I cast her a long look.

What's next is all hers.

And hell, I'm not going to stop her. She deserves her moment in the sun.

"Adriana," she says, and the other woman stops glaring at me just long enough to look at her. "You must have been so scared when you got the news. I'm sure you've been expecting cops any day."

Adriana cranes her head like a snake, fighting back her nerves.

"I really don't know what you're talking about. I don't have time for games," she says stiffly.

"Oh, really? That's funny. I have to make time for a new game every night, where I hold my dog when she wakes up howling, traumatized from almost being drowned." Destiny frees her hand from my arm and stalks over to the large table, trailing her nails along the black metal and glass.

I'd bet anything it isn't used for eating. Just business plans and posing Meghan like a doll for pretty pictures.

My anger returns, thinking about Molly, though I keep it in check.

The husky started howling twice a night the next day after we got home. Her vet tech friend thinks it's a sort of PTSD, and we're doing everything we can to help.

I was up with Dess at three o'clock, walking Molly outside for a quick game of tug and a frozen banana ball in the moon-light, before we helped her back into bed and waited for her to fall asleep under a blanket.

Personally, I'm only offended by almost dying.

But the fact that the world-class bitch staring at us tried to send Dess and Molly to an icy unmarked grave...

I take the seat opposite her, gesturing for Adriana to sit down before I say, "Cutting the fuel line. That was fucking low, especially for someone like you. Couldn't you have at least had the dignity to put a little poison in our dinner?"

Adriana's chest heaves. She shakes her head violently.

"No, no, you've got it all wrong. Jesus, I—"

"Yep. No class whatsoever. Where'd you find the guy who slashed the fuel line, I wonder? Was he sleeping in the dumpster behind your favorite dive?" Destiny's gaze cuts up and down Adriana's figure with sweeping derision.

The older woman regains her composure, just enough to flash us a sickening smile. "What would someone like *you* know about class anyway?"

"Have you met Cole Lancaster?" I ask, raising an eyebrow. "I had the pleasure the other day. We had words. More importantly, he doesn't take too kindly to anyone who tries to murder his daughter with a technique right out of a cheap slasher film."

"Oh, yes," she flings back. "I'm sure he's thrilled at what his daughter's been up to."

Destiny doesn't flinch.

"He called me on the ship. Dad wanted to know what was going on, but I told him we were fine, in case you were wondering. I'm not the kind of girl who runs off asking my parents to bail me out. I like to take matters into my own hands."

Shit, she's on fire.

I don't need to add anything.

I barely knew about the call home she had on the boat.

That's not going to be a comfortable conversation when we get down to it, after all of this is over.

Cole Lancaster threatened to tear my throat out with his bare teeth twice, and I don't blame him. I'd like to think the fact that I brought Destiny home in one piece won some reprieve.

Mr. Lancaster is famous for his temper, and right now, I'm second place in the firing line.

I'll worry about the fireworks with him later.

Still facing Adriana, Destiny doesn't back down. Her blue eyes are sharper than swords. There's no green in them, no softness with her today.

She's thinking about Molly.

A part of me enjoys seeing her righteous anger unleashed. She's a little cherry bomb, deceptively small and bright yet so deadly.

Is it wrong to say it turns me on?

"You know what the worst part is?" Dess asks. "If you hadn't cut corners using a desperate kid from the docks and you'd found someone who was just a teensy weensy bit more careful at covering his tracks, we might have never known. You might've been able to claim it was all a freak accident," Destiny says. "Oh, but then there's Meghan."

Adriana's brows rise, waiting.

"Your lovely daughter sent me a message just before we boarded the yacht, telling me not to. Weird how she knew our plans. Even weirder that she told me not to go with Shepherd right before we got into a really ugly storm..."

Adriana scowls.

She backs up a step like Dess just slapped her across the face.

"What do you want?" she snaps. "If it's a retraction, fine. I'm convinced. I'll have Meghan work night and day to scrub away every trace of your little scandal. I'll... I'll even pay damages. A reasonable sum we can agree on, I'm sure."

Poor, devious little witch.

It should be more enjoyable, watching her squirm as it sinks in just how fucked she is.

I've met people like Adriana Cerva before. They were as common as crows in Uncle Aidan's world. Cold-blooded, ruthless, dangerous when cornered, always willing to draw blood to shut you up.

Only, unlike my uncle's soldiers, I'm positive she didn't think far enough through the consequences of her actions.

That's natural when you've never had to face any karma before. Until now, she's gotten away with all the shit she's pulled.

She still thinks she can bargain her way out of this.

Best of all, she still thinks it's about fucking money.

I touch Destiny's leg under the table, just to reassure her.

Let's bring this home.

Together.

Her foot nudges mine, and I keep my face expressionless as I stare at Adriana.

Her throat works, but she can't quite clear it.

Her voice comes out gravelly and broken when she says "Jesus, what do you people want? Tell me!"

"Confess," I bite off like a gunshot.

Again, she shakes her head like it's falling off, unable to even process what I'm asking.

"Confess *what?* I didn't do anything!" she snarls.

"Meghan sent me a message," Destiny tells her. "The kid you hired to cut the fuel line confessed everything yesterday. We know he came aboard to load food and beverages. We already have the written statement, so you can quit pretending."

Adriana breathes raggedly through her nose. "That... that doesn't prove anything."

Why do they always do this? Deny?

She's cracking up like a thawing lake.

I can see the fear snapping in her eyes, the panicked way she looks around the room like she's searching for an escape.

Destiny senses it, too, as she grabs her phone and sets it neatly on the table, tapping at the screen to open the recording app.

"A verbal confession. That's all we're looking for, Adriana," she tells her. "Let it go easy and we'll get right out of your hair."

Adriana's face twists like she's possessed.

I stiffen in my chair, ready to throw Destiny out of harm's way the second Miss Cerva looks like she's about to go full stupid.

The woman takes a deep breath and steps forward, her eyes glinting as she looks over her shoulder at a rack of knives.

Just then, the door flies open.

What fucking timing.

Meghan Cerva stands there with her red hair gnarled, dressed in a threadbare pajama top and shorts that expose her midriff, looking younger and more bird-thin than ever.

Her eyes, the same color as her mom's, are even wilder.

They're haloed by red, deeply etched tear tracks.

Dess pushes her chair back as Meghan glares at us, right before her gaze falls on her mother.

"Mom, stop. Stop lying!" Her voice breaks on the force of that word. "Tell them. Just fucking *admit it*. They have everything and even if they don't, I'll... I'll give them the rest if you won't. I hate that I ever went along with it, but it's over. You're done now."

"Meghan, Meghan, you're still sick, aren't you?" Adriana's harsh laugh sounds like it scrapes through a cheese grater. "Go back to your room."

"Not this time, Mom." Meghan shakes her head, splattering tears on the floor.

When Destiny approaches her, she backs away, throwing her hands out, her eyes still leveled on her mother.

"You're going to listen to what I've got to say for once. You tried to *kill* them."

Adriana storms toward Meghan so forcefully I'm under a second away from throwing myself between them.

"You're such a little mess when you're off your meds, dear. Go back to bed. This doesn't involve you." Adriana flattens her hand against her daughter's forehead like she's feeling for a fever.

Meghan swats her hand away.

"Shut up. Shut. Up! I know what you did and you—you can't lie to me again. There's no way out of this." Meghan turns to Dess, who's standing right behind her, so much sorrow in her eyes. "Mom engineered the whole campaign. She was livid when I got passed up for Young Influencers, and she launched this gross pressure scheme. She coached every video. She wrote the scripts. But I did her bidding and I feel so much ick. I can't do it anymore. I won't. If they want a statement, they've got mine."

"Ignore her!" Adriana screeches, pulling at her bleached hair.

Goddamn, what a mess.

I grab my phone and punch a single contact covertly under the table, still ready to step in at a moment's notice if this boils over.

"When that guy she got to steal the drone blew it, she panicked. She sabotaged the boat to cover her tracks. I swear, I didn't know she planned anything that awful. Whatever she had coming, I knew it wasn't good, but oh my God..."

Meghan almost doubles over now with grief, reaching for Destiny.

Like the perfect angel, Dess takes her hands, holding her up.

"There's plenty of time to sort this out, Meghan. Don't worry. It's okay, it's okay..."

"Get away from my daughter now," Adriana whispers, contorting into the perfect narcissist.

I only have a split second before she launches herself at them.

Fuck, she's unhinged, her hair whipping around her face.

I push back from the table, roaring Destiny's name.

She twists her head, sees Adriana moving, and spreads herself protectively in front of Meghan.

The girl is in pieces, screaming and sobbing incoherently.

I knew there was a real chance this could be a total shit show, but I never imagined this.

It's like time slows, and my brain does the math.

It knows before I do that I'm not going to beat the rampaging demon.

Not before Adriana grabs Destiny by the hair, tearing her away from Meghan. Her other hand crashes down in a slap that echoes.

That fucking does it.

I'm human lightning, bolting in, crashing into Adriana so hard she spins across the room.

After today, I'd like to think she'll eventually thank her lucky stars that I don't pick her up again and chuck her across the room like a piece of rotten driftwood.

Meghan screams, covering her cheek. It's already red, the fingermarks distinct even in the scuffle.

Adriana struggles as I twist her arm behind her back, pushing until it hurts.

It's like holding a rabid fisher-cat.

"Dess," I say urgently. "Sweetheart, are you all right?"

Adriana's laugh is high and half-insane. "Sweetheart? I fucking *knew* it."

I ignore her shit.

"I'm fine," Destiny says quietly, freeing herself.

My attention shifts to the swaying lunatic in my arms.

"You just had to add assault and battery to your charges, didn't you?" I tell her.

Just in time.

Thankfully, I don't have to bother figuring out how to secure her when the door bursts open and Seattle police start piling in. My call worked.

Ideally, I wanted the confession first, though we guessed we had a fifty-fifty chance at best of her caving.

We didn't expect this fray.

Not that it matters.

After today, we have everything we need to make sure Adriana Cerva enjoys a nice long stay behind bars.

I release Adriana as soon as the cops surround us.

She points at me, her mouth twisted, living proof that some people just don't know when to shut it. "He assaulted me! Attacking me and my daughter..."

Meghan jumps up and goes into a flurry of denial, giving them a quick, messy version of everything that happened.

With Adriana cornered, we can finally breathe again.

"I think that's a wrap," Dess says happily, making a face as she fingers a few torn ends of her hair.

A detective with a craggy face nods at me, then gestures at Adriana. The two cops accompanying him pin her arms behind her back.

"You have the right to remain silent," he begins, rattling off her Miranda rights. "Anything you say can be used against you in a court of law..."

"I didn't do it!" Adriana shrieks again as they try to pull her. The woman's voice could shatter glass. "I'm being framed. It wasn't me, I swear, I never did *anything*. Help me, help!"

Stoically, the cop continues reading her rights before dragging her away.

A female officer remains with Meghan, kneeling beside her. She declines a check from EMTs, but they'll need to get that cheek photographed.

I wish I could say it's a happy ending, nice and neat.

For Meghan Cerva, it's only the beginning.

She'll need a lot of help, gobs of soul-searching, and a metric fuckton of therapy to rebuild her life.

Still, with her mother out of the picture, she's finally free.

Destiny moves closer, and I wrap my arms around her out of habit.

"Will she be okay? Is there anything we can do?" she murmurs, looking at Meghan. Her sobs have finally quieted.

"I think so. We'll let her tell the cops if she has any friends or family she can stay with. If she doesn't, I'll put her up somewhere safe."

"God, Shepherd." Dess shudders against me and I hold her tighter. "Even after all the horrible crap, I didn't think she'd go psycho on her own daughter."

"She tried to kill us over a damn contest gone bad," I remind her. "Psycho is an understatement."

"But the storm was kind of dumb luck. Do you really think she meant to kill us or just send a message?"

I smile because we've gone back and forth over the same question for days.

That's my Dess, always thoughtful, even when some wackjob tries to off us.

"She certainly wouldn't have minded if we never made it home." I pause, lowering my voice so Meghan doesn't hear. "Frankly, I don't think she gave a fuck what happened as long as we were out of the way."

When she looks up at me, there's a gleam of pity in her eyes.

"I can't believe I just thought Meghan was snarky and obnoxious all these years. Her own mother... Poor thing."

I hold Dess closer as we watch an officer escort Meghan out of the apartment.

She's so quiet now, but with the glossy, hurt eyes of someone who hasn't processed their life changing in an instant.

"Here," Destiny says, handing another officer her phone. He bags it and thanks her, telling her he'll get it back to her as soon as possible.

We travel to the police station to give our statements, and then we're free to go.

Adriana Cerva now faces a litany of charges ranging from assault, extortion, criminal stalking, attempted homicide, high seas terrorism, and intent to commit fraud.

As for Meghan, I already know Dess will be a friend wherever she can.

When we get back to my place—no question asked, we came back here—she looks at me. It feels like I haven't slept in weeks.

After Molly comes flying over and we make it through a hundred mandatory licks and paw prints, we settle in on the sofa.

"So, now that *that's* over." The sound of her uncertainty lingers in the air.

I know the feeling.

Our future is still written on blown glass, and if we're not careful, we could shatter it, but I want that future more than anything.

"It's over," I repeat, pulling her into my arms.

I kiss her nose first, memorizing every single one of her freckles that make her uniquely Destiny.

To hell with the age gap, she's so young and fresh and light.

To think she'd even want to be with a man like me feels like living a miracle.

And if I'm lucky, I'll worship that miracle every day she allows it.

"It doesn't seem real. None of it." She looks up at me. Blue-green eyes, that perfect shade of ocean glass. Freckles. Full lips. Gold hair. I could look at her face forever. "But what do we do now?"

"The future, Miss Destiny."

"Together?"

"Is there any other way?" I'm screwing with her, but I hide the nerves behind my question.

The tiniest hint of a smile curls the corner of her mouth. "After everything we went through... yes, Shepherd. I think we'd better do the rest together."

I grin like a deranged fool.

"There's something I need to tell you. I meant to find the perfect place—actually, I haven't known you long enough to plan it properly, and I want to do right by you, but..."

Fucking hell.

Why am I tripping over my own words?

There's nothing as right as having her in my arms.

"I know." She smiles and leans up to kiss me.

The feel of her lips on mine is an explosion, glowing with pure bliss.

"I love you, Destiny Lancaster. You've heard it before, but it's important I say it when we're alive and well," I say against her mouth. "Love you, woman. So much I can't remember life before I did."

"I know, I know," she whispers sweetly, pulling back to give me a teasing grin and eyes shining with relief.

Yeah, fuck me, there's nothing I wouldn't do for this woman.

No pain too great.

No burden too heavy.

No mountain unturned.

It's not just her body or her mind.

She's more than walking sunshine and a giving soul.

Like me, she's suffered, and she knows what to do with it. She'll feed that energy into fixing the world, and she has the passion to do it, too.

I just want to be by her side while her dreams come true, piece by blazing piece.

Maybe, in time, those dreams will merge with mine.

Her lids lower as she watches me.

Sexy, yes, but so intense it burns me to my core.

My heart doesn't know what to do with this look.

I just know I feel every booming thud bone-deep every second she looks at me.

Hot intent scorches her eyes, dousing me in flames.

I've never doubted her, even when I had my head stuffed up my own ass, thinking she was too young and pure.

Now I know better.

Before she says the words, *I know.*

"I love you, too," she tells me. The best fucking words I've ever heard, whispered in a voice like music. "So much it hurts."

"It won't hurt anymore, sweetheart. Never again."

Her smile is so beautiful it almost breaks me as I stroke her hair.

Honest to God, I'm floating and I don't care.

That's what falling does.

Especially when love takes you down so hard you can't tell where the sky meets the ground anymore.

We've been through so much in one summer.

I reacted like I was allergic to her very presence, attacked her like a creature of pure lust, learned to appreciate her quirky names for cars and otter obsessions, and almost watched her die.

She's scared me shitless many times.

And yet, this moment right here, this is what kills me.

It doesn't feel real.

Like any second, some catastrophe might come along and steal her away.

I'm not taking any chances.

I'm making her mine, here and now.

Day one of eternity where I hang up my life as a corporate monk and make time for a new life with her.

"You know I can't promise what's going to happen from here," I say slowly. "But I'm going to do my damnedest to protect you. Don't care if that means tromping around in the rain after otters or digging a foxhole while your old man tries to blow my head off. I promise you'll always have all of me, Dess."

"Shepherd... are you trying to kill me today?" Her voice cracks.

"No. I'm trying to find a way to make it work. It's all I'll ever ask for."

Her hands skim my face, touching my scar.

She feels it sometimes. Kisses it, too.

She just has this way of looking at me like I'm flawless, just as untouched by violence and bad decisions as her, even when I know she's what holds me together.

I'm a rusty fucking hammer in a princess' hand, and I love it.

I love her.

So fully and completely and overwhelmingly it's blinding.

"You're stuck with me now, so we'd better make it work," she tells me.

Damn her, I laugh.

That's my Dess, all sweetness and spice.

I love the little slice of crazy she is, even if I wonder if I'll ever get used to the weight of those words.

I *definitely* won't get used to hearing her say them back.

With too much said and not enough kisses, I shove her fingers through mine and we head upstairs to the bedroom.

Molly twirls around in giddy circles around us before she settles on her dog bed in the corner.

The future I never imagined has only begun.

XXIV: A LITTLE SECRET (DESTINY)

Okay, so it's probably pretty cheesy to say I've never been happier in my life.

There were always little pockets of happiness before. Moments I remember. Times I'll never forget.

But with Shepherd, it's different.

With him, all my smiles are condensed into one long beautiful moment.

Maybe because I'm an active participant in my own joy this time around.

Because this is the happiness I've chosen.

Every day I wake up and choose Shepherd Foster over and over again, and he's standing by with a thousand reasons why.

He makes my breakfast in the morning while I make his coffee.

We go for power runs on the beach with Molly. She nibbles at his shoes if we leave her next to his feet for too long, and he always just has a kind word and the sweetest chuckle.

He even helps with her training, drilling her through command routines with a tug rope in his hand or a pile of smelly salmon treats in his pocket.

That's definitely love.

I love my dog, but some of her snacks will send your gag reflex into overdrive.

Who knew stinky fish pellets could make a girl's heart flip?

Every time I think I love him to my limit, I find out I'm flat-out wrong.

And my heart grows a little bigger, lost in the good times with my boyfriend and Molly, the dog runs and home-cooked dinners and three-hour ecstasies in bed that take me on a tour through every tier of heaven and send me gliding back home to his arms.

Holy hell.

My boyfriend.

I'm still getting used to that.

Once we wrap up all the police interviews and Adriana gets formally charged with the world's creepiest mugshot, Shepherd surprises me with a trip to Hawaii.

My family's place is in Kona on the Big Island, so it's nice to bum around Maui instead. We go diving and snorkeling, then we enjoy a sunset picnic on top of Mount Haleakalā.

When I post snippets of my new life for my fans—which have exploded since the truth about our little near-disaster came out—I don't hide anything.

I just wish Shepherd was a little less scowly when I drag him into a few shots.

What can I say, he's man candy for my lady followers. I also don't mind showing the whole world he's mine.

I deserve *one* indulgence after everything we've been through.

And I get one more when Shepherd practically drags me onto the ferry to Lanai one day for a sunset dinner overlooking a beach bursting with sea turtles.

"They've been an important part of your life," he explains, reaching over to gently finger my turtle necklace. "If I've got to share you with anything that has a shell, I'll damn well make sure you're spending time with both of us."

"You're jealous of my turtles? Really?"

One look at his gruff face leaves me in stitches.

And there's a lot more laughing and a few more tears as we flop down on a hill with a blanket, watching the turtles lounging under the stars, and I share everything.

I tell him how the necklace was the only thing I had left of my mom, and when the original was stolen, my stepmom jumped in to find a replacement that was just as meaningful.

You can't hold on to material symbols, no matter how rare or special they are.

That's how I learned it's the meaning behind them that lasts, the memories and feelings and soul.

And even if he doesn't know it, he's giving me a thousand more as I rest my head on his shoulder, watching the turtles move like beautiful black animated stones on the beach.

"Never thought I'd say it, but I've had my fill of turtles for one evening. Thank you again for... for everything. For loving me," I whisper.

"Dess, you make it too easy." Growling, he rolls until he's on top of me, pressing me down into the sand under the blanket. "Since you've already got that necklace and you'll put up a fight if I mark your neck, will you settle for a kiss?"

I answer with a smile, wrapping my hands around his neck and bringing his hungry lips to mine.

I'm just not sure if I'll ever understand how I deserve so much love from a man overflowing with this much passion.

* * *

It's NOT all fun and games and turtle picnics ending in honey-sweet kisses, though.

Honestly, the one thing that risks throwing a wrench in what we've built is the day when Shepherd meets my dad.

People know Cole Lancaster for his business record first and his stormy temperament second. In the coffee world, he's somewhere between just king and king-sized jerk.

To me, he's always been a softie who never gets tired of hearing me joke about the grey in his hair and the way he moons over Eliza.

But I've never brought a boy home before.

Certainly not a *man* who's almost twice my age, and closer to Dad's.

When I was a kid, he used to have conniption fits over the distant possibility that anyone would want to date me someday.

I'm not a flighty teenager anymore, but somehow his overprotective dad side still hasn't gotten the message.

And even though Shepherd is ready to be perfectly diplomatic the second we walk through Dad's door, I know he's guarded in his own way while I'm drowning in nerves.

Hey, it's not like I left everything to chance.

I gave Dad a heads-up about what to expect.

I mean, the fact that the rumors were kind of true and I'm really dating Shepherd now got this off to a rocky start from day one.

Not an excellent sign.

At least they made it through one phone call without breaking into a screaming match, though. I'd like to think that the whole saving my life thing bought Shepherd a crumb of goodwill—or at least a teeny-tiny chance to explain himself in front of a one-man firing squad.

I'm expecting Eliza to fling the door open with a sunny hug and a dozen questions, but it doesn't happen.

It's just Dad who bellows "come" the second he sees us step up to the door.

He's waiting for us in the hall, arms folded in a white buttondown with his sleeves rolled up.

For the longest second of my life, he raises his head and looks at us.

And *looks*.

Well, crap.

Maybe this meeting was doomed from the start, no matter how much Shepherd paid his good karma forward.

Still, he sticks out his hand and approaches my father, fearless and undaunted.

"Mr. Lancaster."

"Foster," Dad clips.

The way they shake hands looks more like two bears fighting over a salmon.

Dad never once looks away from Shepherd, his eyes flashing like gunmetal.

Oof, this is bad.

As far as Dad's concerned, I'll be his little girl until the day he dies. He's an open-minded guy and not a complete Neanderthal, but I worry he'll never get over the age gap.

It's hard not to cringe, just imagining what kind of cradle-robbing sex fiend he imagines Shepherd to be.

A squeal from upstairs saves us just in time.

Eliza sails through the door with my little brother, Elijah, her airy perfume swirling around her. The wide smile on her face could tame a hurricane.

"Shepherd! The man of the hour," she gushes.

The way Dad's evil eye softens ever so slightly tells me that we just might survive this. Thank God for his wife.

If Eliza decided she's giving Shepherd a fair shake, there's no freaking *way* Dad will pull out a loaded shotgun.

He'll never admit it, but he can never hold out against her, and it's comically adorable.

Shepherd's face relaxes into a smile as Eliza embraces him warmly.

I grab his hand, lacing my fingers through his. I squeeze like I'm hoping I can transfer every bit of goodwill in my bones.

"Something smells tasty," I say, sniffing the air. "What did you make us this time, Eliza? New drink?"

"Let her show you. She's only been fussing over it all week," Dad grumps, leading us inside.

He leads us to the great room with a palace-worthy fireplace and mantle while Eliza disappears into the cave-sized kitchen.

I sit beside Shepherd and my knee knocks against his.

Dad notices the contact like an owl spotting a field mouse. I can practically *feel* his brain blowing a fuse at the mere thought that we ever do more than hold hands like Amish kids.

Nope, he doesn't like that.

Or the rumors, the pictures.

Oh, God, has he *seen* the pictures?

I swallow, smothering the awkward cough.

"I heard Miss Cerva already accepted a plea deal," Dad says, choosing each word carefully.

Shepherd nods. "Didn't have much choice. I put my best guys on the case, but she threw herself on the mercy of the court. Still, don't think she'll get up to much trouble if she's let out on parole in thirty years, totally bankrupt."

"Not a bad outcome, especially for this judicial district. I looked at your legal team. Impressive credentials," Dad admits.

Oh, boy, so he's decided to be all business.

I guess that's better than yelling.

Still, I roll my eyes.

If they're going to talk status the whole time, we're never getting anywhere.

"Yes, guys. The wicked witch is gone and even Meghan got a happy ending. She's rebranded to show off her healing, talking through her problems and her experiences with therapy, hoping it'll help other folks with abusive situations. I'm proud of her. But can we get off the big bad? Like, why don't we talk about the fact that we're dating?" I say brightly.

"Dating," Dad spits.

His face tightens like a lion's, trying to decide if that pesky hyena is worth the mauling.

I barely refrain from reminding him I'm a grown woman,

totally capable of making my own decisions—and choosing who to date, with no shotgun approval from my father necessary.

"It's good to finally meet you," Shepherd says, still formal. Still wary.

When he said he knew it would go well and that he didn't need my dad's permission, I didn't believe him.

This is way more intense than I expected. I'm practically sweating, even if I'm the one egging them on.

"It's not good," Dad growls.

My heart stops. I fight the urge to pinch my eyes shut, bracing for impact.

Oh, yup, here we go...

"You saved my daughter," Dad says abruptly. "She told me everything that happened on the yacht. After I got past the urge to dismember Miss Cerva with my bare hands, and then Destiny herself for lying to me while she was trapped on a sinking ship, I decided I wanted you a little less dead, Foster. You saved her life."

What what?

That's—not what I expected.

My heart flutters hopefully.

"He did," I manage. "Without Shepherd, I would've been fish food for sure."

"I'm glad to hear you can tolerate me breathing, Mr. Lancaster. However, even if you planned to throw me off Mount Rainier one bloody chunk at a time, I'd have saved her anyway. There's no way I'd ever let anything happen," Shepherd says, glancing at me and squeezing my hand so tightly.

There's a glimmer in his glacial-blue eyes like spring, and his mouth curls up very slightly.

It's the kind of smile he only ever gives me.

Our secret smile, and I love it.

Dad just watches us, steely at first, but then his face slowly relaxes.

"We have that in common, I suppose," he says. "Rescuing

women from maniacs in the worst storms to hit Washington in the last fifty years."

"Yes, sir." Shepherd nods slowly. "I heard about your situation. Not an experience I'd ever recommend."

"Wasn't my favorite time," Dad agrees.

"But we got through it, didn't we?" It's my turn to squeeze his hand.

His thumb traces over the back of my palm.

Even with all this tension, he makes me tingle.

God, I love him.

Love him.

Like, we're not even at the six-months together mark, but in this small, tucked-away part of me, I already know this is forever.

A forever I could never experience with anyone else.

"Cole, let me be frank," Shepherd says, going straight for the first name. Risky. "I don't need your blessing to date your daughter, but I'd like it. I respect you for raising an angel who's only thirty percent brat."

I dart him a dirty look.

Dad's eyes narrow and his lips thin.

Yeah, there's no way he's happy about this. I just hope he can respect another man who shoots straight.

Please be cool. Be reasonable. Be fair, I plead silently. *Dad, don't embarrass me.*

"Damn. There's no disputing the fact you saved my Destiny," Dad says after the world's longest silence. "Whatever, *Shepherd,* you get one chance. One. Don't fuck it up and make me regret giving you a green light."

Holy hell.

Another grim silence.

Shepherd weighs his words. I don't know how to tell him that coming from Dad, this is basically the most generous thing ever.

Thankfully, he doesn't need the memo.

"You won't be disappointed, Cole. Thank you."

"See that I'm not." Dad's eyes rake Shepherd again before he stands and extends a hand.

They shake hands again, and this time it's a little less like two snapping bears.

Fortunately, Eliza walks back into this weird-ass manly ritual with a tray full of steaming coffee mugs, banishing the awkwardness.

"It's sweet, it's steamy, and it's full of blueberry goodness straight from Alaska! Come try my latest creation," she sings, pressing a mug into everyone's hands.

Her eyes twinkle and she gives me a wink.

He's hot, she mouths.

I have to agree.

Shepherd is a meteorite, scorching and fallen and brilliant, all blaze in body, mind, and soul.

I'm not sure if I'll ever fully get used to how he loves me, though.

I'm still smiling into my first sip of the new blueberry brew. Eliza has a real 80-20 thing going on with her coffee creations, but this one's an instant winner.

I can't tell if it's the sweetness of the drink that makes me so giddy or the fact that the two men in my life can finally make eye contact without looking like it's pistols at dawn.

After another hour of polite coffee talk with them, we make our escape.

I rest my head on Shepherd's arm as we walk the gardens stretching down to the water behind the house, hand in hand.

"That went well!"

"Did it? Sweetheart, you can't ever cry again in front of Cole. Not even happy tears. He'll put my head on the wall."

I giggle. "Aw, he's not so bad. He didn't start brandishing his Navy knife or anything."

"Not yet," he says dryly.

"Shepherd, he gave you his freaking blessing. That's massive."

He glances down at the top of my head and studies me. "Is he always like this?"

"Wanting to skin my boyfriends alive? Yeah, pretty much. And you're the first one I've ever brought home."

Honestly, my other dates were only that. Never boyfriends.

Boyfriend, boyfriend, *boyfriend*.

The word feels equally alien and spectacular when I just want it to feel real.

Somehow, though, it also doesn't quite feel permanent.

Will boyfriend always be enough to contain what he means to me?

This is so much more than a fickle high school relationship or a steady college guy with an expiration date.

It's bound by real emotion, tears and tragedy and drama and even a little blood.

It's like calling an old giant sequoia tree a shoot.

Still, I love how his hand tightens around mine, and his thumb does that thing again, caressing my skin.

Tingles.

The man makes me a human lightning rod, and he's the only storm I'll ever need.

I haven't told him how much I like it, how much it makes my stomach swoop, but I'm sure he knows.

And I wouldn't change anything about it for the world.

"It went well," I repeat again, papering over the moment just in case he feels as weird about 'boyfriend' as I do. "Trust me. Give it a few months and you'll be best friends."

"You're full of it." Shepherd snorts. "He doesn't even like me."

I hold up a finger. "Doesn't like you *yet*. But he doesn't hate you. You have to do something really atrocious to lose Dad's trust. Once you're in, you're in. Plus, I'm sure this is only a conversation you'll ever need to have once. He basically said you've got the green light to go ahead and m—" I stop right there.

I wasn't really about to say *marry me*, right?

407

Because that would be preposterous.

Totally. Bonkers.

We're just easing into the reality of us with all its quirks and kisses and little spats over where to go for dinner. I should *not* be imagining myself in a white dress right now.

I should *definitely* not be imagining Shepherd in a tux, casting his eyes down like he'll spend the rest of his natural life devouring me.

Oh, God.

He looks good enough to eat even in this goofy fantasy.

My phone chimes with an alert. I pull it out and see a link from Meghan with her latest video.

The therapy is helping her a ton, I think, and sharing her journey banishes the pain faster.

I wait until after dinner with the fam to play it while we're on the way back to Shepherd's place.

"Hey, guys, sorry for the radio silence," Meghan says. She's abandoned her usual sassy, bold look for soft pastel sweaters and a fresh face not plastered with makeup. Honestly, it makes her look younger and infinitely more real.

I smile at the screen.

We've kept trading messages over the past couple months. I think we're moving past that phase where she keeps apologizing while I insist she doesn't need to.

We're slowly becoming real friends.

Shepherd scrubbed the drone pics from the web as much as he could, though they occasionally resurface. When they do, they're no longer a scandal worth circulating.

Just half-dead rumors drained of their dark energy.

While I watch Meghan's latest video, I wonder if this might be the thing that ends them once and for all. I know she's been building up to this for a while, and she's decided that today is the day.

"As some of you know, I've had a mountain of family drama," Meghan says calmly. "I don't want to rehash the deets—watch my other videos for that—but as bad as my mom was... I have some things to own up to."

She pauses and clears her throat just as we pull into the driveway.

Shepherd stops the car and watches with me.

"First, I want to reiterate that *all* of the allegations I made against Destiny Lancaster and Shepherd Foster were completely false. Mom wrote the scripts and coached me on lines with her brand consultant, but I was the mouthpiece. I made them viral. I took the videos down the instant I came to my senses so I wouldn't perpetuate those hurtful lies any longer, but you've probably heard of them and wondered. Maybe you read the news and put two and two together, but that isn't enough. I told the whole world Destiny slept with Shepherd Foster, CEO of Home Shepherd, purely to get her Young Influencers position. That was toxic and inexcusable."

My throat tightens at the way her eyes fill with tears.

She really means this, making amends.

All her apologies, her regrets, feel so sincere it makes my heart bleed.

Meghan stares at the camera. "I was manipulated into saying it, yes, but I never should have. My courage came too late, and the lies my mother made me spread hurt people. I'm deeply ashamed, and I won't ever let it happen again."

"Brave girl," Shepherd growls sincerely, glancing at me with his usual intensity.

I nod.

"Have you reached out yet?" he asks.

"I will in a second. She just posted a few hours ago. I'll comment on the video, too, when I can think of something to say. Just so everyone knows there are no hard feelings."

As Meghan continues talking about her struggle, we head inside. Molly jumps up from a nap and licks my hand, and I walk over to the back door to let her out.

Outside, it's blue as far as you can see, sky and water and crisp fall air mingling together.

One day, I'll get back on Shepherd's yacht and enjoy a closer look—this time without any worries about an untimely date with the crabs. He's just had the ship repaired.

But not today.

Not yet.

"I also wanted to let you guys know something important..." Meghan continues. "After I finish sharing my Journey with Tea, I've made the hard decision to retire. The content will stay up."

I actually gasp.

"I know, I know," she goes on. "Maybe you think this is a huge mistake, but... I've realized it's time to step back and reassess what's really important to me. Destiny taught me that." Her smile, despite the tear tracks down her face, is huge. "I'm going to take some time off and find myself outside the public eye. Maybe I'll volunteer for a bird rescue or something since Mom never let me have a parrot. It's something I've always wanted, and I know I still have a ton of work to do, but... this is my moment. My life. And I'd like to thank you for sharing so many moments with me, and I hope my final videos over the next few months will help bring everybody out there some peace. I owe you one, Dessy, for helping me give myself a second chance."

Damn.

She's so sweet it breaks my heart.

Oh, and she's not finished.

"By the way, guys, in case you don't know, Destiny's passion for wildlife conservation is legendary. She's brave and feisty and so, so smart. Since she's been a big part of inspiring me to get my crap together, go check out her stuff. It's not all about the cute animals. Check her stuff out and take this opportunity to see what difference *you* can make in the world."

I lean over, beaming at Shepherd. "You know, that gives me an idea to celebrate..."

He groans. "No. We're not getting involved with birds. I already funded one big search effort, and you're stuck with Molly and your otters."

* * *

A SLIGHTLY HARASSED man in a blazer and rumpled suit checks my mic, making sure it's attached securely and ready.

Shepherd, beside me, wears one of his customary charcoal suits. Classy and gorgeous and decently intimidating.

"You can't scowl at her the whole time," I say.

"I don't scowl in court." His brows inch down even lower.

"C'mon, Captain McSnarly, that's your favorite expression, and this is the court of public opinion." I preen at him.

Miracle of miracles, he laughs.

"Please try to look friendly," I tell him. "Be approachable."

He snorts. "The fact you're doubting my ability to do either of those things is insulting."

"Nope, it's realistic." I adjust his tie, though it doesn't need me to. He's handsome and polished, as always. "I know you, mister."

"Good. Then you'll know I'm perfectly capable of being polite—when the occasion demands it."

Right.

His version of polite is shooting death rays from his eyes.

Vanessa Dumas, of course, likely knows what to expect.

I imagine he was that version of polite with her once, too, back when they were together.

Not *together*, though.

Not really, I remind myself.

But when he took her places and behaved like they were more than friends, he probably had his professional mask clenched tight.

It's an attractive mask, for sure, but there's no way she

411

mistook his professional façade for any sort of *feelings.* Or even the hint of attraction.

I know him too well by now.

Well enough to be here while we tie up the last loose end in a nice little bow.

I have to search his face for the softness I adore, somewhere behind the steely blue eyes and the hard, handsome face that's chiseled by life.

Just for me, he cracks another almost-smile and his hand finds mine.

"Let's get this over with. You ready?"

"On a scale of one to ten, how bad will it be?"

His grip on my fingers tighten.

Bad, then.

"We'll live," he says casually. "It's a decent improvement over surviving a near drowning and convincing your dad I have a right to breathe in your presence."

Liar. Now he's just being sweet.

"Whatever happens, I'm here, Shepherd," I whisper.

I'm not nervous.

We haven't been hiding our relationship from the cameras or anyone, really.

I've deliberately put him in a ton of my stuff on Insta and TikTok.

Whenever anyone asks, we admit the truth, and we've been seen in public by people who like to talk plenty of times.

For Shepherd, he's actually been out a lot. Another big change. His life doesn't revolve around the office anymore.

So, why are my palms so sweaty I can barely cling to him?

"Sorry." I look up at him and grimace.

"We don't need to do this, Dess," he whispers. "We can still back out."

"No way! Hannah assured me it was the best way to put this to bed. So, yeah. Let's get it done."

The harassed guy holds up five fingers and gestures at us.

Five minutes until showtime.

A muscle tics in his jaw.

The reason we're here isn't to rub salt in the wound that is Vanessa Dumas' failed attempts to get with Shepherd. Or even to trumpet our relationship to the entire world—though that's *exactly* what we'll be doing in practice.

No, the real reason we're here is to prove her wrong.

To clear Shepherd's name and make people understand what a decent human being he really is.

No freaking way I'd ever back away from that.

"How are you feeling?"

"Like the luckiest man on Earth." He's totally deadpan, looking at me with nothing except the barest flicker of amusement he tries to hide.

"Dick."

"We'll have to hope they don't get that on camera."

I pinch his arm, but his teasing helps settle my jitters.

It's certainly not my first time being in front of an audience. But given everything that's happened, I know the stakes, and I want to get this right.

So we wait quietly, still holding hands, until we're given the signal to move to the staging area where the red couches are waiting.

Vanessa already had her chance to deliver her side of the story—pretty much the same version she spat out months ago.

Shepherd used her for sex, promised her marriage, and dumped her.

And with our whole fiasco, she's used it to cement her position, even as she's fallen out of the spotlight.

Shepherd is the bad guy.

But not after today.

As we walk onto that stage, though, her eyes widen when she sees us holding hands.

I know right then we've got her.

She never expected us to be together. Not for real.

She thought the rumors were as flimsy as the lies she's been parroting ever since Shepherd rejected her. And the fact that we're still so clearly together obviously stings.

Good.

The host greets us with a wide smile. Cameras swing in our direction and I have to fight not to acknowledge them. Shepherd, typically, doesn't bat an eye.

"Mr. Foster," she says in her cheery mom voice. I swear, these morning human interest hosts all sound the same. "Miss Lancaster. I'm thrilled you could both make it."

Applause rolls through the live audience.

I'm pretty sure someone screams my name and it's hard not to be surprised.

Oof. The audience factor makes this a little more difficult, but I pin on my bravest grin.

Shepherd smiles pleasantly at the host, Tiffany. Her lipstick is such a vivid blood-red, it makes the other colors in this place seem faded by comparison.

"Call me Shepherd," he says.

"Thanks so much for having us, Tiff." I beam.

"Yes, yes, and won't it be so good to hear your side of the story." Her eyes flick between Shepherd and me. "Does this mean you're dating?"

"We totally are," I confirm.

Damn, that feels good.

Shepherd turns his smile on me and whatever cold nerves I had melt away.

Yep. I would sell my kidneys for this man.

Vanessa snorts so loudly it sounds more like a cough. I'm almost certain she's hurt herself.

"Oh, whatevs. So phony. They'll be over tomorrow," she whispers, her sympathy as fake as her overdone hair extensions.

Shepherd turns to her. "Vanessa, can we talk?"

I can't tell if that's a smile or a silent snarl she throws back.

"Um, yeah. I wish you'd done that earlier. We could've

avoided a big ugly mess." Her eyes fill with the cheesiest tears. "Instead of you leaving me like—like you did..."

God, people eat this stuff up?

It's bad acting at its finest. Like Z-level stuff.

"Enough is enough." He sighs impatiently. "Look, we both know that what you're doing isn't fair to me and it isn't fair to you either. Do you want to be remembered as the girl I didn't want? Is that what you think will send your career into the stratosphere?"

Her mouth drops.

I don't think she's expecting a direct hit.

He turns and speaks to the camera now.

"Miss Dumas has claimed for months that I did the same thing to her as to Destiny Lancaster, but while Dess and I are together now, we never met before my assistant hired her as part of the Young Influencer program. Meghan Cerva has publicly retracted her allegations, on record."

"Yes," Tiff chimes in, pausing as the big screen next to us displays a bullet summary of the drama. "Quite a wild ride for our happy couple lately. But tell me, Shepherd, at the end of the day, we're still left with a lot of uncertainty about your relationship with Vanessa, aren't we? So much 'he said, she said' it could choke a horse."

The audience jeers. A few people clap and laugh obnoxiously.

Torture.

"You paid them off," Vanessa snaps—but she sounds unsure.

Tiffany whips toward her and waves a hand. "Now, now. Shepherd and Destiny's relationship really isn't in question when there's a pile of legal records and witness testimony to back it up. Adriana Cerva, as you'll recall, is just beginning to serve her sentence."

Vanessa's face whitens behind the red.

"Back to your point, I want to come clean," Shepherd cuts in. "Yes, Vanessa and I had an agreement once. I was tired of dating

415

and being swarmed all the time after—" He pauses and inhales deeply. "After Serena."

"Your ex-wife?" Tiff leans forward in her chair intently.

"Yes. Your viewers might not know she was killed suddenly. I surprised her in bed with her lover, we had words, and the guy pulled a gun on me."

Loud murmurs roll through the audience until Tiffany quiets them down.

I look at Shepherd, my eyes big and pleading.

Stay strong. You're doing amazing.

"What I'm trying to say is, Vanessa was a stand-in woman. A mistake I made so I didn't have to face reality. It was a stupid idea. When she wanted more and I turned her down, she ran with stories about us being madly in love. And while she might've ran with those fables, I'm the one who tried to run away. All I did was flee from my past—until I met Destiny."

His eyes meet mine.

I can't bring myself to care that we're on live TV.

I walk over, lean down, and kiss him deeply.

The audience goes absolutely ballistic. They're still shouting and talking loudly as the show pauses for a commercial break.

Next, once we're back on, Tiffany video calls a few people who met Vanessa while she was on Shepherd's arm. We were practically buried in requests from people volunteering to corroborate the truth after they found out about Adriana.

And the two people Tiffany pulls up both say the same thing —there was never any indication that they were dating.

No ring.

No stolen kisses.

No secret smiles I know too well.

Tiffany finally turns to me, the smile on her face undaunted by Vanessa steadily deflating.

"Tell us your story," she says. "How do you feel about these allegations?"

"Well, I know they aren't true, for one. Anyone as work-focused as Shepherd doesn't have time for a relationship. And trust me, he needs some serious persuading to relax."

The easy laughter that follows is sudden.

I prod his leg. "But he's very sweet about it. We didn't plan this. It just sorta happened, like love always does."

"How did you two get together?" Tiffany asks.

"Um. Otters?" And I tell them the story of our camping trip, taking Shepherd's hand as I recount how we couldn't stand each other until that weekend.

"But even then, we still had our doubts. We needed everything that happened with Adriana Cerva to see the truth." I give Shepherd a soft smile. "Plus, he gets major points for loving my dog."

"Well, what more can a man do?" Tiffany laughs. "So your relationship happened after the allegations?"

"I had a crush on him almost from the beginning," I say. "Who wouldn't? I think he took a little longer to come around, but in the end, he did."

"So you pursued him?"

I cock my head as I look at Shepherd thoughtfully. "No. I think we both came together when the time was right."

Tiffany turns to Shepherd. "And no ring this time?"

"Not yet," he says after a moment. My heart races as he continues, "I'm here today because I'm ready to get on with my life, and I think, deep down, Miss Dumas is too. I'm willing to drop all defamation charges if she'll agree to let this go."

Tiffany turns back to her. "Vanessa? What do you say?"

The silence is deafening.

I think she knows she's cooked. The evidence is crystal clear, and with Adriana going down and Meghan's statement, she has even less of a leg to stand on with her lies.

She knows it and so does the world.

So does Tiffany, whose smile is steady and unrelenting.

The next question is going to be devastating.

"Is there any particular reason why you claimed Shepherd

Foster pursued a sexual relationship with you? And if there isn't, why not just take the olive branch?"

"I... I didn't come here for this. The nerve of this man, cornering me like this after everything, after—I simply won't be put on the spot!" Vanessa's expression falls as she stands unsteadily.

I find Shepherd's hand.

After so much misery, it should feel good to see her humiliated like this.

It actually doesn't.

I feel sick.

Her hands ball into fists as she storms off stage, wiping at real tears. The cameras follow her.

It may be what she deserves.

But I don't have that smug sense of satisfaction or victory I expected.

"Tiff, here's her reason. People do stupid things when they're hurt," Shepherd says. His hand is so warm and steady around mine. "She had illusions about us falling in love, and I tried to talk her down. I don't suppose she ever thought it would come to this. Don't suppose she wanted it to, either."

I nod. "It's not something I hold against her."

"Well, that's that, folks. It's all up to the lawyers now, but I think we know where this is going. I'm wishing you both the best, and thanks so much for joining us today to clear the air," Tiffany says, looking between us like she doesn't understand what just happened either.

I know I don't.

Not until two days later, when Shepherd's lawyer gets a note that says Vanessa is retracting her claims, effective immediately.

It feels like the end of the beginning as I drop my phone and leap into his arms the second he walks through the door.

The whole time we kiss, Molly wags her tail, thumping the nearby chair like our little celebration has its own rhythm.

XXV: A LITTLE FATEFUL
(SHEPHERD)

*L*ife is a messy damn blur and I'm loving every smear of it.

For the first time in forever, there's a reason to leave work early.

Hannah has already had enough of my slacking and she teases me relentlessly, of course, but I make no apologies.

I've simply become the guy who leaves at five o'clock sharp unless he has a loaded gun pressed to his head.

Hell, I barely answer my phone anymore on weekends barring an emergency.

Mostly.

Monday to Friday, seven to five is my life in the tower, hashing out high-tech camera systems and adapting drones for peace.

The rest of my time, like my heart, belongs to Destiny Lancaster.

"What do you think?" she asks, blotting at the ice cream on her nose.

This weekend, we took a drive up to Anacortes and stopped off at a small-town ice cream parlor. It's this old-timey place with hipster flavors like curried Elvis and midnight chocolate plum.

It's enough to activate any dormant sweet tooth, though mine isn't obsessed with the ice cream today.

I can't keep my eyes off this woman to save my life.

She's wearing hip-hugging jeans and a t-shirt that's just tight enough for me to see the slight protrusion of her nipples.

Fuck, sometimes I have to pinch myself *hard* to remember she's mine. Then I wonder how I ever got so lucky.

"I think we should go back to the car," I tell her matter-of-factly.

There's probably a secluded parking lot somewhere, right? Behind a building will do just fine.

Or hell, we could just stay where we are, consequences be damned.

She raises a tanned arm, shielding her face from the autumn sun. "Why? It's such a nice view."

I grit my teeth.

There's no argument there with sailboats and green islands and fifteen shades of blue between the sky and the placid waters below.

Still.

I can't just pin her to the wall of the busy grocery store or the burger joint next door, although it's mighty tempting. There's a lot of elderly folks milling around the narrow streets, and I won't be liable for triggering any heart attacks.

I bend down, pressing my mouth to her ear. "Because if we don't go back to the car right now, I'm going to fuck you right here in broad daylight."

Her eyes pop.

I fucking love the fact that I can still make them do that.

It's like I can see the desire flaring in her veins when she smiles. It kicks my own heart and spikes my adrenaline to eleven.

Since getting together, I can't keep track of the number of times we have sex during any given week.

It's probably unhealthy and absolutely indecent.

Completely inappropriate when she wakes up with my tongue already working on her clit. Every time she comes into the office, the blinds snap shut and she leaves teeth marks on my wrist from stifling her moans.

Almost every day and it's still never enough.

I'd say she enjoys the routine as much as I do.

I think a few people have gotten the message. Hannah noticeably takes her lunches away from her desk anytime Destiny visits.

I don't blame her. I also don't care.

Frankly, I'm just glad she hasn't handed in her notice after watching her boss transform his office into a naked freakshow.

That isn't even touching the number of times I've had her outside.

On the grass, the dock, the yacht, once I managed to lure her back on it after we triple checked the weather for clear skies.

Throbbing flesh does a lot to chase away bad memories.

So do a few hours in my cabin with the glass walls, where the only storm is us, gasping and sweating and groaning each other's names through clenched teeth.

She always comes so sweet for me.

When it comes to Destiny, I'm as shameless as I am fucking insatiable.

And right now, I *need* to have her again. Simple as.

She looks me up and down, a smile quirking her lips, nodding at my hard-on. "Careful, boy. I almost think you want us to get slapped with indecency charges."

"There's an easy workaround, and it involves dragging your cute ass back to the vehicle right this second," I growl.

"One that won't get us arrested? It's a busy place with the fall tourists and all..."

"I'll drive off-road, dammit. Into the trees, the brush, where there's no one around to see."

"Hmmm," she mutters thoughtfully, holding my gaze as she licks up the cone, drawing the ice cream back into her mouth with a curl of her tongue.

Little she-devil.

She's about to find out I'm willing to face the rap for public indecency if she keeps teasing me like that.

"Tell me," she says, not looking away. I'm too caught up in the way the sun reddens her nose and highlights her freckles.

"Tell you what?" I ask.

The sun gleams on her hair and fuck, I want to thread my fingers through it and *pull* until she tilts her head back and exposes her throat.

All the better to bite you, my dear.

I want a hundred, a thousand, terrible, filthy things.

"When will you get tired of me?" she asks, but her voice is a whisper.

My brows go up.

"Never. How is that a question?"

"Can't blame a girl for asking. I almost believe you."

"Almost?" I snort. "If there's any room for doubt, then someone needs a nice, long reminder of just how obsessed I am, Dess."

I watch her shudder, hiding behind her blooming red cheeks and sunrise smile.

For a second, I think that's it, that's all she's going to say.

Then she nods. Just once. Decisively.

"Well, okay. Let's go find where we parked and—"

I don't let her finish.

She's airborne as I lift her out of the chair and we take off through the hilly streets like teenagers playing tag. I don't even care that my hard-on makes it damnably awkward to run, or that she's giggling and playfully fighting back when I finally grab her.

I don't even care that this is the most ridiculous—and possibly the horniest—I've ever been in my natural life.

All I want is this bright young thing who makes me feel twenty years younger.

No, better, when my life at twenty-one was a living nightmare.

Dess gives me the laughter and the enjoyment I never had when I was truly young, and she's so worth the wait it leaves me dizzy.

We're both winded by the time we reach the car, but it still doesn't slow me down.

No driver today, just us, so no one inside will get the shock of their life when I throw her against the passenger door and kiss her life out.

Goddamn, this is good.

Every time we kiss, I feel like a starved man settling down for dinner as she kisses me back, my own steaming madness igniting her desire.

For her, I boil over.

Every. Damned. Time.

Soft lips move against mine with butterfly beats, and soon my tongue slides into her mouth, laying claim for the thousandth time.

It never gets old.

Apparently, I need to mark my territory daily.

Her moan is decadent. Absolutely fucking luxurious.

Honest to God, I could feast on her mouth forever.

But my body has other demands, and while I devour her, my hips wedge against hers, making her feel how hard I am.

She never stays quiet for long. She gets ten, maybe fifteen seconds in before she has to break away and tuck her head against my shoulder, gasping too loudly.

I don't care.

A sinister part of me wants to make her scream, to show the world just how much she means to me.

I only hold back for her sake, knowing she won't take kindly to being hounded by small-town cops.

She leans back, her eyes gleaming as she looks up at me. "Guess what?"

"What, sweetheart?"

"I love you."

My dick likes hearing that a lot.

Almost as much as it likes the cradle of her thighs as I grind against her again.

Fuck, she'll be my destruction, and I'll go happily like a moth into the furnace.

I pull her up so her legs are folded around me, sinking my fingers into her thighs.

Still too many clothes, but I'm sure this isn't quite breaking any public decency laws.

Probably.

Her mouth meets mine again, hungry and eager and so succulent.

I kiss back until I forget the heat of the sun and the distant clammer of the seagulls soaring high overhead through the trees.

Everything fades out except Destiny's sweetness and all the myriad ways I want her.

"God, I want you," she murmurs, rubbing her fingers along my bristly jaw.

I rake my stubble against her throat, knowing it drives her wild.

"Your wish is my command, ma'am," I rumble. "Into the car."

For once, she doesn't argue.

Despite the fall coolness, I crank up the air-conditioning before throwing the seat back and slinging her across my lap.

"Fuck," I grind out as she shifts against me, fully straddling me. "Holy shit, Dess."

"I want to do this for the rest of my life," she tells me, then freezes, her arms still locked around my neck. It's clear she thinks she's gone too far.

The rest of our lives.

I smile like a fool. I can definitely handle that.

That's more than fucking okay.

"Pants off, beautiful," I tell her. My fingers find the waistband of her jeans and undo the button. It's our go-to response to big, scary news. "You make me want to live forever if it means fucking you to cinders every day."

I inhale her as I slide her pants down her legs.

She shifts, allowing room, opening her legs slowly and sexy as hell.

It's her eyes that really slay me, though.

The girl has the most beautiful eyes.

Every time I think I'm at full capacity, I fall for her a little harder.

"Every fucking day, Dess. No question," I whisper.

She catches her breath as I slide my fingers through her slickness, sinking in deep.

This, right here, is everything I'll ever need.

Her mouth parted and her eyes restless.

Her hair tangling up in my fist, dragging her head back so I can suck her throat.

Her tits rising and falling, impatient to be next, waiting for my mouth.

Her tight little pussy, aching to be filled, quivering against my fingers as I work them deep inside her.

Fuck.

The entire rest of my existence is nothing but noise.

Her looks, her moans, her shudders will always take priority.

And she grips my shoulders, her eyes hazy with unrepentant lust.

I'm damn glad we have tinted windows. Otherwise, we'd be giving a few stragglers wandering off the main path a show they'd never forget as I unhook her bra and tug her top away to reveal the most perfect nipples.

I suck one and get back a sigh so erotic I almost come in my pants.

Her body welcomes me, hot and wet as ever, writhing against me like pure sin.

"You already have the rest of my life," I tell her. "You had it from the start. I was just too stubborn to know it."

She whimpers.

"Shepherd!" Her fingers grab my shoulders, almost painfully hard.

"Sweetheart, if you want something, take it."

She grabs my wrist and removes my hand. Then she unbuttons my pants and frees my cock, rubbing it against her entrance. We don't bother to work off my pants.

She's so fucking wet for me, and I'm transfixed.

"I want you," she says fiercely. "That's it. No games. Just you."

And just like that, she slides on top of me, engulfing my cock.

The sugar rush of slick heat down my shaft short-circuits my brain.

Her feet are braced on either side of me as her hips plunge down, swing up, and come down so quickly, greedy for more.

One hand presses against the window as she finds her balance. There isn't enough space for me to do half the things to her I want to, but we'll make it work.

Even so, it's some of the best sex ever in our hyperactive love life.

No, not just sex—this is soul.

My body welded to hers, our lips fused together, rocking gently as she gasps and moans and clenches.

I groan my delight into her mouth.

She nips my bottom lip.

I bite back harder.

We wrestle for control just like we always do, racing to the finish, a contest I won't let her win, but God help her, she tries.

That's one of the things I love about her most.

And there are so many little things on a list the size of the Mississippi.

Even through her moaning, her pleasure, the insistent motion of her hips, her eyes wet as she meets mine.

I know then that this means as much to her as it does to me.

When she picks up speed, her counter-thrusts turning frantic and messy, she lets out a tiny mewling sound.

Close.

So fucking close.

I have to clench every muscle in my body to hold back as her pussy grips my cock.

"I know, sweetheart," I whisper, holding her close, shrugging off my shirt so we're skin to skin. "Let fucking go. Come for me, Dess."

With both hands, I squeeze her ass, guiding her movements, dragging her over the finish line.

There, there.

Fuck, there.

She tightens around me again right before the white-hot ecstasy consumes her.

"Fuck!" I bury her lips under mine again as she goes off like a cherry bomb.

I swallow every breathless moan spilling out of her as her pussy tries to rob my soul, giving back punishing thrusts that drive her higher, *higher.*

There's no sweeter sight than driving this woman stark raving mad with pleasure.

"I love you," she pants when she can finally speak again.

That's all it takes for both of us.

She clenches again, the sound she makes ripped straight from her heart, and then I fall the fuck apart.

My balls rip lighting up my spine, and soon I'm one long human current, pure magma that only exists to fill her.

Every part of me, hers.

Body and soul and mind.

She has my all, and I wouldn't have it any other way.

We come together just as she goes off again, so intense I forget how to breathe.

At first, I was amazed at how the energy between us never diminishes no matter how many times we do this. I thought it was a law of human nature.

Now, I know it's going to be like this for the rest of our lives.

She said it herself.

But it's about time I did something about it, I think, coming down from my high with my cock still rooted deep inside her.

And not just because I don't want any shit from Cole if I beat around the metaphorical bush for too long. He's not the type who'll take kindly to any man stringing his daughter along.

I told myself marriage wasn't something I'd ever do again. Not after my last one ended in a catastrophic heart-fuck.

Yet as Dess brushes her messy blonde hair out of her eyes and smiles down at me like paradise, how the hell can I ever do anything else?

"I think loving you might be a health hazard," she whispers.

I'm still inside her, but she doesn't seem to want to move.

Fair. I don't know how we'll clean up the mess we've made either, but right now I don't care.

I pull her in with a hand on the back of her neck, kissing her deeply, drinking my fill.

"Why's that?" I ask.

"Because. I just came so hard I left the known universe."

I chuckle. "That's the kind of warning label I don't mind wearing, woman."

"Only for *me*," she warns.

I snort loudly.

Like I'd ever waste a second on another woman.

"No jealousy. I'm yours," I promise, holding her close— because let's face it, there's going to be a round two in the not-too-distant future—and I think about all the ways I can show her I mean it.

I'm a man who lays claim.

I never imagined giving myself up could be so satisfying, too.

Still, as we trade hot kisses and roaming hands through the lazy evening, I think I'm ready.

For Destiny, I'll throw myself down on the altar and offer her everything.

* * *

THE WORLD KNOWS THE TRUTH, the whole truth, and nothing but by now.

Destiny Lancaster won her Young Influencers position fair and square. Hannah, who came out on record to confirm this, was the person who selected her.

We did not get together until *after* the event.

And now, after that final confrontational interview with Vanessa, everyone knows how deeply in love with Dess I am.

I've made it perfectly clear that it was always her passion and heart and dedication to conservation that made me fall so hard.

Not her looks.

Not her family.

Not her age.

The person she is on the inside.

That's why I'm encouraging her to film as much as she wants on our latest trip to the South Carolina shore to see dolphins. I know it's something she'll want to share with her followers, and that's fine.

If I'm something she wants to share, that's fine too.

At least, I'm learning how to make it *fine.*

I'm coming to terms with the fact that the woman I love has to put herself out there to make a difference in the world.

Destiny swings her phone up to capture me on camera.

We're in the water after diving off the ship. Any second now, I have a feeling some of the nearby dolphins will swim in closer to investigate.

"I know what it looks like," Destiny says in her live video. "But I *promise* you he's having fun."

I make a contorted face at her.

She laughs and turns her attention to a lone dolphin approaching us, stopping less than ten feet away.

"Oh, wow, look!" she squeals. "They're coming."

"Point and shoot. Don't miss anything."

"Oh my *God*." I think she might be crying. "This is so cool."

The guys on the boat are prepped and ready. She doesn't know it yet, but I want everything recorded.

Not for her followers this time.

For me.

For us.

I want to show this video to our kids someday.

"The perfect ending to a perfect week," she murmurs, ending her video with a panned shot of the dolphin before she tucks her phone back in her waterproof grip. "Shepherd, holy crap. I can't believe we're doing this."

Surprisingly, the dolphin isn't done. It comes closer and Destiny makes first contact, gently trailing her hand across its back.

Her other hand is cupped over her mouth.

Shit, I didn't plan this part.

Not that it matters, I'm not having my thunder stolen away by Flipper the nosy-ass dolphin.

"Holy hell," she whispers. "Are you getting this?"

"Every second," I tell her, holding up my camera.

"This is just surreal," she whispers, grinning.

I wonder what she'll say a minute later when she's living a fairy tale.

The dolphin chirps then and we both duck underwater.

I slip on my goggles, watching as she dips under to marvel at the sight.

Dolphins and brightly colored fish dart past, and below, on the seabed, there's an explosion of life. Coral, seaweed, crawling crabs and shimmering fish and so many different colors it would take a year to describe them.

Another dolphin swims up behind me, bumping right into me.

I'm pretty sure it laughs—if dolphins can laugh. Cheeky little punk.

Destiny is giddy.

Yeah, fuck it, so am I.

The perfect moment. The perfect day. The perfect everything.

What better way to start forever?

When we surface, she's laughing so hard her face turns bright red, and I pull her against me. She wraps her arms around my neck.

"Thank you. This entire week has been incredible, but today was the best by far."

"Do you know what today is?" I ask cryptically.

"What?"

"Six months to the day since we went on an otter hunt," I say against her mouth. "Six months of loving you."

She laughs. "Come on, you didn't love me then."

I pretend to think.

"Not like I do now, no." I hold her tighter. "Still, that was the start of me coming to my senses. The first inkling I couldn't live without you."

She laughs again as more dolphins splash around us and one nudges my back.

Another taps Destiny's arm, and she looks down, her brow furrowing in surprise and concentration.

"Um. Is there something in its mouth?"

"Why don't you find out?" I tell her.

"Wait, what? Is it a dolphin? The size seems a little off and—oh, its eyes are weird too." She stares at the fake dolphin before she reaches for the snout.

"Home Shepherd can't improve on nature's perfection, but

we can mimic it. You're looking at the first trial run of our new underwater environmental surveillance drone. Today, it's been painted and designed to mirror the local sea life in stunning detail."

She looks up with saucers for eyes.

"Get out! Shepherd, you're a genius."

I smile and we lock eyes. "Nah. Someone much smarter gave me the idea about six months ago. I almost had to make Carol sign her name in blood to keep it a secret."

Laughing, she holds out a hand as the fake dolphin lets her unhook the small box tied to its clawlike jaws. That's mostly for appearance, but it does do an excellent job of grabbing small objects.

"Oh my God." Destiny makes a strangled sound and stops cold, bobbing in the water.

That's my cue to take over.

I pry the box from her frozen fingers and open it.

It's a pearl engagement ring, a custom design.

I even found that pearl myself years ago on a trip to New Zealand. It was just after the legal circus following Serena's death, when I took a solid month island hopping around the Pacific to clear my head.

The pearl was my only keepsake. The only thing that made me forget my demons for a few minutes. The large, striking pearl washing up on the beach was truly a unicorn event and it made me marvel.

Who knew I was actually finding an engagement ring for my future wife?

Or maybe it found me.

Now, as I watch her eyes glistening with a thousand emotions, I finally understand why.

"Shepherd," she says again, her voice hushed and fingers trembling as she holds them to her lips.

Her wide eyes dart to my face.

Okay, showtime.

I take a deep, rattling breath and—

Fuck.

Silence.

I must've planned this in my head a hundred times. Exactly what I'd tell her and how I'd ask.

I love you.

I need you to be mine for the rest of our lives.

Will you marry me?

After the real dolphins mingling with our robot, it feels a tad anticlimactic.

Still, there's no turning back now, and she needs to know how much she means to me.

"Destiny Lancaster," I say, trying not to choke.

They're filming this from the drone's camera eye, too. I decide I won't mind it years from now if we play this back and I have to watch myself going to pieces.

Just as long as she says yes, dammit.

Just as long as this Destiny is mine, now and forever.

She grips my hand like the little mind reader she is, willing me to carry on.

"I love you more than life itself," I tell her. "You know me. I'm not good with big, feely speeches and I'm not perfect with fancy words, but you already know you're the most precious thing in my life. The second closest treasure is that pearl, and it's got nothing on you. I want you to take it. I want to make you mine every day I'm breathing. I want to come home to you. I want the laughter, the tears, the love, the sex, the disagreements that'll have us ripping our hair out. I want everything. I want all of you, Dess, and I think you know I've already handed over all of me."

Her eyes are huge and sparkling and she doesn't say anything.

Radio silence.

I've had more affirming food orders.

Maybe I'm overzealous, but I take her hand and slide the ring on, still beaming a question into her eyes until it burns.

It fits too well, the pearl's shimmering contrast with the tan of her hand.

Then I wait, looking at her with my heart in my throat, aging a year every second until the woman I love finally says yes.

She doesn't say anything, though.

She *squeals* so loud my ears are ringing.

Her hand shakes as she clamps it over her mouth and she stares at the ring on her finger for a heartbeat too long.

I kiss her jaw, smiling as she melts into me.

"Dess," I murmur. "I need words. Was that a yes?"

She laugh-cries and presses her face against my neck. "You never asked properly!"

"I can't get on one knee while we're in the water, brat."

"Fine. I'll settle for the question then."

"Oh, all right." I catch her chin in my hands and look down at her as she grins. "Destiny Lancaster... will you marry me?"

There's the slightest pause as she stares up at me with her whole heart, and my nervousness evaporates.

"Of course I'll marry you!" she rushes out.

Then we collide like shooting stars in a mess of lips and tongues and hunger that probably isn't appropriate for the video I'm filming for posterity.

When we pull away, I'm grinning so wide my face hurts.

"You planned it all, didn't you? You took me to the ocean so we could get engaged?" she demands.

"Had to pick a place you love."

"There are *dolphins*."

"I know. It all went off without a hitch, everything except for them butting in. Rude little pricks."

She beams at me, and I smile back just for her.

"Just so you know," I tell her, nodding to the cameraman. "You're on video. The drone's equipped with cameras on all sides."

"What? You didn't!" She clutches me and laughs madly before we turn. All the guys are lined up on my charter boat, Captain

Juan and the rest who came along to crew it. They wave to us wildly and one guy whistles as I call, "Thanks, wingmen! I appreciate your help."

I don't think they can hear me, but they get it just the same.

"So, what now, fiancé?" she asks sweetly.

"Now I'd better tell your dad you said yes so he can stop worrying. He thought I only had a fifty-fifty chance."

"What? Rude!" She bursts out laughing again and pushes her hands against my chest. "You really asked Dad?"

"Not *exactly*." I grimace. "I told him I was planning on asking you either way, but I wanted his advice. Just between you and me, I think he liked that."

"He knows how much I love dolphins," she muses.

A dolphin surfaces on our right side then and looks at us with wickedly intelligent eyes. I wonder if they can feel the love, too.

"Nothing would make you happier, he said. After today, I'm inclined to agree." I raise my eyebrows. "So, how'd I do?"

"You want a rating? 'Wonderful proposal technique, excellent setting, ten out of ten, would say yes again?'"

"As long as that yes is forever, sweetheart."

"Well, yeah. That's what marriage is for, right?" She smiles and then her face drops. "Oh, no, I didn't mean—"

"Forget it. That's what marriage is supposed to be. This time, I get to do it with the right person."

She beams like the sun.

"That's what Dad and Eliza taught me. I was old enough to really *know* when they got together, you know? I saw what their love was like—what it still is. That's how I knew what I wanted more than anything when I finally found it?"

"Yeah? What's that?" I nudge my nose against her neck.

"You," she says simply.

XXVI: A LITTLE VOW (DESTINY)

*S*o, here's the thing about my wedding.

Unlike some girls, I never really planned for much in my head before I wound up engaged.

I know.

I know it's meant to be this big pinnacle of life and love and blah, blah, blah. Something every girl dreams about from the day she's old enough to play with Barbies, but I'm not like other girls.

I always figured that once I met the man of my dreams, our wedding would just be this day to pledge my undying love to him, accept the ring, and that would be that.

Happy finito.

The end.

But it turns out that once you're engaged and *planning* a wedding, your brain chemically changes.

Once Shepherd asked me to marry him, it was like flicking on a switch.

Suddenly, I had opinions on flowers and dresses and freaking champagne. I had to pick bridesmaids and decide what I was walking down the aisle to—I went for "Sunshine on my Shoulders" by John Denver, because who doesn't love a classic?

And there were all the tiny details, too.

Dad basically demanded we put the entire wedding on his tab, traditionalist that he is, but the decisions are all on Shepherd and me.

Well, Shepherd agreed, after I backed him into a corner and forced him into accepting my father's generosity.

Billionaires and their egos. Woof.

But the biggest surprise is Hannah, the real MVP.

When Shepherd gets bogged down in meetings about new tests for the underwater sensors, she takes my calls and gives her well-researched opinion on caterers, water-wedding venues, rings and flowers and cakes and music.

She's the one who sends the invitations after I help design them, and she suggests a custom website to help with RSVPs and logistics like a custom web domain for our guests.

I don't know why she's being so nice until she drops the bomb.

"Because he's finally happy," she says simply. "Frankly, I didn't think I'd ever see the day. It's none of my business, his life, but when I've spent as much time this close, I've seen him suffer. He's been hurting so much. You broke the cycle, Destiny."

I try to protest.

I try not to get choked up.

I try to explain that she doesn't have to be our auxiliary planner.

But she's insistent, telling me she's doing it as a friend and not just his executive assistant.

It's her job to handle his company's affairs.

And making sure we're happy?

That's human.

Honestly, with all the wedding planning stress, having her help is invaluable. Also, I like to think we're actually becoming friends.

We've even gone out for coffee a few times without Shepherd anywhere in sight.

It's been good getting to know her off the clock. Even if she and Shepherd aren't close in the traditional sense, she's important to him. She's someone he could depend on during his personal storm, and even though it's passed, she's not someone he'll ever forget.

Plus, it's important to make an effort with the very few people who mean so much to him.

Shepherd being Shepherd, there aren't many of those.

I've also been pretty selective with what I share online. Shepherd certainly doesn't mind our relationship being public—and if he was trying to hide it, coming on live TV and confessing we're dating with a big dramatic display isn't the way to go about it.

But, out of respect for his privacy, I've been picking and choosing my cute moments to broadcast to the world very carefully.

Fame, like infamy, always comes with a cost.

We both know that. It's just the sad reality of what I do, but if there's any way I can protect him from any future unintended crapfests, I will.

Fortunately, the drama is pretty low-key these days when my channels are a mix of travel, animals in peril, and showing off how lucky I am with my man.

I love how much he respects my dreams and what he's prepared to do to make them happen. It's just thrilling to see everything I want coming together, and how supportive everyone can be as our future comes closer.

THE MORNING OF MY WEDDING, I wake up in Shepherd's arms.

Yes, tradition says we should have spent the night apart.

But it's not like we haven't slept together before and even one night without him feels like an eternity. You only get to live the best day of your life once.

I can't imagine starting it any other way than waking up beside my future husband.

"Morning, sweetheart." He drops a kiss on the end of my nose.

"The birds are singing." I lie back and listen, then wiggle my way up.

Oh, God, this is happening.

I'm so excited I can't breathe.

"Just a few more hours." Shepherd leans over, rubbing his bristly chin all over my chest, making me squeal.

I wrap my legs around him and that familiar heat enters his eyes.

The first time we slept together, I was sure it was a one-off.

A flippant mistake we'd struggle to forget.

Yet here we are, still ravenous for each other, and counting down the seconds until the knot is officially tied.

"Not now. We have to wait until after the wedding." I twist away from his searching mouth.

"Why, dammit?"

"Because. Tradition."

"Fuck tradition." He growls the word into my shoulder and bites down gently. "Woman, don't you know better than to tease me like that?"

"I'm not teasing you! I'm bringing us good luck." I'm also breathless. Heat curls through my veins, pooling between my legs.

"You're about to be my wife," he rumbles. "Give me one good damn reason why I shouldn't throw you down and make you scream my name right now."

"Because anticipation makes it sweeter?"

"Anticipation isn't what I call limping through my own wedding vows with balls so blue they look like they're ready to be made into a pie."

I laugh at how he pouts, letting my head fall back, and he chuckles down at me.

That's another lovely thing about Shepherd.

He doesn't mind it when I'm blatantly messy.

I told him once that I was considering not shaving and he told me I'd be just as beautiful with or without hair.

Right now, though, I'm waxed bare. Not a single hair out of place, and I don't want him to see it until the wedding night.

"You're a dirty fucking tease, Miss Lancaster." He grabs me and presses me into the mattress with his weight.

Molly watches us from the floor before lying back on her side with a sigh. By now, she's used to these long, lazy mornings.

"You love it anyway. And you'd better not go back to Miss Lancastering me again. Today definitely isn't the day, dude."

"I suppose not, considering the name expires in a few more hours." He kisses my collarbone so reverently I shudder. "By sunset, these will belong to Mrs. Foster."

He rubs a thumb over my nipples.

If they weren't hard before, they definitely are now.

"Don't be—ohhh."

"If I can't have you now, you're going to suffer right alongside me. Touché."

"Cruel man."

"I do have a reputation to uphold as head of a premier security company. Can't let the world think I'm all fluff as a married man."

Right.

He definitely doesn't look like the stern, stonehearted man everyone thinks he is—Mr. Ex Mafia Brat Perma-Grump.

In my eyes, he's the kindest man I've ever known.

I reach up and kiss him. "I can't wait to marry you."

"Good. Now you know how impatient I feel." He kisses me back before lifting me up and slapping my ass. "Now get yourself put together. Hannah will be here in twenty and she's *never* late."

Oof, like I don't already know it.

I think I love her, just a little bit. Even if she'll give me the evil eye if I stagger outside late—it wouldn't be the first time.

I grumble to myself and him as I walk around his enormous bedroom, collecting my stuff.

He's had a whole new closet built for me and my things, and I make sure my back is to him as I collect my special 'fuck me in my wedding dress' lingerie.

I just *know* he'll love it.

Shepherd chuckles and disappears into the bathroom wearing only his boxers. I run for the guest room shower.

At eight o'clock on the dot, Hannah arrives.

I'm barely showered and out of my pajamas, dressed in something presentable, before I hear the doorbell and race down to get it.

"Do you have the dress?" Hannah looks at her smartwatch and sighs. "You have two minutes."

"Yes, *Mom*." I grin at her before flying back upstairs and grabbing everything I need.

Hannah being Hannah, she has everything mapped out with devilish precision.

First, it's breakfast with my parents and Lena, my maid of honor.

Eliza cries happily over the world's most delicious strawberry shortcake waffles.

I cry.

We all cry.

Tears of joy, of course.

This sense of giddy rightness with the world, of belonging, of being ecstatic with something so perfect.

And I know I deserve this happiness, too.

I'm just thrilled that the people I love are here to share it with me.

Soon, Dad and I duck out for a quick stop at the memorial where Mom is buried. It's just her ashes in this mausoleum. Her real memorial is in Hawaii.

Although we weren't close, and she was gone when I was so young, I still try to pay my respects every so often.

Dad stands behind me silently with his hands clasped while I lay flowers.

I tell her about Shepherd and all the hopeful, happy things happening with my conservation work. I'm not Catholic, but it's a little like how I imagine a confession might feel, and it's fitting for today.

Not goodbye, but closure.

When I was a kid, I always wondered how weird it would be not having a mom to gab over wedding plans with or share my tears as I walk down the aisle. In times like these, I miss her, never mind the fact that I never knew her too well.

It's a lump in my throat. Hard emotion that won't budge until Dad lays a firm hand on my shoulder and squeezes.

"Come on, love. Wherever she is, I'm sure she warmed up to Shepherd faster than me," he jokes.

We walk back to the car.

Later, I find out my mother's absence isn't weird at all.

Because I *do* have a mom, and Eliza bawls like a baby the minute I show up at our venue. I think I even catch Dad turning away a few times, muttering about allergies making him all misty-eyed.

The dress takes over an hour to squeeze into.

I went for a white slip, roaring twenties style.

Lena wears an orange jumpsuit dress she loves as she fusses over me and brushes Molly. I'm a little glad I don't know what Shepherd's wearing.

By the time we get to the docks in the stretch limo, I'm fizzing with excitement.

We've gone for a water wedding. What else?

That means ignoring the blustery weather and venturing out on the Puget Sound.

It's where our story began, out on the water, the day I

bumped heads with a man who only had a kayak and a death wish.

It feels right having our wedding here, even if it's a chill autumn day.

Eliza and Lena fuss over me like bees, making sure my veil is perfect, not caring that the wind will probably blow everything out of place. Dad stands in the corner with Molly and my little siblings, watching them as they stroke the husky and get a thousand face licks back.

"Are you ready?" he asks once Eliza goes back to her seat and it's just us.

The deck sways gently underneath us with the swell, but surprisingly, my mind doesn't go back to that stormy, scary evening.

Adriana Cerva has lost her power over us.

My chest fills with so much happiness I'm pretty sure it's close to actual bodily harm.

I don't care.

"Sunshine on my Shoulders" begins playing gently from the speakers with everyone assembled.

I squeeze Dad's arm as we turn, step onto the main deck, and walk up the makeshift aisle.

We're just in time for an afternoon sun full of oranges and yellows, emerging from a slate-grey Seattle wall of clouds.

It's brilliant and extra special for this time of year, but it's got nothing on *him.*

Shepherd waits for me like a god made flesh.

His eyes are blue smolder, his hands clasped in front of him. His fitted suit looks sewn on, and his shoulders span the horizon.

But I'm not really looking at that beyond a glance.

The only thing I really see is his smile.

Wide.

Open.

Beaming, just for me.

You'd better believe I'm smiling right back with my entire soul.

I love you!

His smile says it back. So does the pressure of his hand against mine as Dad hands me over with a murmured, "Treat her well, Foster. Or else."

So does the way his fingers slide through mine.

So does the deep cadence of his voice as the ceremony begins and lurches forward in a haze, and before I know it, he's saying his vows.

When we first met, we truly thought the worst of each other.

He thought I was vain and nosy and a spoiled brat.

I thought he was heartless and crude, a typical hardass CEO who only cared about money and nothing more.

Then we accidentally gave ourselves a second chance.

Thank God.

He chose to see me for who I am, and I saw past his defensive façade, straight to the vast, vulnerable lion's heart underneath.

We fell in love and the rest is history.

This is our whole future, standing here in front of everyone we love, declaring our love to the world.

The mood lightens and I'm struggling a little less against blazing tears as our ring bearer appears.

Molly—who else?—trots down the aisle like we trained her to.

She does a fabulous job, even if she gets a little distracted along the way.

She only pounces on an impressive two people for quick pets —including Dad, whom she adores—before she arrives by our feet, tongue lolling, the ring box swinging from a small clip attached to her collar.

Shepherd grabs the rings and gives her the sweetest kiss.

Oh great, I'm tearing up again.

"Here's to the rest of our lives," Shepherd says as he slides the platinum band on my finger.

His hands are broad and strong and calloused.

They still do obscene things to my stomach. My lady bits practically burst into flames as he runs his fingers along the inside of my wrists.

Sir, we are in public.

The secret smile he gives me says he knows exactly what this does to me and he's enjoying it.

Oh, I'll make him pay for that later.

Then it's my turn to slide the ring onto him.

I'm pretty sure the seabird above us cackles with delight. The sea quiets and the sun burns hotter, or maybe it's just my blood.

I know it's not truly official until the wedding certificate gets filed.

But this—*this here*—feels like eternity unfolding.

The rings. Binding ourselves to each other. One fate and two hearts and so many heavy words.

Pure magic.

Um, I also had no idea I'd turn so sappy. Captivated, I stare up at Shepherd, looking into his eyes.

This man is everything, perfection incarnate.

His eyes sparkle gently as he looks back at me for the first time as something new.

My husband.

Holy hell, that sounds amazing.

"You may now kiss the bride," the officiant announces happily.

Shepherd must have been waiting for it all day. He takes my waist and dips me back in the most outrageous move ever.

I melt in his arms all the same.

His mouth crushes mine.

Urgent and sweet and fierce, although there's no tongue— probably a good thing. If there was, I'd definitely risk becoming a human fire hazard.

"You are so damn beautiful," he whispers fiercely as he pulls away. But although his voice is low, total midnight seduction, the look in his eyes is gentle adoration. "Love that dress. Pity it'll be on the floor later."

When he helps me up again, I'm laughing.

I twirl one more time as we present ourselves to the crowd for the first time as husband and wife. Everyone laughs as Shepherd pretends to swoon.

Then he reels me back in for another kiss like he can't help himself.

How does it feel so different, kissing my husband?

It's more permanent, somehow, even if it's all in my head and heart.

Hello, forever.

It's a promise I'll die for before I break it.

* * *

AFTER THE MAGIC EVENING, we're plunged into one long dream.

We start our honeymoon on the Vaadhoo Shores in the Maldives.

My idea, seeing as Shepherd came up with the robo-dolphin proposal. I figured I should start pulling my weight in the creative department.

Also, as a bonus, it's one of the most breathtaking places I've ever seen in my life.

The overwater bungalows we've booked are perched over perfect turquoise waters. The resort is full service with massages and spa treatments and day trips, and the scenery—it's not fair.

I can't believe a place this beautiful exists and I've waited this long to see it.

Mostly, though, we make our own way.

The world feels so big on the open sea where it's nothing but islands.

We spend our first few days exploring white-gold beaches framed with palm trees, swimming whenever we feel the urge in balmy waters that feel like one endless warm hug.

Shepherd brings me a colorful drink as I sit with my feet dangling in the water. The sunset shimmers through every shade of red and gold, and my body feels pleasantly sore and tired.

Five days of being a married woman.

Well, six, I suppose, if you count my wedding day.

I glance down at the gleaming metal around my finger. The band slots perfectly against my engagement ring, my tan skin so warm around it, the pearl and silver shades flickering in lovely contrast.

I swing my legs, enjoying the sea against them.

The sun feels like a hot evening kiss against my shoulders, and Shepherd sits behind me with his huge legs splayed.

He smears cool sunscreen against the back of my neck and I shudder.

"You'll burn up if you're not careful," is all he says when I wiggle in protest.

Predictably, I feel his reaction against my butt.

The man has always been insatiable, but on our honeymoon, it's been incessant.

I never knew a human being could have so much stamina.

I mean, he's even giving me a run for my money, and *I* can have multiple orgasms.

Still, my body softens as I lean against him, gazing out across the tranquil sea. The island we're on curves away, outlandishly pale sand set against emerald greenery of trees.

Exquisite.

I'm happier than I've ever been with this trip, this husband, this *life*.

And I almost have to pinch myself to remember we get to wake up and do it again tomorrow.

Against the fading light, the sea glimmers. Faintly at first, then brighter with every wave.

Vaadhoo beach is famous for its 'sea of stars,' a series of bright lights on the ocean. It's actually bioluminescence created by some special plankton.

It's one of nature's biggest miracles.

At night, it's like diving into starlight.

When I turn around, I find Shepherd already grinning at me.

"Dinner can wait. Let's go," he says.

We shut Molly in the bungalow before we go diving in—a little too quickly.

Water sprays up my nose and plasters my hair to my scalp, and I come back up a sputtering mess.

Shepherd makes it look too easy.

He slices through the waves, his body sleek and strong and heroic, drawn like a bow.

It reminds me of when he first taught me to kayak and insisted on proof I could swim.

Back then, I thought he was a stubborn safety freak. Obsessed with minor details and things that didn't even matter.

Could he not just take my word for it?

Now, I appreciate the caring heart he hides behind all those layers.

And okay, fine, so maybe it was sensible to not just trust my word.

I cut through the water after him, letting it stream past my body. I force my eyes open and look at the royal-blue fish darting around us.

I'm living in a painting now, vibrant and colorful and alive.

Just like everything about being with Shepherd Foster.

We paddle out into the bay, hearts pounding, laughing through mouthfuls of surf. When he flings a few handfuls of water my way, I scream and toss a few back.

He takes a direct hit in the face and goes under.

For a second, I'm worried—until he pops up and splashes a wave over me.

I'm still screaming as he takes me in his arms, the little water spat over. We swim through the sea of stars and so many laughs.

The glow is ethereal against his bare chest.

He doesn't look like a man here. He could be something

otherworldly, every muscle bathed in luminous light. The starlight highlights all his perfections—and there are plenty.

He takes a lock of my hair and twirls it, staring. "Have I told you how beautiful you are?"

"Only every hour." I preen. "But you can tell me again anytime."

"Dess, you're fucking gorgeous."

The last sunlight disappears around us in a symphony of color and the bugs start up their night songs as we kiss in the ocean's second sun.

Bioluminescence coats my hands as I reach up to cup his face.

Soon, we're both smeared in it like war paint.

I wrap my legs around him and we kiss.

It's heady and intense and I think we'll never get enough. Then we go deeper, hand in hand, cutting through the silky waters and bobbing under the rising moon.

This is, without a doubt, the happiest night ever.

Later, when we head back inside, Molly bounces like a rubber ball in excitement. After greeting her, Shepherd drags me into bed, impatient as always but not just possessed by physical need.

This is real life.

It's never just been about the sex.

It's always been infinitely more, right from the start, even before we could admit the truth and put a neat label on it.

His face is so handsome, cut from pure granite in sharp lines of adoration and heat.

Inside me, I feel him pulsing, grinding me so deep with slow, deliberate strokes that mark me from the inside out.

"Shepherd," I whimper.

"Patience, sweetheart," he growls. "We've got all night. I want to take my time watching you go over."

It's not wild tonight.

It's slow and steady, building so perfectly I know I'll go to pieces when I finish.

And when it hits, I'm too shattered to even scream.

I just catch a final, searing glimpse of his eyes as his thrusts quicken, as he makes me come, as he empties himself inside me with a rough noise like a mountain falling down.

Holy buck falls.

I guess this is my wedding present.

Without doubt, one of the best orgasms of my life, and that's saying something for a relentless beast who delivers them daily.

After we come down from the high and clean up, I'm tangled in his arms. I smile as his fingers skim my thigh, stop between my legs, and squeeze.

"This is mine. And this is yours," he says, keeping his eyes locked on mine as he grabs my hand and lays my palm on his chest.

His heart drums like a machine.

Yours.

I smile up at him. Our shower washed off the bioluminescence, but his eyes still glow sharper than the starlight.

"Mine," I echo. "I'm a lucky, lucky girl."

"Every part of me, Dess."

"You know I'm yours, too," I whisper.

His eyes close. "Tell me again."

"Yours. Now and forever."

He pushes inside me to the hilt again.

Yeah, I think I want to stay like this forever.

Right here, on these white linen sheets, the ocean dampness still clinging to our hair and our skin bronzed from the sun.

Right here, with my husband inside me and his eyes so warm and every shade of blue flashing in them.

Right here, with our love woven around us so tightly I can't tell where it begins or ends.

Because it doesn't truly matter.

We're now bound by the same beautiful thread of fate.

And as always, he knows what I need.

He sucks my breast, his teeth insistent.

I fall apart and cling to him as he starts to thrust, hard and steady.

Before, it was slow and sweet, but now I let him take and take until these sweet, messy kisses are all we have left.

When he goes over the edge, I'm with him again, and I float in his arms with a lovestruck smile.

Soon, we're dozing, until a pile of husky leaps up on us, licking our faces and panting with excitement.

The last missing piece.

We collapse with my new family in my arms and more love than any human heart can hold.

The last thing I hear before I drift off for a quick nap before dinner is Shepherd whispering to Molly.

"Deal with it, girl. We're sharing her now. As long as I'm breathing, I'm going to love your mama to the stars and back. And if we're lucky, we'll both drive her crazy for a good long while."

FLASH FORWARD: A LITTLE BLESSED (DESTINY)

Years Later

*M*ost women say they have the best husband.

At least, the happily married ones.

They probably mean it.

It's probably true.

But I, Destiny Foster, *actually* have the best husband ever to walk the Earth.

I cradle my hand across my stomach as we stand outside the nonprofit marine wildlife reserve that we built from the ground up. More acreage than the naked eye can even see, all dedicated to preserving over twenty different species and pioneering entirely new types of research with the most cutting edge tools.

Technically, this entire thing was my idea. It's been my wildest dream ever since I was old enough to start dreaming I could make an impact.

But with Shepherd, I was able to make this happen ten times faster. He had the money and connections and presence to hook just the right powerful people into organizing this big land grant along the Olympic Peninsula. It's also so much bigger than I ever could've imagined.

This wildlife reserve alone is *huge.*

But when the right people heard about solar powered drones, cameras so concealed they might as well be invisible, and a research facility with ample white collar employment opportunities and running completely on renewable energy?

They pushed it through the legal labyrinth faster than any other environmental initiative of this size in the last thirty years.

We're going to save lives from today forward.

We're *already* saving lives.

Home Shepherd has an entire production line of sophisticated drones and conservation equipment that's sold to us and anyone else who'd like to use them at the price of production only.

No profit.

And me? My channel is still going strong with over fifty million followers.

I'm still hitting the ground and the lenses as a married woman, boosting public awareness for everything from endangered monk seals to pygmy rabbits.

Until *very* recently, I've traveled North America and even hopped overseas a few times, visiting world-class sanctuaries and conservation teams to stuff my brain full of their superpowers. We're all in this, no matter how separated we are by specialty and distance, and I'm so grateful for the extra time to sharpen my own expertise.

Never mind the fundraising, which has been the master key to everything.

Again, Shepherd came charging to my rescue, lending his name and network to pulling in famous headliners and glamorous venues that probably tripled our dollars alone like the Winthrope Chicago Hotel.

It's not just the fact that he's been with me, holding my hand every step of the way.

It's that he's been there physically, too, right by my side on every continent.

When work allowed, he traveled with me, using the trips as business excuses and sometimes stretching the truth—all so he could see what our conservation push truly needed.

We're a kickass team.

Though when this project started down its final leg, aside from being one of my major backers and helping me figure out the logistics, he's been content to stand in the background. He wants me basking in the limelight while he supports me from the sidelines.

He's made it crystal clear to everyone—press monsters included—that this reserve is my baby. I dreamed her, made her, lived her, breathed her, and put all the work into making her a reality.

Now, here I am with a pair of oversized scissors in my hands, cameras flashing like lightning as I stand beside the ruby-red ribbon. Behind me, a pair of electric gates lead into the reserve, and the plaque glows like polished gold.

The Destiny Foster Wildlife Reserve.

Yeah. It's going to take a long flipping time to get used to that.

My cheeks ache as I grin, and off to one side, I see Shepherd standing with his hands tucked behind his back.

Has any human being ever aged more gracefully?

Somehow, he's gotten more lickable with age.

His hair more distinguished with a creeping smattering of salt and pepper.

His body trimmer, still built like a solid brick with oak branches for arms and legs. That big marathon he organized last year to top off our fundraising goals sent him on a fitness kick he didn't need, but it's paid off massively.

He's bound in a navy-blue suit today, just as handsome and unapproachable as when I first saw him.

But this time, I know the only faces he'll bite off are the ones that dare suggest I didn't work myself to the bone to secure every precious inch of this place.

When he sees me looking, his mouth curves into his signature secret smile.

Still just for me.

Goosebumps, everywhere.

Well done, he mouths. *I love you like crazy.*

I don't need to be a lip reader to make out the words.

I know the shape of them. We've been in public a lot since our marriage with so many wary eyes on us, so I've had to get used to plenty of affection.

What was strange at first rapidly became second nature.

He always makes sure I know I'm loved.

A squeeze of my hand, a breath in my ear, a gentle word.

No matter where we are, he makes sure I *know*, and I desperately hope I do the same for him.

I wield the scissors awkwardly. You'd think I'd be used to all this pomp, having grown up with Cole Lancaster, but nope.

This sort of thing is never smooth when I'm the center of attention.

"Thanks, everyone. By the power vested in me by the great state of Washington, I declare The Destiny Foster Wildlife Reserve officially open!" The snipping scissors accent my proclamation.

Everyone bursts into cheers, clapping their hands.

Shepherd doesn't whoop half as loud as Eliza, but he's still smiling just the same, and his eyes are so soft I could melt right into them.

Then a whole bunch of other stuff.

One thing about pregnancy I didn't realize until now, in my second trimester—it can make you hornier than a goat cactus.

And when you're happy and hitched to a man like Shepherd who hasn't lost a bit of his appetite for hearing me moan—

I don't care.

I don't care that the mechanics are slightly more awkward

now that I've got a belly sticking out, but the doctor assured me it was perfectly safe to have sex up until the end, so I'm enjoying this feeling right now.

As everyone congratulates me, thrusting friendly hands at me and shouting congratulations into both ears, I pick my way across to where Shepherd stands and link my arm with his.

Cameras keep popping, but I ignore them. It's easier when I'm with him, especially when he throws a protective arm around my shoulders immediately and ushers me away for some privacy.

"How are you really holding up?" he murmurs.

"Excellent. We're officially open."

He holds his phone out and taps the screen. There's a map with the name of the place showing up.

"The Destiny Foster Wildlife Reserve. It's got a real ring to it, don't you think?"

We decided on the name over a year ago but I'm still overheating, feeling the blood roaring in my cheeks.

You can guess who insisted on the idea.

It seemed silly, in a way, to put my name on a place this special, but meeting Shepherd, all of this coming together... I have to admit, it does feel like destiny. No goofy puns intended.

He glances at his watch.

"I have an interview with CNBC at three so I can't stay too long."

"You'd better not. My handsome, clever husband, turning his company into the world's top name in green technology." I reach up and kiss his cheek. "Just go. I understand. I'm just glad you came."

He snorts. "Like I'd have missed it for anything, woman."

This morning, after a shareholder meeting, he flew in so he didn't miss a thing.

Have I mentioned I love this man?

"Will you be okay while I'm gone?" he asks.

"I'm pregnant," I say dryly, "not dying. I'll be *fine*." I drag my nails down his tie. "I'm looking forward to seeing you tonight."

His eyes heat, blue flames dancing.

"Can't wait." His gaze bounces from my eyes to my lips and finally down to my baby bump.

I'm wearing a wrap dress that does nothing to hide it, and at roughly six months, it's really starting to show.

Getting pregnant *exactly* when I did wasn't the plan.

I think it was our trip to Arizona, the Sonoran Desert, where we stayed in and made mad, mad love for a whole day for no other reason than we could.

But I couldn't be happier it happened like it did.

Make that two of us.

It's a family. What I—and we—always dreamed of.

I step closer, and with his hands on my waist, he leans in for a kiss so deep that Dad clears his throat loudly behind me. The whole family turned out for the big opening today, of course.

We break apart and I turn to beam at them. They're hand in hand and look just as thrilled as I'm feeling.

Eliza hugs me and Dad smiles at us both. Once the two men stopped eyeing each other like wild dogs, they started getting along.

Who knew they'd become fast friends.

They've even started playing golf together in a twist that still has Eliza and me in stitches.

"Congratulations," she says, pulling back and looking at me.

"Thank you, Liza. I'm pumped you guys could make it."

Dad rolls his eyes. "You say that like we wouldn't be here for you, Dess."

"A little birdie told me *some* people get private tours. Is it true?" Eliza asks, looping her arm through mine.

"That little birdie would be right. Come on. Let's get a few more photos and head inside."

Little Nicole and Elijah start jumping, both of them ready to go combing the forest for otter sightings.

Dad and Shepherd make a similar groaning sound, and Eliza's laugh rings high above the rest. We drag our reluctant men in front of a few more flashing cameras again and smile. Shepherd's hand creeps around my waist to sit on my bump, just resting there.

People are going to notice, and so be it.

I can't even *imagine* the comments that are going to come pouring in from the trolls online. I have to remember most will be positive, though.

It takes some serious time getting used to total strangers telling you how beautiful you look.

I have the best fans, though.

Definitely the best husband.

Oh, and it's a boy, by the way.

A perfect little boy that Shepherd can teach to kayak and I can teach to love conservation. I think, in the end, we'll have two, and I secretly hope our second is a girl.

What could be better than having a mini-Shepherd for a big brother?

I can see it now. They'd tease like crazy and pull each other's hair, but when it came down to it, he would stand up for her with everything he had.

Also, two kids feels like the magic number. I've seen how dynamic Eliza's kids are together and I've been the only child growing up.

Dad and me, we were a team. I would never go back and change what we had.

But I want my kids to have siblings.

I want a good-sized family with all the love and light he's given me.

I laugh to myself, just thinking about our future as we walk through the gates leading back inside the reserve.

There are roads and paths snaking out from the research center, of course. There's even a visitor's center nearby, looking out across the ocean.

"Oh my God," Eliza gushes as we look through the trees and the twinkling lights beyond. "This is so gorgeous."

"That's the wolf enclosure. A special project," I say, nodding to a fence. "We only have two, but they're a breeding pair. We're hoping they'll build up their numbers and some day we can release them back into the forests. We don't have a lot of animals in enclosures around here, but when Shepherd heard about a chance to host the wolves, he couldn't turn it down."

He gives a slight smile. "It's important. The closer they are, the easier we can study them, and figure out what technology works best. We can know their movements and their well-being. That's one of the things I've had Home Shepherd working on this past year."

I walk on, leading them on the tour, linking my hand with Shepherd's. So many prototypes have been put to good use here, and all donated for free.

"What's in that building?" Eliza asks.

"Special amphibian center. We have a few things in there from around the country on loan from other wildlife reserves. The Mississippi Gopher Frog, for example. There's only a few left, and they're exclusively in Mississippi, but we've simulated their natural habitat. Do you guys want to see?"

The kids try to outdo each other shouting.

"Dess, I want to see *everything*," Eliza beams.

I can't help the smile that takes over my face.

I take them all inside. The small enclosures vary from being fully external—places where the species can roam and breed as they usually would, giving them enough space that they're not overly restricted—and internal enclosures.

No matter where they are, though, we've spared no expense, from bringing in experts in the field to setting up microclimates that mimic their natural habitat right down to lighting and environment.

We're going to make sure every creature here has a fighting chance.

✱ And if they're lucky, we'll live long enough to see a few of them *thrive*.

I check the time and click my tongue.

"You should get going, honey," I tell him. "You're going to miss your interview."

Dad pointedly looks away as Shepherd scoops me into his arms. My bump presses against his flat stomach, and by the look on his face, he likes it.

Horny Destiny likes it, too.

Emotional Destiny, even more.

"I'm going to miss you like hell," he tells me.

"It's only for a few hours, wuss," I tease.

"Brat. You'll pay for that tonight." When he kisses me, though, I can feel his smile, and it fills me like sunshine.

"I'll see you later. Have fun. I'll be tuning in."

"I'll be hating every second," he grumps, scratching my face with his scruff one more time.

"I know. Just try to smile sometimes or you'll scare people."

With one more dirty look, he bends to kiss Bump.

We haven't chosen a name yet.

Every time I think I'm sure, I change my mind again.

Right now, I'm thinking Cyrus. Or Soren. Maybe Milo.

We'll figure it out.

"Bye, Eliza," Shepherd says after he gives me one last, lingering look and heads out. "Bye, Cole."

They wave him off and I continue my tour, explaining my hope that one day we can foster a colony of Franklin's Bumblebees somehow, if they still exist. They haven't been spotted since 2006.

Finally, we walk through the research areas, where a few hardworking scientists and interns are skipping the ceremonies to continue doing what I hope we'll do best.

My life is complete.

One day, I hope the world won't need places like this. I hope time and human interference stops leaving such scars on the world, and we won't have to do our best to protect them before it's too late.

Just like it's too late for so many species.

But for now, it feels incredible that we're helping in one of the most important ways we can.

While this place is running, all the animals we're protecting are safe.

And so is my heart thanks to one snarly, special, and always unbelievable man.

Shepherd Foster has given me perfection.

I have love, a growing family, and a chance to make the world a better place, all with a man who lights up *my* world.

How could I ever ask for a greater blessing?

ABOUT NICOLE SNOW

Nicole Snow is a *Wall Street Journal* and *USA Today* bestselling author. She found her love of writing by hashing out love scenes on lunch breaks and plotting her great escape from boardrooms. Her work roared onto the indie romance scene in 2014 with her Grizzlies MC series.

Since then Snow aims for the very best in growly, heart-of-gold alpha heroes, unbelievable suspense, and swoon storms aplenty.

Already hooked on her stuff? Visit nicolesnowbooks.com to sign up for her newsletter and connect on social media.

Got a question or comment on her work? Reach her anytime at nicole@nicolesnowbooks.com

Thanks for reading. And please remember to leave an honest review! Nothing helps an author more.

MORE BOOKS BY NICOLE

Bossy Seattle Suits

One Bossy Proposal

One Bossy Dare

One Bossy Date

One Bossy Offer

One Bossy Disaster

Bad Chicago Bosses

Office Grump

Bossy Grump

Perfect Grump

Damaged Grump

Men of Redhaven

The Broken Protector

Knights of Dallas Books

The Romeo Arrangement

The Best Friend Zone

The Hero I Need

The Worst Best Friend

Accidental Knight (Companion book)*

Heroes of Heart's Edge Books

No Perfect Hero

No Good Doctor

No Broken Beast

No Damaged Goods

No Fair Lady

No White Knight

No Gentle Giant

Marriage Mistake Standalone Books

Accidental Hero

Accidental Protector

Accidental Romeo

Accidental Knight

Accidental Rebel

Accidental Shield

Stand Alone Novels

The Perfect Wrong

Cinderella Undone

Man Enough

Surprise Daddy

Prince With Benefits

Marry Me Again

Love Scars

Recklessly His

Enguard Protectors Books

Still Not Over You

Still Not Into You

Still Not Yours

Still Not Love

Baby Fever Books

Baby Fever Bride

Baby Fever Promise

Baby Fever Secrets

Only Pretend Books

Fiance on Paper

One Night Bride

Grizzlies MC Books

Outlaw's Kiss

Outlaw's Obsession

Outlaw's Bride

Outlaw's Vow

Deadly Pistols MC Books

Never Love an Outlaw

Never Kiss an Outlaw

Never Have an Outlaw's Baby

Never Wed an Outlaw

Prairie Devils MC Books

Outlaw Kind of Love

Nomad Kind of Love

Savage Kind of Love

Wicked Kind of Love

Bitter Kind of Love

Printed in Great Britain
by Amazon